Praise for Karen Chance's previous novels

'Ms Chance is a master at fleshing out her secondary
characters and keeping her storyline moving at a
lightning-fast pace . . . This is a series well worth
getting hooked on' *Fresh Fiction*

'Chance is a great writer of supernatural fantasy that is on
a par with the works of Kim Harrison, Charlaine Harris
and Kelley Armstrong' *The Best Reviews*

'A really exciting book with great pacing and a huge cast
of vivid characters. This is one of my favourite reads of
the year' Charlaine Harris, *New York Times*,
bestselling author of *Definitely Dead*

'A grab-you-by-the-throat-and-suck-you-in sort of book,
with a tough, smart heroine and sexy-scary vampires.
I loved it – and I'm waiting anxiously for a sequel'
New York Times bestselling author Patricia Briggs

'Exciting and inventive' *Booklist*

KAREN CHANCE

Midnight's Daughter

PENGUIN BOOKS

PENGUIN BOOKS

Published by the Penguin Group
Penguin Books Ltd, 80 Strand, London WC2R 0RL, England
Penguin Group (USA) Inc., 375 Hudson Street, New York, New York 10014, USA
Penguin Group (Canada), 90 Eglinton Avenue East, Suite 700, Toronto, Ontario, Canada M4P 2Y3
(a division of Pearson Penguin Canada Inc.)
Penguin Ireland, 25 St Stephen's Green, Dublin 2, Ireland (a division of Penguin Books Ltd)
Penguin Group (Australia), 250 Camberwell Road, Camberwell, Victoria 3124, Australia
(a division of Pearson Australia Group Pty Ltd)
Penguin Books India Pvt Ltd, 11 Community Centre,
Panchsheel Park, New Delhi – 110 017, India
Penguin Group (NZ), 67 Apollo Drive, Rosedale, North Shore 0632, New Zealand
(a division of Pearson New Zealand Ltd)
Penguin Books (South Africa) (Pty) Ltd, 24 Sturdee Avenue,
Rosebank, Johannesburg 2196, South Africa

Penguin Books Ltd, Registered Offices: 80 Strand, London WC2R 0RL, England

www.penguin.com

First published in the United States of America by Onyx, an imprint of
New American Library, a division of Penguin Group (USA) Inc. 2008
First published in Great Britain by Penguin Books 2008
1

Copyright © Karen Chance, 2008

ISBN: 978–0–141–03951–0

www.greenpenguin.co.uk

Mixed Sources
Product group from well-managed
forests and other controlled sources
www.fsc.org Cert no. SA-COC-1592
© 1996 Forest Stewardship Council

Penguin Books is committed to a sustainable future
for our business, our readers and our planet.
The book in your hands is made from paper
certified by the Forest Stewardship Council.

To Anne Sowards, a great editor

Chapter One

My least favorite dead guy had his feet up on my desk. I hate that. His boots were probably cleaner than my blotter, but still. It showed a lack of respect.

I pushed the offending size tens onto the floor and scowled. "Whatever it is, the answer's no."

"Okay, Dory. Your call." Kyle was looking amiable—never a good sign. "I should've known you wouldn't care what happened to Claire. After all, there's not likely to be any money in it"—he paused to glance around my rathole of an office—"and you don't appear to be in a position to do anything gratis."

I had been on the way to my feet to haul his undead ass out the door, but at his words I slowly sat back down. Kyle was a real lowlife, even for a vamp, but once in a while he heard something useful—which explained why I hadn't yet given in to temptation and staked him. And where Claire, my roommate and best friend, was concerned, I'd take anything I could get. She'd been missing for almost a month, and I'd already gone through every lead I had. Twice. Before loser boy showed up, I'd been about to start through the file a third time in case I'd somehow missed something, even though I knew I hadn't. And every hour that passed made it less likely I'd be pleased with what I found at the end of the search.

"Talk," I said, hoping he'd make me beat it out of him. I had a lot of pent up frustration that needed to go somewhere. But, of course, he decided to find some manners. Or what passes for them in our circle.

"Word is, she's alive. I thought she'd have been juiced and packed up for sale by now, but talk on the street is that she wasn't kidnapped at all."

By "juiced" he meant a disgusting black-arts process in which a projective null, a witch or wizard capable of blocking out magical energy for a certain radius, is made into a weapon known as a null bomb. The null's energy is siphoned away to make a device capable of bringing all magic in an area to a standstill. How far and how long the effect extends depends on the strength of the null being sacrificed—the younger and more powerful, the more energy she has to give. And Claire was both very young and very powerful.

Making her even more attractive was the fact that the harvesters, as the mages who specialized in the very illegal practice were known, could currently command a premium for their wares. The Vampire Senate, the self-styled guardian of all North American vampires, was at war with the dark mages of the Black Circle, and the price for magical weapons had gone through the roof. The idea that someone had taken Claire to make into a tool for their stupid war was the main reason I was running myself ragged trying to find her

"The rumor is that she ran off with one of Michael's crew," Kyle was saying. He leaned in to smile in my face, showing enough fang that I knew how much he was enjoying this. He'd tried to chat me up when we first met and hadn't taken my screams of laughter well. He'd been waiting for something to throw in my face, and this was his big chance. "Seems she got knocked up."

I smiled back. "That little lie is going to cost you," I promised, slipping a hand into my desk drawer. Claire, the witch with girl power practically stamped on her forehead, running off with a lowlife connected with Michael's stable? Didn't think so.

Kyle held up grubby hands with telltale brown stains on them. Leftovers from whoever had been lunch, I guessed. I would have advised him that his love life might improve if he paid someone to scrape the dried blood out from under his nails once in a while, if I hadn't thought he'd eat the manicurist.

"No lies, Dory. Not between you and me." He sat back and crossed his legs, looking far too much at ease for my taste. "And you haven't heard the best part yet. Rumor has it that the father's not exactly human, if you know what I mean." His grin turned feral. "Passing me up because you were afraid to bring another half-breed into the world was a waste of time, wasn't it? Looks like you're about to be auntie to a bouncing baby dhampir."

I didn't have to glance in the mirror behind his head to know that my expression hadn't changed despite the shock. After five hundred years of practice, anyone can perfect a decent poker face. Even someone as naturally . . . expressive . . . as me.

"Actually, I shot you down because homicidal psychos with dog breath don't turn me on," I said pleasantly, pulling my hand out of the drawer and throwing an unstoppered vial in his face. The holy water stuff is a myth, but there are other concoctions that don't sit too well with the smarmy undead, and that was one of them. The dragon's blood wouldn't kill him, but he wouldn't look too good for a few days, either. Of course, since it was Kyle, it was a good bet no one would notice the difference.

I tossed his screaming body out the window after he gave up the rest of the few facts he knew, like the name of a bar where I might locate a few of Michael's thugs. He bounced off the sidewalk three stories below and slammed into a parked car, denting the metal with his forehead before crawling off down the street. Too bad it wasn't daylight.

If Claire had been harvested, she was almost surely dead by now. But there was a slim chance that Kyle the perpetually smarmy had actually heard something useful. And any lead, however slim, was better than what I had.

I paused only long enough to grimace at my reflection, which looked almost as bad as I felt. I needed makeup to conceal the dark circles that were currently almost as black as my eye color, and washing my greasy brown hair for the first time in a week wouldn't hurt, either. No chance of doing the femme fatale thing tonight, but that was okay by me. I get cranky without a full eight hours a night of beauty sleep, and since I'd had maybe that much in the past week, I was feeling surly. I picked up a length of lead pipe and added it to the collection under my coat. There were plenty of other ways to get information.

An hour later, I was sitting on a pile of corpses, frowning. The bar where I'd found two of Michael's stable feasting on a half-dead teenager was now a wreck of shattered tables and broken glass. I shifted to avoid the pool of multicolored blood seeping from the bodies under me and stared into the darkness outside. Kyle, it seemed, had not been lying about everything. As one of the boys had helpfully explained after I introduced his head to the bar top a few dozen times, Michael did have Claire. And if Kyle hadn't lied about that, there was the teeniest chance he hadn't lied at all. But I'd still have to see it to believe it.

I tossed a handkerchief at the dazed boy leaning on the body of one of his recent attackers. He looked at it blankly. "For your neck," I explained. Vampires didn't have to bite to feed—in fact, it was against the rules, since it left hard-to-explain corpses behind if they got carried away. But no one had been paying much attention to the law lately. Usually, that was the way I liked it, but it did leave me with a dilemma now.

Normally the mages would be willing to help a witch in a jam, especially a powerful null like Claire. If for no other reason, she was a useful tool they didn't want to lose to the magical black market. The Silver Circle, the so-called white-magic users, would doubtless have sent some of their thugs after Michael in more-normal times, but I doubted they could spare any at the moment. There was a war on, and they were allied with the Senate against an array of forces that were scary enough to make anyone blanch. Not to mention that they hated my guts. If I wanted Claire back, I was going to have to manage it myself.

"What—" The boy stopped, swallowed and tried again. "What were those . . . things?"

I got up, moved around the bar and reached for the top shelf. What the hell, I was going to torch the place anyway. "You want a drink?"

He tried to get to his feet, but was too weak and collapsed again. "No," he said dully. "Just tell me."

I threw back a double of Tanqueray and slid the rest of the bottle into one of the deep pockets in my black denim coat. I ignored his question and walked back around the bar. My sense of smell can usually tell a human from anything else from across a room, but the state of the bar was interfering. Dust and smoke hung in the air, and rivers of blood and bile, and whatever fluid several of the odder demon races used as fuel, ran underfoot. I was pretty sure I knew what I was dealing with, but wanted to be certain.

I kicked the head of a Varos demon out of the way and crouched in front of the boy, sniffing cautiously. A gout of blood—green, so not his—had splattered in the direct center of his chest. It stank to high heaven and explained my confusion. I took the unused handkerchief from him and wiped it off. Even after all he'd been through, he didn't look afraid. Being five feet two and dimpled has long been one of my chief assets.

"You were here for a while, right?" I asked. It was a stupid question—he had six sets of bite marks on his skinny nude body, and none of them looked to be the same size. Vamps have to know one another pretty well to do group feedings, since it's considered an intimate act, so he'd probably been lying around as the free bar snack for a few hours at least. But I wanted to start slow to give him a chance to gather whatever was left of his wits, since there was a chance he'd heard something useful. The two vamps I'd found had told me that there had been a third, who left a half hour or so before I arrived, and that he was one of Michael's lower-level masters. That didn't mean he knew any more than they did, but he could hardly know less.

"I don't get it," the boy told me shakily. "You killed them. You killed all of them. Why couldn't I do that?"

"Because you aren't dhampir." The voice that answered for me was pitched low, from near the shattered door, but it carried. I knew that voice in a thousand moods and tones, from the chill whipcrack of anger to the warm caress of pride, although the latter had never been directed at me. I tensed but didn't bother to look up. Wonderful. Just what I needed to make my day complete.

The boy was staring at the newcomer with relief. Sure, I thought sourly, I do the work, but you save the worshipful looks for the handsome devil with the charming smile. Just don't forget that he could rip your throat out with a single gnash of those pearly white teeth. For all the charisma and expensive tailoring, he's a predator.

One even more dangerous than me.

I busied myself pouring some of the expensive alcohol in my pocket over the clean portion of the handkerchief and pressed it ruthlessly to the worst of the boy's wounds. He screamed, but neither of us paid any attention. We were used to it.

"He'll need medical attention," the voice said as the dark-haired vamp who owned it crossed the room carefully to avoid messing up his two-thousand-dollar suit and Ferragamo loafers. He smelled of good brandy, nicotine and fresh pine. I've never really gotten that last one, but it's always there. Maybe it's some terribly costly cologne, mixed at an Italian perfumer's shop for his exclusive use, or possibly it's just my imagination. A memory of home, maybe.

"I'm sure the Senate can arrange something, considering that they went out of their way only last month to proclaim that this sort of thing doesn't happen anymore." I sloshed a bit more alcohol onto the bite marks at the boy's neck and breast, before moving on to the ugly tear in his thigh. He fainted a few seconds later, which left us with an—on my part at least—uncomfortable silence. I broke it first, more interested in getting this over with than winning some kind of power play. "What do you want?"

"To talk to you," he said calmly. "I need your help."

I did look up at that. In five hundred years, I had never heard those words pass his lips. Hadn't ever thought to, either. "Come again?"

"I will be happy to repeat myself, Dorina, but I believe you heard me the first time. We need to talk, and the young man needs attention. We can obtain both at—"

"I'm not going there."

"At my apartment, I was about to say. I am well aware of your sentiments toward the Senate."

I refrained from glaring, but doubted that my vaunted poker face was good enough to fool him. It had never been before. Besides, he could hear my heart rate speed up with the extra adrenaline of anger, and probably detect the telltale flush my pale skin couldn't hide. I told myself I didn't care. It had been twelve years since I saw him last, and that had ended with my threatening to kill him— for something like the thousandth time—and storming out. He always got to me. Always. Even when he wasn't trying. I didn't think this was likely to be any different.

He reached out to take the unconscious boy in his arms, assuming with that unchanging conceit of his that I'd agree to whatever plan he made. I didn't object, since taking the kid to a local hospital would entail explaining who or what had done this to him, something that would challenge even my ability to stretch the truth. And running to the Senate's local branch was definitely out, considering what had happened the last time I dropped by. Insurance had probably covered the damage, of course, and the place had needed remodeling, but I doubted they saw it that way. I could take the kid back to my house, but although I could deal with his physical injuries, I couldn't erase all this from his memory. But the overgroomed bastard at my side could manage it with little more than a thought.

"I didn't know you had a place in New York," I said, and that worried me. There was no reason for him to be here, much less with what was probably an outrageously expensive Central Park–view apartment. Vamps tend to be territorial by nature and usually stick close to home. Of course, the Senate outlawed the old boundaries some time ago to cut down on feuds, so technically he could go wherever he wanted, but as far as I knew, he had no business or personal interests in New York. Except maybe me.

"It's a recent acquisition."

I narrowed my eyes and followed him out the door. That could mean a lot of things, from him getting a lark to spend some of the millions he'd accumulated through the centuries to dueling another master and acquiring his possessions. I really hoped it was one of those and not some plot to keep up with me. I was well aware that I was dealing with a Senate member, one of the most powerful and dangerous vamps on the planet. I'd been underestimated too many times myself to ever do it to anyone else, no matter how human he looked. Especially not this one.

"Well, I hope it has a shower," I said, pouring the rest of the booze over a nearby pile of highly flammable vamp bodies and tossing on a match. "I need a bath."

*   *   *

The apartment was posh, Fifth Avenue, and did indeed have a park view. I was relieved to see that it was also furnished in the designer-bland beiges and creams meant to be acceptable to virtually any taste—other than mine. That meant he hadn't been here long enough to impose his personal style, so maybe he hadn't been spying on me. I didn't waste breath sighing in relief, but focused on the only other occupant of the room. I hadn't been dragged off to the Senate's local base of operations, but unless I was mistaken, at least one of its members was sitting on a pale camel-colored sofa waiting for us.

The strange vamp flowed to his feet when we came in, his eyes sweeping over the boy before coming to rest on me. I braced for the usual reaction, but didn't get it. That told me either he'd been warned ahead of time, or he was even better than me at the whole poker-face thing. Not surprising—since they don't have to breathe or have a heartbeat unless they choose, most vamps don't have a lot of tells. Especially not the old ones, and I was guessing from the sense of power this one wore like a cloak that he was a lot older than his thirty-something face appeared.

I examined him with interest, since I'd never seen him before. That was unusual, if he was as old as I thought. The newbies come and go, most of them dead before they manage to outlive a normal human—so much for immortality—but I try to keep up with the major players in the vamp world. There aren't that many first-level masters out there, but this one was not in my extensive mental filing cabinet. I quickly added a new file.

He was dressed in an understated outfit my host might have worn if he'd decided it was casual day, one designed to enhance what nature had bestowed with a liberal hand. The off-white sweater was tight enough to show off a nice upper body, and the tan suede pants hugged muscular thighs. A spill of rich auburn was trying to escape from a gold clip at his nape. It looked like the kind of hair women on shampoo commercials have—luxurious, overabundant and shiny. It should have looked effeminate on a man, as should the long-lashed blue gray eyes, but the broad shoulders and strong, arrogant jaw were all male. I frowned at him. Vamps had plenty of advantages already; they didn't need good looks, too. I cataloged his scent—a combination of whiskey, fine leather and, oddly, butterscotch—for future reference, and returned my attention to his companion.

"There is a shower in the bath down the hall, or you may use the one in my room if you like," I was told. "It's through the bedroom at the end of the corridor."

My host placed the boy on the sofa, heedless of the expensive upholstery, and whoever the auburn-haired vamp was, he moved to help without a word. He didn't even bother to keep an eye on me as he did so, which I found vaguely insulting. I'd killed his kind for half a millennium and I didn't even rate a blink? He must figure the odds were in his favor. Considering that I was in a room with two first-level masters, he was probably right.

I went down a hall that smelled faintly of some generic air freshener. They probably advertised it as "lilac-scented," but it reminded me more of vats of chemicals than wide-open fields and flowers. There is a downside to supersharp senses, as with so much else about me.

Of course, there is an upside, too. I cocked an ear, but there was nothing much to hear. A girl was on the phone next door, complaining about some guy to a girlfriend, and someone down a floor was either talking to his cat or having a psychotic episode, but both voices were clearer than the soft noises coming from the living room. The vamps were presumably cleaning the wounds better than I'd been able to do at the bar, and bandaging him up. I knew nobody was planning a snack—it would be like offering people used to beluga caviar and Dom Pérignon a sack of stale Fritos and a flat Coke. Sloppy seconds weren't likely to appeal.

I let myself into the big master bedroom and looked around. Opulent, understated, rich. What a surprise. In here the decorator had gone out on a limb and chosen a gray color palette, everything from charcoal on the bedding to ash on the walls. I frowned around with distaste and craved my paints so badly my palms itched. A good half hour of work on the bare stretch over the bed would make all the difference. I've never gotten a security deposit back yet, but then, in my line of work, that was pretty much a given anyway. And I've never lived with flat, gray walls.

The bathroom was all blinding white subway tiles in what I guess was supposed to be industrial chic. I took white—of course—towels out of the closet and got my filthy self into the chrome and glass shower. At least it was big.

I leaned my head against the soon-steamy wall and tried not to imagine Claire with a tiny version of myself in her arms. Dhampirs, children of human women and male vampires, were never a good thing. Luckily, we are really rare, since dead sperm don't swim too well. However, there were a few cases where a newly made vamp just out of the grave had been able to sire a child. The kids were usually born barking mad and lived very short, very violent lives.

Of course, not all dhampirs were the same. Just like

with human children, you never knew how the genes were going to combine. I'd known a few rare ones who took after their mothers and managed to live—mostly— normal lives. Other than for heightened senses and strength, you might never have known what they were. But were even rarer than the rare breed itself, and I somehow doubted Claire would get so lucky.

I knew her. Whatever the story behind her child's conception, she would love it, nurture it and defend it fiercely, at least until it grew up enough to throw her off a building in a fit of rage it wouldn't even remember. I really, really hoped Kyle had been lying. Otherwise, I was faced with killing my best friend's kid, along with any affection she'd ever had for me, or waiting for her violent death.

It would be useless to try to talk to Claire. She'd never understand how much danger she was in, nor be willing to take the necessary steps to ensure her safety. It was that damn respect for life she was always lecturing me about, the same one that made her a strict vegetarian and forced me to have to sneak out to eat bar-b-que. After all, I could hear her argue, I've known you for years and you've never wanted to kill me. She'd only be hurt and confused if I explained just how wrong she was. Whatever control I may have acquired through long centuries of practice, I'm still a monster. And like the one who sired me, I'll always love death and destruction a little bit more than anything, or anyone, else.

I don't know much about my mother, except that she was a young serving girl dumb enough to believe that the local lord's handsome son wasn't just having a good time with her. They'd been together for several months before he was cursed with vampirism, a state he failed to recognize immediately. Unlike the usual way of making a vamp, the curse took a while to complete the transformation. There was no big death scene and no dramatic clawing his way out of his own grave. Instead, he'd shrugged off the Gypsy's mutterings as the ravings of a madwoman and gone about his usual, love-'em-and-leave-'em lifestyle for a fateful few days. Fortunately, I was the only one to whom he'd passed his newly acquired vampiric genes in the meantime.

Long story short, nine months later, after he'd gone off to get his undead head together, a bouncing baby me entered the world, only to find that the world wasn't happy to see me. The humans where I grew up were pretty savvy about all things vampire and figured out what I was the first time they saw my baby fangs. Mother was told to drown me in the river and save everyone a lot of trouble. I don't know to this day whether I'm happy or not that she gave me away to a passing Gypsy band instead. She died in a plague some years later, so I never knew her. And my father—well, let's just say we have issues.

I don't guess that is too surprising considering that dhampirs and vampires are mortal enemies. Some legends say that God lets dhampirs exist to keep a check on the number of vamps out there. A more scientific explanation is that the predator instinct in vamps is necessary to allow them to feed, but it plays hell with a body that has an adrenal system to overload. But I think at least part of the anger we carry is a natural reaction to being forced into a world where we have zero chance of ever belonging. Vampires hate and fear us, and usually try to kill us on sight. Humans think we're one of them for a while, until one of the rages takes us and our true nature becomes all too obvious. Then we're on the run again, trying to avoid angry mobs of both species while attempting to carve a niche out of their world for ourselves.

Most of my kind burn out early, either by overtasking their systems or—far more often—by dying in a fight. I know of only one other dhampir as old as me, a batty Indian fakir who lives in the desert of Rajasthan, as far away from human habitation as he can get. It took me more than two months to find him the only time I'd bothered, and he didn't have much useful advice to impart. He manages to keep a lid on things by meditating the centuries away, controlling his true nature by simply denying it any contact with possible prey. That really isn't my style. I prefer the traditional method of letting my second nature out occasionally to hunt, providing that it kills only the undead. Or demons, or the occasional were, or pretty much anything that isn't human. It's messy, but it works, and it even led to my current job.

I soaped up my greasy hair and wondered if that was why I'd been tracked down. It seemed unlikely. If the Senate wanted someone dead, they sure as hell didn't need to hire me to do it. They had plenty of their own muscle and an intelligence department second to none. One cut-rate assassin they could do without.

There was also the little matter that I had a habit of refusing assignments unless I knew the circumstances involved—all of them. I had promised myself to limit my sprees to those who, as the saying goes, needed killing. I figured that since it was my hand on the ax—or the stake or the rifle or whatever—it was up to me to be certain I didn't take out someone who had merely irritated a local loan shark. But that nosiness, as the Senate would view it, would have put me off their list of hired talent even if the accident of my birth hadn't already made me persona non grata in a big way. So my skills at the hunt were probably not what was needed here.

I couldn't for the life of me figure out what else it could be, though. Occasionally I earned a few bucks checking the supernatural underground for people with problems that the human authorities couldn't manage or even understand. But again, there was nothing I could offer that the Senate couldn't do itself and probably far better. All things considered, I was stumped. Not that it mattered anyway. As soon as I got a few answers out of buffet boy, I was off hunting Michael. Whatever the Senate wanted, it could damn well come up with some other way to get it. And as for my host, he could drop dead. Again.

Chapter Two

"This is Louis-Cesare. I would appreciate it if you refrained from attacking him while under my roof."

I had slipped back into the living room unannounced, but of course I'd been heard. I was relieved that at least they hadn't smelled me coming—or not as easily as before—since I was clean for the first time in days. I was also wearing one of my host's pristine white dress shirts over my blood-spattered jeans, which he refrained from commenting on, although he did tighten his lips somewhat. I grinned. It had probably cost as much as my rent for the month and it hung down to my knees, but I hadn't had a great selection to choose from. The closet in his room had been almost bare, another good sign, since the guy is a clotheshorse. If he'd been near the New York shops for more than a few days, the place would've looked like an Armani boutique.

"I'll keep that in mind," I told him, sauntering over to the bar and mixing myself a double. With my metabolism, alcohol burns off too fast for me to get drunk—one of the few perks of my condition. "Where's the kid?"

"I've arranged for his care. He was taken away a few moments ago."

I tightened my grip on the bottle and counted to ten. It wasn't a record—he'd managed to get under my skin faster on previous occasions—but it was close. "I needed to talk to him," I said carefully, turning around. "He was the only lead I had. You had no right to—"

"He retains his memories, for the moment," I was told. "You can speak to him later if you must. For now, there are more important matters."

I looked down at a crunching sound to see that I'd cracked the bottle. I set it carefully on the bar and ignored the single malt draining away over the dark wood. Five centuries of fighting for control, and it was all I could do not to smash the thing the rest of the way against his head. How did he do it? No one else caused me to reach boiling point this fast, at least not anymore. "I'd prefer to speak to him tonight," I said evenly. "I'm in something of a hurry."

I noticed that the redhead had closed in a little, as if he thought his buddy might need backup. I repressed a smile. At least I had his attention now.

"He has been heavily medicated, Dorina. He won't be able to tell you anything for approximately eight hours. If you wished it otherwise, you might have mentioned the fact."

I felt my stomach twist into a knot and my heartbeat speed up. I tried to slow my suddenly accelerated breathing, knowing what was coming if I couldn't get a grip, but all I could think about was Claire. I thought of the past month, of the useless leads and the sleepless nights, of calling in every favor I had and promising more to entirely the wrong types for information that had turned out to be useless. I thought of Kyle's smarmy face as he told me a worst-case scenario that still had me wanting to scream, and then a familiar rushing sound filled my ears and I blacked out.

It happens that way sometimes, although mostly these days I keep it under better control. But that night was like old times, when I'd gone on rampages that sometimes left dozens dead, and I was never able to remember more than flashes later. It was the real nature of a dhampir and the reason no one ever trusted us, especially the vamps, who were our favorite prey. It was one of so very many reasons I hoped Claire had been a lot smarter than Kyle had said.

I came around eventually, which rather surprised me. One of these centuries, I fully expect to die in the middle of some berserker rage and never even know when it happens. I've come close more times than I can recall, waking up broken and bleeding, surrounded by bodies in places I didn't recognize and sometimes days later than my last memory. This was better than most. There was something sharp pinning my shoulder to the wall, and the burn of familiar pain helped me concentrate enough to pull the rest of the way out of the trance.

I knew when I'd succeeded by the fact that my shoulder suddenly felt like it had caught fire. As an added bonus, I was the proud owner of an aching jaw, a pounding headache and a severe urge to vomit. The redhead was holding the rapier that had me skewered like a butterfly on a pin, rendering my left arm temporarily useless, and my host was using both hands to hold my right. I was glad to see that they looked more than a little beaten up. The redhead's pretty white sweater was stained with blood that didn't smell like mine, and the brunet had a

long gash down one side of his face that had barely
missed his right eye. It wasn't deep, though, and it started
to close over as I watched. Damn.

"My lord, I do not mean to interfere, but perhaps
restraints . . . ?" The voice had a faint French accent,
which explained why I hadn't known him. The redhead
was a Senate member, but from the European version, not
the North American. And I hadn't been to Europe since a
very memorable visit during the Great War. He was looking a little spooked, which would have pleased me under
other circumstances. At the moment, however, I was distracted by my host moving one hand up to grip me around
the throat.

"I would put you over my knee if I thought it would do
any good," he told me grimly.

The other vamp looked like he'd just been slapped. I
laughed. "He thinks you're being kinky," I said, pausing
to spit out a tooth that had come loose. No worry. I'd
grow a replacement soon enough, and at least it was a
back one this time. I grinned at the French vamp, who
looked vaguely ill at the thought of anyone doing anything with me, except maybe planting a stake in my ribs.
"You didn't tell him, did you?"

The brunet sighed and released me, pausing to yank
out the rapier as he did so. I didn't wince. At the moment,
the pain almost felt good, a reminder that, once again, I'd
beaten the odds and lived. Not that I'd been in serious
danger this time. He wouldn't kill me when he needed my
help. Well, at least not until I turned him down.

"I was planning introductions, had you given me the
opportunity," I was told acerbically.

The redhead's expression was now bordering on revulsion. There must be a brain inside that pretty head, be-

cause he appeared to be putting things together, but not willing to believe what his instincts were telling him. I decided to help him out. I turned to my host, who was looking down at me with an annoyance he wasn't bothering to hide. I threw my good arm around his neck and gave him a robust kiss on the cheek. "Hello, Daddy!"

Fifteen minutes later I was lying on the floor howling, and it wasn't from pain. I hadn't laughed that hard in years, to the point that I almost couldn't breathe and my ribs actually hurt. Of course, that could have been from one of the new bruises I was sporting—between the bar fight and blacking out, I was a little under the weather—but at the moment I didn't care. I wiped my streaming eyes and tried to sit up.

Mircea, better known as Daddy dearest when he bothered to acknowledge the connection, was sitting on the sofa with folded arms, waiting me out. The French guy had poured himself a drink—stiff even by my standards—and taken it to the floor-to-ceiling windows overlooking the darkened cityscape. He had his back to us. I wasn't sure whom he was trying to block out, the abomination or the one who made her.

I crawled into an armchair and valiantly fought to restrain myself. It was difficult, with what I'd just been told. I don't have a chance to do this often, so I savored the moment. "Would it be out of line to say I told you so?" I asked, with almost a straight face.

"I have never known you to be concerned with proprieties," was the caustic reply.

"*Du-te dracului,*" I said automatically, before realizing how ironic telling him to go to the devil was under the circumstances.

"I am proposing to send you to him instead," Mircea replied evenly.

I nodded at the other vamp. "You tell your friend there that this is a suicide mission?" I glanced at the handsome vamp. "Got a death wish, buddy?"

The Frenchman ignored me, but Mircea decided to be contentious. As usual. "He won't be going alone. That is why I went to the trouble of locating you. His job is to trap Vlad. Yours is—"

"Did you tell him that you could've taken Uncle Drac out last time, but were too busy seducing some Senate member to bother?"

"—to keep him alive. He doesn't know my brother; you do."

"Which is precisely why I'm not going anywhere near him." I stood up, stretched and looked around for my coat. Claire had bought it for me after a hunt ruined my last leather number. She'd hoped it would be more resilient, being washable and all, but I wasn't so sure. My wardrobe is constantly updated since I trash clothes like other people throw out Kleenex—a hazard of the job. The last time I saw the coat, it had been covered in goo along with my T-shirt. I decided that I must've left them lying in the bathroom.

"Where do you think you're going?"

"To see if my dry cleaner can get out whatever it is Varos demons secrete when they spit at you. Pinkish purple ooze, smells like a family of skunks and eats into fabric like acid."

I headed for the door, but before I could get there, Daddy was in the way, reclining against the doorjamb. "Sit down."

I sighed. I hadn't really expected it to be that easy.

"There's no point." Mircea just stood there, so I elaborated, more for the benefit of the idiot who'd gotten roped
into this mess than for dear old Dad. Maybe the poor bastard could still weasel out of it. For his sake, I hoped so,
since he was certainly doomed otherwise.

"London, 1889. Dark and stormy night. Ring any
bells? I think the exact quote was, *'If you do not finish
this tonight, if you leave him any avenue by which to return, I wash my hands of the whole affair. Next time, you
will hunt him alone.'"* I glanced at the French guy, who'd
turned around to stare at us. "I was a lot more pretentious
back then," I explained, "but you get the drift. Barely survived the last go-round, not doing it again, especially
when all you're planning is to put him in another of those
oh-so-secure traps and wait for him to find another way
out. And that's assuming he doesn't eviscerate you and
anybody dumb enough to follow you first. Now get out of
the way, Daddy dear; I have a real job to do."

"This is your job, until I say otherwise."

I smiled. I was feeling fairly mellow for a change. I
wasn't sure if that was because of all the violence earlier
or the laughing fit, but either way, I actually didn't feel
like tearing his head off. "And you used to have such
good hearing."

"You will not defy me on this."

I waited for a minute, but he just stood there, looking
all grim and macho. It was the face that usually caused
other vamps to sink to their knees, babbling apologies
and trying to kiss his expensive, leather-covered toes. It
had never worked on me. "Um, I'm assuming there's
another half to that sentence. Because I'm really not
seeing—"

"Claire." That one word stopped me in midrant.

"I had better be misunderstanding you," I said softly.

"You are fond of the human, aren't you?"

"If you had anything to do—"

"I did not take her," he said calmly, "but I could arrange to get her back for you. I can call on the Senate's resources, which you must admit are far greater than your own."

"I'll find her myself."

He arched a dark, expressive brow and gave me his patented condescending smile. "In time?"

I didn't answer for a moment, my brain being busy with a replay of that night in London. All I could hear was the faint sound of bootheels on cobblestones, far away but getting closer. That even, measured tread had echoed in my head for years. I didn't think about what had happened after the steps stopped, right in front of where I was concealed. No. I never thought about that at all.

"Uncle Drac," as I flippantly referred to him to keep myself from gibbering, was the only thing on earth that truly scared me. I think my laughter earlier had been less about Daddy finally admitting I was good for something, and more hysterics from the thought of going up against Drac again. I had lobbied hard for the final solution to the problem more than a century ago, since trapping him had been as much about luck as skill. With nothing else to do to while away the decades, he must have dissected that night a thousand times, analyzing it in that brilliant, broken mind of his, figuring out exactly where he went wrong. Dracula deserved his legend, however mixed-up much of it was due to that Victorian hack writer. He wouldn't make the same mistakes twice; in fact, I doubted he would make any at all.

A mental picture of Claire's face wavered in front of

my eyes. She was one of the few friends I'd ever been able to hold on to for more than a few months. It wasn't that the rages didn't scare her, but rather that she had never been exposed to them. I had never thought of myself as a magical being before I met her, but there was no doubt that she had the same calming effect on me as on a spell or ward. Living and working alongside her had given me the closest thing to peace and a normal life I'd ever known. I still had occasional fits, but only when outside her orbit, and even then, they were rarer. The idea of never seeing her face screw up in thought as she surveyed my latest painting, trying to figure out what the hell it was supposed to be, was brutal.

But Claire was more than my friend; she was also the only chance for me to master my rage once and for all. She's from one of the oldest magical families on earth, House Lachesis, who specialize in healing. They have access to ancient lore that even the Circle itself doesn't know. Claire once told me that there is a branch of the family that does nothing but scavenge, in areas so out of the way as to make Antarctica look like Forty-second and Broadway, for unusual cures, potions and amulets. Another branch researches new treatments, and yet another comes up with debilitating spells to sell to malevolent types to ensure a steady supply of wealthy afflicted.

Despite the fact that she had worked in the business side of things rather than in research and development, she'd been using her contacts to try to find something that would decrease my fits. Because of my metabolism, human drugs don't stay in my system long enough to register. I was hoping a magical solution would have more effect, but no one had ever thought to develop anything for dhampirs. There are so few of us as to make it impractical, and we're not exactly top of the popularity chart. There was a good possibility that Claire's work was the first of its kind ever done. And if I didn't find her soon, it might also be the last.

I *would* find her—I had no doubt of that—but Mircea, damn him, was right. I might not manage it in time. Michael was only a low-level master, sixth at a guess, who ran errands for a couple of vamp bosses in Brooklyn. He was nothing I couldn't deal with half-asleep, but the information I'd gotten from his thugs was that he'd recently skipped town. No one knew where he was, and tracking him with only my own resources to draw on was going to take time. Time Claire might not have.

Mircea, on the other hand, could put an organization on the search that made the CIA, the FBI and Interpol look like a bunch of retarded children—even more so than they usually do. By this time tomorrow, she could be back in our dilapidated house, clucking over her herb garden and two spoiled cats. And, if the pregnancy thing wasn't a figment of Kyle's warped imagination, I'd have time to talk with her and explain a few hard truths.

I glanced at the other vamp, only to see him regarding me with faint contempt. He probably thought he was hiding it, but I'd learned a few things about reading expressions over the years. Or maybe he didn't care if I knew he thought me a coward. He was, after all, quite correct, at least when it came to my scary uncle. Anyone who wasn't afraid of him was either a lunatic or really stupid. I wondered which type Mircea was trying to foist off on me.

"I'd want her back first. Payment only on delivery."

"No." Mircea didn't even bother to look regretful. "Vlad has been on the loose for over a week. To give him more time to lay his plans is folly."

"He's had more than a century to plan already," I pointed out. I didn't like the Vlad reference. If Mircea would just once forget that the monster we were discussing was his brother, it would make things so much easier. But he has this weird affection for family that I've never understood. It ensured that he tracked me down every few decades, even knowing we'd end up in the usual knock-down, drag-out, and it had kept him from staking Dracula when he'd had the chance.

"True, but we dismantled his support network, if you recall. Unless he plans to move entirely on his own, he will need time to find followers. At the moment, he should be vulnerable. But he will not stay that way for long."

I didn't bother pointing out that "vulnerable" and "Dracula" really didn't belong in the same sentence. At no point in time had he ever been anything but utterly capable and completely ruthless. But Mircea had a point. If I had to take on Drac, I'd vastly prefer for him not to have found any helpers. He was bad enough on his own, but the stable he used to control had been another source of nightmares, to the point that I'd spent more than a decade hunting the worst of them down. It had let me sleep a little better afterward, although only a little. Knowing that their lord and master was only one step away from being back in business had never gone down well. I felt my temper rising at the thought that if, just once, Mircea the perpetually hardheaded had listened to me, Dracula would be in a coffin permanently right now and none of this would be necessary. Of course, in that case, I wouldn't have help with Claire.

"Fine. But if I start hunting him tonight, I want the search for Claire to start at the same time."

"Done."

I didn't ask for surety. Mircea is a lot of things, but he keeps his word when he gives it. You just better be damn sure you know what that word is, because he is one of the slipperiest bastards out there when he wants to be. I decided I wanted things spelled out a little more. "If she's alive, I want her back. If not . . ."

"Would you prefer to deal with the parties responsible yourself, or have us do so?"

"What do you think?"

Mircea smiled slightly. "I will order them held for you. I take it we have an agreement?"

I looked at the French guy and wasn't pleased at what I saw. Yeah, there was enough power emanating off him to rival Mircea's aura, which raised hairs on my arms every time I got within five feet of him, but taking down someone like Dracula was going to require more than raw power. A whole lot more. "Yes, but I'd prefer a partner I already know," I said, trying to blunt the insult. "We won't have time to learn each other's styles. What's Marlowe doing?"

Kit Marlowe, vamp, playwright and onetime Elizabethan bad boy, was head of intelligence for the Senate. He was one evil son of a bitch, as I could testify on a personal level, and we weren't exactly buddies. But if I had to track the meanest vamp on the planet, I'd like to have one of the runners-up at my back. As long as he wasn't gunning for me this time.

"We are on a wartime footing, Dorina. I can hardly pull the chief of security away for a personal errand at such a moment."

"It's not gonna stay personal for long," I pointed out. "Our names may head Uncle's list, but we're hardly the only ones on it. The war may seem like a sideshow if he really gets going."

"Nonetheless, the Consul would never permit it." Even Mircea would think twice about bucking the Senate leader's orders, and I couldn't blame him. I'd met her only once, and that had been more than sufficient. My personal opinion was that she was crazier than Drac, but no one had asked me.

"So who is going with us, then?" I hoped he had some better backup in mind than the guys I normally used. One or two could handle themselves in some pretty tough situations, but nothing like this. The only connections I had who might have been useful were currently incommunicado— locked away for crimes the vamps or mages didn't like, but hadn't viewed as being serious enough to merit a cell six feet under. And since the war had intervened, their trials were on permanent hold—there's no such thing as habeas corpus in the supernatural world.

"I would prefer to keep this in the family," Mircea said.

I snorted. I didn't doubt it. Anyone not under his direct command would have no compunction about staking good old Drac at the first opportunity. It was certainly my plan. Assuming he didn't get me first.

Something occurred to me. "So what's he doing here?" I jerked a thumb at the fashion plate. I wasn't on great terms with the family, but at least I knew who was who. And Mr. Lack of Congeniality wasn't on the list.

"I told you," Mircea said in that überpatient voice he reserves for me and the mentally challenged. "This is Louis-Cesare." I looked expectant. He sighed. "Radu's get."

I gave the pretty vamp another, more interested look.

"I wasn't aware my marginally sane uncle had any off-spring."

I was being kind. Radu—Mircea and Dracula's younger brother—was a real weirdo. Not in the contender-for-homicidal-heavyweight-title kind of way like Drac, but almost as creepy. For one thing, he insisted on dressing like a reject from a Three Musketeers film, only reluctantly putting on up-to-date clothes when strong-armed into it. Some vamps liked to dress as they'd done in life when out of sight of humans, but Radu had been brought up in fifteenth-century Romania, not seventeenth-century France—hence, the weird. For another, he'd never, or so I'd thought, made another vamp in his life, although he had been a second-level master for centuries. Someone that powerful without a stable was unprecedented. Followers gave you income as well as protection, and who would voluntarily forgo both? He used Mircea's stable almost like it was his own, but sponging off elder brother would have gotten tiresome to me. But then, nobody much cared what the skeleton in the closet thought.

"This is the only one." I waited, but Mircea didn't elaborate. Again, no real surprise. Why tell cannon fodder any more than she has to know?

"Okay, I understand you want him along, and that's fine. I'm sure I can find something for him to do, but—"

"I think you are laboring under a misapprehension," the Frenchman interrupted, his accent a bit more obvious than it had been before. "You speak as if you will be deciding strategy. You will be under my direction, not the reverse."

I slowly turned to face him, and something in my expression caused him to lower a hand to the hilt of his rapier. He didn't draw it, but he didn't take his hand back, either.

"I don't know who you think you are," I informed him evenly, "and I don't care. But I take direction from no one. Are we clear?"

"We most decidedly are not," he responded, equally crisply. It would have been funny at another time, our trying to out-enunciate each other, but at the moment I didn't feel like laughing. This was going to be hard enough without backup who couldn't follow orders.

"Then we have a problem," I told him honestly. I looked back at Mircea, who was wearing an expression that on anyone else I would have described as petulant. "You know what's at stake here. I know you don't like me any more than I do you, but we have worked together before. I think it was luck, but maybe we'll get lucky again. And you already know how I operate."

Mircea was shaking his head before I even finished. "Normally that is the way I would choose to proceed. But not now."

"Why not?" I thought my question was reasonable, but he suddenly looked angry.

"After all these years, can you not follow a simple command?"

"Not when it's likely to get me killed, no." I looked between the two of them, trying to figure out what unspoken communication was going on. For a brief moment I felt something—not anger exactly but something more elusive—that Mircea and this stranger could communicate so easily without words. Because that's exactly what they were doing. A normal human wouldn't have noticed the few, almost-too-quick-for-the-eye glances, but I did. That was one of the harshest parts of the dhampir experience: the fact that your senses never allow you to be oblivious, never let you for a moment fool yourself into thinking you belong.

Once, when I was very young and even dumber than I am now, I actually let a vamp try to turn me. I'd just reached the century mark and seen my mortal acquaintances age and die before my eyes, with the last one buried earlier that week. I was all alone and tired as hell of it. Not that I'd ever fit in with humans very well, but, God, how I had tried. So I figured, why not? I'm almost there anyway, why not cross over and actually be part of something for a change?

I knew it was a risk, of course: even if the vamp didn't just bleed me dry and leave me to die, most vamps spend eternity tied to a master they can't disobey. They are little more than slaves until they reach master status—which few ever do—and even then their responsibility to their master remains a debt that can be called in anytime. But at that moment, I didn't much care. Turns out, though, I had chosen well, and he gave it his all, I guess hoping for whatever fame would come out of being the first on record to turn a dhampir. But the next morning I woke up exactly as I'd been before, a little light-headed from the blood loss, maybe, but not changed one iota. So add another rule to the books: dhampirs can't be brought over. This meant that, after torturing me for a few days or weeks or whatever time he could spare, Drac wouldn't even try to add me to his new stable.

"I'm risking a lot here," I told them in what had to be the understatement of at least my last century. "I don't think it's asking too much to know why I can't have decent backup."

I never saw it coming. Despite the fact that I've sur-

vived longer than anyone would have bet by being unbelievably paranoid and very good at defense, I didn't see a
thing. I also didn't hear, smell or otherwise have a clue
what was happening. One second I was facing off with
Mircea, and the next I was facedown on the ground, being
pinned very effectively by the hard body pressing into
mine.

My reaction was immediate and unthinking. When
you've been in literally more fights than you can count,
often against opponents much bigger than you who have
no compunction at all about fighting dirty, you learn a
few things. I used them all and then some, yet the face-
to-the-carpet thing didn't change. I was stunned almost
into disbelief. This simply wasn't happening. I would
have believed that Mircea was helping out, except that he
had moved off to lean against the bar. I could see the toes
of his perfectly shined shoes and the knife-edge pleat of
his trouser cuffs, meaning that I was, incredible as it
seemed, being held by only one vamp.

Son of a bitch.

"We can continue this as long as necessary," an infuri-
atingly calm voice said near my left ear, "but we are wast-
ing time. Agree to my mastery and we can begin to plan
how to overcome our prey."

"Bull*shit*!" I tried unseating him again, but no luck.
The asshole was strong, but no way would any single
vamp have pinned me if I'd been expecting it. I tried to
ignore the little voice reminding me that one of the first
lessons I had ever learned was to *always* expect it.

"You cannot seriously believe you could lead a mission of this magnitude," he continued. "You know your
place, dhampir. Stay in it and you may be of some use to

the family. Fail to do so and I will be pleased to remove this stain on my lord's honor. Permanently."

"You will do no such thing." Mircea's less-than-pleased voice startled both of us. "I want your word, Louis-Cesare, that you will neither harm nor allow harm to come to my daughter if you can prevent it."

"My lord, you know what she is!" The voice above me sounded startled, as if he hadn't thought twice about threatening Daddy's little girl in his presence. Apparently, he didn't understand Mircea's family obsession. Which was odd, considering that, as Radu's get, he was part of our dysfunctional clan.

"Your word."

It sounded like Frenchie was choking, but he got it out. "You have it."

I bit back a smile and took advantage of his distraction. I relaxed all my muscles as if I had fainted, which, considering that most of the air was being pushed out of my lungs, wasn't far from the truth. The best I'd hoped for was that he would let up on the pressure enough for me to get a little room to maneuver, so it was a real shock when he suddenly pulled away altogether. "I do not question your judgment, my lord," I heard from far above my head, telling me that the idiot had actually stood up, "but obviously this . . . woman . . . is not up to the task. May I suggest—"

I never found out what he had in mind, because I seized the opportunity he had so foolishly provided. Two seconds later, pretty boy was finding out what the rug smelled like as I ground his head into the pile. "I DO question your judgment," I told Mircea, "at expecting me to work with anybody this stupid." I paused to let Frenchie experience more of the pleasures of rug burn.

"I thought you two would get on," Mircea murmured.

"Hey, still talking here. If you want me to do this, I do it my way. If you aren't available 'cause your manicurist can't switch appointments or whatever, fine. I'll put a team together. I have a couple names in mind already—all you need to do is get them out of jail for me—and I'm sure Marlowe can come up with a few more. I heard there was some sort of dueling whiz over from Europe to help the Consul with a challenge. Someone like that might be able to keep Drac busy long enough for me to deal with him."

"I quite agree," Mircea said, pouring himself a drink.

"Then get busy and see about finding him," I said testily. I wanted things arranged before I let the sneaky creature beneath me off the floor.

"I don't need to find him," I was told calmly. "I already know where he is."

Good, at least one problem was out of the way. "Somewhere nearby, I hope."

Mircea downed a generous measure of scotch in a single gulp. I grinned—most unmannerly. But the pleasure quickly faded at his next words. "Oh, yes. You're sitting on him."

Chapter Three

"Watch your step." I pushed open the kitchen door and skirted around the hole in front of the threshold. A Loray demon's head had leaked enough acid to eat through the worn wooden boards of the floor, leaving a burnt-edged gap that visitors had to hop over in order to enter. Claire had demanded to know why "that grisly thing" had been left there, and hadn't seemed to understand my explanation about rare-poison extraction.

I made it as far as the fridge before a hand clamped over my mouth. I struggled, but the body behind me might as well have been carved from sun-warmed stone; I couldn't budge him. Frenchie had his head tilted as if listening for something, but although I strained, the only threatening sound was the ancient fridge's death rattle. As it had sounded like that since I moved in, I wasn't too concerned. Louis-Cesare abruptly released me and drew his rapier. Before I could warn him about the house, he'd slipped through the door leading to the hall.

I stared after him for a few seconds, then mentally shrugged. I turned my attention to tossing out some perishables and pouring a week's worth of cat chow into the two misshapen lumps in front of the fridge. Claire had suddenly announced some months back that she was going to be a potter. She'd bought a wheel and paints, and used the kiln at a craft store to fire them. The results were . . . unusual. But what they lacked in quality, she made up for in sheer quantity. We had the poor, deformed creations sitting around everywhere. The cats seemed to like them, though.

I hesitated, scowling at the last few days' dishes in the sink, but in the end I went ahead and washed up. Housekeeping definitely wasn't my thing, but Claire hated a mess. I'd probably done more cleaning since she disappeared than in the whole time we'd roomed together. For some reason, a dirty house made it seem that much more empty, as if I didn't believe she'd be back to scold me about it.

I finished drying the last saucer and went in search of my unwanted partner. I found him safe and sound in the living room having a staring contest with Miss Priss. She was managing to look down her elegant feline nose at him despite being curled up on the couch. After a tense moment, she added to the insult by beginning to lick a dainty white paw as if bored. Jackanapes was less brave, the only indication of his presence being two narrowed green eyes that peered out from under the chintz curtains. He emerged when he saw me, but continued to stare suspiciously at the newcomer.

"They are yours?" Louis-Cesare asked after a pause. He seemed surprised that I'd do such a normal thing as keep a pet.

"No. Claire's. She inherited this place from an eccentric uncle and didn't think it fair to throw his pets out when they'd lived there longer than she had." I took in his posture, which was still tense, almost battle ready. "Relax. The war isn't going to follow us here. This place used to belong to a mage—it's well protected."

It was a serious understatement. Claire's uncle Pip had warded the place like it was Fort Knox, despite the fact that most of his stuff wouldn't have interested even a non-magical thief. He'd had the power to spare because the house had been built right on top of two ley lines, the vast rivers of power where worlds overlap. They crossed and pooled their energy right under the foundation, forming a deep well of power that Claire's uncle had used for everything from providing the engine for his wards to fueling the portals he'd littered about the place. And because they had an alternative power source, his enchantments hadn't decayed after he died, as most spells would have done. I resisted an impulse to invite the vamp to finish his solo tour.

"I'm going to go pack," I told him. "You might want to wait here. The house doesn't like strangers."

"Very well. Be quick." The vampire clipped every word, barely pushing out the correct amount of syllables as if it pained him to converse with me. It was something of a surprise—not that he'd feel the same instinctive animosity I seem to cause all vamps, but that he would show it. Most masters are excellent liars, right down to their facial expressions. Of course, maybe he didn't think I was worth putting on a facade.

I blew him a kiss and sauntered upstairs at a deliberately slow pace. I found my backpack under the bed, with a few surprises still inside from my last expedition. I long ago decided that if the choice was either get in trouble for owning illegal weapons or die because I didn't have one when needed, I'd gladly take the former. As a result, I never go on a serious hunt unaccompanied by my big khaki-colored knapsack. It looks like it's been through a few wars, which it has, but it securely holds some stuff that isn't exactly considered light magic. When people are trying to kill me, I don't worry too much about what I throw at them.

I changed into a white T-shirt, a black leather jacket—since the demon goo had reduced my denim coat to so much lace—jeans and black boots. Then I packed a few essentials and emptied the contents of a hidden cupboard into the remaining space in the pack. If I was going after Drac, I was taking my whole damn arsenal with me.

I hefted a short sword, but regretfully decided I'd have to do without it. Nothing else was fitting in that pack. I propped the sword against the wall, where its surface reflected the vivid colors of the mural I'd recently completed. It had surprised the hell out of Claire, not so much for its postmodernist edge, but because the house had permitted it.

Claire was in a constant struggle for dominance with her legacy, which her uncle had given the personality of a crotchety old woman. Yellowing antimacassars remained on the furniture despite the fact that she hated them, because they reappeared whenever she moved them and shortly thereafter something of hers would go missing. Yet I'd slapped paint all over the place and suffered no ill effects. Maybe the house hadn't liked the faded cabbage rose wallpaper, either.

I had just finished packing when I heard a yelp followed by a series of thumps. From the landing, I saw Miss Priss sitting in front of the cellar door, looking smug. I went to the kitchen and got the key and a lantern, since Claire's uncle had never run electricity down there. Then I went to rescue the Senate's great warrior.

He was at the bottom of the cellar steps, lying in a heap. The last person to piss off the house had been one of my clients, who had tried to go upstairs without an escort. He'd not only been transported to the basement but ended up stuffed into a small trunk in the corner. The trunk had since been moved—I was using it for a nightstand—so the vamp had fared better. The only obvious harm was to his hair, which had come loose from its clip and fallen all over his face.

"The house is a little . . . temperamental," I explained as he got his long legs back under him.

"What is this place?" He looked around, eyes bright with interest.

I glanced at the dark cave, trying to see the attraction, but it looked as bad as always. The only saving grace was that the dim light hid the peeling, bilious green paint that had been applied around the time Eisenhower was president, and shadowed the rusting metal hulk in the corner. It didn't help to conceal the heaps of crates, however, since they were scattered all over the place. Claire had been planning to clean them out, assuming that the house was amenable, for fear that they constituted a fire hazard. "The basement. The stairs automatically send trespassers here."

"It is far more than that," he said, picking his way through the crates to where an old set of shelves held bottles of various colors. Claire's uncle had fancied himself an alchemist, but had never found the secret to turning lead into gold. Or much of anything else, according to her. "Your friend made this?" Louis-Cesare had picked up one of the delicate blue glass vials that had always reminded me of oversized perfume bottles.

"She's a null. She can't do magic."

Louis-Cesare inhaled. "Magic was not required here. This is art."

"I don't know that I'd get too close to that, if I were you," I advised. Moisture had beaded the outside of the glass, and his fingers left prints in the damp dust. I didn't know what it was sweating, but it was better to be safe than in a hundred pieces. I'd probably have a hard time explaining to Mircea why his red-haired boy hadn't even made it through the first day. "Pip's experiments could be a little . . . volatile." As demonstrated by the multicolored stains on the basement walls, courtesy of years of explosions.

"I sincerely hope so," he said obscurely. To my consternation, he opened the vial and ran a fingertip over the wet end of the plug. Before I could stop him, he brought it to his lips.

"Pip was an alchemist," I informed him, resisting the urge to step back. "Anything could be in there."

He raised a dark brow. "Alchemist? Is that what they call them now? The last time I visited this country, there was a more colorful term in use. Moonshiner." He went back to browsing the shelves, exactly like a connoisseur in a wine shop. I narrowed my eyes at the pile of metal in the corner—the still, I presumed—and suddenly a lot of things made sense.

"You're telling me these crates contain booze?"

"Booze." He rolled the word over his tongue as if he liked the sound. "Yes, I remember that one. And 'giggle water,' and 'hair of the dog' and, my personal favorite, 'hooch.'" I stared, both at the oddity of hearing those words in his accent and for the realization that some of the slang wasn't exactly current. I scowled. Thank you, Mircea. If Louis-Cesare's knowledge of the rest of the country was as archaic, he was going to be just a huge help.

Before I could comment, there was an unearthly wail from upstairs. After a start, I identified it as both of Pip's cats suddenly deciding to mew in unison. I told Louis-Cesare to help himself—Claire had crates of the stuff— and ran upstairs to find the two miscreants sitting in the bay window, screeching steadily.

"Cut it out!" They ignored me as usual. "No tuna for either of you for a week," I warned. "You'll eat dry food and like it." The threat had no discernible effect, and I decided that a little rough love was in order.

I'd reached out to snatch Jackanapes by the scruff of the neck when a face suddenly appeared in the window. Ancient pewter eyes, clear and cold as spears of ice, met mine. I stared at the handsome face, but made no move to let my visitor in. Unlike the Dark, who tend to populate the same corners of the world where I frequently hang out, the Light Fey are rarely seen. And it usually isn't a good thing when they do show up.

When another alabaster face joined the first, my unrest turned into something darker. I felt rather than heard Louis-Cesare come up behind me. "We have company," I said unnecessarily.

A third Fey joined the others in my front yard. He caught the eye the way a newly drawn sword does— beautiful and deadly. His hair was the same cold, bright mantle as the others, and he was dressed similarly in nondescript gray. So how did I know he was the leader? It might have had something to do with the power that hit me, even through the wards, like a slap in the face.

"Send out the half-breed, vampire." The leader's voice was musical, with an odd lilting accent.

Louis-Cesare caught me by the wrist, keeping me from retrieving a little present for our guests from my pack. "What do you want with her?" he demanded. I struggled against his grip and found myself unable to break it. That was getting old, fast.

The Fey ignored the question. "We have no quarrel with you. Do not give us one. Send out the half-breed or we will come in and take her."

"Let go of me," I told Louis-Cesare quietly. I had no idea why the Fey were so interested in me, but if they wanted a fight, I'd be more than happy to give them one.

Instead of answering, Louis-Cesare increased the pressure on my wrist until I dropped the weapon. He bent his head until his lips found my ear, and even then, his words were so soft that I felt more than heard them. "The Fey are neutral in the war. I believe Lord Mircea would prefer to keep them so."

"That's his problem," I said in a normal voice. I didn't give a damn if the Fey heard me or not. I smiled at the leader. "I've always wondered what color you bleed. What say we find out?"

I didn't get a verbal answer, but the fist he raised to smash my window was clear enough. So was the response to the assault by the house, which didn't like trespassers any more than I did. The offending Fey ended up in the branches of a mulberry bush, halfway across the yard, an expression of slight surprise on his face. His companions did nothing, but their very stillness seemed a threat, especially when their eyes swiveled in unison back to us, silent and unreadable. The cats screeched on.

Louis-Cesare abruptly turned and headed for the hall, dragging me with him. I didn't resist because I thought he was about to help me teach the Fey a lesson about name-calling. He stopped just inside the kitchen, and we both stared at the pale face that had appeared in the glass pane of the back door. "Is there another way out?"

"Let go of me and I'll clear this one," I told him irritably. I would complain—forcefully—at another time about being dragged about like a doll, but for the moment I preferred to save my strength for fighting Fey.

"Answer the question!"

"The front is impassable." It had long been blocked by heaps of crumbling furniture that Claire wanted gone but that the house seemed to like exactly where it was. After a lengthy struggle, they had reached a compromise: the furniture stayed, and she kept the door to the entranceway closed so we didn't have to look at it.

"There are no hidden ways?"

"No." I managed to swing my pack around to where I could reach the contents with my left hand. The sound of shattering glass let me know that someone had figured out how to get past the ward on the living room window. "Except for the portals," I added.

"Like the one at the foot of the stairs."

"Yes. There's another in the pantry. Claire and I use it to take out the trash the easy way. It lets out in back. And there's one in the cellar." I stuffed weapons into easily accessible inner pockets of my jacket, and grabbed a kitchen cleaver for good measure. "I'd take the one in the pantry if I were you."

I started for the hall, but my collar suddenly bit into

my throat and I was yanked back against an unyielding chest. "You are not going to attack the Fey," Louis-Cesare informed me tersely.

I jerked away from him, glaring. We were going to have to talk about personal space. "That's not your call."

The sound of splintering wood whipped me around to see the Fey breaking through the ward on the kitchen door. He looked a little frazzled, with all that silver hair a crackling nimbus about his impassive face, but he was still standing. A second later a sword appeared in his hand as if by magic, which it probably was.

Louis-Cesare plucked the cleaver out of my hand and got a grip on the back of my jacket, pulling me off my feet like an unruly kitten. I dangled there, torn between outrage and discomfort, unable to do much about the interloper. Luckily, the house took care of the problem, deluging him with a hail of pots, pans and kitchen utensils. He staggered backward and fell into the demon hole, which contracted around one of his legs, trapping him. Another Fey, a new-comer with long black hair, appeared behind his shoulder and began trying to tug him out, while two more slipped past him. The last thing I saw before the door to the hall swung shut was the ancient iron stove advancing on them menacingly.

Louis-Cesare headed back toward the living room with me in tow. "I'm not a member of the goddamned Senate!" I said, tugging backward for all I was worth. "I'm not starting a war. I'm defending private property!"

"You are a member of Lord Mircea's household and your actions reflect on him."

I grabbed the edge of the lintel over the living room door and held on for dear life. One of the silver-haired Fey was still at the bay window, muttering something under his breath. It might have been a spell, or a string of expletives. The window's jagged glass shards had formed themselves into a mouth that appeared to be trying to eat the arm he'd thrust through it. I looked for the leader, but he was no longer sticking out of the bush.

"Dorina—," Louis-Cesare began warningly.

"I am not letting them trash Claire's house!" I told him furiously, kicking out with my feet.

He caught my legs and gave a yank. The lintel came off in my hands, along with a good chunk of plaster, and I hit the floor with a thud. He grabbed me before I could scramble away, and dragged me to within an inch of his face. "You will do as you are told. We will inform the Senate of this and demand an explanation from the Fey. But we will not start a war!" With that, he threw me unceremoniously over his shoulder.

I beat on his back, but it was like hitting concrete. He made it to the cellar stairs, but I braced my feet against the sides of the wall, blocking him from going down. "Listen, you crazy son of a bitch! Claire and I sent things through that portal, trying to figure out where it went, but we never found any of them again. What if her bootlegger uncle linked it to an incinerator somewhere? Or a deep pit in the sea? The cellar was his workshop—he might have needed a fast way to dispose of unstable mixes!"

"Why did you not mention this before?" Louis-Cesare demanded.

"I didn't know you planned to run before!"

I'm not sure if it was my argument that halted the stubborn vamp or the deep growl, like that of an angry tiger, that suddenly replaced all the caterwauling. It echoed around the room loud enough to jar the china figurines on the mantel and to vibrate through the soles of my shoes. I jerked my head around to see an enormous white cat appear out of nowhere to swipe a paw the size of a sofa cushion at the Fey who was crawling through the window. I stared at the oddly fluffy creature as I was carried back toward the hallway again. It had a small blue ribbon dangling off one giant ear. Miss Priss had been wearing one just like it.

Another oversized feline, black with familiar green eyes, swished a massive tail and the hall door slammed shut behind us. The sounds of a giant cat fight joined the racket caused by screeching metal and loudly ricocheting kitchen implements. It sounded like a small war was taking place on either side of us, with much hissing and yowling and bumping of large objects.

"Where is the pantry?" Louis-Cesare's voice was calm, but a muscle worked in his jaw.

"Put me down and I'll show you."

He ignored me. With both doors closed and a broken overhead light socket, the hall was almost as dark as the cellar, but he moved easily, managing to avoid the doily-covered tables and hard-edged chairs the house insisted on keeping in the narrow corridor. He found the pantry door on his own, probably by smell.

"Where is the portal?"

When I didn't answer, the hand on my butt tightened painfully. "It's camouflaged as the third set of shelves to the right," I said resentfully. "You'll feel a tingle as soon as you get close."

Mages skim along the top of ley lines all the time, using them like their personal superhighway for fast, un-obstructed travel. But portals are a little trickier. They actually permeate the ley line itself, forming an energy sink

that propels the user into the no-man's-land between re-
alities before spitting them out the other side. Sometimes
that's a few yards away; sometimes it's in another world.
Because they take so much power, portals are pretty rare,
and most people are a little nervous about entering one.
Assuming he'd need to work up his courage, I'd planned
to escape as soon as Louis-Cesare put me down. But the
damned vamp dove in headfirst.

For a second, I was caught up in a maelstrom of
activity—energy hummed inside my bones, sound
roared in my ears and a swirl of colors flashed before
my eyes too swiftly to sort out. Then I was bouncing on
something soft and damp and odorous, bits of which
clung wetly to my fingers. Once the world stopped spinning, I identified it as the sauerkraut I'd just cleaned out
of the fridge. Damn—I'd forgotten that Claire had
started a compost heap.

Before I'd even gotten my feet under me, a couple of
Fey were rounding the house like silver blurs. My face
was forced into the kraut by a strong hand, so I felt rather
than saw the curse fly overhead. It burst against the trunk
of an oak a yard behind us, causing it to catch fire and explode outward. One of the burning bits of bark set a tuft
of compost in front of my nose alight.

Louis-Cesare released me, and I bounced up with a
snarl. "OK. That's it." I grabbed a very illegal weapon
from my jacket, but didn't get a chance to use it. An arm
circled my waist and suddenly we were airborne. It took
a moment to realize that he had actually jumped the six-
foot fence separating Claire's house from the one next
door. We landed in Mr. Basso's flower bed, Louis-Cesare
hitting the ground first and rolling to take the impact.

"You have my word that the Senate will reimburse

your friend for any damage," he hissed in my ear as I
struggled to my feet. "Now, must I carry you from here?"

A Fey appeared on top of the fence, and another
jumped over it with the easy grace of a leaping deer. Neither was the leader, and either they didn't speak English
or they weren't feeling chatty. I silently opened a palm to
show them the small black orb I carried.

Louis-Cesare had drawn his sword and begun backing
toward the Senate's car, a BMW four-door. The driver
must have figured out that something was wrong, because
I heard the engine crank to life behind us. The Fey didn't
so much as glance at Louis-Cesare's nice, shiny rapier.
Their eyes never left the dislocator in my hand.

We reached the car and Louis-Cesare stuffed me in
ahead of him. He hadn't even shut the door before the
driver was tearing away from the curb, tires screaming. I
twisted around in time to see the leader join the other two.
Our eyes met, and his seemed to have darkened. They
looked almost inky now, black as the deepest part of the
sea, and as pitiless.

His power flowed after us, filling the air like a clammy
fog. It took the form of a human hand, shimmering with
the gases that formed it like a glittering shroud. I got the
definite impression that it would be a very bad thing if it
caught us. It wasn't even at the car yet, but I could feel
the coldness of it, a chill that reached all the way to my
bones. I could sense its intent—to search, to find, to kill.
It flowed over a flowering shrub, frost furling the leaves
like autumn had come in a moment. And when it passed
on, there was nothing left behind but dried sticks and
fallen petals.

One insubstantial finger barely touched the bumper of
the car, and I was suddenly engulfed by a chill so great I

would have thrown myself into a fire had one been available. In a heartbeat, it made me certain that warmth would never come again, that I would never do anything but shiver and watch ice creep farther along my bones. So cold.

Strong hands seized me, jerking me across the seat, and lips pressed to mine. Warmth suffused my mouth and began to spread, pushing against the chill shuddering through my body. I came back to myself with a jolt, looking into Louis-Cesare's worried face, as the driver floored the gas pedal. We rocketed through Claire's normally quiet neighborhood like all the hounds of hell were after us, outracing ancient magic with a lot of modern German engineering. I clutched Louis-Cesare's shoulders and shuddered with just the memory of that deadly touch. What had I gotten myself into now?

Chapter Four

An hour later, Louis-Cesare and I were on a plane racing the sun for California. If we didn't win, it was no big deal. We were ensconced in a private jet, owned by the Senate, that was equipped to keep its occupants from ever experiencing unfiltered sunlight. Not to mention that the vamp sitting in one of the luxurious swivel seats across from me was perfectly able to stand the sun if need be. All the older ones could, at least for a while, although they paid for it in enormous power loss. Since I had a vested interest in keeping Louis-Cesare's power level at high, I was glad for the tinted windows.

I wasn't pleased at the way things were shaping up, but at least we were going to be meeting José and Kristie at the end of this jaunt across the country. The Senate had pulled some strings and gotten Kristie away from the mages, and had released José from their own holding cells. The two miscreants had been told that if they helped me complete my mission satisfactorily, all charges would be dropped. I'd talked to them by phone at one of the seedier clubs in Vegas where they were celebrating the news. I didn't object, since they could catch a plane in an hour or two and still beat us to 'Frisco. I was just hoping their party didn't turn out to be in lieu of a last meal. Neither of them knew what the mission was yet, and when they found out, they weren't going to need me to tell them the odds on all of us coming back.

The sound of a phone being snapped shut caused me to look up. Narrowed blue eyes bored into mine. I raised an eyebrow in a deliberate imitation of Mircea. "Yes?"

"We need to discuss your involvement with the Fey," Louis-Cesare announced.

"I don't have any involvement," I told him, getting up. There was nowhere to go, but I needed to move. My hands wanted to shake, my skin felt twitchy and my mouth was bitter with adrenaline. I was all wound up with no one to pound.

"You have not perpetrated any attacks on the Fey?"

"No." As evidenced by the fact that I was still alive. I was enough of a predator to know when I met a greater one, and the Fey leader had shaken me more than I wanted to admit. I don't like running, but in this case retreat had been a good idea. Of course, I didn't intend to admit that to Louis-Cesare.

"Then why did they assault you?" His voice held the same faint sneer he'd used in Mircea's presence, the one that indicated disapproval of everything I was and had ever been. It would have made me uncooperative even if I'd had a clue. Since I didn't, blowing him off was easy.

"You heard their ambassador. We imagined the whole thing, or else the Black Circle fooled us with an illusion to fracture our alliance." I hadn't been privy to the conversation, held via cell phone once we were airborne, but with my hearing, eavesdropping was easy.

Louis-Cesare made a sound that, by anyone less elegant, would have been called a snort. "The Black Circle is the bête noire of the magical world, and so a convenient scapegoat. Those were no mages today."

I didn't say so, but I secretly agreed. Human magic had a very different feel. What I couldn't understand was why either the mages or the Fey would concern themselves with me. Maybe I'd managed to piss off somebody important lately, but no one came to mind. The kind of creatures I hunt, most people are glad to see dead.

Louis-Cesare let the subject drop, but immediately switched to another equally annoying. "Lord Mircea has briefed me on what he knows of his brother's tactics—"

"I very much doubt that." I managed not to grimace. My nerves needed a break, not a reminder of how much trouble we were in. I prowled around, but it didn't help. I still felt like my skin was on too tight.

I flipped through a stack of uninteresting magazines the steward had provided, wanting to feel them tear under my hands. It wouldn't have been much of a loss— apparently the Senate doesn't read *Rolling Stone*—but I carefully replaced them in their little rack. It had been a while since I was wound this tight, with everything an itch: the breath of air from the overhead vents, the smooth vibrations of the plane beneath my feet, the crackle of ice cubes as Louis-Cesare poured himself a couple fingers of something.

I needed a drink. Or a fight. Yeah, a good fight would be just the thing.

"Pardon?" Louis-Cesare looked irritated when I confiscated his glass, downing the stuff in a gulp. It was clear, with little smell or taste, but it could have etched metal.

"They have too much history to have laid it all out for

you," I gasped, "even if Mircea talked nonstop for the past few days. What you got was the *Reader's Digest* condensed version." And probably not even that—Drac wasn't exactly a popular topic round the dinner table.

Louis-Cesare drew his brows together and found himself another glass. "I am a member of Lord Mircea's family. I think I know enough to—"

"You're a first-level master. Radu probably emancipated you ages ago."

"That is irrelevant." He was interrupted by the buzzing of a timer on the table by my elbow. He scowled at it. "We must discuss strategy. Lord Dracula will not be easy to find—"

I barely restrained a hysterical laugh. "Oh, I don't think that will be a problem." I walked into the plane's roomy bathroom. The Senate obviously didn't hold to the idea that deprivation was good for the soul, but at least the marble and gold-plated elegance was quiet. I unwrapped the towel around my head and frowned at the result. I'd had to go with a more subtle shade than I'd have liked, since the drugstore at the airport had had a limited supply of dye. It wasn't a true purple, more of a black with aubergine highlights. Maybe it would brighten when it dried. If this was going to be my last hurrah, I wanted to go out looking good.

I reentered the main cabin after rinsing off and combing my short hair. "Would you kindly stop doing that?" Louis-Cesare's voice was his usual measured tones, but a finger was tapping crisply on the side of his glass.

"Doing what?" I felt around my jacket pockets for one of the special joints Claire makes up for me. She's a master herbalist and although her concoction, like alcohol, has a very limited effect on me, it does soothe my temper.

I had a feeling I was going to need all the help I could get not to rip my new partner's throat out.

"Interrupting me. I would like to be able to finish a sentence."

"You just did." I lit up and smiled as the familiar haze wreathed my head. Bliss. A second later, the joint was pulled from my lips and crumpled into small bits by an angry vampire.

"I need your intellect, such as it is, clear and able to concentrate!" he informed me, right before I sent him sailing down the length of the plane. A worried steward peered out from behind the curtain separating the cabin from the galley, but quickly withdrew. Louis-Cesare jumped to his feet and I lit a replacement.

"Mess with my weed again and I'll be informing Daddy that there was an early casualty on the mission." I saw him wince at my designation for Mircea and grinned. He was hating it that the head of the family had such a black mark against his name. Probably thought it made him look bad, too. "As I was saying, we don't have to worry about Uncle Drac. He'll find us soon enough."

"Don't call him that." Louis-Cesare was looking less pleased by the moment.

"What? Uncle?" I shrugged. "Why not? It's true enough." I blew smoke in his direction and watched him struggle not to comment. "Ah yes, my dear demented relatives. Drac, the homicidal maniac, Radu, the poncy lunatic, and dear, cowardly Daddy, sending us off to manage what he doesn't dare to face himself." I smiled, deliberately provocative. "Just imagine, I'm actually the normal one. Sort of like that blond chick on *The Munsters*."

This time, when Louis-Cesare went for me, I was

expecting it. I wanted a fight—needed one after the day I'd had—and he was the only fair game around. He was also, I discovered, a fast learner. Maneuvers that had taken him by surprise before, he countered easily now, forcing me to improvise wildly. He managed to pin my arms to my sides momentarily, pulling me hard against him in the process. I hadn't had a real sense of his power before, but now it crackled along my skin, warring with my own. I tried to knee him in a sensitive area, but he slipped a leg between mine, crushing me between his body and the bathroom door.

The fight paused. I couldn't break his hold, but he couldn't press his advantage without risking me slipping away. His breath was coming fast and I had a second to enjoy the thought that at least I'd winded him. Then the feel of that solid chest moving up and down against mine brought on another emotion altogether. My entire body clenched, breath coming faster, nipples hardening. I shivered, caught between fury and arousal, and stared up into a face that reflected the surprise I felt.

Louis-Cesare's grip tightened, setting my pulse pounding in my ears. I wasn't accustomed to encountering someone stronger than me, to being unable to break away. The fight-or-flight instinct kicked in, and despite the unexpected attraction, it took all my willpower to force myself to melt against him.

It wasn't a big change, as we were already pretty much as close as we could get, but it felt very different. A second earlier, his body had resembled carved rock; now it was warm, muscled flesh that was very definitely male. His hold loosened, changing into something closer to an embrace. It felt achingly, shockingly good. I shifted luxuriously against the muscular thigh that spread my legs, and slid my arms out of his grasp. I ran them up his chest, and the prick of his nipples through the thin cashmere brought a sudden surge of desire, hard and piercing. I quickly moved on, twining my arms around his neck.

Some of his hair had come loose and was falling about his face in a cloud of shimmering bronze, gold and copper. I wondered briefly if it was as soft as it looked, my fingers flexing with the sudden desire to bury themselves in that shining mass and tangle in a fist. . . . I gently pulled the clip out instead, freeing his hair to tumble around his shoulders. "Louis-Cesare," I murmured, "I have to tell you something."

A shaft of light from an overhead fixture illuminated the sensual blue of his eyes. The brows over them rose and a wry smile tugged at his lips. Oh, yeah, he knew exactly how gorgeous he was. "And what is that?"

I whispered my lips along his neck in a soft kiss, breathing in the warm, sweet scent of the man, the one my brain had stubbornly labeled butterscotch. His smile grew wider, softer, more genuine, forming dimples at the corners of his mouth. Curling a hand in the silken weight of his hair, I pressed still closer, until the curve of his ear was against my lips. "You've underestimated me again."

I jerked down hard on my handhold, forcing his head back, and moved my other hand to the center of his chest. At the same moment, I spun, using my momentum to propel him back against the door with enough force to crack the plastic. I pressed myself against him and pulled down harder on his hair, drawing his head back so far that he was staring at the ceiling. "That's why I always keep mine short."

"Thank you for the tip," he said, through gritted teeth. In a lightning movement, he hooked his foot behind my leg and jerked back, unbalancing me enough that I ended up on the floor. I couldn't stop the fall, but I still had hold of his hair and I dragged him down with me. He landed on top, his weight causing the air in my lungs to come out in a whoosh. Before I could regain my feet, Louis-Cesare had pinned my arms and straddled my thighs, effectively immobilizing me. The few blows I managed to get in were ignored, and within seconds he had captured my wrists and forced them to my sides.

For a moment, we stared at each other, the only motion the faint vibration of the airplane's floor beneath us. "I will not be mastered, manipulated or controlled by a . . . dhampir," he finally said, his voice rough. "Regardless of her parentage!"

I bucked, but his thighs flexed, pinning me on either side. "Ditto," I told him furiously, "except substitute 'arrogant vamp' in that sentiment."

His eyes dropped and almost tangibly caressed a path across my body. "You seem well mastered to me. And if I may offer some advice, your close-combat skills require work."

I arched up against the weight that held me down, deliberately rubbing against unmistakable evidence that his body disagreed with him. "Really? I've never had any complaints."

Anger and heat flashed in his suddenly storm-colored eyes, but his response wasn't what I'd expected. One moment to the next, something changed. It was nothing I could name, beyond a collection of gestures: one eyebrow rising in an elegant arch, a barely there, Mona Lisa tilt to his lips, a slight fall of lashes as long as a girl's. Inconsequential details, but the air between us suddenly went electric, as quickly as if he'd thrown a switch. I was straining toward him before I knew it.

I clenched every muscle to halt the movement, while Louis-Cesare, damn him, was smiling. He slid a hand across my shoulder to my neck, his fingers tangling in my hair as he cupped the back of my head. I don't like feeling overpowered, and when it happens, I fight back. But I wasn't fighting now. I'd let him maneuver me into position and now I was letting him touch me. I remember thinking, Oh, no, he isn't—even as he pulled me the rest of the way up. He dropped his other hand to my waist, settled my body firmly against his own and kissed me.

Such perfect pressure on my lips, such a skillful tongue in my mouth . . . it had been a long time since I'd been kissed with expertise and passion. A warm tongue expertly twined around my own, sending signals all over my body. I hadn't paid much attention to the brief embrace in the car. I'd been stunned and freezing, and more interested in the Fey than in Louis-Cesare. He had my full attention now. A strong hand slowly moved downward until it gripped my backside, pressing me close.

I told myself not to respond, but my body wasn't listening. My hands, no longer restrained, were pulling him closer, my fingers twisting in the decadent softness of his sweater, and I was kissing him savagely. I was furious with myself, knowing in a moment he'd push me away, but even knowing, I couldn't seem to stop. My left leg hooked itself over him, pulling him hard against my body, and we began moving against each other, craving friction, craving intimacy.

Then he shifted, just right, and a jolt of bone-dissolving pleasure wracked my body. My breath squeezed out of my throat in a broken, shaky groan as his lips found my

ear. The tip of his tongue began to trace the whorls delicately, a barely-there sensation in stark contrast to the
feel of him, huge and persistent, pressed hard against me.

"Dorina." He delicately licked along the soft curve,
slowly, down to the lobe, which he caught between his
teeth sharply enough to make me gasp. Then his tongue
plunged inside, tracing the inner channel and leaving a
slight wetness when he withdrew. His breath over the
moist center made me shiver helplessly. "Neither have I."

It took me a second to realize what he meant; then I
was assailed by a vision of strangling him until he turned
more purple than my hair. The maddening, adjective-
inspiring, devious son of a bitch! I managed to get a foot
into his stomach and pushed hard. Because of the awkward angle, he didn't end up sailing down the aisle again,
but it did send him forcefully back into his chair.

When he made no immediate attempt to get up, I
righted myself and moved away a few steps on the pretense of picking up my joint from the table. I needed it to
steady my nerves, and I preferred having something to
look at besides him. I realized I was shaking, and it pissed
me off. One kiss and my brain almost trickled out my
ears! It had simply been a long time. A very long time, I
realized, since I'd known the taste of another's breath in
my mouth, the feel of a nipple hardening under my
tongue, the way that muscle at the top of the thigh jumps
when you bite it. . . .

I sat down and took a long drag. For once, Claire's
skillful concoction didn't seem to be working. "That was
fun," I drawled offhandedly, amazed that my voice
sounded so normal. "Of course, the last vamp who kissed
me ended up with a stake through his rib cage."

I swear, I didn't even see him move. Before I could

blink, he was bent over me, hands braced on my shoulders, forcing me back against the seat. I caught his wrists, my grip as hard as I could make it, and we paused, staring at each other.

I don't know what I looked like, but Louis-Cesare's pupils were dilated, wide and dark, and his lips were parted. I felt my body react to the heat in that stare, and a shiver spilled through me. It was probably just my usual perverseness kicking in—Daddy's pet vampire was the last person I should even think about getting involved with, so of course my libido had latched on to him.

"Do not provoke me, Dorina." The voice was harsh, but not entirely steady. So, he wasn't as unmoved as he'd like to appear. It wasn't much of a victory, but at the moment, I'd take what I could get.

"Don't provoke you?" I stared at his lips. I couldn't help it; we were close enough to kiss. Do it, my pulse was beating. Do it, do it, do it. "Why, are you really that easy?"

Louis-Cesare flinched as if I'd slapped him. His expression changed, and for a split second he actually looked stricken. No, I thought. No, no, *no*. I felt like I'd twisted a knife in my own gut, when I should have felt triumphant. What the hell?

Louis-Cesare abruptly pulled away. He ran a hand through his hair and stared at me while I tried to get my breathing under control. When he finally spoke, it was nothing I'd expected to hear. "Why did you say that Lord Dracula will come to us?"

I searched around the carpet by my feet and found my joint. I took another much-needed drag before answering. My pulse was pounding hard enough that I could barely hear, but Louis-Cesare already had himself back under control. His sweater had recovered from our little tussle without anything so déclassé as a wrinkle; other than for slightly mussed hair, he looked like nothing had happened.

Damn vampire.

God, he could kiss, though.

"Because three people put him away last time, but only two are family," I managed to say evenly.

"Then, logically, he should go after—"

"I wasn't finished. His warped idea of logic only makes sense if you know his history. Radu betrayed him half a millennium ago, leading a Turkish army to force him off his throne. He spent years in exile, plotting revenge. By the time he got back, Radu had joined the life-challenged segment of the family—he'd picked up a bad case of syphilis and Mircea brought him over because at that time there was no cure. But was that good enough for Drac? Hell no."

I stubbed out joint number one after using it to light number two. I was going to need to score some weed in 'Frisco at the rate things were going. It wouldn't be as good as Claire's stuff, but hopefully she'd be back tending her highly illegal herb patch soon. "The only reason he didn't take Radu out immediately was that an assassin in the pay of some local nobles got in a lucky shot. Unfortunately, Daddy chose to bring Drac over instead of leaving him to die. And as soon as he rose, he started in on Radu as if nothing had changed. He wasn't strong enough to kill him, being only a baby vamp, but he didn't let that stop him from hiring others to attempt it."

"But that did not succeed." Louis-Cesare looked like he had forgotten to whom he was speaking for a minute, and actually seemed to be listening.

"Nope. But Drac doesn't get over things. Didn't as a human, doesn't now."

"Yet he did give up eventually. Radu is quite well today—"

"Because of luck," I said flatly. "I don't know what you were told, but Drac never did stop his games. He was finally locked away because it came out that he was the one who set a mob on Radu in Paris, leading to a very nasty imprisonment for your sire that almost got him killed."

"I know." Something about the way he said it made me glance up sharply, but there was nothing in his expression to tell me anything. I wondered exactly when he and Radu had met, and under what circumstances. It was possible, I decided, that Louis-Cesare might know more about Uncle's stint behind bars than I did. But I knew better than to ask.

Most of the older vamps carry a lot of baggage. Humans are amazingly adaptable, able to reinvent themselves when times change, but vamps have a harder time shrugging off the centuries. Some cope by keeping their function constant over the long haul: Mircea is the Senate's chief diplomat, for example, and has been for some time. The world might change, but people's basic natures don't, so their lives have a sense of continuity. Others, like Radu, drift along in some kind of denial, trying to recapture a past in which they felt at home. And some, like Drac, never stop trying to make the world over in their image. I really didn't care which category Louis-Cesare fit. His baggage was his problem; I had enough of my own.

"And then, when Drac escaped a little over a century ago, what do you think was the first thing he did?" I continued. "Went straight back on the hunt as if nothing had changed. We were able to catch him again by using Radu as bait."

"No." Louis-Cesare sounded adamant. "I will not allow my old master to be subjected to that level of risk—"

"Radu is perfectly safe, at least for the moment. He isn't Drac's chief target anymore. Don't misunderstand—I'm certain he'll get around to him in time—but his isn't the first name on the list."

Shrewd eyes that were, thankfully, back to blue, met mine. "And who does have that honor?"

I watched my smoke being pulled into odd patterns by the plane's air-conditioning. "You're looking at her."

Chapter Five

The Electric Hedgehog is a punk cybercafe run by a couple of British guys Kristie knows in a backstreet near the Bay. It's a funky little place where you can log online, get a body piercing and buy some weed under the table, all at the same time. One-stop shopping; I like that.

Believe it or not, I hadn't come just for the weed. I also needed a safe place to meet the rest of the team and Kristie had suggested the Hedgehog's back room. It was a testament to the very different attitudes and styles of its two owners. While the front was all black walls and neon graffiti, the back was hippie coffeehouse chic, with vintage shag carpeting and Che Guevara posters.

I passed the time sipping some really nasty chai, which was the most appetizing thing on the menu, and watching the colors cast by the iridescent bead curtain separating the rooms. Louis-Cesare preferred to pace back and forth like a big cat in a cage. We were the only ones in the back at the moment, which wasn't surprising as the coffeehouse didn't usually rev up until nightfall. Since it was currently seven a.m. 'Frisco time, there weren't too many people interested in bad coffee and worse poetry. After tasting the former and reading samples of the latter that the proprietors had scribbled on the walls, I decided to be long gone by nightfall.

"This is the most irresponsible—"

"Would you calm down?" He didn't seem to be the patient type. "They'll be here. And quit pacing. You're making me dizzy."

"And that could not possibly be the result of the enormous amount of marijuana you have smoked in the past eight hours, or the half bottle of tequila you called breakfast."

"At least I didn't snack on the owners." I'd noticed the length of the handshake he'd given Alan, the taller proprietor with the tongue stud. The older vamps don't have to use fangs to feed. A touch of skin or, in the case of really powerful ones, just proximity to the victim will do as well. Louis-Cesare had had to endure sun at the airport and in the taxi all the way here, and he'd been hungry. It hadn't been hard to guess.

"That was well within the guidelines." He meant that he hadn't taken enough to be harmful and that the owner was none the wiser. It was the PC way to feed, and he'd managed it without a hitch. That didn't make me view it as less of a violation.

I lit up the last of Claire's joints and smiled at him. It was either that or ruin the Hedgehog's back room trying to take him apart. "Whatever."

"The point I was endeavoring to make," he said after a moment, "was that unless your friends—"

"Acquaintances."

"—are even more irresponsible than I was expecting, they should have called by now. There is a very good chance that they have absconded."

I shook my head. "No way. Not that they wouldn't double-cross the Senate or the Circle in a heartbeat, but they made an agreement with me. They know what I'd do if they broke it." I got up and stretched, feeling my spine snap back into place. "Besides, they don't know what the assignment is yet. After they do, we may need to watch them."

Actually, I doubted that. I'd picked José and Kristie as much for their attitudes as their skills; they were the only two I knew crazy enough to think that going after Drac constituted a challenge. It also helped that they had never actually met him. Anyone who had would be a much harder sell.

"Then where are they?" Louis-Cesare was back to pacing again. I glanced at the clock and felt a slight twinge of concern. True, José might be passed out under a table in a dive somewhere, but that wasn't Kristie's style. And even if she'd gotten hung up, she'd have phoned. No way would she risk going back into the Circle's tender care if she could avoid it. Unless something was wrong, she'd be here.

"Maybe they decided to drive and then broke down. José thinks he's a mechanic and usually rides around in some old clunker he's trying to fix up." I didn't really believe it, but it was vaguely possible.

"And neither have cell phones?" Louis-Cesare demanded.

"They just got out of jail," I reminded him, but it didn't ring true to me, either. Kristie had stayed a step ahead of both the Senate and the mages for years, dealing in all kinds of illegal magical items. She wasn't the type to take chances. No way would she have agreed to cross the desert in one of José's rattletraps without stopping at a convenience store for a prepaid cell phone first. "And my phone's on the fritz half the time," I added, trying to convince myself more than him.

Louis-Cesare looked pointedly at the phone sitting behind the bar. Okay, point taken. But pacing a worn spot in the rug wasn't going to help.

"You know," I said, getting to my feet, "I think breakfast sounds like a plan. I saw a bakery down the street when we came in—"

"You are not going alone," I was informed.

"Suit yourself." I picked up my big bag o' toys and slung it over my shoulder. I told Alan we were going for a walk and to tell Kristie we'd be right back, if she showed.

"You want that eyebrow pierced later?" he asked. "It'd look good on you." What a businessman, always trying to make a sale.

"I'll think about it," I assured him. Alan nodded cheerfully and I shook my head. A punk morning person was just wrong.

The bakery had the advantage of a few tables outside with a clear view of the Hedgehog's front door. I let Louis-Cesare have the seat near the café's wall, as it was the best shaded, and immediately regretted it. I felt the familiar prickle of nerves between my shoulder blades as soon as I sat down, the awareness of how bare my back was with nothing to cover it. I scooted my chair over until Louis-Cesare and I were practically side by side, and ordered three doughnuts, a croissant, a ham and cheese bagel and a real, honest-to-God latte.

Louis-Cesare watched the load the waiter set before me a few minutes later with slightly widened eyes. "Metabolism," I said, before he could ask.

He leaned back in his chair as I slathered butter on the bagel. A shaft of sunlight was seeping through a gap in the awning, but he didn't move to avoid it. Show off.

"Are you really going to let that man prick you?" he finally asked.

I choked on my latte. "Excuse me?"

"With the needle. *Comme ça.*" He gestured at his forehead.

I laughed in spite of myself. "No. I heal too fast." He looked a question. "The one and only time I tried earrings, I had to tear them out of my flesh after it grew over them. It took about an hour." I really didn't want to know what ripping off half my eyebrow felt like.

"You heal faster than a human, but slower than a vampire, yes?"

I stared at him suspiciously. I hoped he wasn't asking for future reference. "Depends on the vamp."

"Then your kind gains in power over the centuries, as we do?"

I didn't feel like doing Dhampir 101. Especially since the answer in my case was no. "Depends on the dhampir."

To my surprise, Louis-Cesare took the hint and backed off. "There are other types of jewelry," he commented, as if that thought had never occurred to me.

"Bracelets and necklaces rattle at inconvenient times and are hazards in a fight," I told him shortly. I'd found that out the hard way, when a vamp almost succeeded in strangling me with my own choker.

"You do not have to fight every day."

"I don't have to eat every day, either, but I get really cranky when I don't."

"*Comment?*"

"Never mind." I could live without rehashing my

physical inconveniences. "Hair color is the only orna-
mentation both my body and my profession can handle,"
I added, to forestall more questions.

"Ah." He looked like something I'd said had finally
made sense. "That explains the purple."

"Aubergine."

Louis-Cesare looked like he was going to argue the
point, but thought better of it. "Who is Claire?" he asked
after a moment.

I narrowed my eyes. What was with the twenty questions all of a sudden? Was he trying to psychoanalyze me,
find some sort of weakness, by asking about my life, my
friends? Had he forgotten already who Daddy was? If any
form of mind games worked on me, Mircea would have
had me fetching his slippers long ago. I gave him a flat
look and munched bagel.

"If we are to work together, we should know something about each other," he noted calmly. He probably
thought he was hiding it, but the lazy regard held cool,
critical assessment. Apparently, my new partner wasn't
convinced that Mircea hadn't saddled him with a liability.
That made two of us.

I returned the appraisal, looking him up and down in a
deliberately brazen way. A sunbeam was dancing on his
hair like a captured flame, highlighting a few shorter
strands that curled just below the strong line of his jaw.
The color went well with the creamy cashmere and the
eyes, which, at the moment, were a guileless, angelic
blue. I concluded my own assessment: sophisticated, dangerous and sexy as hell.

Something must have shown on my face, because he
smirked slightly. Smug. Good looks aside, I decided furiously, Louis-Cesare really didn't have much to offer. He

was a judgmental, condescending, self-important son of a bitch. Like every vamp I'd ever known, come to think of it.

I leaned back in my chair, stretching luxuriantly, deliberately letting my jacket fall open. Predictably, his eyes moved down my body—some things outlast even the change. I grinned and he looked away, a rueful smile twitching at his lips. I finished breakfast in peace.

When I'd polished off the last, calorie-laden bite, I pulled out my pathetic excuse for a cell phone. As expected, it had gone belly-up yet again. Portals play hell with anything magnetic, not to mention that the evil thing had come with a couple of built-in quirks. On Drac's trail, the last thing I could afford was faulty equipment, but my nerves were in no shape for fine-tuning anything. I went through the usual routine, and when it still wouldn't come on, I slammed it down on the table and glared at it.

Louis-Cesare picked it up. He looked it over, then quirked an eyebrow at me. "If I can repair this . . ."

"Yeah?"

"Then I choose the topic of conversation."

I gave him a look. Most centuries-old vamps didn't even know what a cell phone was, much less how to fix one. Technological troglodytes, almost every one. "You think you're up to it?"

"Are we agreed?"

"Sure. Go for it."

He regarded the small white devil for a moment, then turned it over in his hands. He pressed, poked and fiddled with the quiet assurance of a man who thinks he knows what he's doing. I watched him, secure in the knowledge that there was no way he'd be able to—

The LED display flickered to life. Louis-Cesare held up the phone. "Fixed," he said unnecessarily.

"My hero," I replied drily. Like hell it was fixed. I hadn't spent months tinkering with the damn thing without learning its vicious little tricks.

"Who is Claire?"

I didn't answer, being preoccupied with an internal countdown . . . nine, eight, seven. . . . When I hit five, I said calmly, "Fifty bucks says it'll die by the time I finish this"—the screen went dark with a cheeky little blip— "sentence."

Louis-Cesare reached into his pocket and pulled out a sleek new cell phone in a shiny black case. He pushed it across the table to me. "Who is Claire?"

I could have pointed out that the bet had been to fix my old phone, not to give me a new one. But he'd been carrying exactly the model I'd been lusting after for months, but hadn't been able to afford. Taking time off to search for Claire had played havoc with my bank account.

"I met her at Gerald & Co.—the auction house." I paused for a minute to pound my piece of possessed circuitry into a hundred pieces. "Gerald's occasionally came across an item that was dangerously unstable but also potentially valuable. They needed a null to keep anything freaky from happening while their people decided if whatever it was could be stabilized. She also worked some of the auctions, to keep the more volatile merchandise quiet while the suckers were bidding on it."

"Why were you there?" Louis-Cesare asked after a moment, his tone managing to convey disbelief that they'd let anyone as disreputable as me into a genteel auction. He'd obviously never been to Gerald's.

"To place a bid." I started fiddling with my new toy, which had every bell and whistle known to man.

"For what?"

"Sweet! This thing even has Internet!"

Louis-Cesare just looked at me. I gave in with a put-upon sigh. "Wallachia's first ruler was a Transylvanian named Radu Negru. Around 1300, he decided to build himself a grand new cathedral at Curtea de Argeş, which is now a two-donkey town but was then the capital. According to legend, construction was going a little slow, and Radu threatened his chief architect, a guy named Manoli, if he didn't start to see some progress. Trying to excuse himself, Manoli claimed that evil spirits were opposing the project. The solution: bury a living woman in the foundation to appease them."

"What does this have to do with you meeting the null?" Louis-Cesare looked like he thought he was being had.

"I'm getting there. Anyway, Radu and Manoli agreed that the first woman on-site the next day would get the honor. As it turned out, the unlucky lady was Flora Manoli. She pleaded with her husband for mercy, and when that didn't work, she cursed him and any other man who touched her grave. Shortly thereafter, Manoli fell off the roof of the cathedral and plummeted to his death." Louis-Cesare was looking confused and slightly annoyed. "Legend says that he hit the dirt right next to the spot where he'd bricked up the missus."

"I still do not see—"

"After a number of suspicious deaths, the stone over Mrs. Manoli was removed and replaced with a new, curse-free version. The old rock was broken up and buried, but enterprising village women located it and sold the pieces. Most of them have been lost over the years, but a few survived. Gerald & Co. somehow got hold of one of the remaining bits." I'd hoped to snag the thing for a song, but someone with deeper pockets had also believed the legend. "I met Claire during the auction and we went for a drink afterward. Turns out she needed a roommate."

Claire was working for a skinflint outfit like Gerald's because the family business was entailed—one heir got control of everything, and the rest were out of luck. After her father died, she and her cousin Sebastian fought over control of the business and she lost. And since rival heirs were usually killed, she preferred to lie low until things calmed down. I'd given her a few pointers about how to stay beneath her family's radar, and in the process learned that she'd recently inherited a rambling old house with lots of spare room and had a pressing need for untraceable cash.

"And now she is missing?" Louis-Cesare prompted.

I scowled. "Yeah." A fact that, among other things, made me look pretty damn incompetent.

Claire had set my rent ridiculously low, saying that she was just glad of the company, and had also told me that I could use the attic for an office. I don't like taking advantage of people, at least not the nice, trusting ones, but I'd needed cheap digs. To soothe my conscience, I'd decided to throw protection into the deal. I couldn't very well act as her full-time bodyguard and still take other clients, but I'd foolishly assumed that, with a dhampir as a roommate, she'd at least be safe at home. So it had come as a rude shock when she was snatched right out from under my nose.

"You are sure she did not leave by choice?" Louis-Cesare asked.

"I returned from a job to find an empty house and no note."

"That alone does not—"

"Claire is like a Virgo on steroids," I interrupted. This conversation was about as comfortable as poking at a bruise. I wanted it done. "Anal-retentive doesn't even come close. One concession I had to make early on was to always leave a note. She worried if I so much as stepped out the door and didn't put a Post-it on the fridge saying when I'd be back. There was no way she would have left without some kind of explanation, at least not willingly."

Louis-Cesare looked at me, but didn't say anything. He didn't have to. A month was a very long time.

My descent into gloom was halted by the sight of three figures disappearing into the Hedgehog's entrance. One of the few constants among all dhampirs, even the mostly human ones, is our ability to spot a vamp under any circumstances. I'm not sure how we do it. I've been in positions before where there was no way I could have smelled, heard or seen anything unusual, and yet I knew a vamp was near. It's like an itch, a sense that somewhere close by, prey can be found. I've never been wrong yet, and every sense I had was telling me that the three heavily bundled figures were vampires. Somehow, I doubted they were stopping in to check their e-mail.

"I'm done," I said, tossing back the last of my latte. "What do you say we take the back way in?"

*   *   *

I'd checked out the back of the club earlier on the pretext of looking for a restroom, having long ago learned that the first order of business in any situation is knowing how to get out of it. I hadn't actually thought I'd need the information. But it just goes to show—paranoid can be a very useful state of mind.

"What is wrong?" Louis-Cesare demanded in an undertone as I paused beside the Dumpster in back of the Hog.

"Three vamps just went in. Leave at least one alive—I have some questions." Before he could argue, I kicked in the back entrance, stake in hand. I felt him grip my upper arm a second later, but barely noticed. I was too busy staring around in rising rage.

"Son of a bitch!" I shook off his hold and ran toward the front, but there was no sign of the three assholes who'd done this. The street out front was empty in both directions, not that that meant anything. They could have disappeared into another alley or shop, or more likely into a waiting car. I should have sent Louis-Cesare around back while I checked on the front. Stupid, stupid!

"What does *'vaca dracului'* mean?" asked a mild voice behind me. I walked back inside to see Louis-Cesare looking at a message that had been written in red across the gold calligraphy of the poetry excerpts. Alan and his partner, whose name I couldn't even remember, had supplied the ink. What was left of them had been dumped in a corner, along with the body of an old man who had been cleaning earlier. Three deaths in what couldn't have been more than a couple of minutes, and they still had time to leave me a message. It looked like Drac had acquired some capable help pretty fast.

"'Devil's cow.' It's his pet name for me." It was actually one of the nicer ones, as I recalled.

"Whose? Are you saying Lord Dracula did this?"

"Not personally." I'd have known if one of the cloaked bastards was Uncle. His presence was unmistakable, especially to me. I'd have been able to taste him on the air, musty and electric-ozone sharp—the smell of madness. I pushed away sickening memories and concentrated on translating the brief scrawl. It was leaking down the walls and was fairly indistinct against the black paint, especially where it crossed the poetry, but I got the idea. "Kristie and José are dead," I said evenly. The note didn't say how, for which I was grateful.

"Dracula knew they were coming to meet us."

It wasn't a question, so I didn't reply. I fished around in my bag and brought out a bottle of tequila I'd ripped off from the Senate's plane. It's always good to have something flammable in my line of work, not to mention that I like tequila. "You might want to wait outside," I said. Vamps tend to burn so nicely.

"How did they know?" It sounded more like he was talking to himself than to me, so I didn't answer. Besides, there were far too many possibilities to count. I splashed alcohol around, except for a mouthful I decided I needed worse than the Hog. I stopped because of a grip of steel on my upper arm. I dropped the bottle and it rolled across the floor, spilling the remaining contents, until stopped by the cleaning man's body.

"What is your problem?"

"We will not continue this way," Louis-Cesare told me grimly. "I may be forced to work with you, but you will show me the proper respect. And when I ask you a question, you *will* answer it."

I glared. The guy had mood swings bigger than his goddamned ego. "Buddy, you are about ten seconds away from getting your ass kicked all the way back to Daddy."

"Do not call him that!"

I tried to rip free from his grip, but this time, nothing happened. My pack was across the room, near the back door where I'd dropped it after seeing the carnage, but I didn't really need it. I had no fewer than three stakes on me at the moment, and I needed only a slim opportunity to slip one between his ribs. Unfortunately, that would leave me with no backup at all and a seriously pissed-off Mircea. I didn't know if reasoning with this lunatic was likely to work, but if not, I could always stake him later.

"Whether you, me or Mircea likes it, he *is* my father. Believe me, I'm not proud of it."

Louis-Cesare laughed bitterly. "No, why should you be proud? Do you have any idea how very fortunate you are? To have a connection with the Basarab line, to have Lord Mircea himself defend you and claim you as his own? If you weren't under his protection, you would have been killed years ago! And what do you do in return? Mock him, belittle him, speak as if he were your equal! You, who have doubtless killed dozens of our kind—"

"Thousands," I corrected, and saw his eyes flash silver. The next second, I was pinned by some invisible hand to the bloody wall, while a psycho vamp stalked toward me. Did the family never make any sane vampires? They really shouldn't be allowed to reproduce at all.

"Some would give all they possess to have what you throw away," he hissed. I tried to move, but got nowhere. That was the problem with the really old vamps. You never knew what kind of extra powers they'd picked up through the years.

"And they'd be welcome to it," I told him frankly. "I don't know what your stake in this is, but I'm here to save a friend. I don't owe Mircea, or you, a damn thing. As for your question, I would guess that Kristie told Drac's guys where she'd agreed to meet us, after some persuasion." For her sake, I hoped she'd talked quickly.

"How did he know to ask her?" I found that when Louis-Cesare had to split his concentration between me and a problem, I got a tiny bit of wiggle room. I started to move my right hand into my pocket. "We have a traitor," he declared, as if this was news.

"No shit. Boy, am I glad you're along to point out these things," I said before I could stop myself. Luckily, he wasn't paying me much attention.

"We have to inform the Senate immediately."

I managed to touch the tiny plastic cylinder of my Bic with one finger. "Yeah, sure, that's the ticket. We'll let the traitor know our next move, so he can tell Drac how to arrange the welcome party."

"And what is the alternative?" Louis-Cesare demanded.

"I'm working on that. All I know right now is that the traitor could be anywhere—in the family, at vamp central, or someone who figured out how to spy on us—we can't be sure." I looked down to see the janitor's lifeless eyes staring up at me, his lips set in a line that almost looked like a sarcastic grin. I hoped it wasn't a sign.

"I promised Lord Mircea that I would keep him informed—"

"He knows me better than to expect that."

"Then it is as well that you are not in command of this mission."

"If we're back to that again, we may as well throw in

the towel right now." He looked confused at the idiom. "We may as well quit," I rephrased.

"You may do as you like," Louis-Cesare said, his sneer informing me that he'd expected no better. "But I do not take my word so lightly."

"You don't know me, but you do know Mircea. Presumably you trust his judgment, right?" My fingers finally got a grip on the slippery plastic.

"Of course—"

"He called me into this because he knew you'd need help. Uncle doesn't fight fair. He uses whatever tactics work. He isn't going to stand there and agree to duel you, best vamp take all. If we're going to beat him, we have to think like him. And besides Mircea, I'm the one most likely to be able to do that."

"You are trying to take control of this assignment," he said stubbornly.

"No, I'm trying to get you to realize that I'm already there. You wouldn't last ten minutes with Drac, no matter how good you think you are."

He looked at me, splayed against the wall, with understandable condescension. "And you would?"

"I have one thing in common with the family."

"And what is that?"

I smiled and flicked the tiny flame to life. "I'm tricky."

Louis-Cesare's response was lost in the roar of flames that caught on the tequila-soaked pile of humanity beneath us and quickly spread across the floor. I suddenly found myself released, and barely managed to avoid falling on top of the burning pile of rags and flesh at my feet. Fire spread through the ruined Hog, licking at my heels as I booked it out the door. I glanced back at the smoke billowing out behind me. "Round one to Uncle," I murmured.

Chapter Six

The Senate's jet sat on the runway, looking pure and innocent under a brilliant blue sky. It gleamed a blinding white, like someone had recently washed it. A fuel truck was rumbling away as we watched, so it was all gassed up and ready to go. It gave me the creeps.

"Are you coming?" Louis-Cesare was impatient, and I couldn't really blame him. I'd been standing behind an empty luggage van for almost twenty minutes, waiting for the refueling to finish, trying to tell myself that it was perfectly okay to go ahead. But the base of my spine wasn't having it. The tingle that had initially made me stop and wait on the humans to exit the area had now become a full-fledged shudder. There was something wrong with the airplane.

I stared at it, ignoring the look on Louis-Cesare's face. It said that he frankly couldn't care less whether I liked it, and was about to go without me. Since wrestling him to the ground was the only way to keep him from doing so, and that hadn't been working so well lately, I was resigned to dealing with whatever or whoever was waiting for us. But I didn't have to like it.

Not that I thought Drac would kill us, even if he was waiting inside. He enjoyed cat-and-mouse games, and he'd only begun to play. He'd want me to pay for those long years he'd spent in captivity, something a quick death wouldn't begin to cover in his estimation. In the old days, he'd had people impaled on blunt, well-oiled stakes, ensuring that it took them a couple of days to die, and that was when he wasn't even all that annoyed. I was pretty sure he had something much more inventive planned for me. But then, that was the problem with maniacs: you could never be entirely certain what they'd do. Maybe he was in a hurry to get to Radu and would mow us down at the first opportunity. I didn't think it likely, but I wasn't willing to risk my life on it.

"We discussed this," Louis-Cesare reminded me, more calmly than I would have expected. "We must contact Lord Mircea and inquire what he wishes to do."

I didn't give a damn what Mircea wanted. My hand stayed on Louis-Cesare's arm, just above the elbow, where I'd instinctively gripped him when he started to leave. "I think there's a problem with the plane."

He tried to shrug off my hand, but I held on. "You are being ridiculous! That is the only secure line to the Senate available to us."

Actually, it wasn't. We could drive out to MAGIC, the Metaphysical Alliance for Greater Interspecies Cooperation, and speak to Marlowe in person. Mircea probably wasn't there, but I wasn't nearly as concerned about keeping Daddy informed as Louis-Cesare seemed to be. Keeping my head firmly attached to my shoulders was more on my mind at the moment, and for that, I needed backup. Marlowe could provide it, and although he'd doubtless give me a hard time first, it was nothing to what

I could expect from Drac. But Louis-Cesare didn't want to leave the area where Dracula's men had been sighted to drive all the way to the isolated canyon near Vegas where MAGIC was located.

"I'm telling you, getting anywhere near that plane is a bad idea. They knew we were meeting at the Hog. Kristie could have told them we were getting there by plane, and that thing is hard to miss."

His lip curled back slightly from his teeth. It made him look more like the predator he was instead of Mr. January. "You're afraid."

I shrugged. "Call it what you want, but I didn't last five hundred years by being stupid. You go in there and you aren't coming out."

"And this would bother you?"

"Not especially," I admitted, "except that I could use help stealing a car."

"For the last time, we are not driving to Las Vegas! It would take all day."

"Not the way I drive."

Louis-Cesare pulled away from me in an abrupt movement that almost left me lying on the concrete. I guess he was tired of arguing. He stepped out of the narrow strip of shade cast by the luggage van and flinched when the sunlight fell directly on him. "Stay here if you are concerned. This will not take long."

I watched him stride away, knowing I wasn't strong enough to stop him. It was an unaccustomed sensation, and not one I liked. Damn stiff-necked vampire. If he was jumped when he got on board, there'd be no way for me to reach him in time. On the other hand, dying alongside him wouldn't help either of us. I suddenly recalled all the reasons I hated working with vamps. Hunting them was a hell of a lot more satisfying.

I watched him walk through the heat haze shimmering over the tarmac and tried to ignore the prickle of worry that had its teeth in my guts. For a moment after he entered the jet, nothing happened, and I began to think that maybe I was being even more paranoid than usual. Then he reemerged, dragging the pilot and steward with him. The steward was motionless, and I didn't like the way his neck was lolling about. He was either dead or giving a good impression of it. The pilot was mostly out of my line of sight, having been slung over Louis-Cesare's shoulder, so all I could see was his uniformed rear and a blood-soaked left pant leg.

I was about to move forward when I noticed several other shapes doing likewise. Within a few seconds, the plane was surrounded by a group of dark figures that, despite my best efforts, I couldn't get my eyes to focus on. Mages, then, under a cloaking spell. This was not good, especially considering that Louis-Cesare had emerged from a Senate jet and the vamps happened to be at war with the dark mages. I thought about the irony of our being killed by someone else before Drac could find us, and bent to open the bag of contraband at my feet.

My hand closed on a small, dark sphere about the same time that the first of the blurs reached Louis-Cesare. I took aim at the circle of shadows that were closing in, and the sphere landed in the middle of a group of them, exploding as soon as it touched the tarmac. A silver flash later, and three of the figures were on the ground. They did not much resemble humans, but considering that they'd just been hit by a dislocator bomb, that wasn't surprising.

One of them had had his head magically reattached to

his thigh, and an arm now grew out of his forehead. Since the arm was the wrong color to match the rest of his skin, I assumed it had recently belonged to the figure at his side, who had acquired a new set of ears on his left cheek but lost his nose. Unlike these two, who were kicking up the kind of fuss you'd expect under the circumstances, the third shape lay still. I realized why as I approached, my remaining dislocator in hand. A large number of once-internal organs were now attached to his outside, and the heart, I saw at a glance, was no longer beating. He was the lucky one; the spell was not reversible, which meant that the other two faced an interesting future.

I ran past them toward where at least six other blurs had reached the ramp and were climbing over a body that partially blocked the way. I hadn't seen what happened, but Louis-Cesare must have killed his attacker, thrown him down the stairs and dragged the jet's crew members back inside. Being Senate property, the plane was, of course, designed to resist certain forms of magical attack, but I doubted its defenses would hold for long against that many mages. Besides, how had the crew been injured unless a way had already been found inside?

I stopped well short of the shapes surging up the ramp and tossed my other bomb. Only half of them managed to get shields up in time. The other three rolled down the ramp to land at my feet, puddles of displaced flesh that in two cases couldn't even scream: they no longer had all the requisite parts in their proper places.

One of the remaining mages, who was either really focused or completely oblivious, kept going for the jet's door, but the other two turned to face me. I didn't wait to find out what the closest one had planned, but rolled another little surprise up the ramp. It, too, wasn't on the approved-magical-devices list, but unlike the dislocators, it was an old invention that I was hoping she wouldn't have seen before or know how to defend against. Either I was right or her reflexes were slow, because the little red marble came to rest beside her booted foot. She instinctively pulled back, but not fast enough.

A curl of crimson smoke engulfed her leg and quickly climbed up her body. An instant later, where a relatively young woman had stood, a wizened old crone remained, her life sucked into the smoke that was now returning to its container. She clutched a withered hand to her breast and sank to her knees as I bounded up the ramp, scooping up my now bright yellow marble as I went. I didn't need the life it contained, but someone else would pay a high price for it, possibly enough to let me recoup my losses on this rescue. Dislocators aren't cheap.

The other mage, the one with leathery skin and a face like a fortyish prizefighter, yelled something. An instant later, what felt like a giant fist slammed into my face, picking me up and throwing me a dozen yards from the plane. I hit the tarmac with a thud, after doing a few disorienting flips midair. The impact resounded all through me, causing me to bite my lip hard enough to taste blood. I looked up at the mage, who was vaulting over the banister toward me like some action-movie hero, and grinned. I never really got into a fight until there was a little pain.

"*Sopor!*" the mage yelled, long before getting anywhere near me. I hadn't known the other word he'd used, but this one was another story. I felt a surge of lethargy start to creep up my spine, threatening to send me off to see the sandman for the very last time, and turning my limbs numb and useless in the process. It might have worked except that I'd dealt with this spell before. I bit down hard on my shredded lower lip and the sharp pain caused the sluggishness to recede slightly.

Fighting mages is never as straightforward as I would like. I prefer a nice physical contest where it's mostly about strength, speed and who has the best moves. With mages, it's about who has the nastiest toys. Considering that I was facing a dark war mage, I had no doubt at all that his toy collection rivaled mine, which was why I ignored the impulse to have some fun and just threw the knife I pulled out of my boot. The guy didn't even flinch or try to duck, acting under the assumption, I suppose, that his shields would stop it. They would have, if I hadn't paid a small fortune to have it enchanted.

That's the problem with magical protection—it's only as good as the mage who cast it, and it is no help whatsoever if your opponent's mojo is stronger than yours. Luckily, my spell had been worth the price. The last emotion on the man's face before he hit the tarmac was surprise as he looked down at the blade that was sticking out of his heart.

I retrieved my knife and ran back to the ramp, shaking my head to get rid of the last of the stupor, but the remaining mage had slipped past the ship's defenses while I was preoccupied. I found him inside, engaged in a tussle with Louis-Cesare. I barely noticed them, or the ransacked state of the plane. My whole attention was focused on the battered pilot, who was staring in horror at a small box wired into the floor near the cockpit. It said 01:34 when I first glanced in his direction, and 01:33 a second later.

The pilot's legs were shattered, with a femur sticking out of the dark blue material of his once nicely pressed trousers. I grabbed him and glanced around. "Anyone else on board?"

He blinked at me but didn't answer. He didn't appear to be in pain, which meant that either Louis-Cesare had given him a suggestion or he was in shock. Either way, I doubted he'd be much help, but figured it was worth a shot.

I gave him a little shake, and pointed at the bomb. "Can you disable that thing?"

"I don't know." He blinked dilated eyes. "If I had more time, maybe . . ."

I took in the guy's dull expression and pale, sweaty face. When I first met him, I didn't think he looked like someone who should be working for a bunch of blood-sucking monsters, with his sandy blond hair, sun-reddened cheeks and heavy squint that somehow failed to clash with his open, friendly smile. He looked more the part now. "Let's go," I said, slinging him over my shoulder in a fireman's carry. It left my hands free for weapons, and I assumed I'd need them.

"Dorina! I ordered you to wait!" Louis-Cesare shot me a look while dodging a blow from the mage in front of him. It looked like a standoff to me, since the mage's shields were deflecting the vamp's blows, but Louis-Cesare was too fast for the mage to hit. The guy might have used something a bit nastier than the long knife he was carrying, had he not been in a magically sealed area. I couldn't risk using my toys for the same reason—it was too easy for them to backfire given the wards the Senate had put up.

"Leave him!" I yelled at Louis-Cesare. "We have to go!"

"You go," he replied, making another useless slash with his rapier. "Jonathan dies today."

I glanced at the mage, whose cloaking spell had dropped, since he was using all his extra strength to maintain his shields. The two men were nearly the same height, but the mage's leanness and slim shoulders made him seem smaller. I cataloged him automatically: short white-blond hair, big gray eyes, even bigger nose, pale face; no, I didn't know him. But then, I try to stay away from mages in general and dark ones in particular.

"We have to get clear before that thing goes off or we'll all die!" I gestured at the bomb, which now read 00:52. "Come on!"

Louis-Cesare and his opponent both looked at the clock; then the mage decided on the better part of valor and bolted for the door. I didn't try to stop him; I was too busy following hard on his heels. Louis-Cesare trailed after me, dragging the limp body of the cabin attendant with him, and the three of us ran full out for the chain-link fence near the runway. The mage, unencumbered by bodies, reached it first and vaulted over. Louis-Cesare dropped the steward and sailed after him, jumping across the eight-foot fence like it wasn't even there.

I dropped the captain beside his coworker just as the plane exploded in an eruption of orange flame and black smoke. Several white-hot bits of metal collided with my back after I moved to shield the captain. I was reaching for the steward when a flying piece of silver sliced through his forehead, scalping him before embedding itself in the fence post behind his head. I huddled over the captain's still-breathing body and waited it out. Some days, it just doesn't pay to get out of bed.

*　　*　　*

Half an hour later, we were in a shiny new Mustang heading for Vegas. It had been chosen because of the heavy UV coating on the windows, but it also came equipped with a manual transmission. I had stared at it doubtfully after we located it in the rental office's vast lot.

"You should have let me steal something. I don't drive a stick."

"I'm driving," Louis-Cesare said, sliding into the low seat as easily as if he'd done it a hundred times. "You're drunk."

I wished. "I had all of two beers, mostly for the water content."

"If you needed water, why didn't you drink water?"

"I don't like water."

"Get in or stay here, Dorina."

I got in. I wanted to be there when he told the Senate that we'd destroyed a million-dollar aircraft in less than a day. I rode shotgun, while our two passengers took up the backseat. One was the captain, who had gone to sleep after a little suggestion from Louis-Cesare; the other was the only dark mage, other than Jonathan, to have survived the explosion. If you want to call it that.

Louis-Cesare had insisted on bringing him along, but the guy was giving me the willies. The foot growing out of the side of his neck and the fact that he now literally had eyes in the back of his head probably had something to do with that. After five minutes of hearing him scream, I'd had enough and knocked him unconscious.

"So, who's Jonathan?" I asked, fiddling with the air vents to get them as wide open as possible. The sun was so hot I could taste it, and the road shimmered in front of us like an undulating black snake. It was the kind of heat that made newspaper headlines and started people making dire predictions about global warming. I had brought the rest of the six-pack along, but like me, the bottle in my hand was already sweating heavily.

The only answer I got was a slight increase in speed. "If we are going to work together, we should know something about each other," I quoted piously.

"The mage is not important."

"You risked your life to try to kill him and he's not important?"

I received only stony silence for an answer. Louis-Cesare's eyes were on the road, but I could see them clearly in the mirror. They were perfect receptors, showing every reaction in those vivid irises. His expression was blank, the planes of his face like those of a statue, cold and unyielding. But when he thought about Jonathan, his eyes were haunted.

"I *said*, you risked your—"

"It is not your concern."

"Really? Because that's not how it looks to me. There was no reason for the Black Circle to hit that airplane. Yeah, it belongs to the Senate and yeah, there's a war on. But they didn't just attack it and leave. They waited for us to come back. They *waited*."

"We already knew we have a traitor."

"Yes, but now we know—" I was interrupted by a gasp of agonized sound from the mage in the back. Considering his current state, I didn't think pummeling him into silence all the way to MAGIC was a good idea, not if anyone wanted to question him later. I found a knockout dart in my backpack and ensured that he stayed unconscious for the duration of the ride.

I turned back to find Louis-Cesare's eyes on me. "Now we know something else, too," I continued. "We have to

conclude that Drac is working with the Black Circle, unless you think we have two leaks, one informing Uncle of
our whereabouts and the other giving the same information to the mages. Personally, I find that a little hard to
swallow."

"It is not impossible," Louis-Cesare said stubbornly.
"There have been cases recently where vampires, some
sworn to first-level masters, have managed to break their
allegiance. A few even attempted to kill their own sire."

My beer had left a ring of condensation on the knee of
my jeans. I rubbed at it and tried to digest this new bomb-
shell. "Why haven't I heard about this?"

"The Senate is keeping it quiet. They are afraid that to
do otherwise would encourage any vampire dissatisfied
with his position to attempt to break their master's hold."
He glanced at me. "You understand the risk?"

I nodded numbly. One of the main things keeping the
vamp world all nice and tidy—most of the time—is the
near impossibility of any vamp breaking the control of
his sire. Each master answers for his or her children, right
up to the Senate level. The only exception to the rule, or
so I'd thought, was vamps who reached first-level status.
I wondered how many would stay loyal if they had an alternative. Why did I think it wouldn't be a lot?

"What is the Senate doing about this?" I demanded. If
the Black Circle had figured out a way to emancipate at
will, we could be looking at chaos—hundreds, maybe
thousands, of disaffected vamps, all making their own decisions, with no regulation other than brute force.

"Investigating. We have reason to believe that the
method the dark was using is no longer available to them.
However, there is no knowing how many vampires were
affected before then. The number is unlikely to be high,

but it is almost certain that we have not yet found them all."

Things just kept getting better and better. "As interesting as all this is, it still doesn't explain Jonathan."

"Jonathan has nothing to do with our mission."

"It looked like he was pretty involved to me!"

A parade of emotion finally flickered across Louis-Cesare's face—pride, stubborness, bone-deep pain—but he said nothing. I'd long ago learned the same lesson—showing your sore spot only allows it to be hit more easily. And Jonathan was obviously a very sore spot for Louis-Cesare. But I had to push. Whether I liked it or not, we were in this together. And there's nothing I hate worse than fighting enemies I know nothing about.

"That hit wasn't meant for me," I said bluntly. "Drac already left me a message, remember? He took out my team and thumbed his nose in my face. Why do that if he was planning to kill me barely an hour later? For some reason, he wants me alive and scared." At least for the moment. "So he didn't order the hit on the plane. The mages cooked that one up on their own."

I waited, but the only response to my nice logical argument was Louis-Cesare's hands tightening on the wheel. "I've had no run-ins with the Black Circle that could explain them sending a whole hit squad after me," I continued. "So they were after someone else. And there's only two of us."

A long pause. "Jonathan is a . . . personal issue," I was finally informed.

"There aren't any personal issues at a time like this."

Louis-Cesare reached over and flipped on the radio. He settled on an eighties station where Eddie Van Halen was going to town on a guitar riff. Nice, but I suspected he just wanted something loud. I scowled at my reflection in the eggplant-colored windows, wondering when my partner had decided that I'd recently been lobotomized.

The plain fact is, anyone the Senate wants dead gets dead. That holds true even for powerful dark mages. It might be more difficult in their cases and therefore take a little longer, but there's no one they can't reach in the end. Yet Jonathan was still alive. Meaning that Louis-Cesare hadn't asked them for help.

Now, maybe he just wanted to take care of the mage himself—he had said it was personal—but I doubted it. I felt the same way about Claire, but if anyone had harmed her, the Senate would hold him for my tender mercies. Taking their help didn't mean ruling out personal involvement. So there was something about Louis-Cesare's history with the mage that he didn't want known.

"You can't hide it from them forever," I told him, just to make it clear that I was keeping up.

"I am hiding nothing." The words were calm enough, but the Mustang was all but flying down the highway.

I was left with the certainty that whatever Louis-Cesare was keeping from me, it was very personal and very disturbing. But there was exactly nothing I could do about it. "If that's how you want it."

His hands flexed on the wheel, their tight clench loosening slightly. "That's how it is."

Chapter Seven

"Hey, Marlowe. You ever consider staking your decorator?" I glanced around the once-immaculate suite of rooms that now, like much of MAGIC, resembled a rummage sale in an inner-city neighborhood. A scorch mark in the shape of a human body marred one wall of the laboratory, next to the hall door that was half-torn off its hinges. And if there was a whole test tube or beaker in the place, I didn't see it.

"Ah." The handsome brunet vamp spun on his lab stool to face us. He smelled of Cuban cigars, cinnamon and some funky ointment with too many ingredients to list. The latter was emanating from the bandages wrapped around his head. His curls escaped from under them in dispirited clumps, but I didn't have the urge to laugh. Any wound that a vamp couldn't heal without resorting to gross-smelling concoctions was enough to have killed a man. It looked like the war had caught up with him recently. "That explains the stench," he said, with a smile that never came close to his icy brown eyes. "I thought something had died in here. But no, that would be in about ten seconds."

"Not unless you want Daddy on your ass," I told him insolently. The few times I'd been to MAGIC had been with Mircea, who tends to make other vamps sweat, crawl and genuflect. I didn't have that advantage now, but figured I could take a half-dead vamp, even Marlowe, if necessary. "I'm here on family business."

"You're a lousy liar."

"Actually, I'm a *great* liar, not that I'd bother in your case. It's much more fun to tell you the truth." I placed a bloody piece of burnt-out metal on the table in front of him. "Speaking of which, the jet got torched. I think this was from the left wing, but I'm not sure." He stared with no expression at the piece I'd pried out of the steward's head. I parked myself on the neighboring stool and tried to look commiserating. "They just don't make 'em like they used to, do they?"

"I most emphatically do not need this," Marlowe said, turning a nearby clipboard over so I couldn't read it. It probably contained nothing more interesting than the estimated repair costs, but he gives a whole new definition to the word "paranoid." He makes even me look laid-back.

"I may have something you do need," Louis-Cesare told him, dumping the still-unconscious mage onto the debris-covered floor. "This one was among those who attacked us."

Marlowe looked the mage over in disgust, while I watched Louis-Cesare. His eyes were perfectly clear, like the sky on a bright June day. He wasn't worried, which meant that the mess on the floor knew squat about him and Jonathan. Those summer eyes met mine over Marlowe's head with a question and I shrugged. I had no vested interest in helping the Senate, and plenty of reasons to enjoy watching them squirm. His secret was safe with me.

"Dislocator," Marlowe sneered after getting a good look at our captive. He glanced at me. "Do you know the penalty for being caught with one of those?"

"Dark mages," I said, shaking my head regretfully. "You can't trust 'em."

"You expect me to believe that one of his allies threw this at him?"

I was surprised, shocked even. "What other explanation is there?"

Marlowe nudged the guy in the ribs with his toe. "Is that what he will say when he wakes?"

"Who knows? Mages, such liars." I wasn't worried. The captain wasn't likely to rat on the person who'd saved his life, and Louis-Cesare had promised Mircea not to do anything to hurt me. Turning me in to Marlowe would definitely go against that promise. It seemed we both had secrets.

Nonetheless, I kept my bag close to hand, since there were some other unsavory devices still inside. There would be a lot more as soon as I got the chance to visit a certain old acquaintance in Vegas. Drac wanted me alive for now, but why? And for how long?

"We do need your help," Louis-Cesare was saying, which seemed to get Marlowe's attention more than my attempts at conversation. I left them to talk things over, because I saw a familiar shadow dart by the door and into a room across the hall. If it had been any farther, I'd have let it go. I have an excellent sense of direction and don't usually lose my way, yet MAGIC's layout seems to change every time I'm there. It could be a spell, one of its many built-in defenses, or simply nerves on my part. I strongly suspected that a whole coterie of dark mages would be more welcome around here than I was.

I met another vamp, one of Marlowe's boys, coming in the door and smiled at him. He bared fangs, but cringed away slightly at the same time, as if I'd really stake him in front of his already pissed-off master. I pushed past him and crossed the hall, noting that it was riddled with bits of serrated iron that were half-buried in the floor. Normally, these form what passes for decorations on the sconces and chandeliers about the place, but in times of attack they become lethal projectiles that target anyone not on the approved list. Since my name was definitely not on that document, I was glad to see that they appeared inactive.

I pushed open the door and saw whom I'd expected. "Hello, Uncle."

Radu, in his usual swashbuckling attire, champagne-colored satin in this case, froze in place. He had the guilty look of someone caught in headlights with a body, a shovel and a big hole. I found his expression interesting, since not much disconcerts the older vamps, especially not ones who have seen and done as much as he has.

I glanced around, but nothing seemed unusual. We were in one of the small, unremarkable rooms that litter the rabbit warren of MAGIC's lower levels. Like the one across the hall, this one looked more like it belonged in a hospital or laboratory than a supernatural stronghold. But there were no alien bodies in formaldehyde or anything else to account for Radu's expression. He smiled nervously, the famous turquoise eyes that had once garnered him the nickname of "the Handsome" wide and scared.

"Stop looking like you expect me to draw a weapon and come after you," I said irritably. I don't know why he does that—I've never actually tried to kill him—but maybe he figures there's always a first time. I sat on the edge of a nearby counter and lit a joint, trying to look casual and put him at ease. Considering the tenseness that practically radiated off him, I wasn't doing so hot.

"You're a brunette again," he said, and then looked flustered when he realized that making personal comments wasn't the best way to start a conversation.

"Temporarily."

He tried widening the smile, but it trembled on his lips and he soon gave it up. "It has, er, been a long time, Dorina."

"Dory, and yeah, I suppose so." I thought for a minute. "Let's see, World War II was still on. I remember because you were bitching about the Krauts sinking some ship with a bunch of your stuff on it—"

"The blockade, you know, around Britain." He gestured helplessly. "Such a bother. Some of the rarer herbs simply aren't available anywhere else."

"Right." I glanced around the room at the rows of shelves holding valuable ingredients. "Bet there's no problem getting unusual stuff now, with you working at MAGIC."

There was no earthly reason for Radu to jump slightly at that comment. The Senate had used him for the last century as one of its brain-trust weirdos, hanging around the lower levels, concocting God knew what. There was nothing new about it, so his reaction interested me. But since I knew I had about as much chance of getting information out of him as of being voted most popular by vamps worldwide, I switched subjects.

"I'm working with Louis-Cesare now—did anyone tell you?"

He nodded vigorously. "Mircea said something about it. How are you two getting on?"

"Famously. Until Jonathan showed up."

I watched Radu carefully, but there was no sign that he recognized the name. And if he had, there would have been. It never ceased to amaze me that he and Mircea were full brothers. "Who?"

"Nothing." I gave him my sweetest smile, and for some reason, he blanched. "I'm glad I caught you, Uncle. I need a favor."

"There are three great houses of the Light Fey," I was told by the nondescript little vamp Radu had dug up. He smelled like old, musty books and dust, and was gray all over—hair, eyes, clothes and teeth. But the bookworm knew his stuff; for once, Uncle had come in handy. "The Blarestri, or Blue Elves, are the current ruling house, but their grip is less than firm because their king has no heir. Or, rather, he does have a son—Prince Alarr—but he cannot rule."

"Why not?" I perched on the overflowing desk, an enormous rolltop like something out of Dickens, that filled most of the tiny office. The vamp was one of Marlowe's beetles, a group attached to the spy network who acted less as operatives than as librarians. He was one of those responsible for keeping track of info on the Fey, and Radu had called in a favor so he'd allow me to pick his brain for half an hour. So far, it hadn't yielded much.

"Alarr is half-human, and the ruler must always have a majority of Fey blood," the beetle explained. "But there are those who doubt that he intends to follow the old ways if they deprive him of a throne. People fear civil war should the king die, for there is another claimant. The king's sister married a Svarestri noble, and bore him a full-blooded Fey son with royal Blarestri blood. They call him Æsubrand—it means the Sword of the Æsir."

"I understood about one word in seven of that," I told him frankly. "Back up. Who are the Svarestri?" The cram course on Fey politics was already giving me a headache. And I couldn't even complain because I'd asked for it.

"The Black Elves, as they are known, are the second great house of Faerie. And because the Alorestri, the Green Elves, have never shown much interest in politics, it is the Svarestri who pose the greatest threat to Blarestri rule. In fact"—he paused to light a pipe—"according to legend, they did rule once, long ago, when the Æsir walked the earth."

"The who?"

"How can you have lived so long and be so ignorant?" he asked tetchily.

"The Æsir were the lords of battle," Radu put in.

The beetle glanced at him approvingly. "Quite. Said to love war more than the very air they breathed—Odin, Thor and the like. They displaced the Vanir, the older fertility gods, and banished their followers, the Blarestri, from Eluen Londe—"

"What?"

"Eluen Londe." I looked at him blankly. "Faerie!" he clarified impatiently. "They gave its rule into the hands of those who pledged themselves to their service—the Svarestri—who ruled it until the Æsir departed."

"Departed for where?"

"But that's the great mystery, isn't it?" Radu asked excitedly. "No one knows. One day, poof. They simply weren't there anymore."

I raised an eyebrow but didn't question it. I really

didn't care where some probably mythical beings had gone on vacation. "Okay, how about more modern history? What's the situation now?"

The beetle looked vaguely perturbed. He hemmed and hawed for a while, but the upshot was that the vamps didn't know squat. There were rumors of turmoil in the Fey capital, and no one had seen the king for weeks, but whether that signified a coup, no one could say. I'd sat through that whole history lesson and learned absolutely nothing useful.

"All I want to know is why a party of Fey wanted to kill me," I said heatedly.

The beetle's lips twisted enough to show fang. "Doesn't everyone?" Radu hustled me out the door before I could find out if the vamp's plump little carcass would fit into his overstuffed desk.

Radu escorted me back to Marlowe's digs, then made his excuses and disappeared into his lab. He closed the door, waited a few seconds to see if I'd follow, and continued toward the blank wall he'd been facing when I'd stopped him. I knew this because I'd left an Eye of Argus charm looped around the back of a nearby chair. As soon as Radu disappeared through the wall, I slipped back into the lab, retrieved my little eyeball cluster and put it back on my key chain. Time to find out what had Uncle so jumpy.

The hidden entrance to a corridor carved out of the local sandstone wasn't warded. I stopped at that realization, more than a little worried since where the Senate doesn't have wards, it tends to have even nastier things. Most wards are designed to keep something or someone out of an area, or to set off an alarm when an intruder passes through them. Booby traps are used when the Senate doesn't care about interrogation, and only wants any snoopers dead, usually in a very unpleasant way.

It took me a long time to get down that corridor, because I was convinced that a trap lay waiting somewhere along it, and had to test every foot before I dared to move ahead. I have a charm that makes any magical traps in a two-foot area become visible, but it takes twenty seconds or so to kick in every time a new reading is needed. I had to move ahead two feet, stop, let the charm do its thing, get a negative reading and start all over again. It was the sort of thing that made me want to scream.

I could tell from scent that Radu had entered the left of two doors at the end of the hall. Oddly enough, since he hates the ocean, Radu always smells like a day at the beach: salt and ozone. Today, that was overlaid with something else, an odd, musty air that I couldn't place. Since my brain's scent catalog is pretty extensive, that should have worried me more than it did. But the nerve-racking pace had made me impatient, which in turn caused me to be more reckless than usual, although things would probably have played out the same way in any case.

As soon as my charm read negative on any surprises, I opened the door and slipped inside. I flashed on that old story about the lady or the tiger, and had time to think that it figured I would pick the latter, before the thing was on me. I smelled the fetid breath of something that had been snacking on raw meat recently and hadn't bothered to floss, felt claws on the front of my jacket and heard the familiar rushing sound in my ears that precedes a period of dhampir-induced madness.

When I came around, it was to find Radu swatting at

me with a stick. "No, no, no!" he was chanting, and from the rough state of his voice, it sounded like he'd been screaming it for a while. Weirdly enough considering the noise level, no one else had joined us, unless you counted the various strange things cowering in the corners. It was difficult to see them because a prehistoric-looking panther the size of a small horse was sprawled across my chest, its body limp in death. Since my hands were still buried in its throat, I didn't have to ask what had killed it.

Radu, I realized as my vision cleared the rest of the way, was attempting to beat the thing off me. But his aim wasn't very good and as many thumps landed on me as on the recently departed. My ribs felt sore enough to let me know that this had been going on for some time.

I sat up, throwing the body away and catching the stick as it descended again. I tried not to notice that several of the creatures in the corners immediately began to make a meal off the remains of the kitty. "Cut it out. I have enough bruises already."

"Dorina? You . . . you're not hurt?" He looked stunned. I don't know how people think I've lived as long as I have. The rumor is that I'm freaking lucky, and while I wouldn't argue the point, it isn't the only reason.

"No, didn't feel like being cat chow." I glanced down at myself, but all parts seemed to be present and accounted for, if not in particularly good shape. There was a lot of blood—not mine for the most part—and a few tufts of fur clinging to my top. "Crap!" I shrugged out of my jacket and held it up to the light. Large slash marks perforated the heavy leather giving me a view of the room in places. Its thickness had spared my body much of the laceration, but that didn't make me feel much better. "This is the second one in less than a day," I complained.

"The Senate's going to get a bill for a new wardrobe if this keeps up."

"You're really all right!" Radu threw his arms around me, causing me to wince when he squeezed the wounds the jet parts had made in my back. "I was so worried, Dorina! Mircea would . . . I couldn't think what I'd tell him if—"

"Yeah, I'd hate it if my death got you in trouble with Dad," I said with undisguised sarcasm. Radu didn't seem to know how to reply to that, not that I gave him a chance. "And what the hell is this place, anyway?" I realized that none of the creatures, some in cages and some roaming free, looked all that familiar.

The two things snacking on the carcass looked like someone had hit a giant rat and the contents of a Dumpster with a dislocator—nothing made sense and nothing was where it was supposed to be. One of the sort-of rats seemed to have gotten hold of a human leg, which I originally thought it was saving for dessert. I looked away when I realized it was attached to the side of one furry hip, and was moving slightly, as if trying to gain a footing on the blood-slick floor.

After five centuries of horrors, very little gets to me anymore. Disgusted I can still do, but I would have said that appalled was no longer on my sensations list. The last time I'd felt it had been during the Great War, when a hunt took me into the trenches in France just after the Battle of the Somme. A mountain of corpses, too battered and blood soaked to reveal what army they had belonged to, fell on top of me while a revenant vamp and I were playing hide-and-seek. Digging my way out had not been pleasant. I still have dreams about it sometimes, of sliding on a bed of churned-up mud, decaying bodies pressing in all around me, someone's soil-stained tibia stabbing me in the ribs, and rats the size of rabbits snacking on the feast man in his infinite stupidity had provided. A few of the men in the pile had still been alive, although they were busy coughing their lungs out in foaming pink shreds, courtesy of a recent mustard gas attack. I made a few mercy killings and got the hell out of there, leaving the revenant behind. It was the only time I'd ever run from a quarry, and I wasn't proud of it. But at least I believed I'd seen the ugliest face of humanity.

I'd been wrong.

I think it was the instinctive knowledge that, whatever these things were, their creation had not been accidental that got me. I watched a thing with a wolf's head and a giant lizard's body pull itself across the floor toward us, its heavy, fang-filled mouth dripping saliva onto the floor, and felt as much pity as revulsion. Both of those were eclipsed a moment later by a rushing tide of pure rage.

"Is this your new hobby, Radu?" No wonder he hadn't wanted to be followed! "And here I was telling someone recently that one of my uncles is semisane. Guess I'll have to rethink that statement, huh?"

"Please, Dorina, it isn't what you think—"

"The name is Dory!" I realized that I had Radu in a grip that would have broken more than a few ribs if he'd been human. I pushed him away from me, and he staggered near the remains of the kitty cat, causing the rat things to chatter at him. He took a few steps back in my direction, but stopped short, as if having trouble deciding which of the dangers was worse. If he'd been doing what I suspected, it was definitely me. "Okay, tell me what I should think. 'Cause you don't even want to know what ideas are swimming around my head right now."

"You aren't supposed to be in here!" Radu wailed, almost in tears. "You weren't supposed to see this!"

"I bet." The stench from the cages and the viscera being chewed over by the rat duo was starting to get to me. Just because I've smelled worse didn't mean I found it pleasant. "Come on. You can explain while I steal a new jacket."

Mircea's quarters in MAGIC were, like their owner, subtle, rich and somehow intimidating. Of course, the sheer size might have had something to do with that last one. There was a receiving room guarded by a stately foyer, an intimate dining room, a library and a bathroom as large as my office. There were two large bedrooms, one of which was Radu's temporary home, and five smaller ones—in case, I assumed, someone needed to house a horde of servants. The only one I'd seen so far was a sour old Englishman—a vamp, of course—that Mircea had long ago loaned his brother. I suspected that had been prompted less by generosity than by the creature's perennially bad disposition. Geoffrey had scowled at me on arrival, but since Radu was with me, he'd had to let me in.

Radu and I ensconced ourselves in the master suite. Walnut panels lined the walls except for where a built-in bookshelf interrupted to showcase an impressive collection of what were probably first editions. An antique Kashan rug in rich gold, brown and cream covered the floor. The bed was enormous and built high off the ground, with sturdy wooden posts at the corners providing anchors for the curtain rods that outlined it. The curtains were plush cognac velvet with tiebacks in a dark brown satin that matched the sinfully soft quilted comforter. So good to know Daddy wasn't depriving himself.

Radu sat on the bed and watched me with apprehensive eyes as I sorted through Mircea's huge old wardrobe. The carvings were traditional Romanian: a tree of life bloomed on each door, around which twisted rope, flowers and wolf teeth in an elaborate design meant to ward off evil spirits. Considering where the thing was located, I thought that was being optimistic.

It didn't surprise me to see it there, though. Mircea loved Romanian folk art, especially anything made of wood, and had assembled a huge collection through the years. His main estate, in an isolated part of Washington State, is filled with everything from priceless antique doors from Maramures, the woodworking heart of the old country, to cheap but pretty hand-carved spoons that had caught his eye. Or at least it was the last time I had been hauled there for a family gathering, back in the eighties. I'll never understand him. Everything I own, except for my weapons collection, can fit in a small car. I like it that way, being mobile, able to pull up roots and leave everyone and everything behind at a moment's notice, driving off into the sunrise. . . .

"I thought that was supposed to be sunset." I didn't realize I'd spoken aloud until Radu piped up.

"Sunrise is better. That way, you have a full day's head start on any nocturnal types who might be in pursuit."

I passed over a forest of coats in expensive materials with soft drapes in favor of something sturdier. "This might do." I dragged a leather capelike coat out of the back of the wardrobe and slung it over my shoulders. It was butter-soft, buff-colored leather with a rich brown lining in what felt like silk. It was too big, of course, but that just meant I could hide more stuff underneath it.

"You can't say anything about what you saw, Dory. You have to promise me." Radu was looking at me the way a small child might regard something sprouting tentacles and oozing pus that had just slimed its way out of a closet. I found myself getting annoyed with him all over again.

"Relax, I'm not going to bite you." You'd think I was the vampire here. How Radu had ever run a country in the cutthroat bad old days was a mystery. The guy got nervous if you looked at him too long.

"I'm not . . . I don't . . ."

"Save it. Just tell me what's going on." I flopped onto a forties-era leather chair. It looked like something Bogie would have liked and was decadently comfortable.

"I'm not supposed to talk about it," Radu protested, glancing around like he hoped for rescue. Not likely. I hadn't seen any servants besides Geoffrey, and he wasn't the hero type. He'd tried to knife me in the back when we first met, supposedly before he knew who I was, but the most he ever did to my face was sneer.

"Try."

"It . . . they . . . were an experiment. Or part of one."

"I didn't know you went in for that kind of thing." It wasn't the first time I'd seen attempted manipulation of species. Demons, for one, were always trying to improve their bloodlines any way they could, to win out over rival clans in the constant infighting, and the Fey had been doing selective breeding for centuries. But those were attempts to improve things, however odd they might seem to outsiders, and nothing I'd seen in the lab looked like an upgrade to me. Not to mention that I'd always thought that Radu, the Senate's resident mad scientist, had an ethical code of sorts.

"I didn't! I wouldn't!" Radu stopped wadding Mircea's nice bedspread into a ball and stared at me in what looked like genuine consternation. "We captured them in a raid on one of the Black Circle's haunts. I was asked to discover the reason they were created."

I was inclined to believe him, mainly because I couldn't even start to guess why the Senate would waste valuable resources, especially during a war, on splicing genes. "You didn't guard them very well if they're some big secret."

"They are guarded quite well!" Radu said, offended. "You were able to pass through the screens only because they are keyed to me—or, more specifically, to anyone with my blood. Since the only other persons who fit that description are trusted family members, it seemed foolproof." He looked grumpy. "We forgot about you."

"You always do. So what did you find?" His expression slipped from righteous indignation into sneaky evasiveness in a flash. I mentally shook my head. "Let me guess. That's the part you're not supposed to talk about."

"I'm not supposed to talk about any of this! And you had better not, either, Dory. The Senate won't like your knowing."

I shrugged. "They basically don't like my breathing, so what else is new?"

Radu crossed the room so fast I almost didn't see him. A second later I was dangling a couple feet off the ground, while those delicate-looking hands shook me like a dog. Just when you forget they're vampires . . .

"Promise me! You can't say anything! The Senate is

deadly serious about this. If they even suspected that you knew—"

"What? They'd kill me? And that would be different from the current situation how?" I wrestled out of Radu's grip and straightened the creases his fists had made in my new jacket. "Speaking of which, we need to talk." I pushed him into the chair I'd vacated, and leaned over as menacingly as I could manage with a straight face. "How about you and I discuss our mutual problem?"

"Wh-what problem?"

"Don't play dumb. I'm sure Mircea mentioned it, maybe in passing? Drac's loose." Radu nodded, gulping. He looked vaguely ill, and I took that for an encouraging sign. It showed he had a brain, and that he knew his brother. "What are you planning to do about it?"

"I've already done it," he told me, gesturing around. "Why do you think I'm here? I don't like this place. Nothing is ever left where I put it, and one Senate member or another is always prowling about, asking for progress reports. I could work much more efficiently at home. But Mircea said Vlad wouldn't try for me here."

"No, I suppose not." Considering that he'd have to wade through the Senate and their retainers, the Silver Circle and its bevy of psychotic war mages and who knew how many weres, Fey and whatever else was hanging around at the moment, it seemed a safe bet. "So the plan is what? To stay trapped here forever? Doesn't sound like fun, 'Du."

"You know I hate that absurd diminutive," he told me irritably. "Why can't you leave people's names alone? Does it physically pain you to utter an extra syllable?"

I grinned. "Looks like I struck a nerve."

"Nonsense!" Radu sat up a little straighter and pushed

me a foot or so back. Talk of his predicament seemed to have evaporated my scare potential—there aren't many things that look frightening next to Drac. "Mircea said you'd take care of him shortly, and then I can go home." He looked testy. "Why aren't you on the hunt, instead of snooping about here? I thought you liked killing things."

"Aha!" I clapped him on the back. "I knew I wasn't the only smart one in the family. You want him dead, too!" I went to pour the guy a drink. He'd earned it.

"Of course I do!" Radu snapped impatiently. "Do you have any idea what he'd like to do to me? He's always despised me."

"So we're in the same boat." He took the glass of whiskey I handed him while I settled onto the hassock at his feet—or tried to before finding myself dumped unceremoniously on my butt. I got up and tried again, only to have the same thing happen. This time, I looked closer at the footstool, a fat paisley-covered pouf with thick tassels at each corner, and noticed something fairly weird, even by my definition of the term. It was hovering a few inches off the ground, its little bun feet not quite touching the rug.

"It was upholstered from an old flying carpet," Radu explained, seeing the direction of my stare, "and tends to be temperamental. I wouldn't—" I grabbed the thing, only to find it suddenly wriggling like an overly energetic puppy. It spurted out of my hands, but I jumped on top and held on. "It doesn't like anyone using it but Mircea," Radu said. "I think there's another chair in—"

"I like this one," I told him, as the bucking-bronco ride I was being treated to careened me into the bedpost, smashing my thigh against the hard wood.

"It doesn't like me, either," Radu said as I grabbed one

of the tiebacks from the bedpost. The plan was to strap it down, but somehow it seemed to know that, and went skittering off in the other direction, jouncing me as savagely as it could manage in the process. "Anyway, I don't think Vlad hates you, Dory," Radu sighed. "Or if he does, it's merely for an accident of birth."

"And the little thing of helping to trap him for a century or so."

"Well, yes, there's that." Radu drained his glass while I struggled to get the tieback looped around one of the hassock's squat feet. I finally managed it, but then I had to figure out where to attach the other end that had a chance of holding it. "But he hates me far more. Mircea and I are full brothers, but he and Vlad were always the soul mates. Two warriors and a bookish runt—it was laughable," he said bitterly. "I tried to keep up with them, at least at first. But I was no good at any of it. Even with the best instruction in the country, my swordsmanship was never better than average and I was hopeless on a horse. Still am, really."

"Uh-huh. Life's a bitch," I commiserated not at all. The hassock rode us by the bookshelf and I got an idea. I snagged several heavy volumes, and sure enough, its antics slowed down perceptibly. I shoved them underneath me and quickly grabbed two more. The hassock slowly started to settle toward the floor and I thought I had it, but then it gave a huge heave and threw both the books and me off. It flounced away, tassels swinging smugly.

"You can have this chair, Dory," Radu offered, starting to rise, but I waved him off.

"No, really. I'm fine." I started stalking the hassock, dismemberment in mind. "You were saying?"

"Yes, well, things deteriorated after Father agreed to

our being hostages, of course. Indeed, they became immeasurably worse. I got out of much of the torture after Father broke his treaty with the Turks and they threw us in the dungeons. I should have been stronger, should have defied them the way Vlad did, but you don't know what it was like." He licked his lips and set the glass aside with a slightly shaking hand. "I saw what some of the older prisoners looked like, those that had been in there for a while. Noses and lips missing, teeth knocked out, limbs torn off, burns everywhere—"

"Yeah, bad stuff." I'd seen things that made the Turks look like children at play, but then, so had Radu. The difference was that he'd been pretty damn young, barely a teenager if I remembered right, to be dealing with that house of horrors. Since he was handling the Senate's menagerie now, something that would have given me nightmares, he must be made of sterner stuff than he looked.

The hassock suddenly reversed course and swept through my legs, knocking me to the floor again. I shot it a dirty glance; even the furniture around here hated me. Then I made an abrupt leap and threw myself on top of it. Turning the wicked thing upside down, I lashed it to the bedpost before it had a chance to try any more tricks. By the time I was finished, it was trussed up in all four tie-backs, the sheet and several items from Mircea's wardrobe.

"There!" I grinned at it triumphantly. "Now try to move, damn you."

Radu sighed and stood up to get a refill. "That's all very well, Dory, but how are you going to sit on it now?"

One of the tassels waved about, giving the distinct impression that it was flipping me off. Fine. It could stay like that until it rotted. I dropped into Radu's abandoned chair and glowered at it. "Were you trying to make a point, Uncle?"

He propped himself against the bar and regarded me somberly. "Only that I was weak. I was offered a way out, and I took it. Vlad never forgave me for that, for sleeping with the enemy, as they say these days. And then, of course, he thinks I betrayed him and stole his throne—"

"You did betray him and steal his throne."

"Well, yes, but only after he went barking mad," Radu said impatiently. "I wasn't stupid, Dory. I knew the Turks were trying to use me, but something had to be done about Vlad. I've never forgotten the sight of the corpses, thousands of them, staked alive on the fields around Tirgoviste. In all the years since, I've never known anything like it."

"There were more killed in some battles in the world wars."

"Yes, but not with the . . . the precision, the intent. You remember—he had the stakes laid out in geometric patterns, so he could climb that tower of his and gloat over the pictures they made."

"No, I don't recall that. I'd been given to a bunch of Gypsies, remember?"

"Oh, yes." Radu looked at me vaguely. "How did that turn out for you, then?"

I stared at him. Five hundred years later and he finally thinks to ask. "Oh, peachy. They kept cats around to keep mice off the food, and me to kill any vamps that tried to munch on them. Fun times." Until they all ended up dead, anyway.

"Oh, good."

I bit back a retort. I was fast recalling why I usually

avoided conversations with Radu. "My point, if you'll let me make it, is that we both have the same enemy. Okay"— I held up a hand to avoid another waltz down memory lane—"Drac may be planning a more elaborate send-off for you, but me being dead still figures in his plans somewhere. It doesn't in mine."

"Then you had best tell Mircea you won't be going after him. He needs to know, in order to plan something else."

I regarded him through the heavy, cut-crystal glass. A dozen little Radus looked back at me, each as clueless as the last. "And what, exactly, do you think his backup plan is? Who would be crazy enough to face Drac? Even if there wasn't a war on, I think it's safe to say that's one commission most people would pass up." I actually knew a few bounty hunters who might be stupid enough to try, for the right fee, but I doubted they'd do more than make Uncle feel insulted that they'd been sent against him. Right before he turned them into meat.

"Mircea would deal with it," Radu offered unhelpfully, "but he's trying to arrange a meeting of the six senates."

"Why?" Having one group of crazed senior vamps around was enough.

"The war, of course. It's becoming quite bothersome."

I decided to let that conversation wait for another time. The less I knew about what Mircea was doing, the better I tended to sleep. "So, anyway, we have a common enemy—"

"You've said that."

I took a deep breath and tried one more time. "The way I see it, we have two choices. We can cower in here until Drac raises enough of a force to come in and get us, or we can go on the offensive. I prefer the latter, since letting him call the shots is a good way to end up dead. Or worse," I added, considering that Radu was probably right about his brother's plans.

"And how do 'we' do that? I told you, I'm not a fighter, Dory. That army I led was Turkish, and so were its commanders. I was mostly there as a figurehead, so the people had someone from one of the old families to consider their ruler instead of a Turkish prince. I didn't make many decisions."

"You won't have to fight him," I assured Radu.

"Oh, good." He looked relieved.

I drained my drink and patted him affectionately on the leg. "You're the bait."

Chapter Eight

As I'd expected, the rub came more from Louis-Cesare than Radu. Uncle was smart enough to realize that if the only choice was either to face Drac when he was unprepared or wait for him to gather more followers, the former was infinitely preferable. The only thing we could come up with that was likely to force him to act before he was ready was the prospect of catching both of us together in an undefended area. And that meant a change of venue.

Not surprisingly, Louis-Cesare wasn't pleased. He didn't like the idea of Radu leaving the relatively safe confines of MAGIC for his country estate, despite the fact that said house and grounds were a maze of magical traps that Radu had spent years developing. It seemed that every time he invented something new for the Senate, he tested it out at his place. For our purposes, it was perfect. Drac would find us a hell of a lot more prepared than he expected. Louis-Cesare seemed unable to grasp that simple point, however.

"I absolutely forbid it! Gamble with your own life if you must, but not with his!"

"That's up to Radu to say, don't you think? Is he your master, or vice versa?"

Radu, who was supervising the loading of a lot of large, smelly cages into a truck, ostentatiously ignored us. He was taking his menagerie of genetic horrors with him, to continue his work from his home lab, and the unusually heavy rainstorm we were getting was making the shift difficult. It seemed the things didn't like getting wet. Contrary to popular belief, the Mojave does get rain from time to time, only the dry, hard-packed soil doesn't deal with it well. I hopped over a fast-forming orange red puddle that was leaching onto the concrete as 'Du jabbed at a giant claw with a cattle prod. It had wormed its way through the bars of a cage and snagged one of his assistants. Obviously, dealing with Louis-Cesare was up to me.

"I am trying to ensure his safety," he was saying fiercely. "Something to which you seem entirely indifferent."

I gave him a flat look. "Our job is to deal with Drac, not to guard Radu."

"I will not sacrifice my master to your revenge," I was informed bluntly.

"This isn't about revenge! It's about saving Claire."

"Then I will not trade Radu's life for the woman's. If we can trap Dracula without endangering Radu, well and good. If not—"

"You'd see him go free?" I stared at him, but his face was utterly implacable. He meant it. The stubborn, condescending, self-important son of a bitch actually meant it. And this was the guy Mircea had sent along to help me! I reined in the impulse to connect Louis-Cesare's head with the driveway a few times and smiled. "Okay. Let's go over it again," I said brightly.

"I have heard more than enough," was the grim reply.

"You are reckless, and a danger to yourself and everyone near you. How—"

"I'm reckless? Who almost got us killed on the plane?"

"—you have survived this long I do not know, but I will not allow you to commit suicide and take Lord Radu with you! Other plans will be made. You will be informed of them when necessary." He turned in Uncle's direction and actually started to walk away.

"Hey!" I grabbed the closest thing, which happened to be his rain poncho. "Did I say we were done here?"

The temperature of the surrounding air skyrocketed. "I would advise you to remove your hand, dhampir, while it remains attached to your body."

"Oh, that's rich, coming from you."

Blue eyes narrowed dangerously. "And what does that mean?"

"It means you have a habit of violating my personal space. Tell me, is that a French thing, or do you just like touching me?"

Blood moved in his face, spreading over his cheeks before draining away and deserting them. "You believe you can say anything you wish to me, and I have no choice but to accept it because of your father."

I blinked in surprise. I'd used that line on Marlowe, but only as a taunt. I didn't make a habit of hiding behind Daddy's reputation. I had one of my own, and there were damn few vamps who forgot it.

"Mircea gets me into a lot more trouble than he's ever gotten me out of," I said tersely. "Current situation included. The only reason he didn't let you stake me in New York was because his ass is in the fire and I'm expected to pull it out. Again."

"You understand nothing!" Louis-Cesare radiated anger

like heat. "I have been told a dozen times today that I was mad to assault you in front of him, mad to think that my opinions might stand against those of his only true child, his only living flesh!"

I choked, caught halfway between a laugh and a curse. "Someone's been pulling your leg, big-time." Louis-Cesare looked confused. "They've been making a joke at your expense," I clarified. "Believe me, the only value I hold for Mircea is whatever I can do for him. I'm another weapon in his arsenal, nothing more, and the whole vamp community knows it."

"And what would you know of the 'community'?" Louis-Cesare demanded. "When did you ever live among us, Dorina? You choose to stay on the fringes of our society so that you may pick off the weak, but you were never part of it!"

Bitterness shivered through me like a chill. "Yeah, I choose. Gee, I wonder why that is. Maybe because every time I get anywhere near it, someone tries to kill me! Unlike you." I looked him up and down, with a sneer I didn't bother to hide. "Basarab line with no taint of bad blood, Senate member, dueling champ. You're a bloody vamp hero, Louis! What would you know of my life?"

"More than you do of mine, it would seem." Louis-Cesare's eyes burned blue fire. "For centuries, my own master refused to have anything to do with me. I was known as the outcast, the one our famous line wanted no part of. While you, a dhampir with the blood of our people still dripping from your hands, were welcomed with open arms! You laugh at them, despise them, threaten to kill them, time and again, and still they want you. Yet every advance I make is thrown back in my face!"

I blinked at him. The fact that I'd never heard of

Radu's offspring suddenly made more sense. "But why spurn you?" Louis-Cesare was the perfect scion, the gallant son whose accomplishments might just cover the blots on the family page. Like Drac. Like me.

His mouth twisted bitterly. "Ask your father if you wish to know. Or Lord Radu. Perhaps they will tell *you* the truth."

"I'm asking you."

"Why? Why ask me anything?" he demanded savagely. "I am merely tolerated for the moment because the Senate is desperate. Too many of their members have already been lost to the war, and others may be so before long. Now they need strength, but when the war ends . . . things will be as they were."

I frowned. That didn't sound like Mircea. Betray him and he'd cut your balls off and feed them to you, but I'd never seen him turn his back on an ally. I doubted very much that I was going to see it now. "When we get through this, I'll talk to Mircea," I began, wondering why I bothered.

I stopped because Louis-Cesare was going purple. "I do not need your pity!" He stepped closer, until his body was actually touching mine, but I didn't call him on it. He'd been so controlled, so smugly superior, in the car; it was good to see some of the arrogance bleed away into a more honest emotion. Nobody else seemed to notice how much of it he carried around, but I knew anger. On most people it was a shallow, washed-out emotion, limp and tepid. On Louis-Cesare it was incandescent.

"What *do* you need?" It slipped out before I could catch it.

Time froze for a long, breathless minute. Then Louis-Cesare's eyes flooded silver, melting into white-hot heat. I was so startled by the transformation that it took me a moment to realize that he didn't look aroused; he looked livid.

"There is only one service you provide to my kind," he said in a savage undertone. "When I am ready for it, I will let you know."

It was like a punch to the stomach, a clean blow that takes the wind right out of you. I honestly had no idea what to say. Then an arm slipped around my neck, saving me the trouble by almost crushing my windpipe.

I couldn't believe anyone had actually managed to sneak up on me; then I heard Marlowe's voice and understood. The damn vamp moved as quietly as smoke—it was one of many things that made him so deadly. "Have more care, Louis-Cesare. Remember what you're dealing with."

Louis-Cesare shot him a purely vicious look. "Release her! This is a family discussion."

"Family?" Marlowe didn't bother to hide his disgust. "You're beginning to sound like—"

I elbowed Marlowe painfully in the groin, then skipped back out of reach. "I don't know what your deal is," I told Louis-Cesare furiously, resisting the urge to rub my abused throat, "but you take it up with Radu. This was as much his idea as mine, and he thinks it'll work. You want to tell your master he's a fool, you go right ahead. Let me know how that goes, if you survive."

Louis-Cesare had clamped a hand around Marlowe's bicep, restraining the enraged vamp, but his eyes were on me. "We are not finished."

Perverse bastard—he'd been the one walking away a moment before. "Oh, I really think we are," I said, and splashed toward the garage.

I was halfway hoping he'd follow me, maybe give me an excuse to run over him. But when I drove out in that year's

Jaguar—so new the leather smell hadn't even worn off yet—he was still standing in the rain, talking with an angry-looking Marlowe. I stopped by Radu, who was giving his battered assistant a lecture on keeping proper distance.

"Your son is a maniac," I informed him.

'Du sighed. "What now?"

"He was raving about not being welcome in the family."

Radu winced. "Not that again!"

"It isn't true?"

"Of course not! We had to keep him at a distance initially, of course, but that's all over with now."

"What's all over with?"

"Oh, that whole time-change thing," Radu said vaguely, as if I should already know whatever the hell he was talking about.

"What time-change thing?"

"Oh, you know. Before, when that Gypsy cursed him."

"Louis-Cesare is cursed?"

"Well, not *now*," Radu said, as if he thought I might be a little slow. "In the other time stream. The one Mircea altered."

"Wait a minute. Mircea altered time?"

"Really, Dory, if you'd keep up with the family, you'd know these things."

"Humor me."

"Originally, Louis-Cesare was cursed, not made," Radu said with exaggerated patience. "Some Gypsy became annoyed with him about something and . . . I don't remember the details. Anyway, after the time change, I ended up being the one who made him a vampire. But we had to keep everything else as close to the way it had been as possible or risk altering the present. And that included me not being there for Louis-Cesare, because of course I hadn't been before, since I didn't even know him." Radu looked at me petulantly. "I explained all this to him, you know."

I blinked. "As coherently as you just did for me?"

"Naturally! Not that it seemed to make a difference."

"'Du," I said slowly, "there's the teeniest chance that he doesn't believe you."

In a positive fugue of gestures, Radu rolled his eyes, shook his head and sighed. "Never have children, Dory. They are no end of trouble."

"I'm a dhampir," I said tightly. "We can't reproduce."

"Well, that's all right, then." Radu waved it away.

"I'm going to spread some rumors about our destination in Vegas," I said, changing the subject before I was tempted to strangle him and save Drac the trouble. "They'll probably take a while to get around, but there're no guarantees. Be careful on the way there. I'll give you a few hours to get under way before I mention anything."

"Kit has arranged an escort for us." He glanced back to where the boys were talking. "Try not to bait Louis-Cesare, Dory. He is . . . somewhat confused at the moment."

"That would make two of us." Mircea was going to have some explaining to do, the next time I saw him.

"Try to understand, my dear. He doesn't know where you fit in. You're a dhampir, which rather puts you beyond the pale in his way of thinking, but you're also Mircea's daughter and therefore someone to whom he owes a degree of esteem. He doesn't understand that you aren't serious when you tease him. He interprets it as a lack of respect."

"Then he's right on the money," I said, and floored it.

* * *

"I don't think you understand my position," I said, signaling the bartender for another drink. The guy was human, yet he didn't so much as blink at the fact that I was talking to a three-foot-tall gnome with a foot-long nose, beady purple eyes and ears that were growing a forest of bushy white hair long enough to braid. It matched his eyebrows and the snowy mop on his head, but the real stunner was the beard. It was pure silver and almost as long as he was tall. I'd seen him tuck it into his belt before, to keep from tripping, but tonight it flowed free, like a river down his chest. It was an oddly beautiful feature on an otherwise unprepossessing body, and always made me smile.

Benny was a fairly standard Skogstroll, or forest troll, and this *was* Vegas, land of the strange. But I was still surprised at the total lack of interest everyone was showing. Things had changed a bit since I'd been here.

We weren't in a demon bar tucked away on a backstreet, but in a poolside lounge at Caesars. I'd been told at his shop that I'd find Benny here, and sure enough, he'd been belting back margaritas for a while, judging by the bleary-eyed look he turned on me. "I get it, all right?" he said, holding up a gnarled hand to keep me from repeating myself. "You got a tough assignment and you need something with more kick than the law allows. But I'm telling you, I got nothing."

"You always say that." I wasn't about to take no for an answer. I needed to restock, and it didn't seem likely that the Senate was going to help me out. Especially since Mircea wanted Drac trapped, not dead, and none of the things I had in mind were the type you walked away from.

"Only this time, it ain't no bargaining tactic. There's this war happening, you know? My inventory was raided by the Senate—they said to confiscate contraband."

Benny accepted another drink from a waiter, whose eyes never quite managed to focus, and licked the rim. "And right after that, the damn black mages hit me for what was left. Don't nobody understand the concept of paying for nothing no more."

"Come on, Benny. I know you. You never have everything at the shop."

"And now I ain't got nothing nowhere else, neither." He sighed and patted my hand. "You been a good customer, Dory, and you know me. I've always played straight with you, right? But it's the times we're living in. Word is, the Senate is vulnerable and its control is slipping. Who knows what's coming? Nobody, that's who. So they all want protection, don't they? A little something extra in case things start to implode. Truth is, my inventory was getting pretty thin even before the raids. And now . . ." He shook his head. "I got nothing."

A harassed-looking mother walked by the bar, little girl in tow with a sno-cone clutched tightly in one fist. The girl's bright blue lips shaped a startled "oh" of astonishment as she caught sight of Benny, who dropped her a friendly wink. "Mommy! Look at the elf!"

"Don't stare, Melissa! And don't call people names!"

I looked at Benny as the little girl was towed away, still protesting that she wanted to say hello to the "nice elf." "I wouldn't call an Occultus charm nothing, Benny," I observed mildly. They were expensive items used to ensure that anyone who didn't already know what someone looked like would see only a projected image. The exception was young children, whose brains hadn't yet formed the preconceived ideas about the way the world ought to work that the charm exploited.

He shrugged, unapologetic. Benny was like most of

his kind when it came to turning a buck. He'd sell his own mother—who had, after all, tried to eat him—if he thought he'd get a good price. Problem was, he didn't think I had the funds for the no-doubt completely over-inflated prices he was getting these days. Most of the time, he'd have been right. But not today.

"Well, that's a shame." I casually placed my shiny yellow marble on the surface of the bar, next to his collection of colorful paper umbrellas. "You know I'd prefer to deal with you, but I guess I'll have to go somewhere else."

His eyes fixed on the small orb and he slowly set his drink back down. "Come to think of it, Dory, I might have a few special items put away."

A little over half an hour later, we pulled up outside a large warehouse. "A few items?" I asked as we climbed out of the Jag.

Benny shrugged and struggled with a heavy lock on the thick metal door. "I've had this place for years. Usually, I keep it at least half-full. Right now, well"—he pulled back the sliding door—"take a look."

A large, echoing space greeted us. Empty pallets were scattered about, along with a lot of crushed cardboard boxes and a rusty forklift. The overhead lights flickered on reluctantly, and I noticed what looked like a small office in back. "This way," Benny said, picking a path through the trash. "Got a shipment in a couple days ago, and lucky for you, nobody's been by to rob me yet."

"Why don't you move your inventory somewhere they can't find it?"

"If I leave some interesting stuff lying around, I stay up and running and don't get dead." Benny's booming voice bounced off the walls. "War isn't a time to have people start looking at you as expendable. The Senate knows I got contacts they don't. That's what comes of trying to put craftsmen out of business for a couple hundred years—they tend not to want to do business when you get yourself in a jam."

After disarming a few dozen protection wards, Benny flipped on the fluorescents in the claustrophobic office and squeezed around the side of a desk even messier than mine. I stayed back a few feet, in case any of the towering piles decided to fall, and waited. "But I wasn't shooting you a line earlier. My selection ain't what it used to be." Out of his old metal desk he pulled a small briefcase. There was a wait while more spells were disarmed, and then the lock stuck. When he finally got it open, I had a hard time keeping a suitable poker face while eyeing the stuff inside. Benny waggled a shaggy eyebrow at me. "Well, Dory. Can we do business or what?"

I bent over for a better look, making sure a few of the items were what I thought they were, and barely kept from grinning like a fiend. Oh, yeah. I really thought we could.

Ten minutes later, I had four disrupters with the power of about twenty human grenades each, and a top-of-the-line morphing potion. The latter was a yellow glop that performed a glamour even on nonmages like me. Spread it over your face and within minutes you could look like virtually anyone. It tended to break me out, but there were lots worse things than a bad case of acne, and with Drac on my back, I needed all the help I could get.

Benny and I were dickering over whether four or five disorienting spheres—which made you either very dizzy (demons), forget why you were fighting (vamps) or pass out (humans)—should complete the deal when a faint whiff of ozone suddenly replaced the dry tang of the desert. I hit the ground and the next moment, the glass windows that composed the top half of three of the office walls shattered inward, and a wave of force slammed Benny against the metal back wall, reducing his oversized head to so much jelly. I started to move about the same time that the glass shards hit the stained carpet squares.

I grabbed the case from where it had been knocked to the floor by one of Benny's thrashing arms, and hopped out a now missing window on the far side of the room. I threw an expensive disorienting sphere behind me as I left the office, since I was now in possession of twelve of them, and took a second to glance about. The office had obviously been an afterthought, perched near the back exit by someone who decided that managers should have a little privacy. It was not near enough, however. I dove behind a bunch of empty crates and wondered if my extensive karmic debt was about to be called in. A foot away, several more crates and half the wall exploded as the giant fist that wasn't there slammed into them.

Have I mentioned that, sometimes, I really hate magic?

The problem was that I didn't have a full warehouse offering plenty of cover—the sad state of Benny's business had seen to that. Since I doubted my ability to survive a blow from whatever was attacking me, the dozen yards to the back door may as well have been a thousand, especially since I strongly suspected that I'd find a welcoming committee waiting outside. Even if I made it in one piece, I wouldn't remain that way for long.

And again I smelled it, a faint flicker of ozone, like the first lick of an approaching storm. I told myself I was imagining things. It *had* rained lately, after all. But, slicked with sweat, I froze in the darkness, muscles locked and singing with strain as icy panic gnawed at my spine.

Another smash of crates, which was close enough to

send splinters into my boots, brought up my other small problem: I might not be able to move, but I also couldn't stay where I was. My usual choice when backed into a corner is to attack everything in sight, but since there *was* nothing in sight, I decided I might have to try something else. The trashing of Benny's office had blown out the lights, so the only illumination was the dim starlight filtered through some grimy windows near the ceiling. Acting on the hope that whoever was out there couldn't see me any better than I could see them, I backed away from the exit toward the forklift I'd noticed earlier.

I kept near to the wall as the area closer to the door was systematically wrecked. One nice thing about all the noise, I didn't have to bother being quiet. I finally made it to the metal monster and climbed aboard. I was not, of course, going to try to drive it. Forklifts weren't likely to be able to outrun even a fit human, and if it was mages with magically enhanced speed, weres or vamps after me, I'd really be toast. It would, however, provide a nice distraction if I could get it to work. I put a couple of Benny's disruptors on the floorboard, emptied the rest of the case's contents into my new coat's roomy pockets, started the engine and jumped out of the way.

When the invisible hand smashed the thing to bits a few seconds later, I was already halfway across the floor running full out for the front door. I'm as fast as all but the oldest vamps when I want to be, and knowing what would happen when the disruptors went off gave me the best incentive I'd had in a long time to break speed records. I was still inside the building when the explosion came, but just barely. The blast picked me up and threw me against the sliding door, which buckled and then tore off its track. The crumpled metal sheet and I went for a wild ride across the parking lot, striking sparks off the pavement, skidded past a group of dark figures and careened into an SUV.

I rolled underneath the chassis of the vehicle but didn't stay there long. A set of powerful hands grabbed me and hauled me out the other side, about the same time that pieces of the warehouse began to rain down all around us. So much for having to worry about disposing of Benny's body, I thought, as I brought a knee up to connect with my captor's groin. He let out a curse, which I barely heard, being temporarily deaf from the blast, but a flaming crate landed almost on top of us at the same moment and I got a glimpse of his face. Uh-oh.

"Dor-i-na." The syllables were like three strokes of a lash. "I have been looking for you."

I swallowed and gave a sickly smile. Ashes and fire continued falling all around us, like a vision straight out of hell, but I barely noticed. Who cares about the setting when you're already looking at the devil? "Uncle."

Chapter Nine

"It is a simple enough bargain, Dorina." Drac sat in his suite at the Bellagio and smiled at me. It might have been more effective if the expression hadn't completely missed his cold, dead eyes. "I would expect even you to understand."

All vampires are technically dead, of course, but most manage not to look like it. Drac didn't bother. There was no reason at all to forget that the slender body draped comfortably over the armchair was, in fact, stone-cold dead. He didn't breathe, blink or swallow. His skin was a matte white a geisha might have envied, and his eyes were a flat, opaque green like the glass on a beer bottle, with no spark whatever in their depths. The smile, the only expression on his face, was so completely without meaning that it could as easily have graced a department store mannequin, except it would have made the customers very jumpy. I was feeling a little like that, too.

"What part of the conversation did you not comprehend?" Drac was speaking Romanian, I suppose because he felt like it. Or maybe he didn't want his goons to overhear. Either way, it wasn't making me happy. My memories of the old country compose a large percentage of my nightmares, even though I haven't been back in almost three centuries.

"The part about me retaining my 'miserable life' in exchange for helping you," I replied. I spoke in English. If he didn't like it, good.

"You think I would betray you?"

I shrugged, trying to seem nonchalant. Vamps are like dogs—showing fear only makes it that much more likely they'll rip you to shreds. "It crossed my mind. I did help to trap you, after all. I doubt I'm on your favorite-people list."

Drac seemed to find this funny. The eyes didn't warm up—I had never seen them do so—but the laughter sounded real. "Ah, Dorina. You do flatter yourself." He sat up slightly and changed expression again. I think it might have been an attempt to look earnest. Mostly, it just looked blank. The newer vampires have that problem sometimes, until they figure out how to get their dead features to form appropriate expressions. Drac had never been real interested in learning.

"Let us be clear, yes? You are a dhampir. A misbegotten creature with no concept of honor, so how can you betray? You acted as you did for two reasons: it is your nature to hunt my kind, and my brother enlisted your aid. I cannot fault you for the first any more than I would a snake for biting me or a scorpion for stinging. I might crush them, under the right circumstances, but blame them? No. As for the second, you could have refused my brother's order, but you would have been foolish to take such a risk on my behalf. I would not have thanked you for it, and he might well have punished you. In your position, I would have acted the same."

"Well, if you aren't carrying a grudge, then I'll be on my way." I didn't bother getting up; it would have been pointless, and the goon behind me looked like he'd appreciate a chance to put me back in my seat. Preferably in little pieces.

I had already calculated the odds of busting out of there, and didn't like them. Benny's stash had been stripped off me along with my other weapons, and I'd been knocked unconscious for the trip here. That isn't easy to do with a dhampir, and my head was feeling like a jackhammer had been at it. When I woke up, it was to find that Drac had a dozen followers in the room, a combo of mages and vamps. Together, they rendered any attempt to run for the door suicide.

I didn't recognize any of the vamps as being from Drac's old stable, but none of them were days-old babies, either. The one behind me, for instance, was at least a fourth-level master, and therefore had to be on loan from someone. I was betting Rasputin, the self-appointed leader of the other side in the war. He had plenty of vamps to spare but had just been given a black eye by the Senate. He must have been over the moon at the chance to unleash Drac on them. He could lie low and lick his wounds while Uncle kept his enemies busy, not to mention depriving them of a powerful member if he got really lucky. The fact that Rasputin was allied with the Black Circle would also explain the mages.

The vamps were standing around seemingly at random, but enough were near the windows to ensure that even if I decided to attempt the ten-story plunge, I'd never make it. My chance of getting away using force was about the same as that of the suckers downstairs winning at roulette. But unlike for them, a loss for me could be permanent.

Drac continued as if I hadn't spoken. "Let us say that, at the moment, you are no more to me than any other dhampir. Normally, I kill all of your kind who are foolish enough to cross my path. It is a precaution, like a farmer putting out traps for mice. But under the circumstances, I am willing to make you the offer of a trade. Your life for assistance with my current endeavor."

"You want me to kill Mircea and Radu for you."

Drac stared at me for a moment before breaking out into laughter once again. At least I was providing entertainment, even though I still had all my internal organs intact. Would wonders never cease.

"I had forgotten how amusing you can be." Drac calmed down after a moment, the nonexpression replacing the previous mirth. "I admit to some surprise that no one has yet managed to end your existence, but certainly you overrate your skills if you believe you have a chance of disposing of either of my siblings. Admittedly, Radu is a coward and a weakling, but he is not stupid enough to trust anyone, particularly one such as you. And Mircea . . . has always been remarkably difficult to kill."

When he spoke Mircea's name, Drac's face finally found an expression—hatred. The depth of his emotion thrummed through the room, like the skull-throbbing sensation of a building storm. And I suddenly realized that maybe I'd been wrong about Drac's main target. "Yeah," I agreed slowly. "You'd think he has some sort of guardian angel."

Drac's face twisted. "He doesn't need one. He has always been able to persuade others to fall on their swords for him. Our father sent Radu and I to the Turks, but his precious heir was kept safely by his side. Mircea lived like a prince while Radu whored himself to get out of the dungeons and I was tortured every day for years!" I didn't need to complain about the lack of emotion now. His eyes were glowing with it. "Even death worked in Mircea's favor," he spat. "When the treacherous dogs of the nobility lynched him, he was saved—by the very curse meant to destroy him!"

I stared into incandescent green eyes and finally understood. What I'd put down to madness was sounding a lot more like out-of-control jealousy. Even weirder, I could sort of relate. Mircea always seemed so sure of his place in the world: he was Mircea Basarab, scion of a noble house and prince of the supernatural world. He wore the assurance of his worth like a cloak, while the bastard he'd sired shivered in the cold. "He always lands on his feet," I said, and not all the bitterness in my voice was fake.

"Not this time." In a flash, Drac's face was once again a bland mask. He regarded me narrowly. "As astonishing as it is, we have something in common, Dorina. One man has plagued both our lives for far too long. He made you the abomination that you are, doomed to live forever alone, shunned, an outcast, while he condemned me to an existence of perpetual suffering for a single mistake."

I badly wanted to ask what he meant, but bit my lip to stay quiet. Questioning Drac was a risky business. You never knew when he would decide he'd had enough and start amusing himself other ways.

"I do not expect you to undertake the risk of challenging him," I was told. "I merely require you to bring both of my brothers together in one place. Somewhere away from the Senate and the protection of this MAGIC enclave. I will do the rest." He thought for a moment, steepling his hands like a bad impression of Sherlock Holmes. "A private residence would be best, somewhere secluded. Mircea's home in Washington State would be perfect, and rather fitting. With the surrounding forest, it resembles the old country."

The conversation was getting pretty surreal. Mircea and I weren't what could be called close, and I'd threatened many times, loudly and in public, to kill him. But this was the first time anyone had ever taken me seriously. Did Drac think I hated Mircea as badly as he did? Had he honestly forgotten London, or did he think a century had blunted my memory? I repressed a shudder. That wasn't the sort of thing that slipped your mind. Not in a century, not ever.

"I don't think it's too likely," I commented blandly.

"There is a problem?" Drac asked, almost politely.

"Yeah. Mircea isn't in Washington right now. The last time I saw him was in New York a few days ago, but I got the impression he wasn't planning to be there long. And he's not in Vegas. He's on some mission for the Senate— I'm not sure what—but with a war on, I doubt he's going home anytime soon."

"Plausible." Drac thought for a moment. "And Radu?"

I didn't hesitate. Radu and company had a four-hour head start, not to mention a Senate escort. Telling the truth simply meant one fewer hurdle—how to get news of the move to Drac. "You might have more luck there. Radu is moving to his place and I've been invited along as bodyguard until another team can be assembled to replace the one you killed."

"Why does he leave MAGIC's embrace now, knowing

I chase him?" Drac looked at me shrewdly. "Did you hope, little dhampir, that I would come after him myself?"

"The thought did occur to me, yeah." There was no point denying it; no other explanation would make sense.

"And Radu's 'place' would be where?"

"He's never invited me over for dinner, so I haven't actually seen it. But it's in California, some old winery he bought for a song back in the sixties."

"Why does he think he will be safe there?"

I couldn't deny knowledge of this, either. As Radu's bodyguard, there was no way I'd have let him choose that location unless I had researched it and determined that it could withstand an attack. "Mircea's a Senate member. He has a lot of enemies, and Radu has always been seen as his weak link. Some major wards have been put up there, almost as good as MAGIC can boast, just in case anyone tries to get at Mircea through his brother."

Drac did not do anything as human as relax back against his chair, but he somehow gave the impression of pleasure anyway. "Good. Then he believes himself secure. As his protector, you will have reason to inquire into the precise nature of these wards. You will communicate that information to me and arrange to have both of my brothers there at the same time."

I fidgeted. "What if that isn't possible? I told you, I don't know where Mircea is. Not to mention that he isn't likely to come running at my call. I could maybe find out about the wards, but—"

"I have other ways past the wards, Dorina," Drac said, and although he didn't introduce his mage friends, we both knew whom he was talking about. "Your information will make things easier, but it alone will not buy your life. An easier death, perhaps, but no more. I want Mircea."

I swallowed. "What reason can I give him, assuming I can find him? He doesn't completely trust me—"

"Of course not. My brother is not a fool."

"But you realize that makes things somewhat—"

I never saw the blow coming, didn't even feel it land. The first clue I had that maybe I was asking too many questions was when my body connected with the wall in a sickening thud. I slid down the tasteful beige wallpaper as a dark figure crossed my blurred vision. "If you wish to live, you will manage. I will be waiting for your call. Do not disappoint me."

One of the annoyances of being a dhampir is that your body just keeps on going. I guess it's a precaution, to be able to push on in really tough situations, but there are times when you need a good faint. The trip back from Drac's was one of them.

I suppose his boys figured he wouldn't be likely to object if they emphasized his point a bit more, since he had come close to bashing my brains out himself. As a result, by the time they finally left me in an alley behind a strip club, I was really wishing I could go off to la-la land until my body started to repair some of the damage. But no.

I would have groaned, but my mouth seemed unusually full of tongue. I tried to lift my head, but it appeared to be welded to something rough beneath my cheek that reeked of old garbage and urine. I finally forced my puffy eyes open and squinted the world into focus through a curtain of lashes.

Dirty water was trickling down a brick wall. I lay in front of some trash cans, bleeding onto a couple of rotting cabbages. Well, that explained part of the smell. A guy darted into the alley, relieved himself against the wall, saw me and ran off. And that explained the rest.

The club's overhanging roof dripped a steady stream of rainwater onto my upturned face. It tasted like tar, and burned whenever it came into contact with one of my various cuts. After a few minutes thinking about the last time I'd ended up in this much pain, and how I'd fervently promised myself never to be that stupid again, I decided to sit up. This required batting away a couple of cats, who'd been hissing at me for blocking their way to the scrap heap, and a lot of swearing. The broken ribs flowering blue and purple through my ripped top didn't like my new position, but I was damned if I'd lie in a trash-filled alley all night, shivering and feeling sorry for myself. By the time I managed a sort of leaning stance against one of the aluminum cans, I had moved past the pain to a nice, slow burn.

If Daddy dearest had listened to me, none of us would be in this position now. And if Radu had bothered to bestir himself just once during Drac's imprisonment, he could have killed the son of a bitch before he had a chance to get out again. Neither of them deserved me getting a paper cut on his behalf, much less my current state. If there was any way to get to Claire without playing these games, I'd have dragged my battered self off and left them to fend for themselves. I could always go on the hunt again later, after she was safe. And if I was lucky, someone would stake Drac for me in the meantime.

Unfortunately, I didn't have a clue where to find her, and without the Senate's formidable resources, I didn't hold out much hope for a rescue. Especially now that my special-weapons collection was sitting on zero. Drac had taken my backpack as well as the items I'd acquired from Benny's case, leaving me without a stake to my name.

I picked a banana peel out of my hair, wincing as my strained muscles put on a vehement protest. It felt like half the ligaments in my shoulders either were out of commission or wished they were, probably the result of having one vamp almost pull them out of their sockets holding me in place for another to pummel. I could only hope I wasn't going to be in a fight anytime soon. But I couldn't afford to hole up somewhere and bleed for a few hours. I had people to see, and the first name on my list wasn't hard to find.

The Strip was alive with flame, from the fireworks detonating overhead to the casino-sponsored floats, each of which seemed bent on outdoing in gaudiness and patriotism everyone else. And, on the Fourth of July, that translated into fire—a lot of it. The red, white and blue bunting surrounding Dante's entrant in the patriotic parade went up in flame as I watched.

Dante's, Vegas' premier vamp-owned casino, also happens to be in the family, so to speak. Its current manager was sired by one of Mircea's less-reputable sons, and therefore might be expected to do me a favor. Assuming I could get to him before the float went to hell and took him with it.

I ran forward and grabbed on to the side of the cheerfully burning float. It was designed to look like a pirate ship—never one to miss a trend, that was Dante's—complete with skeleton crew. The crowd lining the Strip applauded and shook sparklers at the harried captain, while his supposedly loyal followers jumped ship. They were humans in black suits painted with iridescent silver. The only true member of the supernatural on board was still there, frozen in place at the mainmast, looking around with a panicked expression.

I understood the look when the ornamental skulls securing the bunting started to detonate. No one else seemed to notice—things were exploding all over the place, after all—but the expression on the captain's face was enough to tell me this wasn't part of the show. Something slammed into the deck beside my hand and I yanked back. It was a burning arrow, the end covered in pitch. I hadn't seen anything like it for centuries. What the hell?

"Casanova!" I yelled to be heard over the fireworks, which were erupting from two barrels on either side of the deck, and the crowd, which was shrieking in delight. A human wouldn't have heard me, but then, the captain wasn't one.

A swarthy face that looked right at home with the puffy shirt and eye patch peered at me over the edge of the crow's nest, where he'd fled in terror. He tossed messy black curls back over his shoulder and groaned dramatically. "Oh, God. Just when I thought it couldn't get any worse."

It's always good to be remembered. "I have to ask you something!"

"Now?!"

"That's the idea." I hopped on board just as the ship started weaving back and forth across the roadway. I crawled across the burning deck as fast as possible with the ship listing this way and that. Luckily, most of the props seemed to have been fastened down.

I grabbed the rigging and started up, only to have an arrow suddenly appear in front of my eyes, still quivering as it stuck out of the mast. I blinked at it, and a second later I was dangling over the burning deck by one arm. Casanova gave a heave, and I landed half in, half out of the crow's nest as a barrage of arrows slammed into the wood all around me. Another heave and he'd dragged me into the relative safety of the oversized basket at the top of the mast. The crowd cheered wildly on both sides.

When I got my breath back, I looked up to find him doing something with the mass of switches and wires jumbled together on one side of the nest. "You could make me feel much better by telling me this is all part of the show."

"And you could make me feel much better by telling me that whoever is shooting at us is pissed off at you," he replied, frantically meshing wires.

"Sorry, not this time." Whoever was attacking the float had already been shooting at him when I arrived. For once, it looked like someone else was the target.

I ducked as another arrow flew overhead, taking out the skull and crossbones flag right over our heads. "What are you doing?"

"Trying to shut down the fireworks. This thing is loaded with them, and if they all go at once . . ."

"Okay, then. Maybe I better ask you that question now."

"Dorina!" The yell came from somewhere in the crowd. I caught sight of an auburn head weaving its way toward us and swore. How the hell had he found me?

"I need weapons," I told Casanova in a rush. "A lot of them."

He glared at me as another barrel of fireworks exploded below, showering the deck and half the street with bright blue sparks. "And you're telling me this because?"

"Because your old boss was a member in good standing of the vampire Mafia! You've probably got more weapons stashed away than the freaking Senate."

"Dorina!" I ignored the very pissed-off vampire yelling at me from what now sounded like the deck. What he thought he was doing down there amid enough fire to roast a few dozen of his kind, I didn't know. Maybe he really was crazy.

"And your point is?" Casanova had given up on the wires and was peering over the edge of the crow's nest fearfully.

"The rumor is, your boss recently skipped town. He's not going to be fighting a war anytime soon. So help a gal out here. I can make you a list—"

"Save it. Go see your usual suppliers." Casanova grabbed a handful of rigging and swarmed to the deck as easily as a seasoned sailor. I grabbed a piece of wood from the side of the nest, snapped off a piece to make a point and followed on his heels.

"My usual supplier is out of business." Permanently.

"Then go plague someone else's life!"

"I'm plaguing yours."

"I noticed," Casanova snarled, glaring at my makeshift stake and doing a mad sort of dance across the deck to avoid the hot spots.

I would have followed, but a hand encircled my arm. "What are you doing here?"

"What are you?" I collapsed to the deck, taking Louis-Cesare with me. A piece of burning sailcloth swept through the air, right where he'd been standing. "I thought I told you to stay with Radu."

"You told me nothing. Nor did you explain where you were going or when you would return! You stole a very expensive Senate vehicle and left, that was all."

"I talked to your sire," I said, trying not to sound defensive. It wasn't like I owed him an explanation. "And you're avoiding the question."

"I came after you!" he said, with a pretty good glare considering that he was pressed flat to the deck. "You informed Radu that you were going to Las Vegas to spread rumors of our activities. I thought it unlikely that Mircea would appreciate my allowing an adherent of his house to walk into a war zone to talk with the disreputable types likely to have Lord Dracula's ear!" He took in my dishevelment with a sneer. "It seems my fears were justified."

"And yet who is rescuing whom?" I pointed out, trying to restrain the need to pop him in the mouth.

"I do not see a rescue," he said, pushing off from the floor. "I see you in a trap, in peril of your life."

"And you're doing so much better?"

"Dory! Some help here!" Casanova sounded less than his usual suave self. I jumped up before Louis-Cesare could grab me, and threw myself in the direction of his voice. If he got torched, my best chance to replace Benny's stash went up in flames with him.

I found him wedged into a small door in the deck, with only his head and shoulders visible. "Do you drive?" he demanded, sounding a little shrill.

"Drive what?"

"This." He jumped out of the hole, showing me a steering mechanism that, presumably, kept the float on course. Everything looked fine except for one slight problem.

"Where's the driver?"

"Deserted, along with everyone else."

"Why?"

"Why do you think? With the boss out of the way, control of the business is up for grabs."

"And someone is trying to grab it away from you." My timing never ceases to amaze me. I slipped into the claustrophobic little space and took a closer look. The float had been built on a tractor bed, which meant that the driving apparatus was a stick. Even worse, we were approaching a bend in the road. Until now, the float had remained more or less on target from inertia, but it wouldn't stay that way for long. A glance out of the small space under the prow showed me what lay ahead if we couldn't get this thing to turn. "I don't drive a stick—"

"Neither do I!"

"But I know someone who does." I pushed Casanova out of the way and grabbed Louis-Cesare by the ankle. "Get down here!"

Thankfully, he didn't waste time asking why. And once he was down, the why was sort of obvious. A large group of tourists had arranged themselves on bleachers for the parade—probably been waiting there half the day to get flattened by a rogue pirate ship. Louis-Cesare cursed under his breath, but slid into the seat while I scrambled out of the hole around him. I dropped the trapdoor closed after me and grabbed Casanova by his pretty lace cravat. "I need a favor."

He said something extremely rude. I just smiled. "I'm not asking for me. I'm on a job for Mircea. You know, family patriarch? And, incidentally, your boss?"

Casanova's attitude changed immediately, an ingratiating and totally fake smile falling over his features like the mask it was. But his answer stayed the same. "I told you the truth. I don't have anything!"

"You lying son of a—"

I didn't get a chance to tell Casanova what I thought of him, because the crew took that moment to rejoin us. Apparently, they'd gotten tired of waiting for the ship to take out the boss and decided to do it themselves. And they'd found friends. Casanova grabbed up a sword that had fallen to the deck, and thrust it in my hands. "I hope you remember how to use one of these," he said, before drawing his own weapon and making a flying leap for the side of the ship.

"I'm not done with you!" I screamed after him, as a figure in a bad Halloween costume took a swipe at me.

Thankfully, the guy in question was human—I'd have been missing a head, otherwise—but my reflexes must have told him that I wasn't. I turned to see fear on his sweating face. He backed away, holding the blade as awkwardly as if he'd never seen one before in his life. I grinned, and his eyes got huge, like two eggs in the dark. He took a few hasty steps back and fell off the float, arms wheeling uselessly in the air before he hit the asphalt. I peered over the edge in time to see him scrambling away on all fours until he was swallowed up by the crowd.

An itch between my shoulder blades told me that someone else had decided to take up where he left off. I managed to get my sword up in time, but the force of the attack drove me to one knee. Then I kept on falling because Louis-Cesare took the bend in the road on what felt like two wheels, barely missing the front row in the bleachers. I managed to grab hold of a skull to keep from being slung across the deck, and got a close-up look at the tourists' expressions as the crisped bunting dusted their tennis shoes black. Luckily, the sudden movement had also caused my opponent to stumble. He went down on hands and knees as I rolled and got my feet back under me.

Unlike the human, this one knew damn well what a sword was for, probably because he'd wielded one for centuries. Our weapons clashed together, high over our heads, as we both vied to trap the other's under our own. I was outclassed strengthwise, and my overtaxed shoulder failed me. The vamp grinned as he twisted my sword downward, and I accepted the inevitable with a grimace. Damn, this was going to hurt. A jarring shock traveled up my arm to my abused shoulder as I buried the stake in his ribs. He stared at me in shock, apparently surprised to discover that I had two hands. He died before the grin faded from his face, little bubbles of blood on his lower lip.

Casanova staggered by, the human attached to his back making a damn good try to saw his head off, while a vamp tried to skewer him from in front. "I thought you'd deserted!" I yelled, as another sailor lunged at me.

"Not for lack of trying," Casanova gasped, prizing the human off his neck and tossing him half a dozen feet at my opponent. The two men lurched around the deck for a few seconds before falling backward off the float. "And I thought you said that maniac could drive!"

I shrugged. "Compared to me . . ." A human jumped me, and had time to see my grin before doubling over in agony as I forcefully kneed him in the groin. I kicked his sword away before he could remember he had one, and followed up with a blow to his temple, rendering him unconscious. I'd had to kick him, because my shoulder was threatening to go on strike if I lifted that cutlass one more time. I stood watching Casanova battle half a dozen crew members, my chest heaving from exertion, and accepted the fact that I couldn't help him.

I pulled up the trapdoor and dropped down beside

Louis-Cesare. "Change places," I said, trying to push his
butt out of the driver's seat.

"*Quoi?*" He looked up from frantically shifting gears.
"What is it? What is happening?"

"Casanova needs help, and I'm in no shape to provide
it. Move!"

To my surprise, Louis-Cesare moved. He launched himself up on deck while I tried to figure out the mess of gears.
He'd gotten us turned, but I was left with keeping us
from plowing into the flag-waving, bunting-covered mass
ahead. I stomped on the brakes and discovered that they
were a lot more sensitive than I'd thought. A crew member
who must have been standing too close to the prow went
sailing past my small peephole into the road. I'd practically
stood the float on its head, but at least we'd stopped.

I poked my head out cautiously, in time to see most of
the crew go over the side for the second time that night.
Several of the rest were down, and judging by their condition, they weren't going to be getting up again. A trio of
vamps were more resilient, and had ganged up on Louis-
Cesare. They were busy regretting that decision. The
damn man was annoying, but there was a slight chance
that he deserved his reputation.

He pinned one vamp to the mainmast by running him
through with a sword, until it came out the other side of the
wooden post. He took the vamp's own weapon from his
thrashing hand to throw at the second. It didn't take him
out, but even a vamp will be slowed down by a cutlass sticking out of his midsection. The third he knocked into the rigging with a savage elbow to the neck. The vamp in question
had been behind him at the time, but his aim was perfect. I
made a mental note not to try sneaking up on the guy.

Casanova had apparently decided that his backup had

things well in hand, and had located a spot where the bunting had all burnt off, allowing him a flame-free zone to drop to the road. I leapt after him and grabbed his hair, only to have the long black wig come off in my hands. I threw it to the asphalt and got a grip on his shirt instead. "Where are you going?"

He shot me an evil glance and retrieved his wig. "Elsewhere."

"Not until I get what I came for! You owe me."

"Then I'll have to keep on owing you. The Circle raided Dante's this morning and confiscated the lot. You want weapons? I suggest you see them."

"The dark wouldn't dare—"

"It wasn't the dark." He began making rude gestures at the float behind us, the crew of which had started yelling for us to get a move on. "Although it's getting a little hard to tell the difference these days."

An angry George Washington hopped down from the next float in line and came stomping over to see what the holdup was. Casanova moved toward him, obviously spoiling for a fight with someone he could actually beat up, but I grabbed his arm. "But that goes against the treaty! The Senate will—"

"Swallow the insult. We're at war, and the Silver Circle is the Senate's ally, in case you've forgotten. They reminded me of that fact at length when I very politely requested reparations. 'We'll address that after the war,' " he mimicked bitterly.

"They couldn't have taken *everything*!"

"If you'd like to search the place yourself, be my guest. If you find anything, I'll be happy to split it with you."

"What's the world coming to?" I raged. "When even the bad guys run out of weapons?"

"I'm not the bad guy—at least, not in comparison."

George had reached us, and he wasn't looking happy. "Get this thing moving! You're holding up the entire—" He caught sight of me and shied back for some reason.

"I'm having a few personnel issues," Casanova said, with an attempt at dignity. Apparently, he'd decided that the man could be useful, because he trotted out charming smile #48: for suckers who are about to give me something for nothing. "You wouldn't happen to have anyone who can drive one of these things?"

George nodded, his eyes never leaving my face as he backed quickly away. "So what am I supposed to do?" I demanded.

A vamp landed hard on the street beside us, and Casanova kicked him viciously in the ribs. "I don't know, but whatever it is, I suggest you do it soon. Everyone who can get out of here is heading for the hills. Except for me," he added, picking the vamp up and slamming him against the ship's hull. "I'm not going anywhere. Everyone may as well understand that right now!"

I sighed and gave up. A quick glance showed that Louis-Cesare had cleared the deck and was tying the only human dumb enough to stick around to a barrel with the remains of the rigging. Time to make my exit.

"You don't know why I was here—I never had a chance to tell you," I instructed Casanova, as a periwigged young man hurried up, only to stop dead at the sight of us.

"Theatrical makeup," Casanova told him, apropos of nothing. "There's a trapdoor in the deck." The guy nodded and scrambled on board, looking a little freaked-out.

I eyed Casanova up and down. He didn't look that bad to me. "Who are you supposed to be, anyway?"

"Jean Lafitte."

"And that would be patriotic how?"

"He fought in the Revolutionary War, and in the War of 1812. On the American side."

"I thought he was a pirate."

"He was." Casanova smoothed his brilliant maroon coat. "I told you. Sometimes the bad guys can be good guys. It all depends on the circumstances."

"Thanks for that nugget of wisdom. I'll cherish it."

Casanova ignored me. "Who is he, anyway?" He hiked a thumb at Louis-Cesare, who was standing on the deck, searching the crowd with a scowl on his face.

"Radu's get."

"Did you say *Radu*?"

"Don't ask. Point is, I doubt he'd make a good impression on my suppliers." Assuming I could find any. Not to mention that it wouldn't do my reputation any good to be seen hanging around with a Senate member.

"I never saw you." Casanova agreed, vaulting back onto the ship, which was slowly starting to move again. He poked his head back over the edge, black curls swinging. "Oh, and *chica*, we're having a special on facials this week at the spa. Think about it."

I scowled, but didn't have time to respond appropriately. Louis-Cesare had spotted me and he looked a little tense. I dove into the crowd and got gone.

Chapter Ten

My mood wasn't improved when I found, after dragging my bloodstained self through a large section of Vegas' demon bars, that most of my old contacts either had left town or were currently doing a Benny impression. It wasn't until the sky had turned a pale, cloudless blue, announcing the official end of the year's rain, that I managed to dig up an old acquaintance.

I don't get out West much—the proximity of MAGIC is a big deterrent—but once in a while a job results in a jaunt to the area. I found one of the guys I occasionally use for backup when that happens in the middle of packing for his patented rat-on-a-sinking-ship routine. Another hour and I'd have missed him.

"Jay, good to see you!" I slammed the door to his cheap hotel room—rentable by anything from the hour to the month—and smiled. It made the sort of impression I was hoping for, mainly because of the dried blood matting my hair and the grimace my split lip made of my grin. I hadn't seen myself in a mirror yet, but the reactions of the crowds in the bars had been enough to tell me that intimidation probably wouldn't be a problem.

"Dory!" The Nsquital demon's face, which was able to pass for human if you squinted, turned violet and sprouted little bumps that looked like acne. They weren't.

"You spray me and I'll kill you before I melt." I flashed a little fang, but held out weaponless hands. "I came to talk, Jay. Relax, would you?"

"I . . . I wouldn't poison *you*, Dory. You know that."

"Sure. That's why I came by." I sat down on the lumpy mattress and thumped his plastic suitcase. "Lucky I caught you, huh?"

"You know how it is." Jay was back to ugly-human mode, his oversize teeth, jug ears and carrot top making him look like a grown-up version of the *MAD* magazine guy. The baggy corduroy trousers—necessary because jeans tended to show the tail—and ratty, oatmeal-colored tee didn't help with the cool, but they did give him a pathetic edge that sort of relaxed me. "I don't like the neighborhood so much now that it's a war zone."

That was probably the truth. Nsquital don't like violence. Their position as the twice damned—the literal translation of the name—ensured as much. They were a motley crew of many demonic races, mostly of the minor-functionary level, who had obtained a measure of freedom because each one had killed its master and fled from punishment. They could be found and dragged back by whatever had replaced their dead owner, but most weren't worth the trouble of hunting. Jay had slaughtered a minor servant at Mammon's court whom nobody had liked much anyway. Its replacement would stir-fry him as a matter of policy if it ever stumbled across him—like in a war zone, for instance—but otherwise he was probably okay.

Unless somebody ratted him out, of course.

"This visit was well-timed, then. If you're leaving, you won't want to drag all that heavy weaponry with you, right?"

He sighed, blinking faded blue eyes that had always reminded me of an accountant's. Of course, that was what he'd once been, sort of. "Aw, come on, Dory. You have any idea how many times I've been held up this week? A guy's gotta make a living."

"Exactly. So why are you turning down a customer?"

Jay look shocked. "You're planning to *pay* me?"

I smiled. He paled again, but never got more than a violet blush this time. "Well, not exactly."

"Dory, you know I don't do credit. This is a strictly cash-and-carry business." It would have been a better line except for the wobble in his voice.

"Fine. Then get me something to carry out of here, and I won't cash in the bounty on your head."

Jay's shoulders slumped in defeat, which didn't bother me much, as it was a standard bargaining tactic with him. But then he started to cry and I got shifty. I hate it when anything cries. I wanted to slap him to make him stop, but there was a chance that would only intensify the waterworks. And I couldn't tell him I'd been kidding about the bounty, since it was the only thing he was afraid enough of to give me what I needed.

"Um, hey. Look, Jay, don't—"

"I knew something like this would ha-happen," he wailed, collapsing into a heap. "I was trying to get out, but I wanted to sell off the rest of my stock first, for traveling m-money. Greed!" he screamed, "I should have known it would get me in the end!"

"This isn't the end, dumb ass," I said, dragging him off the floor. "Would you shut up and listen? I am not having a good day. Make it better and nothing bad is going to happen to you."

"But I don't have h-hardly anything left!" he moaned. "I told you, I spent most of the night s-selling out. Bargain-basement prices, too. I'd have kept something back for you, Dory, I promise! But I didn't know you were in town!" He started to leak again. I looked around for a tissue but couldn't find one.

"So tell me who is left that can help me. All my contacts beat you out the door." I was facing a personal apocalypse and was all but defenseless. Typical, but so not good.

Jay wiped his tears on the rough bedspread and looked at me with watery, hope-filled eyes. Maybe the nasty, blood-covered freak wasn't going to kill him after all. "Not many," he finally said. "The dark mages have been stockpiling everything they can get their hands on, and once they figured it out, the Senate started doing the same to try to keep as much as possible out of the mages' hands. Then they both began threatening anyone who supplied the other, and then started stomping on them. That's when I decided to get out of town."

"The Black Circle is planning something, then, something soon."

He nodded, eager to be helpful now that he'd decided he had a decent chance of living through this interview. Why did people always assume I meant them violence? Even a dhampir can have a mellow day.

"Word is, they've got some powerful new ally, only nobody is naming names." Considering that I'd just left Drac surrounded by dark mages, I didn't really need one. "Most people think they're going to hit MAGIC again, but I'm not so sure. The rumor is that someone let them in the first time—that they had a mole who gave them the keys to the wards, but of course they've all been changed since. Going after that place now would be nuts."

"What's your theory, then?"

"Me?" Jay suddenly seemed to recall that having opinions wasn't usually healthy in our circle. "I don't think anything. I only want to get out of here before—before it gets worse."

When the demons start leaving, it's not a good sign. I sighed. Vegas was going to have to fend for itself; I had other problems. "Okay, how about this? Where is this stockpile the dark mages are making?" He stared at me for a minute, and then his lips started to tremble. I thought he was about to start blubbering again, so was sort of relieved when I realized he was laughing. Even if it didn't make sense. "What? Are you stoned?"

Jay just laughed harder. While I waited for him to get himself under control, I took the opportunity to rifle through his suitcase. He was right: other than a few human weapons I could steal from any sporting-goods store and a cloaking spell in a crusty old vial that looked like it might have gone off, he was clean.

"You . . . you're really going to do it, aren't you?" he finally gasped.

"Do what?"

"Hit the mages," he said eagerly.

I shrugged. "Depends on how hard it'd be. But I'm going to need a lot of stuff, and they have it."

Jay licked his lips and darted a nervous look around. "I've heard some things. Nothing definite, but I might have . . . an idea. The mages, they don't . . . they worry about the Senate, you know? And the Silver Circle, of course. But the rest of us . . . they don't think we matter."

There was a tinge of anger to that last comment that interested me. "Like they robbed you at will," I said slowly, watching his reaction, "and killed Benny without a second thought."

"Benny?" Jay looked shocked, and I remembered that they had worked together off and on. Might should have left that out. "He's . . . dead?"

"That's why I look like this. I went to him first for supplies, but when we were making a deal last night, a group of dark mages torched his warehouse with us still inside. I got out, but Benny . . . sorry, I know you liked him."

Jay didn't cry again, but he stared at the stained carpet like he didn't even see it. "I told him he should get out," he said softly. "But he said it would be okay. That I should leave, because of the bounty, that it was getting too hot for me here. But he wouldn't go himself."

I put an arm around his bony, hunched shoulders. "I thought you'd have heard. The warehouse went up like a Roman candle."

"No. I ran out of stock around midnight and dropped by a place, got some Chinese." I hoped he meant takeout. He saw my expression before I could hide it. "Mu-shu pork!" he told me indignantly. "And then I came back here."

"Well, I'm sorry I had to be the one to tell you."

"I'm glad you did." This was said with a note of unusual—for him—resolution. "I'm glad I didn't leave sooner." He hopped up from the bed and hefted the suitcase. "There's something I need to do before I go. Something for Benny!"

I grabbed his arm. "That's great and all, Jay, but you're forgetting—I need some information."

"Don't worry," he assured me, throwing his remaining possessions haphazardly in the already stuffed case. "I'm going to do more than tell you where you can find those bastards. I'm going to show you!"

That's how I came, three hours later, to be leading a bunch of motley-looking trolls, demons and a few humans—mostly friends and ex-employees of Benny's— toward a boarded-up bowling alley in a bad part of town. I really hoped this plan wasn't as psychotic as it sounded, but for once at least it wasn't mine. Jay had dragged me to see Benny's secretary, a large female Bergtroll, or mountain troll, named Olga. She had a broad nose shaped like a squashed mushroom and an impressive golden beard, and her tiny eyes were still red from crying. After hearing our proposition, she had grabbed her battle-ax and her Rolodex and started organizing some payback. I'd spent several hours feeling pretty useless, waiting for the troops to assemble and some semblance of a plan to be formed, although Olga did show me to her bathroom, where I managed to get most of the blood off.

Once everyone assembled, the pace started to pick up, and so much swearing, weapons waving and mage bashing had been going on that I hadn't actually heard the plan. I just intended to grab whatever I could while the troops took the mages apart, assuming vice versa didn't prove to be true. In my own defense, I did try to talk them out of it, but the lynch-mob mentality had taken over and there wasn't much I could do. Olga had merely crushed me to her enormous bosom and promised to see that no one hurt me. I grabbed a couple of knives and a .44 automatic out of Benny's office equipment and silently returned the sentiment.

It was almost funny, as our crew of forty or so pissed-off amateurs and a few gimlet-eyed professionals surrounded the small buff building. "Stay behind me, small one," Olga said, then eschewed subtlety to bash in the door with her ax.

The rest of the crew took their lead from her and made doors for themselves through windows, service hatches and, in the case of one particularly large mountain troll, a brick wall. I followed Olga in as soon as her considerable girth managed to squeeze through the door. It was a bit of a letdown to realize that the building was empty. Even worse, it had the feel of a place that had been so for a while. No electricity lit the overhead lights, a fine layer of dust coated everything and the only discernible odor was a faint reek from the rows of red and blue shoes behind a low counter.

I leaned against one of the concrete block walls and watched the mob take the place apart. "No one here," Olga said, squinting about with her inadequate eyes. I doubted she could see very well despite the numerous holes that had been knocked in the place, letting in midday light, but her sense of smell was probably as good as mine and I didn't smell anyone.

"Should we tell them?" I asked, lighting up.

"No, let them have fun." She hopped up on the counter, which groaned slightly under her weight, and watched the destruction. "What you think?" she demanded when I didn't comment.

I closed my eyes and mentally filtered out the smell of weed, mildewed pleather and sweaty troll. A faint but discernible trace of stale air wafted to me from somewhere nearby. I opened my eyes. "I was wondering what's behind all the shoes."

Olga hefted her ax and swung around to face the

collection. She cleaved the center section clean in two. "That," she said helpfully.

I regarded the set of stairs going down into bare earth with disapproval. I hate dark staircases, especially when I know I won't like what I'll find at the other end. I glanced at Olga. "It might be better if we don't try to take everyone down. Don't want anyone blocking the exit."

She nodded and called a huge troll over. He had on a pair of jeans, which surprised me, since I hadn't known they made them in that size, but no shoes. I caught myself staring at his knobby feet, which had the usual number of toes for a troll—three—and made myself stop. "Wait here," she told him sternly. "Don't let others pass. If we not back in half an hour, come down and kill everything."

He grunted, which I had trouble deciphering, but Olga apparently understood. No one else appeared to have noticed us, which wasn't surprising considering that the demons were setting the red pleather booths on fire and the trolls had started throwing bowling pins through the unlit beer signs. Their aim was pretty lousy, but there were a lot of pins, and the resounding crashes and tinkles of glass seemed to amuse them. Troll bowling.

I turned to Olga. "There's no chance in hell anyone down there doesn't know we're coming. Let's take a quick peek, but if I tell you to run back up the stairs, you do it, no arguments. Okay?"

"You funny little woman," she said, and started down the stairs. I sighed and followed.

I have better-than-human eyesight in the dark, but even I couldn't see much on those stairs. I don't doubt that Olga was completely blind, but she never faltered. Trolls aren't exactly graceful, but they have a low center of gravity for climbing around mountains and fjords, so I figured I was more likely to fall than she was. Luckily for me, four hundred pounds of troll stood between me and whatever was down there, something I found vaguely comforting.

When we finally ran out of stairs, we found ourselves in a tunnel carved out of the local sandstone. It looked like some of the deeper areas of MAGIC—those the vamps preferred to the upper levels belonging to the mages—except for the claustrophobically low ceiling. There was only the faint illumination from the stairway to guide us, and I couldn't see a candle or lantern lying about, which was odd in a place even infrequently used.

Olga and I changed positions, after I explained that I might have more luck detecting the various nasty surprises a group of dark mages could have left for us, but she chafed at my pace. Drac had taken my key ring and its charms along with everything else, but I compensated somewhat by scattering clumps of dirt ahead of us to see if any obvious traps had been left. Nothing happened— not even a minor early-warning ward sizzled—which made me steadily more nervous as we progressed. It didn't help that the farther we went from the stairs, the harder it was even for me to see anything.

Because of the almost nonexistent light, I found the rockfall by running into it. Olga plowed into me and I got a mouth full of sandstone dust before we sorted ourselves out. So this was why nothing had tried to stab, incinerate or crush us on the way in.

"Rockfall," I said, spitting. "There must be another way in, on the other side."

"Yes, but where?" Olga asked sensibly, pushing me to one side. "We go through here." With sheer brute strength, she hacked her way into the blockage, clearing a path twice as wide as me through a six-foot-deep pile of rocks and dirt. Even at my best, it would have taken me thirty minutes or more of hard labor to make that hole; she managed it in about two. I made another mental note: avoid wrestling trolls.

When I stopped choking on clouds of dust, I found that I could see again. Olga's patient expression was visible in the light of a nearby lantern tucked into a nook. It threw hard shadows on the walls, showing us a wide, innocent-looking stretch of corridor that I didn't trust at all. The mages might have caused the fall to block off a vulnerable entrance, but any regularly used areas were going to be guarded by someone or something. And since these were dark mages, it would probably be something lethal.

"We're going to have to be more careful from now on," I told Olga, who gave me an impatient look. I noticed that she had her ax in hand, and nodded. We were on the same page.

It took us almost ten minutes of very cautious movement to get to the large cavern at the end of the hall. But maybe ten seconds after we entered, I got two big clues as to why nothing had grabbed us. A complex ward called the Shroud of Flame leapt up behind us, blocking the way back, and a wall of emotion hit me so hard that it literally knocked me off my feet.

The sensations were familiar, and highly unwelcome. So was the scene that accompanied them, superimposed over the real one like a movie shown on a see-through screen. I could still see the cavern, but most of my attention was caught by the images of my past that flickered and changed in front of me. It was like someone had accessed the part of my memory labeled "good riddance" and was doing a top-ten most-hated-events countdown. Only it seemed they were starting with number one.

A dark-haired child woke up in a nest of blankets next to a fire. It was summer, so there was no need to sleep inside one of the cramped wagons, which always smelled of body odor and garlic, in the surrounding circle. The only others up at this hour were two camp dogs worrying something near the edge of the clearing. The girl threw off her blankets and smoothed her clothes before going to see what it was. The food was usually hung from tree limbs to keep animals out of it, but sometimes a rope would break, and she knew she'd catch hell if the dogs were eating the smoked ham they had acquired at the last village. I wanted to scream at her to run and not look back, but knew it wouldn't do any good. She couldn't hear me, and even if she could, she was far too stubborn to listen. Then or now, I thought as my eyes followed her small form toward the two large dogs.

The shaggy gray creatures were part wolf—wild, half-feral things, kept around by more food than they could scavenge, and used to scare off interlopers. They were about as far from domesticated as they could get, but it had never occurred to her to consider them dangerous. Dogs of any kind don't usually bite the hand that feeds them, but Dili, named after the fact that he had never been quite right in the head, was gnawing on something that looked a lot like a human arm. Baro, his huge mate, had something in her mouth, too, which a beam of early-morning sunlight showed clearly as the head of a middle-aged, bearded man.

The girl screamed then, at the sight of Tsinoro, leader of their kumpania, being breakfast for dogs. She screamed for quite a while before she realized that no one was coming out of the brightly painted wagons littering the small clearing. Her cries would have raised the deaf, much less a company of people used to reacting quickly to any sign of trouble. She should have been able to sense immediately why no one had come—her sense of smell was good enough to discern the miasma of blood and feces that radiated out of the small wagons even without her entering them—but she wasn't thinking clearly. Wasn't, in fact, thinking at all, being in a panic to find someone, anyone, still breathing.

She ran to the nearest wagon, one of the largest since it belonged to Lyubitshka, the chovexani of the clan, who was respected for the power of her magic. But it quickly became obvious that it had not been strong enough to help her this time. The girl stared at the mutilated body of the most powerful person she knew, and began to shake. She was afraid, not only that whatever had killed the wise woman would come for her, as well, but also because Lyubitshka had yelled at her just the day before for tearing a hole in her favorite blouse when laundering it, and now there was no way to obtain forgiveness. Having someone so strong go into the spirit world angry with you was the worst thing her young mind could imagine. Lyubitshka would make a powerful muló, a vengeful spirit that returned to seek out those who had wronged it in life.

After stumbling down the steps of Lyubitshka's wagon and looking wildly around for the angry muló, the girl went a bit mad. She ran to throw open the doors of each wagon, but found only more corpses inside. After her increasingly panicked investigation proved that she and the dogs were the only living things left in the kumpania, she collapsed near the fire, exhausted, tearstained and shivering in shock. Even after her natural resilience kicked in *to calm her slightly, she didn't bother to wash herself or even look for salvageable items to pack. She was not so young that she didn't know the proper way to treat the dead, and there was no one else to do it.*

I watched her dig a pit in the middle of the clearing, to which she dragged each body after wrapping it in a blanket to avoid handling it directly and risking marimé, *or uncleanness. They should have been dressed in their best clothes, but there was so much blood, and some were not even whole anymore, that she didn't know where to start making them presentable. She arranged the bodies in the hole, and piled on top of them their extra clothes, jewelry, tools and best dinnerware as custom required. There was no beeswax to use to close their nostrils and prevent an evil spirit from entering them, but considering how many wounds most of them had, she doubted the spirits would find animating these bodies very useful.*

As she piled earth on top of the heap of the dead, she sobbed for them, even those who had considered her unclean because of her parentage. They had been her family, or as much of one as she had ever known. And now they were gone. Sweat and dirt mixed with her tears, and her nose started to run, but she didn't wipe it away. She wasn't finished yet.

She turned the horses loose and ran them away from the camp, since tradition allowed their continued survival. But everything else had to be destroyed. It was a laborious process, but she finally managed to break every remaining plate and glass, kill the two dogs and pile great armloads of brush around each wagon. She lit the fire and stood off to one side, watching everything she had ever known go up in flames. She would soon start to feel hungry and worry about how she was to survive when all the money and salable objects of her kumpania *were now cursed and useless. She would wonder who would take her in, since the other Gypsy bands would certainly blame her for the tragedy, just as she was starting to blame herself.*

She was not very old, but she knew what they whispered about her when they thought she couldn't hear. She knew why they had taken her in, and what she could do. Killing the occasional vampyre who tried to hurt the kumpania *was no more difficult for her than any of the other chores— gathering firewood or doing the wash—that were regularly demanded. She remembered nothing of the night before except going to sleep as usual, but there had been other odd periods of blackness in her life, and stories told of actions she had taken during them that she knew nothing about.*

And one irrefutable fact stared her in the face: she was the only one left.

The fire spread to some nearby trees as she stood there, but she made no move to escape the heat. I felt again her despair, and knew she wouldn't have cared much if the fire had consumed her, too. The kumpania *had fed and clothed her for years, and all they had asked in return was protection. She was there to ensure that the ancient nightmares that walked abroad at night, the things that even the strongest Rom man couldn't fight, did not decimate their small group. The group had not always been kind, but they had kept their bargain. What did it matter if she had to drink from a separate bucket or if they went out of their way to keep from touching her? They had seen to it that she never wanted for anything. And how had she repaid them? With the very fate they had been trying to avoid. She ought to let the fire take her. They were right—she was unclean, and her birth had ensured that she would never be anything else.*

Chapter Eleven

I came around to find myself sobbing against a vast, hairy expanse, and vaguely realized that it was Olga's beard. For a second, the grief continued to pound against me, hot and fierce. I swallowed and tried to concentrate enough to throw it completely off. I took a deep breath, then another. And as the sea of memory retreated, an odd thought occurred.

Whatever spell this was, it couldn't manufacture such accurate memories, not of events that no one else had ever seen. It had to be pulling them from my own mind, and if that was true, what I had just seen had been created from what my eyes had recorded long ago. And that left me with a very important question.

"Where was the blood?" I croaked, sitting up.

Olga looked at me strangely, and I stared back at her. Of course, she hadn't seen the vision, or at least, not the same one I had. But she didn't ask any questions, which was good because my brain was already crowded with them.

I'd deliberately refused to relive those memories after I escaped from that cursed forest. They'd sat in the back of my mind like a fresh bruise, tender and unpleasant every time I touched them. But maybe it had been a mistake to shy away. If I was the killer as I'd always assumed, why had I not been drenched in blood? Everyone else had; even the dogs had looked like they'd been soaked in it. But when I smoothed my apron down that morning, there had been no sticky residue on my hands, no splotches of dried brown on my clothing. And even I couldn't manage a slaughter like that without leaving traces, especially not in one of the berserker rages.

But if I hadn't done the deed, I should have woken up during it. Even without enhanced sensory perception, it would be hard to sleep through something like that. But if there was no blood . . .

"You through?" Olga inquired patiently. "Lars will come soon if we do not return, and make much noise."

I suddenly noticed that, unlike me, Olga had not broken down into a huddled mess. "Why isn't the spell affecting you?" I demanded.

She looked at me levelly. "My husband die today and my business ruin. What could be worse?"

I started guiltily. I hadn't known Benny had a wife. No wonder the spell didn't work on her—she was already living her worst day. Any memory the spell brought up would probably be a relief if it blocked out the present. I, on the other hand, had five hundred years of nightmares for it to pick among. I could still feel tendrils of the spell trying to weave their way around me, but the shock that my biggest fear of all time might have been a lie allowed me to push them aside. Sometime very soon I was going to sit down and ask myself some hard questions about that night, but now was not the time.

I got a good look around and realized that someone

else had been trapped by the spell. Louis-Cesare was huddled in a corner with his back to me. He must have been following right on our heels to have made it through the door before the spell blocked the way. It looked like he was wishing he'd been slower.

I saw him shudder, a slow vibration that started at the small of his back and ran up his spine. His once-pristine leather jacket and slacks looked like someone had been clawing at them, and one glance at his broken and bloody nails told me who. He didn't appear to have enjoyed the show any more than I had.

He began slowly rocking back and forth, the muscles of his back clenched tight, only the graceful curve of his neck visible under the curtain of hair that hid his features. He was moaning softly, and said something, to some figure from his past, presumably. My French is adequate if not elegant, but he was slurring his words too much for me to understand. Then he began to laugh, a broken, bitter sound, like glass under boots. It hit my raw nerves like fingernails on a chalkboard. I reached for him, not thinking, just wanting to stop that awful sound. The minute my hand touched his skin, I was dragged into his little corner of hell.

A darkened cell, where he lay helpless and bound. The jailers stripped him roughly, tearing at his clothes, the knife at his neck a silent threat. It didn't stop him from trying to fight, from thrashing until they beat him almost senseless, fists and fingernails gouging mercilessly. Eventually his limbs refused to obey him and the taste of dust and straw and the metallic tang of blood filled his mouth. The hitching of his breath sounded far away; he could almost imagine that it came from someone else. Until a new pain started, something they had not dared before, that snapped him back into himself in horror.

Clamping his teeth on a scream, he panted in a red haze of pain and fury as his body flinched away from invasion, its desperation beyond his control. He couldn't master the shaking in his limbs, the reflexive struggle or the half-choked gasps, but he wouldn't scream. The humiliation settled like stone in his gut, blending with the agony as they took their turns and their time. One of them laughed, and he could feel it in his belly, letting him know this wouldn't end anytime soon. Bile burned the back of his throat, but an icy calm settled over him. He would find a way out of here, he promised himself, and when he did, no one would ever make him a victim again.

I jerked away, shivering in a cold sweat, damning whatever mages had set this trap all to hell. After my breathing returned to something like normal, I borrowed a handkerchief from Olga and wrapped it around my hand. No more skin-on-skin contact, not here.

I squatted and tried to make eye contact, but I couldn't see his face until I brushed a snarl of hair back from his forehead. His usual pale perfection had faded to chalk white and his eyes were bruise dark. I felt a surge of unaccustomed compassion. He looked so young, without the superior, closed expression he usually used around me. He didn't look like Louis-Cesare, Senate member and arrogant bastard. He looked like Louis-Cesare of the auburn hair and the blue eyes and the devastating smile. I reached out, my finger tracing the line of a single tear down his cheek. Then I slapped him.

The first one didn't have much of an effect, but by the fourth, I'd gotten into the swing of things and his head was thumping the wall each time it rocked back. A slender hand reached out and latched on to my arm before I could deliver a fifth. "Have you snapped out of it yet or should I hit you some more?" I asked. "'Cause I don't mind. Really."

His mouth curved into a painful expression that might have been a smile, except for the awful brightness in his eyes. "Dorina."

"That would be me."

"Thank you." There was a quiet gratitude in his voice that made me grin like an idiot, and some of the bleakness in his expression faded.

"You know," I said, glancing at another Shroud of Flame spell that blocked the door behind him, "you could really make my day and tell me you have something to counter that."

He blinked at the thick wall of fire as if surprised to see it there. "No."

"Then we have a problem." It was an understatement. Now I knew why the mages didn't bother to waste manpower guarding their backs. Anyone who sneaked in here was trapped until one of them came along and finished him off, or left to rot. Neither option appealed to me, but neither did getting flame broiled. I might survive the Shroud, but I'd spend a month helpless thereafter from having every inch of skin barbecued. Olga might also live through the process—the thinnest troll skin is approximately the consistency of rawhide—but no way could Louis-Cesare manage it. Vamps burn like they've been soaked in lighter fluid even without magical help. We needed an alternative.

Louis-Cesare had regained his feet, but was leaning heavily against the wall, resting his head on his forearm.

"Merde." I decided to see if Olga had any ideas; he looked like he needed a time-out.

I eyed the cavern walls speculatively. "Olga, do you think you could hack through that?" She didn't have a pickax, but then, she hadn't had one earlier, either.

She shrugged. "In time. But Lars come soon." Lars hadn't struck me as a mental giant, and he'd let Louis-Cesare slip by, but maybe I was missing hidden depths. I must have looked skeptical, because she waved at the wall. "He make new door." Okay, that I could see. Mages tend to forget that there are other ways to solve a problem than magic. You can put all the spells you want on a doorway, but if someone kicks down the wall and makes a new one, it doesn't matter much, does it? I just hoped Lars didn't bring the ceiling down on top of us in his enthusiasm.

"Where are we?" Louis-Cesare had decided to join the conversation.

I turned on him, and for a moment had the disorienting sense of double vision, seeing someone who was the same as ever, and yet so very different. I forcibly squashed the empathy that wanted to dull my edge. I couldn't afford that now. "I didn't know I was coming here until a few hours ago," I accused, my voice harsher than I'd intended. "How do you keep finding me?"

Louis-Cesare's expression shifted from the dullness of shock to arrogant exasperation. "That is hardly relevant at the moment."

"It's relevant to me!"

He apparently decided that answering was easier than arguing. "Because of the cell phone I gave you. The Senate was able to use it to pinpoint your location."

I fished it out of my jeans and stared at it. The sleek

black case gleamed innocently in the dim lighting. I should have known. I ground the traitorous device under the heel of my boot with a scowl.

Louis-Cesare watched, a wry curve to his lips. "I am beginning to understand your difficulties with electronics."

"Very funny."

"Lars is here," Olga suddenly announced, getting heavily to her feet.

"You brought *trolls* with you?" Louis-Cesare had apparently just noticed the two mountains staring at each other through a curtain of fire.

"It's more like they brought me." I left him to his own devices and went to see what Olga thought Lars could do.

"Get the others," Olga was telling him. Lars obediently turned and lumbered back down the corridor, shaking the floor slightly as he did so. "It not be long," she said, glancing past me to Louis-Cesare. "You know this vampire?"

"Unfortunately." Her teeth bared and I hastened to explain. "He's okay. He just whines a lot."

Under the drained and the pained and the fed up, Louis-Cesare almost looked amused—until Olga thumped him on the back. The comradely gesture would have shattered a human's spine. "Good. I hear rumors," she informed us. "They say the rebel vampires and dark mages work together. When Lars come back, we break through these walls. You," she told Louis-Cesare like a general addressing a private, "sense any vampires, awake or asleep. We kill them first. Then we take back what is ours."

"Who is 'we'?" Louis-Cesare asked incredulously. "The Senate itself wouldn't dare to attack such a place, at least not yet. But you propose to do so with what? A band of trolls?"

He'd addressed the question to me, but Olga answered. "If you afraid, you go," she said with a shrug.

Louis-Cesare's mouth opened and closed a few times, as if he was having trouble processing the fact that a wild-looking bearded lady had just called him a coward, but I didn't let him get going.

I turned to Olga. "There could be a complication."

She raised bushy eyebrows and I started feeling guilty. I probably should have mentioned this earlier. "There's a chance that the mages and vamps are getting a little extra help these days." I spent the next five minutes filling her and Louis-Cesare in on my recent adventures. "Don't get me wrong—if you still want to kick some vampire butt, I'm your girl. But I don't think your crew is ready to deal with Drac just yet." I managed not to mention that I didn't feel much like it myself, either, although I think the point came across.

"You knew where he was, even to the room number, and you said nothing?" Louis-Cesare demanded. "Do you wish to trap him or not?"

"Not!" I responded heatedly. "That's Mircea's thing. I want to kill him. I think I've been pretty clear on that. But I'm only going to get one shot at it, and I'm not exactly prepared right now. That was the point of coming here in the first place, to get some decent weapons."

"The Senate *has* weapons!"

"And I'm sure they'd be thrilled to turn them over to me. Besides, they don't have the kind of stuff I need. Or if they do, they aren't likely to admit it."

"That was why you did not want me with you. You were planning to buy illegal weapons!"

"Until Benny got dead, yeah. That was the plan. The plan now is to steal them."

Olga's massive forehead was wrinkled as if thinking was causing her pain. When she spoke, though, it was clear that she'd followed the conversation well enough. "This Drac you speak of, he killed my Bienvior?"

"Yeah. He had mages with him who did the dirty work, but he was in charge."

Olga nodded, as if that was all she'd needed to know. "If he here, I kill him for you," she said simply.

Louis-Cesare and I exchanged a glance. "Um, Olga . . ." I stopped, both because I had no idea how to explain how unlikely that was and because the crew had arrived. At least, I supposed they were behind Lars, but his bulk filled the doorway, making it impossible to tell.

"Take down wall," Olga told them, pointing to a spot beside the doorway. "Then we kill things."

What we found after hacking through two walls of solid rock was a warehouse. But it wasn't anything like I'd expected. Stretching in a long line down either side of a rough-hewn corridor were tiny, shallow cells, barely more than indentations in the walls. Most were empty, but a few were not. And one caught my attention immediately because, although it was at the end of the corridor, the scent emanating from it was unmistakable.

The cell was empty, but the scent was strong. Too strong for the occupant to have been gone long. The trail led to a door, which even before I reached it I realized was heavily warded. I cocked my head, filtering out the sounds coming from behind me, and concentrated. Yeah, I'd thought so.

I ran back to the other end of the corridor, dodging trolls and demons and the assorted creatures they were releasing from the cells, and grabbed some of the larger chunks of rock from around our newly created doorway. Running back the way I'd come, I managed to avoid Louis-Cesare, who was standing in the middle of the corridor watching me with a bemused expression, and reached the door again. I heaved the rocks at the warded door, every nerve ending singing at me to hurry.

The wards held firm, as I'd assumed they would, but the guard on the other side, who had been jingling change in his pocket and humming off-key, suddenly came to attention. He might not be able to hear through the door, but he could certainly hear the strident alarm that had gone off when the wards were tested. "Come on," I said under my breath. "You can handle this. Probably just some stupid slave got loose. Did you double-check the last door you closed? Because if not, and you go for help, you'll catch hell. Come on in and check it out on your own. Then no one needs to know."

I don't have the kind of mind-control abilities that vamps do, but if I concentrate really hard, I can manage to plant a basic idea in someone's head. It doesn't have the compulsion behind it that Mircea's thoughts do—no one has to act on any of my little doubts, but people often do, anyway. Especially if they sound like something they might have thought up themselves.

Louis-Cesare came up behind me, but for once he refrained from saying anything. A moment later the wards fell—I could feel tendrils dissipating like smoke about us—and the door opened. The guard wasn't a complete idiot. As soon as he heard the cacophony that a dozen trolls make when ripping apart steel doors, he tried to shut the heavy metal slab again, but my foot was in the way and a second later, my hands were around his throat.

"You have got to be kidding," I said in disgust after

riding him to the floor. Underneath me lay a human, plain and simple. I sniffed him to be sure, but there was no doubt about it. "A norm? What, are they nuts?"

It shouldn't have surprised me, since a vamp would have been unaffected by my mind games and a demon would have thrown them back in my face. But I still had trouble believing that the Black Circle had left a norm on guard duty. They're even more contemptuous of regular old garden-variety humans than most mages. They call them dims and, for the most part, ignore their existence.

Louis-Cesare managed to squat elegantly alongside the norm. "He could be booby-trapped."

I shook my head. "No." I'd seen such things before, mages using humans like trip wires, with a spell designed to detonate if the norm's heart began to race or at some other indication that trouble was near. But I knew the signs, and this one had none of them. He smelled of fear and sweat, of socks that had been worn too long without laundering and of the sausage and onion sandwich he'd eaten earlier. I could tell what shampoo he used and that he'd massaged Ben-Gay onto his left calf today, but there was no stench of dark magic around him. In fact, there wasn't any that I could detect anywhere, which was more than a little odd in a Black Circle stronghold.

"Look, t-take whatever you want. Just d-don't eat me, okay? I had garlic for lunch," he said, so panicked that the whites showed all the way around his watery gray eyeballs.

"Good. I love it when dinner's already seasoned." I snatched the creep to his feet. "One chance. What's going on here? And I'll know if you lie to me."

"Th-the auction. It's almost over, but you can probably get in on a few lots if you hurry." He looked at something

over my shoulder and what little color he had went on vacation. "O-or just take what you want. Anything, really."

I glanced behind me to see that Olga had joined
Louis-Cesare, with a crowd of assorted creatures behind
them. One of the smaller trolls had something by the
hind foot that I eventually identified as a were cub. It had
taken me a minute because the full moon was several
weeks away, yet the small snarling creature was in full
wolf mode and currently attempting to bite through the
troll's tough skin. The troll cuffed it hard enough to send
its head cracking against the wall, leaving it dazed and
slightly more subdued.

I looked at Olga. "No eating," I said, hoping she'd
agree since there wasn't a lot I could do about it if she
didn't. "We have to find out what's going on."

She had a muttered conversation with the troll, who
scowled through his beard and defiantly bit off one of the
were's toes. The small creature howled in pain and started
thrashing about even more, while Olga sent troll boy
face-first into the cave wall. She slammed a foot down on
him when he bounced off, putting her considerable
weight onto his torso, and he let go of the were. Crazed
with pain and fear, it began slashing at anything within
reach until Louis-Cesare grabbed it by the scuff of the
neck and knocked it out.

I turned back to the human, only to find that he'd
passed out on me. I sighed and gave him to Olga, who
was steadily grinding the troll's face into the hard cavern
floor. "I'll be back," I told her, and she nodded pleasantly.

The tunnel let out onto a much larger one, which in
turn led to what looked like a naturally formed cavern,
about a story below the mouth of the tunnel. Crude stone
steps had been carved into the side, leading down into the

gloom. A few lights—some magical, others more prosaic—
lit the place in patches, especially the small, cleared area
serving as the auctioneer platform. I could see even in the
shadows, but was soon wishing I couldn't.

"The human was right," Louis-Cesare said from over
my shoulder. I nodded, trying to keep a grip. Some kind
of illegal auction was going on, and it wasn't for bootleg
cigarettes. A lot of the heavy cages ringing the platform
were empty, but some still had creatures in them. The fact
that a few of them looked suspiciously like the deformed
things in Radu's laboratory made my stomach begin to
sink. But even worse was the fact that I caught two very
familiar scents on the air. One was the same as in the
holding cells: Claire had been here, probably within the
last hour. The other was Drac's.

Tamp it down, I told myself sternly, sinking fingernails
into my palm hard enough to break the skin. I wouldn't do
Claire any good by freaking out, if by some chance she
was still here. "An unusual specimen," a human announcer
was saying. "Half-Duergar, half-Brownie—quite the combination. It will protect your property better than a pack of
guard dogs and fix you lunch to boot. What am I bid?"

A small, dark gray creature, all of about two feet high,
stood in the blinding circle of light, vainly trying to shield
its large eyes. It was shaking in fear and making a high,
mewling noise that sounded like a cross between a child's
wail and a power saw cutting through metal. It made me
wince and apparently the buyers didn't like it any better,
because no bids were forthcoming.

The auctioneer kept trying for another few minutes,
while I stood there and used every trick I knew to keep
the crashing tide in my head from taking over. Had Claire
stood in that circle, being jeered at by the motley crowd?

Had she been beaten like the tiny crossbreed was currently being, as the auctioneer tried to get it to shut up? The thing must have been stronger than it looked, because it managed to get the stick away from the human wielding it. The creature wrenched it through the bars of its cage, then turned it back on him, getting in several good licks before the man scrambled out of the way.

"That's it, Marco—I'm done. Put a bullet through its brain and let's move on." The auctioneer had shut off his microphone before making the comment to a nearby goon, but it echoed in my head like he'd screamed it. At the image of someone putting a gun to Claire's head, the tidal wave came crashing through my defenses and I was suddenly drowning in a sea of red.

"Dorina!" I heard someone call my name, but there wasn't enough sanity left for me to respond. The familiar, killing rage rose up like vomit in my throat. I fought the bloody tide for another few seconds, but that was as useless as it had ever been, and I knew in that instant that Claire was either dead or long gone. There was not the smallest, lingering shred of her blessed calm to help me hold my ground, and with that thought, I gave up trying. If these things had killed her, let them join her. We could all go to hell together. After all, I already knew the proprietor.

Chapter Twelve

I woke up to disorientation and extreme pain. The first was because I was upside down, hanging halfway off an overturned cage with my butt in the air, and the latter because I was bleeding from, at a guess, half a dozen wounds. Most of them felt fairly minor, however, compared with the metal rod that Louis-Cesare was trying to pull out of my side. It had gone completely through me to pierce the top of the cage. He gave a final heave and the thing tore loose with a sound of screeching metal and splitting flesh. With nothing holding me in place, I slipped to the floor, bleeding in more places than I could count.

"Are you sane, or what passes for it with you?" he asked in a strangled half lisp. I recognized the sound—that of a vamp with fully extended fangs—not that I'd heard it often. Mostly, when they get to that stage, they aren't much interested in talking.

I nodded weakly. The animal that clawed through my veins was gone—for the moment. I could feel the ragged remnants of confused rage, but that was normal. It would pass, and even if not, I doubted I'd be doing further damage anytime soon.

Before he could reply, the Frenchman was airborne, landing several yards away. Two huge brown eyes appeared in my field of vision, peering at me out of a small, misshapen face. Shaggy gray hair obscured most of the features, including any sign of a nose, but there were a few scraggly fangs poking out of the fuzz. I noticed that several of them were pointing the wrong way, heading upward like tusks, while a few of the others had grown in such a way as to be more a threat to the creature than its prey.

I stopped wondering if I was about to become something's lunch and struggled to sit up. Unfortunately, that made the room tilt violently and my blood seep out even faster. A tearing, sharp pain bit into my side every time I moved or breathed.

"Lie still if you want to live!" Louis-Cesare ordered harshly. "And call that thing off or I will be forced to kill it. I cannot help you while constantly fending off attack!"

"What is it?" The room kept swimming in and out of my vision, but I managed to focus on the hovering gray thing. It reminded me of a Mr. Potato Head doll assembled by a two-year-old. All the parts were there, but they weren't necessarily in the right place. The comparison was strengthened by its incongruously long, sticklike arms and legs, which poked at sharp angles out of the fur. Its knees were currently up around its head as it squatted protectively beside me, close enough that the stench emanating from it made my eyes water.

"A lot which failed to sell. It was about to be killed when you went mad." Louis-Cesare nudged it cautiously with a toe and it snarled at him so viciously that one of its bent fangs pierced its bottom lip, causing a trickle of black blood to join the matted dirt and who-knew-what on its chin. "It appears to be under the impression that you saved its life." A misshapen appendage that only vaguely resembled a hand reached out to pat my hair. "How touching. Now call it off!"

"How do I do that?"

"Improvise." He had his hand on his rapier, and I didn't doubt he'd use it.

I sighed. "It's okay," I told my little groupie. "If he lets me die, Daddy will kill him for you."

The thing must have understood something, because it shuffled back a few paces, letting Louis-Cesare get close enough to examine me. I lay back against the floor while he touched my cheek gently, then stroked along my throat. Light mental fingers danced past my tattered shields and suddenly I could breathe without pain. His hands were warm on my skin and his touch swept away the last of the confused frenzy. They made me feel steadier, anchored, and I realized that he'd hit me with a suggestion. Normally, that sort of thing wouldn't work, but my shields were in shreds. And since it took most of the pain away, I didn't feel like protesting.

I closed my eyes and let a wonderful numbness creep down my body from neck to knees. The room was spinning to the point that I knew I'd lost a lot of blood— enough to be dangerous even for me. I didn't try to catalog my wounds, since I couldn't seem to concentrate, and decided to use what little mental capacity I had for more important things. "Claire?"

"She was here, but not by the time we arrived. There is a note for you, when you are well enough to read it."

"A note?" Trust Claire to find time, in the middle of a slave auction, to leave a note! The girl needed therapy. I laughed, but it hurt, so I stopped. "I feel well enough now," I said, and made the mistake of trying to sit up again. The room did some kind of weird kaleidoscope thing and started to grow dim.

"Stay put!" I was told savagely. "You will never read it if you are dead!"

I decided he might have a point, and lay back again. The twisted hulk of the cage loomed over us, and I had to be careful not to move much or I came into contact with some of the hundreds of pieces of splintered wood that littered the place. I eventually identified them as the remains of the folding chairs the bidders had been using. Olga's group must have gone nuts.

I'd lost Mircea's coat somewhere and now Louis-Cesare tore my T-shirt in two. "We haven't even had dinner yet," I protested weakly, and he glared at me out of eyes lit by an inner glow. "Daddy's turn gold," I told him confidentially, and giggled.

"You should be unconscious by now," he muttered.

"Dhampir," I reminded him. Louis-Cesare didn't answer, but he upped the amp on his suggestion. I found myself staring into eyes like starlit steel, some unsuspected poetic part of me whispered, or lightning cutting across a summer sky. They really were amazing, those eyes. "Pretty," I observed, which seemed to startle him.

Olga appeared behind him, her bulk dwarfing him as if he were a child. She bent over to see me better, close enough that her golden beard tickled my chin. "She alive?"

"For the moment." Louis-Cesare's voice sounded strained.

"Good. That vampire, he not here," Olga informed me. "Where we hunt now?"

"I'm working on that," I told her. She nodded, satisfied, and lumbered away.

Louis-Cesare began digging around in my chest for

something. A bullet, I remembered vaguely. The auction-eers had had guns, and judging by where his impromptu surgery was taking place, someone had been a good shot. It had missed the heart, but not by much.

"We cannot take her along," he commented. It took me a moment to realize he was talking about Olga.

"Sure we can."

"You know nothing about her!"

"I know Drac killed her husband. I don't think she has a chance of bringing him down, but it's her right to try." Humans might be willing to fight their battles in court, and for lesser things the magical community followed suit. But for this, someone would bleed. I just hoped it was the right someone, as the idea of Olga writhing away her final hours on one of Drac's special poles didn't appeal.

"She is a Bergtroll," he informed me, as if there was any chance I'd failed to notice.

"Uh-huh. A really pissed-off one. You don't want her to come, fine. You tell her. I've had about all the violence I want for today."

Louis-Cesare looked like he was going to argue, so I distracted him with a pitiful groan. Too bad it wasn't faked. He went back to surgery, and in return for my agreement to stay still while he patched me up, he filled me in on some of the stuff I'd missed. "It seems we disrupted an illegal auction featuring failed experiments by the Dark Fey. They gave them to a group of humans they use to do some of their errands as—what do you call it? A bonus," he said, dropping the bullet he'd extracted onto the floor. "The pris-oners said that there were no mages here, only humans. I believe the Dark Circle abandoned this location as too vul-nerable, and that the wards we found were some they did not bother to remove when they left."

"And what did the humans say? If they work for—" I broke off at a particularly painful dig.

"We would have asked them had your allies left any alive," was the acerbic reply. Another little bullet hit the floor. No wonder I felt like crap. Even I usually manage to avoid getting shot twice in the chest on the same day.

Then what he'd said registered. I looked around and for the first time noticed that the man who had attacked the little crossbreed was now draped across a couple of cages—on opposite sides of the room. Pieces of the auctioneer and his staff were everywhere, with an arm still clutching a gavel about a yard away. While Louis-Cesare stitched me up, I watched Olga's little troll, appearing unaffected by his obviously broken nose, tuck it into a basket alongside other mangled bits. Takeout, I presumed.

"Wait a minute." My sluggish brain finally threw up the obvious question. "If this was some bargain-basement slave auction, why was Claire here?" The idea of her in what amounted to an odd bin was ludicrous.

Louis-Cesare didn't reply, being too busy digging a .22 out of my thigh. Before I could press him, someone came into view who drove the words right out of my head. "Shit!" I tried to rise, but Louis-Cesare held me down.

"What is wrong with you?" I just stared past his shoulder at the new arrival. Either I was hallucinating or the threat wasn't as great as it seemed. I really hoped it was the latter, since I was in no shape to defend myself.

The newcomer knelt gracefully beside me. I tried not to stare, but I don't think it worked. At least he was worth it, being quite simply the most beautiful man I'd ever seen. Golden hair spilled over his shoulders and in the dim room it seemed to glow with an inward light. Eyes so dark green they were almost black provided a startling contrast, especially framed by gold-tipped lashes. But his face was the most surprising thing about him. Faint laugh lines crinkled around his eyes, and his smile revealed even white teeth. Despite the perfection of the features, the first word I'd have used to describe him would have been "pleasant," something I'd never have thought to associate with a member of the Light Fey.

The Fey's otherworldly looks did not keep him from being attacked by a growling gray blur, however. "What do we have here?" The light, musical voice sounded amused, and a softly shimmering hand plucked the creature out of the air. "Ah. An infant Duergar. Is it yours?" I just stared as he held the poor Duergar securely by the nape of its neck. It tried to scratch him, but the Fey's arms were even longer than its own and kept it just out of reach. "But this cannot be the fearsome warrior," the Fey said, his eyes widening as they took me in. "She is too young, and far too pretty."

"She is five centuries old," Louis-Cesare replied tersely.

"As I thought," the Fey said. "A mere child." He lifted my hand to his lips and if the dried blood on it bothered him, he didn't let it show. "I believe you are called Dory, am I right? I am known as Caedmon, at least in your world."

The Duergar seemed to object to Caedmon touching me, and started flailing its sticklike limbs in a frantic attempt to scratch his eyes out. The Fey glanced at it. "They can be very useful: resistant to poison and most magic, fierce in battle, extremely loyal, and many are skillful smiths. I once had a wondrous belt with a gold buckle—exquisite work—made by one of their renowned artisans. But if you'll forgive the observation," he added, "this is a poor specimen."

I grabbed the snarling thing away from him, and it

quieted after wrapping two spindly arms around my neck. "It's only a baby," I said defensively.

Caedmon nodded. "True, but without the proper training and the supervision of its people, it will never acquire their skills. And I think it unlikely to be welcomed among them. There appears to have been some mixing of bloodlines. It would almost certainly be viewed as an abomination. It would be a kindness to put it out of its misery."

I hugged the Duergar and fought not to gag. After a bath, he'd kind of look like Animal from the Muppets. I always liked the Muppets. "I think I'll call him Stinky."

Louis-Cesare rolled his eyes, but Caedmon merely smiled. "How apt."

"What are you doing here?" I asked, doubting he'd come to buy anything. The Fey tend to be a bit more particular about their slaves.

He gave an elegant shrug. "It seems we have a common purpose: I, too, am looking for your friend."

"The Fey Council sent him," Louis-Cesare explained, shooting the newcomer a dark look. Apparently, they'd met before I woke up, and it didn't look like Louis-Cesare was impressed.

"To investigate this unfortunate matter," Caedmon added. "I am greatly concerned for your friend. She must be found, and the sooner the better. I thought I had discovered her whereabouts, but was too late."

"Why are you interested in Claire?" She'd never mentioned a connection with the Fey. And here I thought I was the one with all the secrets.

"I greatly look forward to discussing that with you," Caedmon said, "but"—his gaze swept my battered form—"perhaps when you have recovered?"

"Tell me now." I put a hand on his arm, and found it al-

most cool to the touch, or maybe that was the liquid feel
of the silk. If any fashion designers saw how he wore his
plain gray tunic and leggings, the medieval look would be
on every runway come fall. I tried to sit up, but still didn't
have the strength. Even the pain from the wound Louis-
Cesare was currently picking at hardly registered. I
couldn't remember a single twenty-four-hour period in
which I'd lost consciousness this often, but it felt like I
was slipping away again.

"Here, allow me." Caedmon laid a hand on my forehead. His power surrounded me, like sunlight on my skin.
Despite the fact that we were underground, it threw a pattern of gently waving branches across my body and
gilded the dusty air until everything glittered. The sounds
of the cleanup became a distant background noise, over-
written by musical laughter and voices singing unknown
songs. I breathed in a rich forest smell, and vague shadows swirled up around me in a storm of green and gold,
like leaves caught in a high wind. For an instant I thought
the cave would disappear altogether; then a phantom leaf
brushed my cheek and I jerked away, scrambling to reinforce my shields. The sensations hadn't been threatening,
but neither is the sun until it burns you.

I didn't know whether the images were deliberate
sendings—an unobtrusive attempt to calm my nerves—or
simply part of what he was. Either way, they passed
quickly, and with them went much of my lethargy. Unfortunately, their passing also broke Louis-Cesare's suggestion, and that meant a return of some serious pain.

I let out a string of Romanian curses I thought I'd forgotten and pushed the vamp away. Stinky hissed at him.
"What are you trying to do, an amputation?"

I looked down at my legs, which a moment before had

been peppered with seeping wounds, only to find that all but one had closed over—the one he'd been digging in. As I watched, a lump appeared under the skin and, instead of staying put, began roaming around in a very unpleasant way. Then out of the wound popped a squashed metal object that I distantly realized was the bullet Louis-Cesare had been trying to locate. A second after that, the wound closed.

I stared at it in amazement. No one healed like that except a first-level master. Or, it seemed, the Fey. My mind immediately began wondering how you'd go about killing someone who could repair major injuries that quickly, while Caedmon helped me to my feet.

"You're a healer."

He smiled, and it was breathtaking. "A minor talent."

"So tell me about Claire."

His smile widened. "You're a single-minded little thing, aren't you?" Since he topped me by at least a foot and a half, I decided to ignore the "little" remark. From his perspective, it was accurate.

"Yeah. Besides, if we pool our information—"

"My thought exactly," he agreed, perching on the overturned cage like he was posing.

Louis-Cesare stood with folded arms, his mouth a straight, hard line. Something about the Fey seemed to annoy him, or maybe he didn't care for the turn of conversation. Finding Claire wasn't his mission, but I was glad to see that he was smart enough to realize that there was no way to prize me out of there until I'd learned all I could. Radu was safe enough for the moment; Claire wasn't.

"It is a long tale, suitable for a bard's song," Caedmon said, his voice taking on a lilt that was almost singing itself. He had no real accent that I could place, but I'd have known blindfolded that English wasn't his mother tongue. "But perhaps it would simplify things if you could tell us what this says?" He pulled a piece of paper out from under the cloak he wore, and looked at it with vague irritation. "Humans are such restless creatures. Every time I visit this world, they have new tongues among them; I no longer attempt to keep up." He handed over the folded scrap, which I saw with surprise had my name on the outside. "It appears that someone knew you were coming."

I sat abruptly on the edge of the cage and opened the letter. It was in Romanian and came straight to the point; Uncle never had been much for small talk. Drac didn't trust me to betray Mircea without an added incentive, so he'd provided one. He'd found out about the auction from his Dark Circle allies and recognized Claire's name. It seemed he had bothered to get my recent résumé, and thought there was a chance I might want my roomie back. If I preferred that to be in something other than a hundred pieces, he suggested I get to work on delivering his brother. Claire was "something to sweeten the deal."

I stared at the words, written with a quill pen in blood. I smelled it, just to be sure, and it was Claire's. Most of the magical community had moved on to using ballpoints like everyone else, but Uncle had always been a traditionalist. Since the letter was basically a contract for Claire's life, I suppose he'd thought it appropriate.

I reviewed my options, and they were universally horrible. I could ignore Drac's command and lose Claire to what was certain to be a particularly gruesome death, or I could betray Mircea and Radu. It had never really occurred to me until that moment to hand over the family. I didn't feel like a part of it—I never had—but it was somehow difficult to think about it simply not being there anymore. I had assumed I would find a way to turn the tables on Drac; now I realized that the easiest way to get what I wanted, maybe the only way, was to go along with his plans.

For some reason, that thought made me almost nauseous. I killed vampires, but my targets were usually revenants, the masterless psychos who were little more than animals. Vamps who stayed, however marginally, within the law had little to fear from me, although I didn't let that get around. And now I was expected to kill those who not only were within the rules but helped to make them?

"Dory." It took me a moment to realize that Louis-Cesare had been talking. Caedmon was regarding me with compassion. I'd probably been leaking my inner turmoil all over the place.

I looked at Louis-Cesare and drew a complete blank. I am usually a fairly glib liar—nothing like dear old Dad, of course, but good enough for most circumstances. Yet I couldn't think of a thing to say. Neither alternative was acceptable, but as least I had options. But if Louis-Cesare discovered what Drac had planned for Radu, I'd never get a chance to figure a way out of this. He'd move him back to MAGIC even if he had to cart him off bodily, and that would seal Claire's fate as surely as if I'd killed her myself.

"Drac has Claire," I finally said, hoping my pause would be mistaken for shock. "He says not to come after him, or he'll kill her."

Louis-Cesare nodded, but Caedmon appeared confused. "Who is this? Another vampire?"

"Dracula," I said, realizing that I'd used the diminutive. Radu was right; it was a bad habit. To my surprise,

Caedmon didn't look like the full name meant any more to him than the short version. So much for Uncle's notoriety. "I want to find Claire because I prefer not leaving my friends to face hideous deaths," I explained shortly. "What's your excuse?"

A puzzled frown creased his brow. "I am looking for my king, of course."

"And you think they're together?"

He looked at me as if I might be a little slow. "One would presume," he said drily.

I had a feeling I was missing something, but I hurt too much to care. "What's this king's name?"

Caedmon shrugged beautifully, causing his velvet cloak to shimmer around him before falling once again into perfect folds. "I do not know."

"You don't know your own king's name?"

"I am not certain the noble lady has yet gifted him with one," he said slowly. He looked at me curiously. "Can it be you do not know?"

"No!" I hopped up and was immediately sorry. The room tilted sideways and I sank to one knee before strong arms caught me. I looked up into a pair of concerned emerald eyes, and discovered that they were even more breathtaking at close range. "I don't know. After a month of searching, I don't know a damn thing. You think you could enlighten me?"

"But, if you are her friend, surely she told you?"

"Told me what?" I was still feeling grateful to him for the revved-up healing, but my nerves had taken a beating. If I felt better, I'd probably have been bitch slapping that pretty face by now.

He seemed to realize that and spread his hands

apologetically. "That she is with child. Your friend is carrying the next ruler of Faerie."

I stared at him for a long moment, then burst out laughing. Claire? In a dalliance, not just with a Fey, but with their king? When did she fit it in, between growing my weed and doing the grocery shopping? I got this crazy image of her taping a note on the fridge in her fine, precise hand: "Out screwing Fey king, be back around eight. Don't forget to feed the cats." It was absurd.

"Is she well?" Caedmon asked Louis-Cesare in an undertone. "I haven't lent energy to a human in some time; perhaps I overdid it—"

"She isn't human," Louis-Cesare corrected him. "She is dhampir."

"Truly?" The Fey's eyes brightened above a surprised smile. "I have heard of such beings, but never before had the pleasure of meeting one." He unfastened his cloak and draped it around my shoulders. It was soft and clingy, and smelled slightly of some kind of subtle cologne, or maybe that was just him. I couldn't seem to get a scent catalog on the Fey. It was like he was a breath of wind that blew scents to me from every direction except his own. It was confusing, but also intriguing.

He peered into my face, eyes literally glowing with curiosity. "My people can never resist any new experience," he said. "We find one so rarely."

"Uh-huh." The idea of seeing just how many new experiences I could show him flitted across my mind. "And how did Claire end up dating a Fey?" I asked.

"That is a very good question," Caedmon replied unhelpfully. He pulled me nearer despite the fact that this also brought him into closer contact with Stinky, who was clinging to me like a limpet. My thoughts were too confused to protest, even had I felt like it. Why hadn't Claire mentioned any of this? And why had I noticed nothing unusual? I thought I'd remember something like a seven-foot-tall glowing Fey hanging out in our living room.

"The Fey will find your friend. You cannot so much as look for her without risking her life," Louis-Cesare commented, derailing my train of thought. "Do you truly think Dracula will hesitate to do as he says?"

No, I didn't. Which brought me back to my previous dilemma. I could ignore Drac's ultimatum, stall for time and hope Caedmon managed to rescue Claire. But however powerful he might be, he obviously didn't understand our world very well, and that gave Dracula a huge advantage. I couldn't leave Claire's fate in the hands of the Fey any more than I could dump the whole problem on Mircea. Somehow, I was going to have to get her back on my own. I just wished I had even a vague idea how.

Chapter Thirteen

Radu's place looked exactly as I would have expected, if I had bothered to think about it. Our car passed through a crumbling stone gate and up a long drive to a graveled parking area. It fronted a complex of outbuildings and a two-story main structure surrounded by colorful explosions from out-of-control bougainvillea, hibiscus and jasmine. Unfortunately, neither the overgrown foliage nor the deep twilight managed to conceal the house. The original Spanish exterior, which had probably featured simple adobe walls, was now thick with Moroccan tile work, carved pillars, gilt cupolas and more wrought iron than a New Orleans bordello.

I would have said as much, but I wasn't looking any better. We were all a little worse for wear—except for the Fey, who was fresh as a daisy, damn him. Of course, he'd had his own seat, while I'd been relegated to the roughly one-eighth of the back not taken up with Bergtroll. Olga had been persuaded to leave her army behind, but there had been no way short of violence to stop her from coming (and even Louis-Cesare had balked at attacking the grieving widow). And then there was Stinky.

I'd had to hold him on my lap due to the lack of space, and even with the window down, things had gotten pretty ripe—to the point that Olga had started edging away from us, giving me maybe an inch of extra space there at the end. When even trolls think you reek, things are bad. The pièce de résistance, however, was the wards. I'd felt them crackle no less than three times on the way in, and had been grateful that we were expected. But even so, everyone's hair was standing on end by the time we finally arrived, and Stinky was little more than a round fur ball with legs.

Louis-Cesare came up beside me and, before I could protest, lifted me into his arms and started toward the house. He'd done the same thing to get me into the car, but I'd been fading in and out and had hardly noticed. I would have told him to put me down, but my legs did feel a little wobbly.

Radu gave us a surprised glance when we got to the door, but refrained from comment. He was dressed in what counted as somber attire for him—black velvet and jet beads that glittered in the light from the old-fashioned lantern he clutched in one pale hand. The absence of electricity told me immediately how serious he was taking this. No plain everyday wards here—the big boys must be online to send us back to the days of candles and lanterns. It did make for a nice ambience, though, since Radu's demented designer had not yet made it inside. Cathedral ceilings with old wood beams met us in the entryway, which featured a simple, open-tread staircase leading to a gallery landing. I spied an ominous sign for the future, however: the classic lines of a wrought-iron chandelier now dripped with a couple hundred rock crystals.

We went right, into a large living room with a huge

fireplace that looked big enough to consume small trees. The only incongruous note in the old-California theme was the painting glowing over the fireplace. It was a copy of Bellini's portrait of Mehmed II, the Ottoman sultan best known for conquering Constantinople and renaming it Istanbul. He'd thereafter considered himself the new Roman emperor, since Constantinople had been the last holdout of the glory-that-was-no-longer-Rome. He invaded Italy, but never managed to take the Eternal City. He did end up with a pretty nifty souvenir, though. I stood looking at it, but although it's well-done—Bellini was no hack—it didn't tell me much about the man who had been Radu's lover and political patron. It told me more about Radu. I supposed it made sense that he'd want a memento, but still. I spared a thought as to what Drac would say if he saw it, and smiled.

"I fail to see anything amusing," Louis-Cesare said stiffly, after laying me on the sofa. I was about to snipe back when I got a good look at him. His usually softly curling hair was a frazzled halo that crackled alarmingly whenever anyone got near it, and his normally pale face was dead white. His eyes were fever bright and there were tired lines near the corners. I hadn't noticed when I was getting patched up, but he'd also been wounded, once in the thigh and again in the upper part of his right arm.

None of his wounds were serious for a vamp, much less a master, but judging by the state of his clothes, he'd lost a lot of blood. And that was after what had to be a strenuous day even by his standards. Yet the only time he'd fed was what you might call a light snack at the Hedgehog. I edged away slightly, perching on the end of the couch with Stinky. I put him down because the couch was leather and could be wiped clean, but he immediately crawled back into my lap. The creature seemed very needy, or maybe it was just scared. Either way, I wanted to get it a bath if I was going to continue to have it draped all over me. Having a supersensitive nose can be a problem.

"Sit, rest," Radu said, fluttering about. "I'll have refreshments brought."

The advice had the opposite of the intended effect on me. "I'm not hungry," I lied. "Is there anywhere I can clean up?"

The rambling old place was staffed by some of Mircea's stable, several of whom came in as we were speaking. Like all good servants, they'd anticipated their master's needs. The one carrying a tray and bottle was well-known to me—unfortunately.

"Geoffrey, can you show Dorina to the gold room?" Radu asked. "Be back in an hour, Dory, or Chef will sulk. He's so pleased to have someone new to cook for, he's been slaving away all day."

"I'll remember," I said, giving Geoffrey the hairy eyeball. It's hard to look dignified in a few rags, a pair of bloody boots and a velvet cloak, especially when you have a filthy fur ball wrapped around your neck, but I tried.

Ever the proper English servant, Geoffrey inclined his head without hesitation, nothing in his carriage giving away the fact that he'd vastly prefer to show me to the closest garbage heap. "Of course, my lord."

I followed Geoffrey out the door as the second servant, a human, started undoing his cravat. He was handsome, with tawny hair and eyes and a healthy, youthful complexion. I hastened my steps, overtaking my guide in my hurry to get away before Louis-Cesare started in on his appetizer.

I took a wrong turn and ended up in a grassy courtyard with a small fountain and a couple of fruit trees. The night sky was dark blue overhead, soft with the glimmer of stars, but the illumination from the house made it possible to see without being obtrusive. A light breeze, cool but not cold, blew in from a small iron gate set in the wall, which was weighed down by a mass of overgrown honeysuckle. It was surprisingly charming.

"Your rooms are this way, unless you intend to bathe in the fountain, miss," Geoffrey commented from over my shoulder.

I thought of the wreck Stinky would likely make of any bathroom. "Yeah. This is good. Fetch towels and some soap, would you?"

Geoffrey hesitated for a full five seconds—a new record—before I heard his quiet "Yes, miss."

I actually did end up bathing in the fountain, although not by choice. Stinky, it turned out, did not like water and was even less enamored with soap. He made it clear that he had no intention of getting to know either of them better. To make a long story short, I insisted, he demurred, I pulled him off me and threw him in the fountain, he leapt out and I chased him around the courtyard and threw him back in. And so on. It ended with both of us soaking wet in a fountain filled with bubbles, but Stinky was going to need a new name. At least for a little while.

I wadded up the Fey's velvet cloak in an attempt to dry Stinky's hair. Since he was basically a fur ball with claws, that was harder than it sounds, but I had started to make headway when I heard a noise behind me. I turned to find Louis-Cesare standing at the edge of a puddle staring at me with a strange expression.

"That garment is doubtless worth a fortune," he observed as Stinky tried his best to shred the Fey's cape. The material stretched but didn't rip, trapping him long enough for me to finish the job. He fled under a pink rhododendron as soon as I let him loose, and immediately began rolling in the dirt. I sighed.

"You planning to rat me out to the Fey?" I demanded.

"No." Louis-Cesare put a bundle of cloth and a bottle of wine down on the edge of the fountain. He saw the direction of my gaze. "I thought we deserved a drink."

I thought that was the most sensible thing I'd heard him say yet. I sorted through the bundle, which turned out to be clothes, while he poured us both a drink and a half. As I'd feared, Radu's idea of appropriate attire was scary. The white linen tunic was okay, with a high neck closed with black ribbon ties and long, full sleeves. But it had been matched with a heavy white wool skirt and two black aprons covered in red and gold embroidery. Traditional Romanian female attire. I refrained from wincing, if only barely.

"Lord Radu said you would find these garments familiar," Louis commented. I looked at him suspiciously. He looked sober enough, so why did I get the impression he was laughing?

"Yeah, that's the problem," I said sourly. Unfortunately, the choice was between wearing Radu's offerings and dining nude. My T-shirt was being held together by a safety pin borrowed from Olga, and the few dry patches on my jeans were stiff with blood.

"Radu has . . . unusual taste," Louis-Cesare agreed, sitting on the edge of the fountain. I realized I wasn't the only one relegated to borrowed attire, although he'd definitely gotten the better of the bargain. A cascade of lace spilled down the front of his antique shirt, and buttery leather pants hugged better legs than any vampire deserved. To go with it, he had a nice peach complexion, the darkest I'd seen on him yet, and his hair was back to its usual shiny abundance. The lamplight from the house filtered through the trees overhead, dappling it with gold.

Not for the first time, I envied vamps their recuperative powers. He still looked a little worn around the edges, more the warrior than the fashion plate, but he'd be right as rain by morning. I doubted I'd be so lucky. I slumped on the side of the fountain, struggling with the fact that I'd gotten winded chasing a baby Duergar. Changing clothes suddenly seemed like way too much trouble, at least without that drink first.

"Where'd you get the wine?" I asked as Louis-Cesare passed me a glass. It turned out to be a dark, fruity red, Radu's own label.

"It was meant for dinner; I found it on the butler's tray."

"So Geoffrey actually did me a favor?" The wine hit my empty stomach hard, but I didn't care. Occasionally my weird metabolism actually comes in handy. "Will wonders never cease?"

"He is yours to command."

"Who? Geoffrey?" He nodded and I laughed. "Sure he is."

"You are Lord Mircea's daughter."

"And the stain on the family honor," I reminded him. "Like a good butler, Geoffrey prefers things tidy."

"He has threatened you?" Louis-Cesare sounded surprisingly grim, considering that he'd done the same himself not too long ago.

"Everyone threatens me; it's not important."

"You deserve his respect!"

"For what? Being the boss' little girl?" I waved my glass, sloshing some wine over the side. It looked strangely like blood in the dark. "'Fraid that's out-weighed by the whole killing-off-his-kind thing."

"I have seen you kill no one who did not deserve it. And you handle your . . . disability . . . admirably." He stopped, looking slightly uncomfortable. "I did not think a dhampir capable of such compassion."

I stared. By God. A *compliment*. From Louis-Cesare. That wine was just going right to his head.

And then, of course, he ruined it. "I am glad you have come to your senses about Lord Radu."

"Come to my senses?"

"To help protect him. It is the only intelligent way to proceed."

"How exactly is letting Drac run free intelligent?" I demanded.

Louis-Cesare's eyes narrowed. "He will be caught eventually. It is only a matter of time with the forces the Senate currently has in the field."

"Except they aren't gunning for him."

"He has shown a lack of judgment in the past, a reputation borne out by his current alliance. He cannot help but run foul of the Senate before long."

"That's one theory." And not one I shared. People had been underestimating Drac for centuries. He might be crazy, but he had the Basarab cunning and was utterly ruthless about how he used it. Not a good combo. "But then, you gotta wonder why, if the Senate can deal with him, Mircea went to the trouble of drafting us."

"He hopes to end this before his brother spills more innocent blood."

"And you don't care about that?"

"Radu's blood is also innocent!" I thought that was debatable, but didn't say so. Louis-Cesare looked like he was getting a little heated again. So much for having a pleasant, low-key conversation.

"Why do you care so much what happens to Radu?" I asked, knowing I'd probably regret it. "Didn't he abandon you?"

"He is also my sire!"

"And Mircea is mine. It's never bought him a lot of slack, actually."

Louis-Cesare gave me a condescending look. "Has it not? You are here now, in answer to his call—"

"Because of Claire!"

"—as you should be. You would not exist but for him, as I would have died centuries ago if not for Radu. We have a debt to the family."

A little wind was playing fitfully through the trees, tossing the leaves about, but when I looked upward, I could see the stars in patches. I took a deep breath of cool night air and told myself not to overreact. "You're confusing me with a vamp," I said shortly. "Just because Mircea donated some sperm doesn't mean I'm bound to him."

"There are other ties than magic. Loyalty, obligation, love—"

"I do not love Mircea!"

"And whether you acknowledge them or not, you feel them, too. You belong by his side when he needs you."

What I felt was a burst of anger, hot and fierce. Damn him for stirring to life that old, bitter craving, the one that wove itself around the word *belong*. I'd never belonged anywhere. It was the first lesson I'd ever learned, drummed into my bones and ripped into my flesh long before the infant that would become Louis-Cesare was even born. And it was the one I made sure I never forgot.

"You'll see how much love I have for the family," I

told him savagely, "when I plant a stake in Drac's cold, dead heart."

"You still intend to go after him," he asked incredulously, "even though it could mean your friend's life?"

"He'll come after us. I thought that was the plan."

"Using Lord Radu as bait was your plan!"

"Which he currently is," I pointed out.

"Dracula will never try to reach him through such defenses! I did not understand until I saw them for myself, but it is true. He is as safe here as at MAGIC."

I didn't feel like debating it. There *were* no defenses good enough to keep out Drac if he wanted in, but convincing Louis-Cesare of that would be counterproductive. And even if I felt like trying, I doubted I was up to it. Even my anger had sputtered out against the overwhelming tide of exhaustion. I stared at a flickering firefly in the grass, feeling oddly dislocated. "Whatever."

Louis-Cesare said something else, but it sounded very far away, like he was speaking underwater. I was so tired my eyes didn't want to focus, to the point that the firefly's path blurred into a long, continuous neon line. And then it happened again. It was like drowning, sinking helplessly down into dark, frozen depths. But instead of water, I was floundering in a sea of memory.

I realized that the drumming sound I was hearing wasn't my heart, but someone beating on a door. It took a moment to realize it was me. The door opened to reveal a pissed-off female vamp in a diaphanous white negligee: Augusta, a Senate member. Her outfit stayed white until I lurched into her, soaking the front of the expensive nightwear in enough blood to indicate a mortal wound. I looked down to find that I was wearing only a man's long overcoat that was gaping open in front. Under that was a lot of blood and what looked to be half of my intestines, which I was keeping inside by pressure from the hand that hadn't been needed for beating down the door.

"My back," I whispered.

"I'll fetch a doctor," Augusta said faintly. She looked hungry, but I didn't care. At that moment, she couldn't have done much more damage. She dragged me over to a big bed and tried to get me to lie down.

I shook my head. "My back," I repeated.

"I know. Don't worry—I won't put any pressure on your stomach."

"No!" I was trembling with the effort of standing up, but I couldn't lie down. "Look at my back. It's a message, for Mircea." The vamp had been paying so much attention to my ruined stomach that she hadn't even noticed that the back of my coat was completely drenched, and not by water.

I was trying to get the coat off, but couldn't manage with only one hand. Augusta helped, then stopped when it was half off to stare in shock. I could see what she saw in the mirror of a small rosewood dressing table, not that I needed the reminder. Someone had carved letters into my flesh, although the blood, part dried and part fresh, blurred them, making them impossible to read.

"Get Mircea," I whispered, kneeling on the floor, gripping the bedpost to stay partially upright. I heard her leave the room, shouting, and for a small woman she had a surprisingly strong voice.

What seemed like only a few seconds later, Mircea came in, shaking black snow off his greatcoat. He smelled of coal dust, horses and cheap perfume. He knelt by my side. "What happened?"

"You sent me to find your brother," I gasped, fighting to stay conscious. *"Unfortunately, I succeeded."*

Mircea began peeling the coat the rest of the way off. His expression was carefully blank, but his eyes were amber fire. Another vamp entered the room, carrying a basin and a towel. *"Master,"* he said, bowing to Augusta but managing not to spill the water. *"I would like to clean up the girl."*

Augusta gave a bark of laughter. *"I'm sure you would."*

"I was an orderly in South Africa, master. I survived the Zulu War; I know something about knife wounds."

That wasn't the only way he knew about them. Jack was Augusta's current pet—and he'd been a monster even before she'd turned him. He stupidly offered Mircea the basin. One savage movement later, both it and Jack went flying against the wall. Jack hit hard enough that his body actually left an impression, tearing away the wallpaper to show the bricks underneath.

He didn't get to his feet, but cowered on the floor where he'd fallen, hands on his head, not daring to look up. He'd have seemed almost pitiful if I'd had any emotion to spare. I didn't, and it looked like Mircea felt the same. *"Do it,"* I told him. *"You have to."*

Mircea's hand smoothed my hair gently. Then he snapped his fingers and Jack reached out a trembling hand to retrieve the basin. He crawled with it to the door and was gone. Faster than I would have believed possible, he was back, with more water and several towels. He also carried a bottle of whiskey, but no glasses.

"No alcohol," Mircea said without bothering to look at him. I guess he must have smelled it.

"Forgive me, my lord," Jack murmured obsequiously. *"I merely thought, to prevent infection—"*

"She is dhampir," Mircea said curtly. "She doesn't contract infections. Leave us."

Jack bowed deeply and backed out of the room, either to show respect or because he didn't dare turn his back on Mircea. There was a vibrating tension in the air, sort of like the tremors before a volcano erupts. I concentrated on staying upright while Mircea carefully washed the wounds on my back, wetting an area, patting it dry, pausing to apply pressure here and there to the cuts that were still bleeding, then starting over again. I wouldn't let him touch my stomach—I assumed I was going to die anyway, so what was the point?

Slowly, the letters began to show more clearly. It took forever and was excruciating, but I was so close to passing out that I barely noticed.

"Can you read it?" Augusta asked when Mircea had finished and set the bowl aside.

"Bandage her wounds," he said after a moment, ignoring her. "See that she lives."

"Mircea!" My lips were numb, but somehow I forced the words out. "If you do not finish this tonight, if you leave him any avenue by which to return, I wash my hands of the whole affair. Next time, you will hunt him alone."

The only answer I received was the door shutting softly behind him. My head drooped to rest on the edge of the bed. My reflection showed that a few of the shallower cuts were already starting to knit together, blurring the edge of some words like random strokes of an eraser. The whole thing would be illegible in a few hours.

Drac had carved his challenge to Mircea into my flesh, then gutted me and left me to stagger back on my own to the house the vamps were renting. And it had worked. Mircea had gone off to meet him, but instead of killing the son of a bitch who had just carved up his daughter, he was going to trap him in some concoction of the Senate's, all neat and tidy and problem solved.

I swallowed bitterness and stared at the door, trembling with exhaustion and waiting to pass out from the blood loss. It had some impressive dents where my fist had hit it earlier, but it was solid. Nonetheless, I could dimly hear a low-voiced conversation on the other side. I was breathing in pants, trying to get enough air into my lungs to satisfy their craving, but I managed to catch snatches of it anyway.

"The Consul grows impatient and demands a solution, or at the very least an update. I have to tell her something—"

"She will have her solution, tonight."

"And what will that be? The dhampir is right. You must kill him!"

"This is a family matter, Augusta—it does not concern you."

Jack's voice sounded again, stronger than the others, perhaps because he was making no effort to be quiet. "Do I have your permission to attend her, master?" I didn't catch the reply, but the door opened a moment later and in he came, with bandages, a new basin of water and a small black bag. I eyed it suspiciously, but he took out only a length of thread and a scary-looking needle. He tugged me onto the rug and examined my stomach with a critical eye.

"He may not have been responsible for the deaths of Jack's victims, but he has been making vampires without permission, and not registering them. For that alone, he will surely be sentenced to death. Kill him now and spare your family the shame of a public execution."

"*Release my arm, Augusta. I do not have time to discuss this with you, even were I so inclined.*"

Jack had started to sew me up, and I badly needed something to distract me from the pain. Why wasn't I unconscious? The needle plunged in and out of my flesh as I stared at the door, straining to hear the conversation.

"*Mircea!*"

"*You do not understand the situation.*" Mircea's voice was calm, but I knew him well enough to recognize the thread of anger running through it.

"*What is there to understand? If he had insulted one who belonged to me in such a fashion, I would crack his skull like an egg!*"

"*And thereby give him exactly what he wants!*"

Jack used fine, even stitches, I noticed in something like a daze. He'd have made a good tailor. "*If he wants to die, he has merely to say,*" Augusta whispered viciously. "*There would be no lack of volunteers to grant his wish!*"

"*And they would be slaughtered for their trouble. Why do you think he provokes me—threatening Radu, attacking Dorina? He wants to die by my hand and no other.*"

"*Then give him what he wants!*" I would have echoed Augusta's sentiment if I'd had the strength.

"*No.*" Mircea's voice was hard as stone. "*Let him live and remember, not die and forget!*"

I heard him stride away and a moment later, Augusta slammed back into the room. "*She will live, master,*" Jack told her, unruffled. "*I swear it.*" He patted my hair almost fondly. "*I am not surprised that the count did not like this one. There is no fear in her.*"

I wondered, as I finally allowed myself to pass out, how anyone could be so wrong.

Chapter Fourteen

"Dorina!" Hands were clenched frantically on my shoulders. Whoever was holding me was shaking. I gripped strong arms in both hands, struggling to reconnect with the present. "Are you all right?" someone demanded.

I was back, I realized. Shocked to the core, but back. "Never better." My laugh sounded thin and ragged even to me. I let it peter out.

My eyes focused enough to see Louis-Cesare staring down at me. He didn't look much more composed than I felt. Panic had washed the color from his face, leaving his eyes insanely blue. "You are *not* all right."

"It wasn't so bad," I said, still half-confused about where we were. My eyes saw grass and stars and fireflies, but my brain kept telling them they were wrong. Only the lighting was right: the dim glow from the house approximating candle flame. "He wanted to be sure I lasted long enough to deliver the message. . . ."

Louis-Cesare said something extremely rude in French. I blinked at him. It took me a moment to realize that he was talking about Drac. But how did he know . . . ? "You saw."

He nodded grimly. I felt the flex of strong biceps under my palms as his grip tightened. "As if the memories were my own."

I peeled a wet strand of grass off my cheek. It felt clammy, like the touch of Jack's hands. "Sorry about that." It seemed pretty inadequate, but it was the best I could do at the moment.

I managed to sit up. The hands gripping my shoulders dropped away, but the fingers dragged almost reluctantly down my arms. It was a tiny thing, lasting the space of a heartbeat, but it sent something weightless coiling through my stomach.

I leaned against the water-slick side of the fountain for support, but it wasn't enough. The scene around me telescoped without warning and I sagged face-first into more wet grass. Louis-Cesare pulled me back into his arms. I should have protested, but the heat of his chest at my back was soothing. I'd get up and face whatever had just happened; I'd force my body to a strength I didn't feel, in a minute. . . .

We sat there not saying anything. I was too confused to speak. I hurt, but not in the right places. I wanted to clutch my stomach, even though it was one of the few parts of my body that didn't ache. But it felt like it should, like those stitches were still being punched through my flesh. Like it had really all just happened again. And then there was the feeling of Louis-Cesare's heart beating against my back, his legs solid on either side of mine. He had dropped his head to my shoulder, and the sound of his breathing in my ear was steady and sweet. "I'm sorry, too," he whispered, and I found I couldn't talk at all.

His thumbs began digging into the knotted muscles of my shoulders, kneading the tension expertly away. After traveling from my neck to the small of my back, they worked their way up again, wringing the aches from my body. I closed my eyes, feeling my muscles relax one by one, and my head dropped forward. I heard my own murmur of contentment, but it sounded impossibly far away, lost in the hypnotic stroking of Louis-Cesare's hands.

There was a sharp callus along the side of his index finger. He flinched a little when I reached out and captured that hand, held very still while I stroked lightly over it. The skin was uneven, just a little rough, and the flesh beneath was hard. He was watching me touch him, and I could hear his breath halt in his throat.

I couldn't remember the last time I'd sat like this with anyone. Kindness after cruelty, warmth in a cold place, tenderness instead of suspicion: none of it was supposed to come to me, and certainly not from a vampire. Uncertainty fluttered through my stomach. What was I doing? I dropped his hand and started to move, to pull away, when his voice stopped me. "Why did Dracula torture you?" he asked softly.

"What did Jonathan do to you?" I shot back, expecting that to end the conversation.

He surprised me. "Something similar. Someone important to me . . . a witch . . . was taken by the Black Circle. They intended . . . you know they steal power, from whomever they can?" I nodded slowly, barely moving my head. I didn't say anything, afraid to break the mood, afraid that he would disappear back inside that shell of his and I'd never find out what was going on. "What you may not know is that, taken to extremes, it kills their victim."

Actually, I did know that. A normal human isn't simply someone with no magic; he is a completely different species. If magical creatures lose all their magic, that doesn't somehow transform them into norms. It kills them, by draining away something they need to exist as much as humans need blood.

"What happened?" I asked cautiously.

Louis-Cesare shrugged, and I could feel the movement along my back. "I offered myself in exchange."

"You did what?" I was sure I'd heard wrong.

"Jonathan is addicted to magic the way some humans are to drugs. But, as with drug addicts, he has difficulty finding a steady supply. Powerful magic users—the only kind that can appease his hunger—are not easy to catch. And even when he is successful, the sacrifice can only provide one 'hit.' Then the subject dies, and another must be obtained."

"I don't understand." So why did I suddenly feel chilled?

"A master vampire can heal almost any injury, even a total loss of magic. He can be drained every night, yet still rise the next, as long as his head and heart are intact. He is the perfect, unending sacrifice."

For a moment, I couldn't breathe; the chill had expanded and everything was frozen, including my brain. I didn't ask for details. I didn't *want* details. I was suddenly hugely grateful that if we'd had to share a memory, it had been mine.

I swallowed. "How long?"

"I was his captive for a month. We had agreed to a week, but Jonathan refused to let me go. He said . . . he said he liked my taste better than anyone he'd ever had." I turned in his arms so I could see his face. One look in those eyes and I knew he wasn't kidding. In the dim light they shimmered crystal, like sapphire viewed through ice, reflecting perfectly every emotion. "If Radu hadn't found me, I might still be there."

"*Radu* found you?"

"Yes. As my master, he was able to track me. I was in a stone-walled cell, too weak to break out during the day, and subject to Jonathan's attentions every night. I had almost given up hope, until one afternoon I heard a voice outside my window telling me to step back. I didn't recognize it—I had not seen Radu in years—but I thought it prudent to comply. Just as I did so, the entire wall broke away, leaving me staring at a dust-covered man trying vainly to control the rearing horse he had chained to the window bars."

"That sounds like Radu."

"Then the roof caved in." It was said so deadpan that I wasn't sure if I was being teased. But Louis-Cesare's lips twitched, softened and curved into a smile. I laughed in relief. "It did," he insisted.

"I've no doubt." 'Du was many things, but a master engineer wasn't one of them. "But I still don't understand what happened at the plane. Why was Jonathan trying to blow you up?"

"He wasn't. He has been trying to recapture me ever since I escaped, but had to be careful lest he risk making war on the Senate."

"We're already at war."

"Giving him the perfect excuse. By destroying the Senate's jet, he hoped to convince the family that I had been destroyed, too—that there was no need to search for me this time."

"But . . . why haven't you told the Senate? Why not let them take him out for you? As you said, we're already at war with his Circle. What's one more dead mage?" I'd be happy to do the honors myself.

"To pull resources away from the war for a personal vendetta would require my explaining the charges against him."

"So?"

Louis-Cesare just looked at me. "How many people have you told about what happened to you that night, Dorina? How many know why it is you hate Dracula so intensely?"

I got the point. "No one. Mircea threatened Augusta with bodily injury if she ever so much as breathed a word. As far as I know, she never did."

"And there was no one else?"

"No. Except for Jack. But as his master, Augusta's word spoke for him, too. Why?"

"The spell we encountered in the caves . . . the only ones I know of are localized—linked to a specific place. We should have left it behind us when we came here. But those were your memories, were they not?"

I hesitated. Part of that scene had been familiar enough—the aftermath of Drac's little torture session in London. But the last bit . . . that was new. I'd always assumed that Mircea wanted Drac kept alive because of some misguided sentiment. Now I wasn't so sure. Maybe the old guy had more backbone than I thought. "Most of it. Maybe all of it. I don't know—I wasn't exactly at my best at the time."

"Some legends say the Fey can induce visions. That they influence people in such ways."

"Caedmon couldn't have brought on that nightmare, even if he had a reason." I slowly got to my feet, testing my body, relieved that it responded, if sluggishly. I was going to have to try to avoid getting beaten up for a few days. "There's no way he could have known about it. No one could."

I reached for Radu's tunic, wanting to get on something a little warmer than a tattered T-shirt, but moved the wrong way. A bolt of pain shot through me—from the shoulder Drac's boys had tried to wrench off. "Son of a bitch!"

"You aren't healed." Louis-Cesare stood up beside me, without his usual fluid grace. I bit back a wry grin—and we were Mircea's invincible champions!

"I'm okay." That Fey magic was something else, but it hadn't replaced the considerable blood loss—only time would do that—not to mention that I'd had plenty of aches and pains even before the fight. But that was nothing new.

"Are you certain? I may have overlooked something."

I didn't answer. A hand had come to rest beside my left breast, and a warm finger was caressing the damp cloth, tracing the almost invisible indentation left by one of the bullets. I started to say something, but my throat felt oddly constricted. Then both his hands were moving over my body, searching for hidden injuries. One finger accidentally brushed across a nipple, shooting sparks all the way to my toes. Calluses, I decided vaguely, can feel very good.

"Your reaction in the caves was worrisome," he informed me.

I was more worried about my reaction now. I found myself wanting to suck those fingers into my mouth, to see Louis-Cesare's eyes grow dark with lust and want. "You can see I'm fine," I told his shirt, fighting a strong urge to take the delicate material in my teeth and rip it off him. It was so intense for a moment that I had to close my eyes and concentrate on why that would be wrong on so many levels: he was Daddy's little spy, there to insure that

Drac didn't get everything he had coming, a vampire and a Senate member. None of those spelled lover in my book.

So why did my hand reach out to push a stray curl behind his ear? To my surprise, Louis-Cesare leaned into the feel of my hand. There was a slightly pink line, warmer than the rest of his skin, on his cheek. The fast-healing injury ran from his jaw nearly to his eye, adding to the pirate effect of the clothes. I traced it lightly with a finger. We were close enough for me to count the shades of blue that blended in his eyes, to see the way the strands of gold and brown and red mingled in his hair. To note the network of lines near his eyes, the fine traces of bitterness at his mouth. It must be the blood loss, I decided, reaching up to press my lips to his.

He went completely still at my touch, then, after a startled moment, gently tugged away. "Dorina, what are you doing?"

"If you don't know, you're the densest Frenchman I ever met."

"You are not well."

"Let me worry about that." My hand tingled faintly where it rested against the flex of his bicep. I moved it to his thigh, finding hard muscle beneath the smooth leather. No softness anywhere, except the velvet of his skin, the touch of his mouth . . .

"You are in no condition to worry about it," he told me, his voice oddly tender. He caught my hands in his. "I had to use power on you earlier, and I am not certain—"

"I can't be influenced." I tried to tug my hands away—there were far more interesting things they could be doing—but he laced our fingers together, tightening his grip.

"If your shields are in place, perhaps not. But they

were not up earlier. And the residual effects of a powerful suggestion can be—"

Need washed through me, rough and wild. I didn't
want a lesson on mind control, damn it! I cut him off by
reaching up on tiptoe and sinking my teeth into that
lovely full lower lip, the one that had been driving me
crazy ever since I met him. I barely had time to taste the
blood on my tongue before his arms went around me,
pulling me hard against him. But he didn't kiss me, and
with his height, I needed his cooperation. He also didn't
let go of my hands, so I was effectively immobilized, my
arms trapped behind my back, our fingers still enmeshed.
That strength that had so irritated me before held me fast,
and I suddenly found it extremely erotic that I couldn't
get away unless he released me.

My hands tingled with the need to run over him, to rip
off those ridiculous clothes and feel warm skin against
warm skin instead of leather against cotton. But he
wouldn't let me. The thought occurred that maybe Louis-
Cesare was right—maybe I *had* been influenced—but at
the moment I really didn't care.

I finally gave up all pretense of control and arched
against him. I was rewarded with a low groan in that rich
voice, all velvet and heat, and suddenly he was kissing
me. The feverish, openmouthed caresses started hard and
got harder, almost desperate. It felt like fire was pouring
through me and tasted of raw power—hot and sweet,
burning and perfect. The heat of his breath was scalding.
God, I was going to go crazy if I couldn't touch him.

Then, just as suddenly, I was alone. After a confused
second, I realized that Louis-Cesare was now standing
on the other side of the fountain, facing away from me,
his back tense. When he turned around, his eyes were

shadowed and his face sported hectic color in his cheeks. Apparently he'd remembered that he was kissing a dhampir, and a bastard one at that.

So much for compliments.

I felt heat closing my throat and had to take a few deep breaths to get myself under control. God, I must be even more tired than I thought. I pulled the hideous skirt on, slipping my ruined jeans off underneath. It wasn't my style, but it bought me a few seconds to rearrange my face.

"Why do you think the Fey is really here?" Louis-Cesare asked. There seemed to be something wrong with his voice.

I slipped on the tunic, hands tingling at the memory of what it had been like to touch him. "You heard what he said. He's looking for Claire."

"You have already told him what you know—that he will find the woman with Lord Dracula. Why is he here instead of looking for them?"

"Why don't you ask him?" It certainly topped my agenda. Caedmon had asked to delay filling in details until we arrived. Considering that conditions in the car had not been conducive to intelligent conversation, I hadn't pressed him. But all bets were now off. I was tired and confused, but I wasn't going to bed until I had the truth about Claire.

"The Fey cannot be trusted. They speak in riddles and half-truths when they trouble themselves to say anything at all! I am responsible for you to Lord Mircea, and I do not trust Fey magic."

"And I don't trust you."

"That makes two of us," he said obscurely, running a hand through his messy curls. "May I see the note the woman left you?" It would have sounded like a non sequitur to anyone listening in, but to me, it made perfect sense. Louis-Cesare didn't trust me, either.

Smart vampire.

"Her name is Claire. And no, you can't."

"And why not?"

"I lost it."

Blue eyes stabbed me with unmasked suspicion. I wanted to look away, but didn't dare. But he stopped short of searching me—I suppose he thought he'd done a pretty good job of that already—and I was careful not to glance at my left boot, where I'd slipped Claire's note. Louis-Cesare probably didn't read Romanian, but Radu sure as hell did. And the last thing I needed was for them to know about Drac's ultimatum.

I fished Stinky out from under the bushes. "Come on," I said wearily. "Let's go get some answers."

Chapter Fifteen

I knew Radu wouldn't appreciate having Stinky at the dinner table, especially since he'd managed to coat himself in mud again, thanks to his frolic under the bushes. But I wasn't leaving the little guy on his own. Letting him run loose, especially when the place was on high alert, was not smart. And 'Du had certainly had worse dinner guests. In fact, out of everyone at the table that night, Stinky was the least scary.

The dining hall turned out to be on the opposite side of the grand entryway from the living room, but we didn't go there. I guess Radu thought the table, which looked like it could seat forty, was a bit much for an intimate party. Instead, I was led downstairs to a wine cellar, where a much smaller table had been set for five. I plopped Stinky down in the seat next to mine and nodded at Olga. She inclined her massive head back at me, and the fact she'd been able to see my greeting tells you how many lamps Radu had burning around the place. He was being the thoughtful host, making sure that, even without electricity, there was enough light for a troll's weak eyes. Geoffrey silently set another place, not deigning to so much as look at either me or the hair ball next to me, then went back to pouring wine.

Louis-Cesare wasn't eating—so much for the stereotype about the French and food—nor was he bothering to conceal his dislike for the Fey. It was a good thing he had the rep of someone who could handle himself in a fight. Not that Caedmon seemed worried.

The Fey had commandeered a place on my right and appeared intent on being the perfect dinner guest. He was voluble in praise for the onion soup and escargots that started us off, and for the wine, some of Radu's best stock. I suppose for an immortal, anything new was good, and that dinner was certainly a new one. At least I doubted that he'd previously sat down at a vampire's table with a dhampir, a Duergar and a large Bergtroll, but then, what did I know? And that was the problem. I didn't like having an ally I knew so little about any more than Louis-Cesare did.

By the time the second course was served, I decided that enough pleasantries had been exchanged. "Okay, Caedmon. We're here. Spill it."

"Certainly." Unlike the rest of us, he seemed to be enjoying the special version of steak tartare that Radu's chef had worked up for the main course. He'd already finished the helping Geoffrey had served us, and now used the end of his knife to spear another of the tiny cows that were wandering around the central serving dish. The rest of the miniature herd scattered, lowing, to hide under the spinach leaves that rimmed the plate. "What would you like to know?"

Louis-Cesare broke in before I had a chance to decide which of the questions crowding my brain to let out first.

"How do you know that Miss Lachesis carries the Fey heir?"

Caedmon swirled his desperately mooing captive around a dish of spicy mustard. Blood mixed with the sauce, creating a spiral effect. "Because she said so. I tend to take a lady at her word about such things."

"To whom did she say it? To you?"

"No. She made the claim to one of the humans conducting the auction. He contacted our delegation at MAGIC, offering her to us—for a substantial price, of course."

"Then how did Drac get to her first?" I was sitting on my hands to keep from wrapping them around that ivory throat, but that wasn't going to work for long. I was bled almost dry and exhausted, enough that my temper should have been calmed at least a little. But no such luck.

Caedmon used his fork to cut off the escape of a couple of cows, which had been making a break for the shadows around the salt cellar. "He reached the auction ahead of me and took her from the auctioneers by force." Caedmon didn't sound particularly put out. He was relaxed, casual even. "Whether he can manage to control one so powerful, I do not know." He shrugged. "Perhaps if he keeps her sedated . . ."

I was about to erupt, but Louis-Cesare beat me to it. "Stop teasing her. Tell us what you know." His face matched the voice—cold, hard and not amused.

Caedmon's friendly expression altered, his smile growing as brittle and brilliant as cut crystal. He didn't seem to like orders. I don't know what would have happened if Stinky hadn't chosen that moment to choke on one of the larger cows—about the length of my index finger—which he'd been trying to shove down whole. Olga clapped him on the back with one enormous hand, causing the creature to fly out of his mouth like it had been shot from a gun. It landed in the tray of Amaretto pears Geoffrey had just brought in. A dozen butterflies, which had been decorating the dish, scattered in a mad fluttering of spun-sugar wings.

Radu looked tragic. Geoffrey didn't look like much of anything, his face a careful blank as he regarded the ruined dish and his splattered shirt. Olga, on the other hand, seemed to find the whole thing extremely funny, judging by her guffaws of laughter. She'd been throwing the miniature herd back like popcorn, not even bothering to chew, and I guess Stinky had been trying to imitate her. I checked on him, but he didn't appear to be suffering any ill effects.

I turned back to Caedmon. "Please—tell us what you know."

He inclined his head in a naturally aristocratic gesture. "Of course." The rich voice wrapped itself around my nerves, instantly soothing. Which was a good thing, considering what he had to say. "I am afraid I have more questions than answers, as does the Domi, our assembly of elders. A child is a great joy among us, not something to be hidden in the dark as if shameful. Yet no one knew until recently that the king was even acquainted with your friend, much less that he may have sired a child with her! And now you tell me you didn't know it, either." Caedmon flashed me a red-toothed smile. "The mystery deepens."

He ripped a leg off one of the struggling creatures on his plate and swallowed it whole. He seemed to like only the haunches. Half a dozen tiny torsos floated on a river of blood in front of him, a few still weakly moving. "Maybe it isn't true," I offered.

"Why would she make up such a fantastic lie?" Louis-Cesare asked.

I shrugged. "Maybe hoping for help in getting away from her kidnappers? Anything would be better than being handed over to the harvesters."

"But why contact the Fey?" he insisted. "They are not known for altruism toward outsiders. If they rescued her and discovered she was lying, she would likely be in even more peril than before."

"But was she lying?" I turned to Caedmon. "What does your king say?"

"I would ask him had he not disappeared several weeks ago. There was an assassination attempt, or so it seems. He went on a hunting expedition with two trusted retainers one afternoon and never returned. We found his horse—riderless—and, after a search, the two retainers—dead. But of the king himself, there was no sign."

I stared at my plate, my stomach flip-flopping like a landed fish. I herded my cows over to Stinky, who appeared to have the appetite of a couple of starving teenagers, and tried to order my thoughts. "So the Domi sent you to find out the truth," I finally said. "Because if Claire's claim wasn't a desperate lie, she carries the heir to the throne." Caedmon's mouth was full, but he nodded. "And if the rumor is true?" He swallowed but still said nothing. "You're planning to take her back with you," I accused.

Caedmon sat back in the hard, uncomfortable dining chair as if on a throne, his legs stretched out in front of him in supine elegance. "The present situation proves that she is hardly safe here, does it not?"

"I believe I'm missing something," Radu announced indistinctly, around the tiny brown leg that was sticking out of the corner of his mouth. He seemed to be having difficulty with his own chef's cooking. A moment before, a bull had fallen over the edge of his plate, and when he'd tried to scoop it up surreptitiously, it gored his finger. "I thought the heir had to have a majority of Fey blood. Why would Claire's child, assuming she is pregnant, be in the running?"

Caedmon shook his head, causing all that golden hair to shimmer like a silken banner caught in a breeze. "Forgive me, but you do not seem to know a great deal about the lady in question. The Domi has recently learned that her mother had a liaison with a powerful Dark Fey noble. If Claire was the result, a child born to her and our king would be three-quarters Fey. And a very strong contender indeed."

I stared at Louis-Cesare, and could tell we were both thinking the same thing. "Half-breed." He said it first.

I nodded. The Fey who attacked us hadn't been after me at all—they'd mistaken me for Claire, the other half-breed who lived at that address. It looked like Kyle had gotten something right, after all. Claire was carrying a nonhuman child, but the father was Fey, not vampire. I felt a rush of relief so extreme that I laughed aloud. This garnered me a few worried glances, but I didn't care. That was one huge weight off my mind. Unfortunately, it wasn't the only one.

"I was under the impression that the Fey took human babies and left changelings in their place," Radu was saying. "Why would a Fey leave a child behind?"

Caedmon made a graceful, indeterminate hand gesture. "Presumably because the lady did not tell him she was going to have one. Perhaps she feared that he would take the child if he knew."

"Then how did the king find out?" I asked. "Claire's mother died when she was a baby. And if her real father didn't know . . ."

"That is one of many questions I, too, would like to

ask, were there any who might answer them," Caedmon said. "Perhaps her mother told her husband the truth before she died. Perhaps he arranged for a test. There are several that could have shown the truth, both magical and mundane. We can only speculate."

Louis-Cesare's blue eyes narrowed as if he didn't like Caedmon's answer. "The Senate believes that the succession struggle has been taken into our world recently. Both Prince Alarr and another contender, a Svarestri noble named Æsubrand, have been seen in New York within the last month."

I stared at him. "Where did you hear that?"

"From Kit Marlowe." I scowled. The beetle hadn't bothered to mention that little tidbit.

Louis-Cesare had the look of someone who was thinking hard. I preferred it to the compassion on Caedmon's face. I didn't want Claire to need compassion. "If the king is dead," Louis-Cesare said slowly, "the throne is in contention. Disposing of Claire, if she is carrying the king's child, would also remove a rival."

"She must be found and the succession issue resolved," Caedmon agreed. "In the last civil war, more than ten thousand of us perished." His gaze went distant, as if he was seeing another time. "Arrows shredded the sky. Blood fell like rain. Smoke from the funeral pyres filled the air until all that was visible was a dirty haze that stung the eyes and stopped the throat." His voice thrummed in the air like a note from a plucked string, and suddenly, I could actually see the scene his words described.

Wind whipped my robes against my sweat-soaked body. Below me, a battlefield flowed away to the blood-red horizon. All around, columns of smoke clutched the sky like leprous fingers. Everywhere lay bodies in still-

*smoking armor, suffocating me with the smell of blood
and fire and burnt flesh. My hands were raw from holding the spear I had used against my enemies, but I barely
noticed. Ashes were in my eyes, ashes that had once been
the body of a comrade, an ages-old life ended by a chance
shot from a green recruit. They clung to my face, stealing
the pride of victory, mixing with my tears, threatening to
choke me—*

"Caedmon!"

It felt like someone slammed a door in my face. I was
back at the table, my heart thudding, my ears ringing, my
vision swimming in pieces. I was light-headed and dis-
connected, as if my mind was trying to occupy two places
at once and it wasn't built for it. My mouth was sour with
anguish over the death of someone I'd never met; my
veins thrummed with adrenaline from a fight I'd never
experienced.

Radu was on his feet, confusion on his face, and
Louis-Cesare was looking daggers at the guest of honor.
Caedmon ignored him, but his eyes were concerned as he
gazed at me. "My apologies, child. I would not have had
you see that."

"What happened?" To my surprise, my voice was
steady.

Caedmon appeared slightly embarrassed. "The Frum-
fórn, what you call the Fey, exist in both planes of being
at once: the physical and the . . . I suppose you would call
it the spiritual. I sit here, I eat, I talk, yet my awareness is
not taken up entirely with such things. It exists—I exist—
elsewhere, as well. And for a moment, so did you."

"Why?"

He lifted his glass slightly. "I have had, perhaps, a bit
too much of our host's excellent wine."

Louis-Cesare snatched up his own glass, sniffing it cautiously. He turned to Radu. "What are you serving?"

Caedmon smiled at his host. "I must congratulate you—smooth, velvety and with a subtle tang that lingers on the palate like perfume."

Radu looked from him to Louis-Cesare, managing to appear proud, confused and contrite, all at the same time. "I thought it appropriate, considering our guest—"

"What is it?" Louis-Cesare demanded again.

Radu was beginning to look cross. Something told me his dinner party wasn't working out quite as planned. "I had Geoffrey dilute it. Most of that is my personal label—"

Caedmon chuckled. "And the rest is some of the best Fey wine I have tasted in many a year."

"So that is what did it!" Louis-Cesare's expression could have cut diamond.

Caedmon's eyes went dark, like underwater jade. "Do you wish to accuse me of something, vampire?"

"That . . . substance . . . tortured us with memories! Made us relive things from the past. Horrible things."

Caedmon's expression was eloquent. Without saying a word, he managed to give the impression that it was an incredible trial to be forced to share a table with one so ill-mannered. Then he sighed and looked at me. "Did you also experience these memories?"

I nodded. "We thought . . . we encountered a spell at the caves. We thought the mages had left it."

"You were likely correct, although our wine would heighten the effects. Have you had any before tonight, say, within the last three days?"

"No. I—"

Louis-Cesare interrupted. "You drank some on the jet,

from my glass. I had filled a flask in the cellar of your home."

"Wait a minute. You're telling me Claire's cellar is full of Fey wine?"

"Yes. I was surprised to see it, for only the Fey can make it. I always wondered why it is so heavily regulated in our world." He stared daggers at Caedmon. "It seems now I know."

Caedmon looked affronted. "In a few days, three at the outside, the effects will dissipate. The strongest will be gone in a few hours."

I sat up, feeling more myself. I sniffed my glass, but there was no sign that we'd been drinking anything dangerous. It had merely tasted like a decent red, fruity and earthy. "What does it do?"

"Nothing harmful," Caedmon assured me. "Under the right conditions, it helps align two people's thoughts or, in lesser quantities, their emotions." Dark green eyes regarded me appraisingly. "Even with a great deal of wine, few would have been able to pull forth a memory so vivid. I could almost smell the smoke."

I nodded, thinking of the molten armor, like a black puddle around one of the bodies, and of the scalding wind. By the time it blew across all the fires, it was like a breeze straight off of hell. It brought back memories of my own, of the trenches in France after a mortar attack, and I broke out in a sudden sweat. My heart leapt in my chest, adrenaline flooding me as my perception began to skew. My throat closed once more, full of pain, choked with ashes—

Caedmon stroked his hand up my arm, brushing power along my body like liquid, dissipating the sensation. "Yes," he murmured, "unusually sensitive." He smiled reassuringly. "Do not let it concern you. What you saw happened long ago, a memory of our last great war. Even then, it took centuries to replace the numbers lost. Now, I fear, it would be impossible. Yet a struggle over the succession could provoke just such a cataclysm. Your friend must be found."

"You read my mind," I said fervently, shivering slightly from the power in that brief touch.

"The Fey don't read minds," Louis-Cesare said harshly, his eyes on Caedmon's hand.

Caedmon smiled, and it was not a particularly nice expression. His grip tightened. "Perhaps not. But we read other things. For example, vampire, I know you have a knife up your left sleeve, even though I cannot see it. The metal sings to me; it is a talent." He glanced at me, and his smile was deliberately provocative. "One of many."

Louis-Cesare's anger suddenly filled the small room like water, and in a heartbeat his eyes went from silver-tinged to as solid as two antique coins. I sat frozen, awash in a sea of power. I was beginning to understand why Mircea had wanted him along, only Daddy had failed to mention anything about the hair-trigger temper. I guess he assumed the red hair would clue me in.

Caedmon sat very still, not offering challenge but not shrinking from it, either. I wasn't sure what to do, with a suddenly homicidal vamp on one side and a less-than-pleased Fey on the other. Rock and a hard place didn't begin to describe it. I glanced at Radu, but he was sitting like a deer caught in headlights, with those beautiful turquoise eyes almost completely round.

In the end, it was Olga who defused matters by letting out a belch that I swear was a full minute long. By the end of it, we were all staring at her in sheer amazement. It's considered rude by troll standards to fail to show appreciation for a fine meal with an appropriate bodily function. It appeared Olga had liked the grub.

She patted her enormous middle and got out of her chair with all the grace of a pregnant hippo. "Good food," she told Radu, who managed to nod his thanks. "I sleep now," she announced, with an almost queenly dignity. Geoffrey scurried to lead the way back up the stairs, and Olga followed him out, her behind brushing the sides of the narrow stone stairwell as she went.

I decided she had a point. If Caedmon knew anything more, I'd squeeze it out of him tomorrow when I could think better. I pulled Stinky out of the cheese plate, where he'd decided to take a nap. "I think I'll call it a night, too," I said, hefting him onto one hip. I didn't bother to say good night. Radu was too stunned to notice, and it wasn't a Fey tradition. Besides, I had a feeling it wouldn't be.

Chapter Sixteen

Branches whipped across my face with a sting like tears. The hard-packed snow slid under my feet as I ran, but I couldn't stop or even slow down. The sky was a pale, leaden gray overhead, but darkening rapidly. There was worse weather coming. I should turn back, return to the dismal but warm interior of the tavern, but I couldn't. I would never go back there, to that malodorous, ill-lit, cramped little place. I couldn't stand to see fear in the eyes of the men, to have them shrink back when I passed, to listen to them whisper about the evil that had come among them. Even though it had been the whispers that told me of what I would find.

I paused on the top of a steep, rocky slope, drawing clear, cold air into my starved lungs. The wind that keened down crags and across frost-armored trees was bitterly cold, but it was blowing the other way. I could see the smoke, but not smell it. Not yet.

The valley stretched out in front of me in wave after wave of white, broadening and finally merging with the plains below. A few snowflakes drifted down, catching on the ends of my hair. There was a haze of white in the air *over the other end of the valley. Soon, it would consume the smoke, and what I sought would be lost until spring revealed the tattered remains. No. I had to get there first.*

I plunged down through the trees, leaping, stumbling, and half fell into a rough clearing. Now I could smell the smoke. The air was filthy with it, its acrid taste in every breath, coating the inside of my throat, my lungs. I knelt down on the hard-packed snow in front of blackened ruins that in no way resembled the village they had once been. Already, delicate crystal flakes were trying to cover the ugly, smoking remains, as if the forest resented the mar on its beauty. Soon, they would succeed.

I cautiously picked a path through the smoking ground toward the only heap that had yet to collapse. It didn't look much like a house—it could have been a storage shed or even a shop—but I didn't have time to search through the entire charred landscape for clues. I tugged on the few intact boards and they fell inward, disintegrating even before they hit the floor.

They left a hole big enough for me to slip through, but there was precious little to see. A few scorched pots, a scrap of cloth that suddenly burst into flame, crumbled to ash and blew away on a breeze. Nothing else.

I crouched among the ashes, sifting through the still-warm remains with my fingertips. What had I expected? The bodies were outside, scattered charred bones and wisps of hair crisped by the heat. Indistinguishable. I could have walked over hers on the way here, unknowing. There was nothing to show that this had once been her house, no object left intact that might have been hers, no familiar scent on the breeze. No memory, however vague, from the time I must have spent here.

Nothing.

Wet flakes melted on my face, running in cold rivulets down my cheeks. A wisp of bitter smoke curled from the rubble, extinguished almost immediately by the plop and hiss of a wet clump of snow. I looked up and realized that it was falling more heavily now, piling up in soft drifts against the black lumps outside. The wind was picking up, too. I should leave—now, before I was trapped in this white hell.

I lingered a few minutes longer anyway, strangely reluctant to go, to admit defeat. But, the cold was running chilly fingers along my body, leeching my heat, making me shiver. I backed out of the tiny space, and immediately the wind and snow reached out to grab me. The village's remains were only dark shapes now, dimly visible through a heavy snowfall. Fierce, bitter cold wrapped around me, and I stumbled over a protrusion, falling flat on my face. A quick pain pricked my palm. I looked down and saw nothing, but my hand closed over a hard, metal shape, long and sharp. My numb fingers recognized the familiar feel of a dagger.

The wind howled around me as I stumbled to my feet, but I made it to the trees and the scant protection they offered. I glanced down at the weight in my hand, and it was a treasure, the blade so bright it reflected the white-flocked canopy above me almost like a mirror. The hilt was engraved, a complex rendering that must have cost a fortune. No peasant's protection this. A grim-looking dragon, obviously carved by a master's hand, clutched a cross, its slit, angry eyes staring outward in obvious challenge.

I shoved it into my belt, glad to have the protection it offered. Even more valuable, it was something to prove to myself that I had been here, that it hadn't been just a dream. I had come, even if it was too late.

I woke up to the shrill sounds of a very unhappy Duergar. When he saw I was awake, Stinky stopped the caterwauling and crawled into my arms. I hugged him, feeling his tiny chest rising and lowering in frightened breaths. As with Caedmon, I couldn't get a clear scent reading on him, but he picked up so many smells it would have been difficult anyway. At the moment he smelled like soap and dirt and raw beef. It was oddly comforting.

I sat staring into the darkness as Stinky slowly quieted. I must have made some kind of sounds in my dream to so upset him, but I couldn't imagine why. It hadn't quite been a nightmare, although it had the flavor of deep sadness, of important things left undone or done too late. And it had been unbelievably real. I could almost smell the charred wood and feel the sharp sting of pine needles across my face. In a warm bed in a well-heated house, my body shivered from biting cold and bitter loss.

I had no idea what it meant. My dreams usually involve things jumping out at me from dark alleys, dragging me off, ripping me open—my subconscious isn't exactly subtle. The things that frighten me tend to be tangible, like the knife. But although it had borne the family symbol, it hadn't been menacing. No one had attacked me and I'd suffered no physical pain, unless you counted the slight sting of the blade's point. And if that was the worst injury I suffered on this job, I'd throw a party.

After a few moments, I gave up and tried to return Stinky to his nest of blankets on the floor. Despite the bath, I suspected he had fleas, and didn't want him sharing my bed. But he resisted, and those sticklike arms were stronger than they looked. I got a good look at him and realized that it hadn't been my distress that woke him up, after all. His little stomach was hugely distended. The

whitish gray skin under the lighter fur on his belly was
pushed out like he'd swallowed a softball.

Pitiful brown eyes stared at me, round as coins, begging me to make it better. I looked helplessly back. I'm
pretty good with battlefield wounds and emergency
triage, but nothing in my long experience taught me what
to do with a sick Duergar. Then he got *that* look on his
face, and I snatched him up and pelted for the bathroom.

Stinky was very sick. Very, very sick. And by the time
I got him and the bathroom cleaned up, I wasn't doing
much better. I'd been sleeping in my T-shirt, which had
been laundered while I was at dinner, but it was unsal-
vageable. I threw it and the bath towels in the laundry
chute and fell into bed, only to feel silken skin slide luxuriously along my own.

I sat up in time to keep Caedmon, who'd appeared out
of nowhere, from taking a swipe at Stinky. To be fair, the
Duergar had been trying to scratch out his eyes. I
snatched Stinky away and scowled at the Fey. "He
doesn't seem to like you."

The moonlight spilling in through the lattice-covered
windows painted silver diamonds across the Fey's chest
but left the rest of him in darkness. Light reflected in
those startling eyes for a moment, causing them to gleam
like a cat's caught in the beam of a flashlight. Then he
moved and was again all silhouette and shadow. "It needs
to learn to distinguish friend from foe."

"And you came by in the middle of the night to tell me
that?"

Caedmon stretched out on the bed, his silver dressing
gown falling around him in perfect folds. He ignored the
spitting and hissing fur ball a few feet away and gave me

a limpid look from under a pale sweep of lashes. "I heard the commotion and feared for your safety."

I narrowed my eyes at him. "Heard it how? The door is solid oak." Louis-Cesare might have managed it, but I hadn't expected the Fey's senses to be quite that sharp. "Are you next door?"

"Alas, no. Your uncle placed me in an entirely different wing. Judging by the smell, I believe it to be near the trash heap."

"And you didn't complain?" Caedmon had struck me as someone used to the best. And he certainly wasn't shy.

He shrugged, causing the neckline of his robe to slide off one shoulder. It was obvious that he hadn't overdressed for the occasion. "I saw no need, as I do not intend to use it."

"The Fey don't need to sleep?"

He laughed, and the old stories are true—it really was like the sound of bells. "Why waste the night sleeping when there are far more pleasant things?" He traced a pattern in the air and a stray moonbeam bent itself into the shape of a flower. It floated slowly down to rest against my hand, and I swear, for a moment it felt as if it had actual weight, before dissipating like smoke.

Stinky didn't seem impressed. He gave a tremendous heave, pushing long, twiglike toes into my abdomen, and launched himself at the Fey. A second later, he was tied securely in the blanket and tossed back in the bathroom.

I hadn't even seen Caedmon move, but there he was, casually leaning against the bathroom door. That robe was thin enough to be declared illegal in most states, I decided, slightly dazed. Then something hit the door behind him with a thud, and he sighed. "Are you certain you wouldn't like me to dispose of that creature for you?"

"I'd think two members of the Fey would get on better than you."

Caedmon tilted his head slightly, regarding me somberly. "I will ignore that," he finally said. "But I would strongly suggest that you never again compare a member of the high court with a dirty half-breed. It is rather like comparing a human to a particularly mangy cur. The nobles who know less about your world would almost certainly . . . take offense."

I sat up. "I've been called a dirty half-breed myself on more than one occasion."

Caedmon didn't reply. In fact, I doubt he even heard me. I looked down and realized that the sheet that had been covering me had slipped when I moved, and that I was currently providing him with a free show. I snatched up the coverlet and his expression tilted perilously close to a grin. I suppose gold velvet wasn't particularly off-putting.

"I appreciate the thought, but adornment is not needed. Bare skin will do admirably." He carelessly let his robe drop and turned in a full circle, hands outspread. He not only hadn't overdressed; he hadn't dressed at all. "Many strange things are said about us," he continued, "but most are quite exaggerated. For instance, the Norse believe all Fey to have a flaw somewhere on their person, a mar to their beauty. Fey women are even said to be hollow, with a beautiful frontal appearance but no backs!"

In the dim light, he burned like a pale flame, his hair a flowing nimbus around his head. And if his body had a flaw, I didn't see it. *"Nici un lucru să nu crezi, cu ochii până nu vezi."* The liquid syllables fell with ease from his lips.

My mind was busy with other things, so it took me a moment to realize what I'd heard. Seeing certainly was believing in his case, but that wasn't the point. "I thought you didn't understand Romanian."

Caedmon sat on the side of the bed, naked and gloriously aroused. "In a life as long as mine, one picks up a great deal of esoteric knowledge."

"You read the note."

He looked slightly surprised. "Of course. Wouldn't you? But obviously I could say nothing around the vampire."

"Louis-Cesare? He's all right," I said absently. Caedmon had started stroking my leg through the coverlet, and it was distracting.

"Then you have told him of the ultimatum?" He saw my expression. "No, I did not think so. I do not trust him, either."

"Why not? You just met him."

"He's a vampire, and others of his kind have been causing considerable trouble at home of late. It is possible that they are behind the current unrest, encouraging those who should know better to try for honors above their station."

This suddenly didn't sound like a seduction attempt anymore, despite the hand on my thigh. "Why are you really here, Caedmon?"

He tried to lift the coverlet, and I slapped a hand down on it. He grinned, unrepentant. "I told you. I have never before had a dhampir—I quite look forward to it. And afterward we can discuss our mutual problem."

"Let's discuss it now."

He laughed. I seemed to be providing him with a lot of entertainment. I hoped he enjoyed it, because it was all he was going to get. After my emotional roller coaster of a day, I was in no mood for games. Especially not with a strange Fey.

"But I think much better after—"

"Caedmon!"

He sighed and lay back, spilling a waterfall of pale hair over the bed and providing the moonlight with a very attractive playground. I could swear the beams seemed to bend a little around him, as if trying to touch as much of that opalescent skin as possible. "We have common cause: we both want the girl," he informed me. "You to save her from this rogue vampire, and I to discover whether or not she carries the heir."

"And if she does?"

"I will see to her safety. You have my word." That should have been laughable—for all I knew, Caedmon was here to kill Claire, not to save her. Not to mention that I never take anyone at his word, much less a very strange stranger. But when Caedmon said it, the hoary old line took on dignity and weight. I found myself oddly reassured, and it pissed me off.

"Won't it be a little difficult to guard her in New York?"

Caedmon sent me an old look. "I will not endanger all of Faerie for one woman's convenience, as you surely must know. But do not be alarmed." He stroked my side as if I were a flustered pet. "It may not be an issue. Perhaps there is no pregnancy at all, or possibly the child is female. Then your friend may stay where she likes."

"What, women don't rule Faerie?"

"Certainly not." He feigned shock. "Or, rather, not in the civilized areas. The Alorestri presently have a female leader—terrible woman—but they have always been unorthodox. It comes from living so near the border, practically side by side with the Dark. They need every pair of hands for defense, and once women are warriors, it is difficult to keep them out of politics."

"How distressing for you."

Caedmon smiled. "Oh, I like strong women, Dorina." I hadn't seen the hand that had wormed its way under the covers, but I felt it when it slid up my calf. "In fact, I prefer them."

I reached under my pillow. "And precisely how can you help me?"

He eyed me in amusement. "Refrain from stabbing me and I will tell you."

I let go of the weapon, but kept it near to hand. Caedmon noticed, but didn't appear worried. "You are in a difficult situation, little one. If you are to get back your friend, you must give this Dracula the lives of two others whom you esteem. Either that or risk attacking him and possibly losing her nevertheless. Is my summary accurate?"

"Close enough." He didn't get any kudos for that; he'd had enough clues from the letter. "What do you propose to do about it?"

"You need two men," Caedmon said. "One is already here, and the other—" He thumped himself on the chest theatrically. "I can be him."

I stared. It was hard to imagine anyone who looked less like Mircea. "You? Not on the darkest of nights! I doubt you could fool a myopic servant, much less his own brother!"

"You forget my people's ability at glamourie. I assure you, I can."

I shook my head. "And you forget the vampire sense of smell. Drac could tell the difference from across the room—from across several rooms! He'd never buy it."

"But I will not be across the room, little one. He will never see me so close—"

I was about to ask how he expected to manage that when I heard something. It was faint, but this house had settled long ago; there was no reason for the stairs to creak unless someone was on them. Judging by the way his hand tightened on my leg, Caedmon had heard it, too. So much for questions about his hearing—it was at least as good as mine.

Or maybe better. "Louis-Cesare," he mouthed. I don't know how he knew, but I didn't question it. The last thing I needed was for Louis-Cesare to think I was in collusion with the Fey. He was suspicious enough as it was. Caedmon seemed to reach the same conclusion, because he tossed the coverlet on the floor, threw a leg over me and started kissing my neck.

I pushed at him, but it got me exactly nowhere. I was getting extremely tired of strong manly types. Whatever happened to the ninety-pound weaklings? The kind I could maybe still beat up? "What are you doing?"

"Providing me with an excuse to be here," he murmured in my ear. Then he bit it.

"Caedmon!"

"Dorina!" Louis-Cesare's muffled voice came through the thick wood. I stared at it, wondering why I suddenly felt guilty.

Caedmon took the opportunity of my distraction to cop a feel. I didn't bother to repress a squeal, since I knew his excuse wouldn't work. I had a reputation for being very cautious about my lovers—with good reason. I'd had more than one try to kill me. No way was Radu going to believe I'd invited someone I'd just met for a rendezvous.

The Fey had started working his way downward. Warm lips slid along my collarbone, putting the long line of his neck directly under my nose. I did the only thing I could under the circumstances. I bit it.

Caedmon leaned into the feel of my teeth in his flesh as if to a caress. It startled me enough that I jerked back, ripping my fangs through his skin instead of sliding them out as I'd planned. Blood dripped down the perfection of his chest in a dark stain, and he groaned loudly. I don't think it was from pain.

The door to the hall burst its hinges and Louis-Cesare stood there, pale and deadly, with eyes like liquid mercury. Someone grabbed me around the waist. It wasn't Louis-Cesare, because he had moved like quicksilver, getting an arm around the Fey's injured throat in a stranglehold. Caedmon didn't appear to have noticed. His eyes were on me, and an odd little smile played about his lips. "If you wanted it rough, my dear, you had only to say."

"Let me go," I ordered Geoffrey. My only answer was having the coverlet, which he'd snatched from the floor, thrown over me. "I mean it! Put me down this minute!" I felt myself being carried into the hallway, but the damned blood loss ensured that there was little I could do about it. "Goddamnit, when I get my strength back—" I heard what sounded like a war starting up behind me, but I couldn't see anything for the damned sheet. I decided on a different tactic. "If you let them kill each other, Radu will stake you!"

"The master's son is quite able to take care of himself. And I very much doubt he will kill an honored guest. Sadly, none of us are permitted to do so." The tone was Geoffrey's usual imperturbable one. But he let my head bounce off a half-dozen walls, vase-topped plinths and wall fixtures on the way to wherever we were going.

Chapter Seventeen

"You should have eaten your dinner, Dory," Radu reproached me. "Chef was quite upset. That is a very complex spell, you know, and he thought you didn't like it. And that was on top of The Pear Incident." His tone gave it capitals. "He'll sulk for a week. You'll be lucky to get a peanut butter sandwich tomorrow."

"That actually sounds pretty good." At least I wouldn't have to hunt it down before I could eat it.

Whatever Radu was about to say was cut off by a loud crash and a curse from above our heads. The sounds of carnage had been going on for the last five minutes. I thought it a shame—if they trashed the place, Radu would probably redecorate. I glanced around, fearful for the tasteful original touches that remained. I wasn't scoping a way out, but Geoffrey tensed from his position by the door. He'd given me the velvet bedspread, which I'd draped togalike around me, but he obviously wasn't going to let me rejoin the fun.

"Since you brought up food—," I began. If I was trapped in the living room with Radu, I figured I might as

well eat something. I needed to get my strength back.
Among other things, I had a butler to beat up.

Radu sighed. "Sit," he commanded. "I'll have something brought. If Chef hears that you were prowling
around his space tomorrow, I shudder to think of the con-
sequences."

"If he's one of Mircea's stable, surely you can order
him to—"

"Of course he isn't," Radu said, tugging on an old-
fashioned bellpull on the far side of the fireplace. "Have
you ever heard of a vampire chef?"

"Well, no, but—"

"Nor will you. Death, you know," he said archly, as a
mirror shattered somewhere above. "Ruins the taste buds."

"But you eat, occasionally anyway, and Mircea—"

"I'm second level, Dory, and your father is a step
above me. With power comes certain advantages, but do
you really think the world's handful of upper-level masters have nothing better to do than braise a leg of lamb?
That's what we were supposed to have tomorrow, by the
way, with homegrown rosemary, but who knows what
we'll get now. Chef threw it out after The Pear Incident."

I waited while a servant came in and received instruc-
tions. Somewhere in the distance, it sounded like an entire
china cabinet had been pushed down a flight of stairs.
After the man left, I glanced at Radu. "What, exactly, is
Louis-Cesare's problem?"

"Which one?" I raised an eyebrow; apparently Radu
hadn't forgiven his son for the scene at dinner. Suddenly,
a speculative gleam lit his eyes. It made me nervous. "He
tends to be very protective of women," he said thoughtfully. "You're a woman, Dory."

"Thank you for pointing that out. But I didn't think dhampirs qualified."

The ceiling shook, so hard that some of the plaster cracked and fell down in small chunks. Radu smirked. "It appears you've been upgraded." I moved my chair slightly, to avoid being directly beneath the large, swaying chandelier, and looked up to see him regarding me with that same disquieting look. "Perhaps he'll finally stop blaming himself over that girl," he mused.

I knew I'd regret it, but I asked anyway. "What girl?"

"Christine, the perpetually tragic." Radu threw a new log on the embers, apparently solely for the chance to stab viciously at it with a poker. He saw my expression. "You haven't heard the tale?"

"Should I have?"

"Not really. It's long and extremely depressing. Suffice it to say that, centuries ago, Louis-Cesare brought her over in order to save her life. She had been tortured because of him and he felt responsible. But he never stopped to consider that she was an ardent Catholic, and moreover one who believed the old stories about us. She thought the change had damned her, and informed him once she rose that she would have preferred a true death."

"So he killed her?"

Radu rolled his eyes. "If only!" he said fervently. He saw my expression and grimaced. "Don't give me that look—you haven't met her. The woman is impossible, always in some trouble or other. Most recently, she was kidnapped by Alejandro." Radu said it like I should know the name. "The leader of the Latin American Senate," he added impatiently when I looked clueless.

"So why is Louis-Cesare here, instead of off rescuing her?"

"Because no one knows where she is, of course!" Radu looked at me suspiciously. "Are you being sarcastic?"

"No, I just can't imagine the family swallowing an insult like that."

"You simplify everything," Radu said crossly. "Not every problem can be solved by whacking it with a stick!"

"No, just nine out of ten."

Radu visibly restrained himself. "An underling of Alejandro's, a vampire named Tomas, challenged him," he explained with exaggerated patience. "Alejandro wanted Louis-Cesare to be his champion. But the rumors about that court—it's disgraceful."

I didn't need to ask what he meant this time. It was infamous for sadism, even among vamps. "I take it Louis-Cesare refused?"

Radu nodded. "He told him that part of the purpose of a challenge was to weed out incompetent, cruel or insane masters—and that if he couldn't fight his own battles, he didn't deserve his position."

I winced. Diplomacy didn't seem to be Louis-Cesare's strong suit. "So Alejandro kidnapped Christine to make it his battle," I guessed. "Fairly standard."

"It is too bad you weren't there to warn him at the time," Radu said acerbically. "In any case, Louis-Cesare defeated Tomas, but refused to kill him, as the man had done nothing wrong. So Alejandro refused to release Christine, claiming that he had stipulated to let her go only when the threat was gone, and that as long as Tomas lived, the threat remained."

"And the Senate couldn't intervene on his behalf," I reasoned. Agreements between masters were rarely challenged by the Senates, especially if the two involved were members of different Senatorial bodies. It was too easy to have a personal quarrel escalate into war.

"Which is why this has dragged on for so long."

"How long?"

Radu flipped a hand. "Oh, a century." I stared while he went blithely on. "And ever since she was taken, Louis-Cesare hasn't been the same. He knows she may be suffering, and he feels responsible for it—twice over, in fact. He's become extremely morose about the whole thing."

"Radu! The woman was tortured, forced to join the undead and kidnapped, all because of him. Has it occurred to you that maybe he has something to feel guilty about?"

"You sound just like him!" Radu said irritably. "He didn't torture her; the Black Circle did."

I blinked. "Come again?"

"They were trying to steal power, as usual. She was an untrained witch, you see, before the change. Very powerful magically, but her faith ensured that she wouldn't accept it. Any manifestations were ignored, or put down to the devil's work." Radu shook his head. "It was only a matter of time before the dark found her."

"Louis-Cesare said you rescued him from some dark mages once. I assume we're talking about the same group?"

Radu looked annoyed. "He shouldn't have mentioned that."

"Why not?"

"Because I promised Mircea not to have any contact with him."

"Because of that time thing," I guessed.

"What time thing?"

"The one I'd know about if I kept up with the family."

"Oh, yes, exactly. But then, when no one could find

him . . . well, what was I supposed to do? Leave him to be tortured to death every night? Anyway, don't mention this to your father. Mircea doesn't need to know everything."

Amen to that. "Did you really bring down the roof?"

Radu ignored the question with aristocratic disdain. "As I was saying, Christine has had several hundred years to recognize that we aren't monsters. I explained to her myself that vampirism is a disease. She doesn't blame weres for transforming into slavering beasts on a regular basis, but she continues to view us as just above Satan himself. It's insulting."

"Maybe weres haven't screwed up her life," I commented, flinching at the sound of glass breaking somewhere above us.

"The point is, he doesn't allow himself to get close to anyone anymore. It isn't healthy!" Radu pronounced, as if he were the poster child for mental health himself.

He started pacing, the hem of his elaborate teal dressing gown swirling around his agitated feet. He looked like a man at the end of his rope and I made a brilliant deduction. "There's more than Louis-Cesare's issues troubling you."

Radu shot me a less-than-fond look. "My brother is trying to kill me—again—and in order to prevent that, I'll likely have to kill him instead. My well-ordered house has been disrupted by some extremely strange, not to mention violent, creatures, and my chef is absolutely livid about—"

"The Pear Incident. Yes, I know." I looked at him narrowly. Something about that list worried me. "You said you had no problem with killing Drac. You agreed with me that it was the smartest course. You aren't getting soft on me, are you, 'Du?"

It worried me that he didn't immediately respond. He had come to rest by the mantel, but wasn't staring at the fire. The portrait above it seemed to have riveted his attention instead. The new log popped and sparked in the silence, while the old one slowly crumbled to a soft redness beneath.

"I was eight," he finally said, "when we first became hostages. Vlad was thirteen."

"Radu! Don't tell me you're getting sentimental." I couldn't believe he was doing this. "He tried to kill you. Repeatedly!"

"It isn't sentiment," Radu insisted, gazing at the still-vibrant colors of the portrait. "Nor some rusty conscience stirring to life. I never really had much of one, you know. Even before the change."

"What, then?"

He glanced over his shoulder at me. "Why do you think I have this painting, Dory?"

"Well, he was your lover. I suppose—"

He laughed, but it was harsh. "We were never lovers. At least, there was no love involved in anything we did." He fiddled with some of the ornaments along the mantel, as if his hands needed something to do. "As a prince, Mehmed had a map, showing not only the Turkish lands but all of Europe, too. He told me that there was destined to be only one empire in the word, one faith and one king. It was the belief that I could forward his ambitions that attracted him to me. There were dozens of handsome *oghlanlari* at court—royal pages—who were better-looking than I. They chose them as much for appearance as ability, whatever they said. And none of them ever took a sword to him."

"You attacked the sultan and lived?" I grinned.

"Sultan's son, as he was at the time, and yes. He propositioned me and I took a swing at him. Not that I wounded him much—I was never a swordsman. And then I showed my true mettle by running off and hiding up a tree. I only came down when he swore a solemn oath not to kill me." He smiled bitterly. "I got off lightly because he knew I might be useful. They needed a puppet prince, and Vlad wasn't cooperating."

"It surprises me that you'd keep a picture of him. Personally, I'd burn it." The servant returned and placed a tray in front of me. It was chicken, and thankfully it wasn't clucking.

Radu dismissed the vamp and joined me on the couch. "I don't keep it out of fondness, Dory, but as a reminder of how easily I was once molded by another. I became exactly what my captors wanted—I dressed like them, thought like them—I even converted. I swear, for a while, I was more Turkish than they were. I keep the painting to remind me of what I was."

I snorted. "Give yourself a break. You were a kid. They brainwashed you."

Radu shook his head. "As much as I would like to claim that, it's only partially true. I was eleven when he seduced me—a child by today's standards, but in the world we inhabited, that was not so young. Mehmed had begun ruling a province of the empire at the same age. I was brainwashed because I allowed myself to be. The only alternative was unthinkable, so I took the path of least resistance. It took me a long time to understand: ultimately, we are all responsible for our own actions."

"As Drac is."

Radu was quiet for a moment. "I sometimes wonder which of us they molded more, myself or Vlad. My delusion was shed long ago, but he is still trapped in his. They made him a monster, Dory, in those dungeons."

I bit back a comment out of respect for what Radu had been through, but I wasn't sure if I'd be able to stay quiet if he elaborated. It wasn't like I hadn't heard the story before. It went something like this: Drac was a heroic teenager who refused to be cowed by Turkish threats. Whenever he was taunted by his guards, he taunted them right back. Every insult of theirs was met with one of his, usually even more inventive because he'd had enough education to provide inspiration. He cursed them, their ancestors and their Prophet. He was brutally beaten, then thrown back into a solitary cell from which he could see the even-worse punishments visited on others. The execution methods varied depending on the extent of the prisoner's offense: some were given a plain old hanging, while others were shot full of arrows, beheaded or, worst of all, impaled.

Impalement was reserved for those guilty of the most heinous crimes, but in a time of war, it ended up being used fairly frequently. The teenage Vlad got a ringside seat for one on a weekly basis, and apparently took notes. He watched the crows pick at the carcasses that were left under the hot Turkish sun until they were only blistered meat. Maybe he managed to endure his punishment by dreaming of impaling his torturers one day—I don't know. But when he finally took the throne of Wallachia, it became his favorite way of scaring away invaders and enforcing his decrees.

Almost any crime, from lying and stealing to killing, could be punished by impalement in Drac's reign. Mircea once told me that his brother placed a golden cup on display in the central square of the city to be used by thirsty travelers. It was worth more than a lifetime's wages for a worker, but it was never stolen. I would be willing to bet that nobody even thought about it.

Even more famously, two Turkish ambassadors to Drac's court failed to remove their turbans in his presence. Drac ordered that the hats be nailed to their heads so they would never have to remove them again. Likewise, he once held a picnic in the middle of a field of impaled bodies just for the hell of it. And, when one of his nobles held his nose to keep from gagging at the smell, Drac had him impaled on a stake higher than all the rest, so that he might be above the odor.

He justified his actions by pointing out the lawlessness of the land before he took over. The problem with that excuse was that Drac's "law and order" had ended up killing far more of his people than even serious disorder would have done. I looked up some statistics once, out of curiosity, and discovered a chilling fact: in his short, six-year reign, he'd had at least forty thousand victims. No, the expediency excuse had never worked for me.

"But, in the end, it was Vlad who chose to use the tactics they taught him, both against the Turks and his own people."

I blinked at Radu, surprised to hear my own thoughts echoed back to me. "It's getting a little hard to follow your logic, 'Du," I told him honestly. "Are you saying that you *are* in favor of killing him?"

Radu shot me an irritated look. "I am saying that, while it may be a necessity, I will take no pleasure in it. Not because I have any affection for Vlad—in truth, I don't believe I ever had any—but because it might have been me. If he had been born with the face to tempt a prince, and I had been left in the dungeons, would our positions be reversed today?"

So that was what was eating him. "I doubt it, 'Du. You said it yourself—you were always very different people."

"True. I doubt I would have survived the dungeons. I have never been brave."

"You would have survived." Louis-Cesare's harsh tones made me jump. I whipped my neck around, and there he was, less than three feet away, and I hadn't heard a thing. If I didn't get some sleep soon, I was going to be completely useless. Caedmon was nowhere in sight, but since Louis-Cesare wasn't covered in blood, I assumed he was still alive. "There are many forms of courage," Louis-Cesare said. "You would have done what was necessary. But no more."

I nodded in agreement and gave Radu a slightly greasy kiss. "The Turks didn't make Drac a monster, 'Du. They just brought out the one that was already there."

Louis-Cesare and I exchanged a look. The expression in his eyes said that Drac was suddenly a lot closer to a permanent resting place. I didn't know what had caused the change of heart, but I wasn't about to complain. For once, we were in perfect agreement.

Radu escorted me back to my room as soon as I finished eating. I waited until I heard his almost silent footfalls fade, then sneaked off to find Caedmon. Or what was left of him.

After a fruitless half hour of searching, I was starting to wonder if Louis-Cesare had decided to hell with the truce and fed him to Radu's little pets. Then I heard a car pull up outside. I made it to the entryway in time to see Caedmon walking out the front door, looking his usual perfect self. There didn't appear to be so much as a hair out of place.

"So you are alive."

"You seem surprised."

"A little."

Caedmon smiled. "Your vampire is overproud of his abilities. It is a weakness. Some would exploit it."

"But not you."

"Another time, I might be tempted."

"And now?"

"Now I am slinking away in shame after assaulting the daughter of the house," he told me cheerfully. "Walk with me, Dorina. Allow me to humbly beg your pardon for my egregious conduct before I depart."

I followed him outside, where a car driven by one of Radu's human servants had pulled up. We skirted it, moving far enough away from the house that, with a little luck, we might avoid being overheard. Caedmon leaned on the fence by the pen where Radu was keeping his esoteric collection. The growls, squeals and shrieks coming from inside provided extra sound camouflage.

"I am likely being watched," Caedmon informed me, "to ensure that my inherently depraved nature—that is a quote, by the way—does not lead me to further indiscretions whilst I grovel in mortification."

"So grovel."

A climbing rose bent in to caress his hand. He stroked its stem affectionately. "You first."

A tentacle covered in brown fur slammed into the wards in front of us and sizzled for a second before dropping to the ground. The air took on the scent of frying bacon. The new members of Radu's menagerie appeared to be fighting for dominance with the old ones, and a couple of the wilder hybrids were attempting to tear each other apart. The less dangerous creatures cowered on the sidelines, probably hoping to snack off the losers.

Caedmon regarded the display with distaste. "Out of curiosity, what are your vampires attempting to create?"

"Nothing. They captured these from the Dark Circle. Or so they said."

"Why would anyone wish to create such obviously useless specimens?" I shook my head. I still didn't have an answer. "If one was of a suspicious bent of mind," Caedmon mused, "one might almost think they are creating the more hideous creatures as a distraction, to ensure that their real experiments, should any be found, are lost in the crowd."

"Maybe. But which are the real ones and which the red herrings?"

"Better to ask why the vampires are so interested in them. They are not known for charity. They become involved with those likely to bring them profit or to pose a threat."

Long talons slashed the earth and great furrows of turf were ripped up, until a huge creature, birdlike only in its overall shape and leathery wings, leapt down from its perch on a small shed. It landed in the middle of the battling group and began ripping into the other creatures with a gleeful disregard for its own safety. It soon scattered them with cobra-swift strikes from its talons and lethal, pointed beak. When the slaughter was over, instead of pausing to feed, it paced the confines of the pen. A long tail slithered across the ground behind it as it searched for a new victim.

"So which are we looking at here?" I asked, strangely fascinated.

The creature's frighteningly humanlike eyes locked with mine. Beside me, Caedmon laughed. "If I find out, perhaps I will tell you. We are partners, are we not?"

"Are we?"

"Certainly." He lowered his voice. "I shall make my ignominious exit, and return tomorrow night as Mircea."

"I still don't think it will work." The bird creature started to feed, ripping great strips off a half-dead furred body that twitched in a vain effort to get away. I was reminded disturbingly of Radu's dinner party, especially since those too-human eyes were still on me. They looked hungry.

"Because I was interrupted before I could explain my ingenious plan," Caedmon informed me blithely. "It is simple enough: Dracula will see 'Mircea' arrive, and shortly thereafter, the wards will fall. Naturally, he will believe that you are fulfilling your part of the agreement and mount his attack. I will have enough of my supporters stationed around the perimeter of the estate to deal with him, and to rescue the Lady Claire."

"And if he doesn't have her with him?"

He sighed happily. "Then we will have to find a way to convince him to tell us where she is." I got a momentary flash of Drac being tortured by the Fey. It was almost orgasmic.

"Sounds great," I said sincerely, "except that there are about a thousand things that could go wrong, starting with your disguise."

"It pains me that you have such little faith," he reproached.

"You have to be seen being welcomed into the house as Mircea, or Drac won't buy it. But if anyone sees through your disguise, the game's up. Louis-Cesare will never let us lower the wards and endanger 'Du's life. And with them still up, Drac can't get within a mile of this place. So unless you have enough retainers to cover a perimeter that large, when we don't even know from which direction he'll come at us—"

"You should trust me, little one. In comparison to the machinations that occur every day at court, this is a minor intrigue. As I see it, there is only one possible snag—interference by the vampire."

"Radu doesn't make a habit of answering his own door. It's Geoffrey you have to fool, at least long enough to get in, and that won't be any easier. He's one of Mircea's stable. I think he'll know his own master!"

"Not him. The other. Louis-Cesare."

I eyed the Fey. I didn't see any seeping wounds or missing limbs, so it looked like he had been able to handle Louis-Cesare well enough. "He isn't likely to be hanging around the foyer, either."

"No, but he may be, as you say, 'hanging around' other places, such as the source of the power for your uncle's wards."

"Which would be?"

"The first thing you will discover for me. The wards should let me in when I return as they already know me as a friend of the house. I will shut them down after I arrive, but I will not have time to search the house. Second, you will need to ensure that Geoffrey is out of the way and that someone with less knowledge of Mircea answers the door. One of the humans would be best. And third, you must distract Louis-Cesare long enough for me to lower the wards."

"Is that all?" I asked sarcastically.

"It should suffice." He smiled with amused tolerance. "I will arrive at nine p.m. tomorrow. That gives you more than twenty hours. I am confident you can manage in that time."

The only reason I didn't bite him was the certain knowledge that he'd enjoy it. "And why should I trust you? A strange Fey I only met yesterday?"

Caedmon smiled gently. "I think you know why."

I thought I did, too. I covered his hand with mine. "As long as we have an understanding about Claire. No forcing her into Faerie against her will." Caedmon gave me innocent eyes. I pushed his thumb onto one of the rose's longer thorns, deep enough to hit bone. "If you betray me, I'll gut you and feed the remains to Radu's menagerie."

Caedmon pulled his hand off the rose and brought the bleeding digit to my mouth, smearing blood along my lips. "You say the sweetest things."

"I mean it, Caedmon."

He bent his head and gently kissed away the blood. The taste of his lips was an explosion of sweetness, like summer condensed. "I know."

Chapter Eighteen

Fresh blood at midnight isn't red. It's a purplish black that easily blends into the shadows. I plunged my foot ankle-deep into a frost-covered puddle of it and swore softly. The upper crust was only half-frozen, and the sticky sludge beneath oozed around my rag-covered foot sickeningly. I jumped to the side, scrambling for purchase on the icy rocks and slippery dead leaves, leaving a trail of dark gashes in the snow.

When I finally forced my eyes upward, I saw what I'd expected. The naked man impaled on a thick wooden stake above me had skin the color of the snow piled all around, and never moved except when the vicious wind tossed his limbs about. The eyes were frozen over with a thin layer of ice, making them glitter with a parody of life in the moonlight. I looked away, but all I saw was a line of similar corpses bordering the path down the mountain, disappearing into the dark. It looked like my quarry was home.

A flight of crows, startled by my presence, left their perch in the skeleton of a tree and wheeled out over the valley, a score of dark shapes dipping erratically in the wind. The full moon illuminated thick woods glittering with frost, cut through by a silver ribbon of river. It would have been breathtaking, if I'd had any to spare. I didn't. I hadn't dared take the main path up the mountain; even on a night like this, it was guarded. I'd had to crawl up a crumbling dirt path engineered by goats and practically impassable by anything not on four feet. The only sight that interested me now was the two cloaked guards standing in the shadow of a nearby stone overhang, the fog of their breath thick as smoke as they stomped their feet, trying to get some circulation going.

The massive slab over their heads had a beard of long icicles, like a mouth with sharp, jagged teeth. It almost looked as if the entryway were trying to eat them. The gray hulk of Castle Poenari rose menacingly behind them, sparkling with the same ice that crunched under their boots every time they moved. A bitter wind howled around the mountain, and I could hear one of them struggle to breathe, the air rattling wetly in his chest. But they hadn't dared to light a fire. Their master frowned on any sign of weakness, and I guess they preferred pneumonia to ending their lives writhing on the end of a stake.

Since I shared that view, I decided that a frontal assault might not be the best plan. I was confident that I could take on a couple of half-frozen guards, but if one managed to raise the alarm, it would put an early end to my evening's plans. I looked for other options, but there weren't many. Despite being located at the peak of the mountain, the castle was surrounded by high, deep walls of natural stone and featured three tall watchtowers designed to keep people like me outside.

I became well acquainted with those walls, since I spent the next half hour scaling them, clinging to the few narrow ridges where the outer stones didn't fit together *perfectly. Every time I stayed in one place more than a few seconds, my hands froze to the rock, ensuring that when I moved on, I left a little more flesh behind. My movements caused chunks of ice to cascade from the edge down the fifty feet of dirt slope that surrounded the castle, to the steep drop-off below. I looked down once, and immediately regretted it. I didn't look again.*

The wind almost knocked me off twice, bringing with it stinging bits of ice that scoured my skin and threatened to blind me. It howled around my ears like an angry demon, seeming to take it personally that I continued to hold on by my fingertips. More than once, I was bashed against the stone hard enough to have me worrying about the state of my rib cage. And when I finally made it to the top, I had to wait, hanging on the almost featureless outer surface of the walls, until the guards on patrol moved away.

As soon as they did, I hauled my half-frozen body over the parapet and dropped to the ground. It was less of an improvement than I'd hoped. The biting wind was gone, only to be replaced by the bone-chilling cold of winter air trapped inside thick stone walls. Even worse, I had no idea where I was supposed to go and the castle was crammed with soldiers. Everywhere I looked, bodies flowed through the shadows before coming out into the moonlight.

I'd hoped that an assault in the middle of the night would find most people asleep, but I should have known better. Considering whom I was dealing with, night around here was probably busier than day. I finally lost patience and crossed the open courtyard at a run. For a wonder, no one saw me. It helped that most of the guards were huddled into their cloaks, more worried about not freezing to death than about possible intruders.

I entered the castle unseen. The cavernous arches of the corridors were immense above me, and even my softest footfall seemed to ring into infinity. I ghosted along the walls and somehow made it to the large main hall without being seen. The air was filled with the clatter of plates and goblets, and lanterns pushed at the darkness, spilling large puddles of light on the floor and dispelling the concealing shadows. It was obvious that I would have to wait for the group of soldiers gathered along one of the room's long tables to finish a late meal before I continued. The smell of their food made my stomach growl; how long had it been since I'd eaten? I couldn't remember, but the scent of beer and cold lamb caused my abdominal muscles to clench uncomfortably.

I turned my attention to the sight of a new-looking tapestry on the back wall. It showed an armor-clad figure at the head of an army, who I assumed was either the father or the son because he was riding a dragon. Both belonged to the Order of the Dragon, a group created to fight the Turks, which had given them their famous nickname. "Dracul" means dragon, so "Dracula" was literally "son of the dragon." It seemed a good bet that the painting was of the son—he was spearing an enemy on the point of a pike.

The soldiers finally left and I moved into the echoing space, trying to keep to places that did not have dried rushes on the floor to crackle underfoot. The ceiling above was so high that it disappeared into darkness, and seemed to pick up every stray echo of sound. At last, I reached a high, arched door, leading to a short, dimly lit corridor. Nearby, a set of stairs wound up into blackness, the lack of torches an encouraging sign, as only my prey was likely to be able to see his way without them.

I reached the top to find myself facing a heavy oak door. It was cracked slightly, pouring a line of orange fire-light over the stones. I edged forward cautiously and nudged the door open with my foot. The room inside was large, but more cozy than the vast dimensions of the rest of the castle, and was perfectly circular. I peered around and realized two things: I was alone and I wasn't likely to stay that way for long. The lit candles told me that much; no one bothered to light an unoccupied room, especially if the means to do so, like most other supplies, had to be dragged sixteen miles up a mountain. Someone was ex-pected. I just hoped it was the right someone, since I really didn't feel like wading through half the guards to get to him.

The room was full of booty. Several dozen plush prayer rugs brightened the walls, helping to insulate the cold stone. Many of the silver and gold vessels scattered about had Arabic words enameled onto them, the carpet was a Persian in blues and burgundies and the shiny brass lamp that hung from the ceiling didn't look local. A sudden wave of exhaustion made the exotic colors run together, and I swayed slightly as the last of my adrenaline was used up. I hurt everywhere, but that was nothing new. What undid me was the sight of a real bed dressed with a pile of lovely furs and blankets, so high that they made a mound. I walked toward it unconsciously, my head spin-ning from pain and wonder.

I must have made it, because I fell onto something soft and squashy that my dazed senses identified as a feather mattress. The impact hurt my bruised ribs, to the point that I think I passed out for a minute. When I came around, I discovered that my first impression had been wrong: I wasn't alone.

I was slumped over a body that was seeping a crimson stain onto what had been clean white sheets. It didn't have a pulse, but that didn't worry me. His kind never did unless trying to pass for human.

My heart was beating so hard in my chest that I thought it might shatter a rib. I noticed irrelevantly that the blood was ruining his clothes. His dazzlingly white tunic had been embroidered at the sleeves and around the slit collar in bright red and gold, but darker patches now marred the pattern in several places. I couldn't tell how bad the wounds were, because although he was in bed, he hadn't bothered to divest himself of his fur cloak. It was so silky that my hands completely disappeared in it. I stroked it softly, unable to believe my luck.

I stared down at my victim, and slowly undid the rag holding a sharpened wooden sliver around my waist. He didn't move, not even to open his eyes. I told myself to get it done, but I hesitated. I'd never killed a sleeping vampire. Their daytime resting places were too hard to find to make it worth the effort; I caught them animated and bent on mayhem, not lying around wounded and helpless. This was so different from the fight to the death I'd envisioned that I simply sat there a moment, staring at him. He wasn't at all what I'd expected.

His face had the same expressive eyebrows and long, dark lashes he'd passed on to me, but with strong, masculine features underneath that made them look quite different. He was very good-looking, but except for shadowy depressions in his cheeks, he was as white as bone. He looked ill, which was absurd, since vampires don't get sick. Of course, the blood might explain it; the coverlet beneath him was virtually soaked with it. I had an awful idea: had someone beaten me to it? Had someone else stolen my revenge, while I struggled not to fall off that damned wall?

My hands started shaking and I couldn't seem to stop them, and my breathing was shallow and uneven. I sat back down on the bed until the room stopped swimming, then started to pull off the remains of his ruined shirt. The wounds underneath were deep, with a few showing bone, but none looked to be in the right area for a heart blow. So why didn't he wake up?

I told myself that a dead vampire was a dead vampire, no matter how he got that way. I got a better grip on my stake and decided to stop worrying about who had attacked him in such a half-assed way and just get it done. I positioned my makeshift weapon over the heart, but again I hesitated. I wanted him awake for this, aware enough to know who was about to end his miserable life and why. It shouldn't happen like this, without him even waking up. Somehow, it seemed almost obscene.

"Are you going to kill me or wait for me to die of old age?" I jumped at the sudden question, and the hand that had been lying so utterly still and limp a second ago caught my wrist. I struggled, but found that I couldn't move. I stared at my arm as it hung there in the air, the strength that had never before failed me suddenly useless. "It will be a long wait, I assure you."

Bright amber eyes looked me over as he easily rose to a sitting position, his other arm grabbing me by the neck like an errant puppy. He smiled, showing fully extended fangs. "You had your chance. Now it is my turn."

I fought and thrashed against the iron hold, but it was no use—I couldn't move. I screamed, as much in rage as in fear, and the hold tightened, tearing more cries from my throat. A hand clamped over my mouth and I bit it.

Someone swore, and it was in French, not a language I'd have expected under the circumstances. It brought me back to myself slightly. I opened my eyes to find Louis-Cesare bending over me, worry clearly visible in his blue eyes. Déjà vu.

"Dorina!" Louis-Cesare's face blurred in and out. He looked like he was struggling to stay calm. He wasn't struggling half as much as I was.

I'd met Mircea for the first time in a bar in Italy, around the turn of the seventeenth century, not in a castle in Romania. Especially that one. Cetatea Lui Negru Voda, the Citadel of the Black Ruler, was the real castle Dracula. It had originally been built in the fourteenth century, but Drac rebuilt and expanded it after he returned from his Turkish adventure. The Turks had let him go after learning of his father's assassination and Mircea's burial alive at the hands of the nobles of the town of Tirgoviste, who supported a rival family on the throne. They knew he'd stir up trouble as soon as he got home, giving the Wallachians something else to think about besides fighting them. And in that regard, Drac hadn't disappointed.

He had decided that the only thing that would protect Romania from outside invaders and inner rebels was a show of strength. On Easter Sunday 1459, he started as he meant to go on. Drac invited the nobles of Tirgoviste to a lavish dinner party. Once there, they were arrested and forced to march fifty miles to the town of Poenari, located where the Carpathian foothills turn into real mountains. Those who survived the trek were put to work building him a fortress on a steep precipice overlooking the Arges River. The job continued for months, until their elaborate banquet attire rotted and fell off their bodies—then Drac ordered them to keep working naked. It was the harshest kind of physical labor, mixing mortar and lugging huge stones and timber up the steep mountainside. Many died of fatigue and illness, but some survived. Drac examined his new fortress, decided there was nothing major left to do and ordered the remaining workers impaled.

The castle had, not surprisingly, developed a bit of a reputation. It was said to be haunted by some of the thousands who had died there. Maybe that's why, when tourists come all agog to see Dracula's castle, they are taken to Bran Castle in Transylvania, even though the only connection with it Uncle ever had was to besiege it once. But it's in good condition, while Poenari's version is a hulking ruin, a great lump of stone and misery, with pieces regularly working loose from the grainy old mortar to drop onto careless-tourist heads.

And Bran doesn't give people nightmares.

"Dorina! Are you all right?" Louis-Cesare shook me, and from his frantic tone, I had the impression that it wasn't the first time he'd asked.

The problem was, I didn't know the answer. I'd been under a lot of stress for a month, without Claire to help mitigate it, not to mention I'd almost died twice in one day. Even with my past experience, that could bring on a troubled night. It could be just a nightmare. But the images had seemed so real, much more detailed than my usual dreams. What if the spell had combined with the wine to dredge up something long buried?

But that didn't make sense. I'd never been to Poenari, not in its heyday and not afterward. And if I'd never been there, it couldn't be some residual effects of the spell. So why could I almost feel the rough texture of the stone under my fingertips? Was it a nightmare, or something more? And if it was more, how was I supposed to find out? I couldn't very well use a flawed memory to search for gaps in the same memory.

Mircea, I thought blankly, what did you do?

"Dorina!"

"I don't know," I answered truthfully without thinking about it, and it wasn't the right answer.

Louis-Cesare began fumbling around in the bedclothes. Hands slid over my body, looking for an injury. I quickly recalled that I wasn't wearing anything but a pair of panties, having not had anything suitable for nightwear after Stinky ruined my tee. I realized when a drop of water hit my nose that Louis-Cesare wasn't much better off. His hair was wet and the only article of clothing on that long body was a damp white bath towel draped loosely around his hips. I couldn't understand why he'd been showering in the middle of the night, until I noticed a sliver of daylight peeking through a gap in the heavy curtains.

It was morning. Morning of the day I was going to get Claire back. I started to get up, only to have Louis-Cesare force me back down. "You will stay here until I have a physician called."

"I'm okay—"

"Which explains why I have had to hold you down for the last five minutes to keep you from tearing at your own skin!"

"—and doctors can't do anything more for me than you already did."

"Dorina! You are ill!"

"Louis-Cesare! I'm a dhampir! I go crazy on a regular basis. Just one of the joys of being me." I tried to rise again, only to find that I couldn't. It was no longer sexy, I decided. "Let me the hell up!"

Louis-Cesare was suddenly attacked by a growling

Stinky, who wrapped his stick arms and legs around the vamp's head and held on for dear life, making a horrible screeching sound the whole time. "Don't hurt him!" I yelled as Louis-Cesare reached for the little guy.

A pair of exasperated blue eyes stared at me out of a mask of matted gray fur. But the hands trying to prize Stinky off gentled. He pried the Duergar away and held him at arm's length. Stinky gnashed useless fangs at him and spat. "It does have a curious charm," he murmured.

"Will you please let him go? He thinks you're trying to hurt me."

Louis-Cesare's face lost its amusement. "You do well enough at that yourself," he said shortly. Stinky was bundled into the bathroom for the second time and Louis-Cesare turned to regard me with crossed arms. I suppose the gesture was an expression of impatience or exasperation, but all my brain could manage to focus on was that towel. It looked to be in immanent peril of falling off entirely, barely clinging to the muscular swell of his hips—smooth-skinned hips glistening with water and flecked with soap suds.

I tried to look away, but the man was perfection, beauty given a face and body. The line of his throat, the sleek muscular sweep of his torso, were pure masculine sensuality. And in the dim light filtering in through the curtains, he almost looked like he'd been oiled. My mouth went dry.

"Dorina!" Louis-Cesare had moved, one of those lightning-fast transitions that vamps use when they can't be bothered to appear human. He was by the bed staring down at me, and that was definitely exasperation on his face. "Have you heard anything I have said?"

"Not really."

I suddenly felt the press of the intimate little room, with its lush carpets, gaudy gold-papered walls and rich, dark furniture. A breeze from the open window shifted around my legs, pushing into the sheet covering me. It was a tentative little thing, just a filmy tickle, but I was cold and he stood there still flushed from the heat of his bath. The soap smelled good on him, and the faint musk rising from all that warm skin smelled better. I shivered, hard.

Louis-Cesare's breathing had roughened as my gaze lingered on his body. "You will not distract me!" His words were a surprise, because that hadn't even occurred to me. Hadn't, but should have. The last thing I wanted was to discuss my dreams, especially the last one.

A smile flirted with my lips. I stroked a hand up the interior of one strong thigh, shivering at the whiplash of sensation, the blaze of skin on skin. "You mean like this?"

I found myself on my back, with Louis-Cesare above me, his eyes flashing blue gray lightning. He looked powerful, hard, aroused. Stunning. "I do not believe that this was one of your fits, Dorina. There was no provocation—"

I took advantage of his nearness to run a hand down his chest and along the tight belly, until I hit the terry-cloth barrier just below the curve of his waist. He grabbed my hands before I could tug the towel off, and leaned over me, trapping them on either side of my head. "So what are you planning to do?" I grinned up at him. "Tie me to the bed?" As soon as I said it, I regretted it. Louis-Cesare looked like a man who has finally heard a good idea. "Don't you dare!"

My arms were pushed over my head. I would have protested, but the action brought that perfect mouth close enough to kiss, so I did. He tasted right the way water tastes right—simple, necessary.

Louis-Cesare leaned into the kiss for a moment; then tore away, his eyes blazing with something wild and seductive. The look alone was enough to send a wash of desire through me. It didn't help that he was close enough for me to reach out and tangle his hair in my fists and pull him close, close enough to kiss again, close enough to make him moan. Just thinking about it made me ache, a sharp knife of want twisting in my stomach. I curled my hands around slats in the headboard to keep from grabbing him.

"I have found nothing else that succeeds with you!" The voice was deep and rough, with only a faint echo of his usual smooth tones. "I make logical arguments, but you do not hear."

"Don't," I warned him in a strangled voice. "I've had a hard month. I ache in more places than I can count. The last thing I need is a lecture."

He hesitated for a moment; then his palms smoothed back down my arms to cup my face. The usually so-controlled features were strangely tender. Those blue eyes met mine, asking, seeking. "What do you need?"

I should have laughed, should have thrown it back in his face as he did once to me. But my gaze had fixed on his mouth, on those impossibly enticing full lips. "Guess."

The softness of his mouth was a surprise. I leaned into the insistent sweetness of the kiss, loving the way his lips caressed mine, how he managed to infuse the lightest of touches with a longing that made me weak. I let go of the slats, wanting to touch him, but he curved one of his hands over both of mine, curling them tightly around the headboard. For some reason I didn't protest, possibly because his other hand had found my hip and slowly moved down until it cupped my backside. His mouth had moved along my jaw to my neck as his hand caressed me, as gently as if I were made of glass.

He didn't ask what was wrong; he must have known I wouldn't tell him. He simply resumed kissing his way downward, until my heart beat rapidly beneath his lips. He met only sleep-warm skin because the sheet had at some point slipped to puddle around my waist. "Everything about you is provoking," he breathed. "Your voice saying outrageous things, your body striding up and down, giving me orders, and your taste—"

The thought skittered across my mind that if this was foreplay, sex with Louis-Cesare would probably kill me. I felt the headboard crack under my hands and decided that there were worse ways to go. And then it happened again. Images flooded my brain, richly detailed and absolutely breathtaking.

Dorina, naked on a bed, head dropped back to expose that lovely throat, luscious mouth open in soft moans, sweat trickling between those perfect breasts, glistening on a waist so tiny I could span it with my hands. There is no part of her I haven't ached to touch: the soft roundness of her cheek, her beautiful throat, her breasts. I am possessed by an angel with ridiculous hair, flashing eyes and a devil's mouth.

Seeing myself through Louis-Cesare's eyes, feeling his emotions as well as my own, left me speechless—and extremely confused. He dropped his head farther, to where the sheet was covering my lower body. I was about to ask him what was happening, when he traced my lower stomach with his tongue, then, with no more warning than a gleam in his eyes, almost roughly plunged it into my navel.

It was a shock, delightful, delicious and unanticipated, sending liquid shivers to the pit of my stomach. No one had ever brought me so quickly and deeply into pleasure, but suddenly my whole body convulsed with it. His lips moved slightly downward, finding the flesh below my belly button, and his warm breath against me made me squirm. His eyes had bled to liquid silver. They held a question, but I couldn't find my voice. I managed to nod, and was rewarded with a smile, heart-stoppingly sweet, as he slowly eased down the sheet.

He stroked the backs of my thighs with his fingertips and I lifted up, letting him ease off my panties. He paused to kiss my lower stomach before baring me completely. His thumbs found the sensitive skin at the backs of my knees, and big, warm hands smoothed up the insides of my thighs in a butterfly touch. They made a more purposeful caress down, in an unspoken appeal. I opened for him.

Louis-Cesare took his time, stroking, kissing and licking a trail upward from my knees. Then his head dipped between my legs and that hot tongue flicked higher. That rough liquid texture explored me, but only briefly, shallowly, teasingly.

The velvets under her are not as soft as her skin. Closing my mouth over the center of her. That racing pulse whispering how fragile she is, how delicate—careful, must be so careful, until she melts with sweetness, like honey on my tongue. He suddenly stopped altogether, and I wondered if he'd noticed that his thoughts were leaking all over the place. No, he couldn't stop now! The heat of his breath over me was enough to rip a groan from my throat. Pleasure and frustration combined to drive me crazy, and he wasn't even doing anything.

Louis-Cesare caught my eyes with his. "I want to part you and open you and go deep." The words whispered their way across my skin as if they had a life of their own. I shivered from his voice alone, and his hands tightened on my thighs. He paused to wet his lips. "I want you to come with my tongue inside you."

We stared at each other for a heartbeat. Whatever he saw on my face must have reassured him, because he made a sound, deep in his throat, then that shining head moved down again. One hand curved around my hip, lifting me up so he could taste me better. *Tongue pressing just so, slipping into the hot slickness of her, drinking deep, hearing her cry out. Her back arching, hips bucking, pressing up against me in a quickening rhythm, her scent maddening me, her taste exploding on my tongue. My blood singing in my ears, racing through my veins faster and faster. Her body is so sweet—*

I started feeling shaky. This was exactly what I'd wanted, just what I'd needed, except that I hadn't dreamed it would feel like this. Too much—it was like looking into somebody's unedited thoughts and it was just too damn much. Every sense was heightened, leaving me able to feel the tiny ridges on Louis-Cesare's fingertips as they caressed me, hear the whisper of his hair over my skin, taste the soap on his body.

Dragging my tongue over her, plunging it into her. I can sense the pace she wants; I know the touch she craves. So beautiful, head flung back, body spasming under mine, sweat sheening her thighs, she is slick under my hands, moaning, straining, tousled hair dripping, hands clutching the headboard desperately. Beautiful, so beautiful.

I gasped, fists clenching with the unexpected strength of the sensations flying between us, no longer quite sure where my pleasure ended and Louis-Cesare's began.

Every touch of his hands was a double sensation—I felt it on his skin, in his emotions, as well as in my own. Double vision didn't come close to describing it—it was double everything. And it was too intense, far too intense. God—I could drown in this, echo after echo, never stopping, until my heart gave out and I literally died of pleasure. But I also couldn't stop, couldn't ask him to stop—the very idea was insane. No one could pull back from pleasure like this.

As its full force struck, I went wild thrashing and crying and coming harder than I could remember. I collapsed like a first-timer, boneless, my heart thundering in my ears. For a moment I thought I blacked out, but I could still feel my heart beating wildly in my chest. Then I opened my eyes, which felt a little odd, as I couldn't remember closing them. Louis-Cesare's face was flushed and wet, his hair stuck to his face in strands and the gray blue eyes glittered. His hand moved to languidly stroke my stomach, while the tip of that talented tongue ran along his full lower lip, as if licking up the remnants of some decadent dessert. It was the most erotic thing I'd ever seen.

I finally found my voice, although it wasn't completely steady. "What . . . what *was* that?"

"Fey wine," he said after a moment, his voice hoarse. "It has . . . lingering effects."

I stared at him, speechless. That had been the remains of a diluted drought imbibed twelve hours ago? No wonder the stuff was regulated! In its pure form, it could drive a person mad.

Even if I hadn't had the memory of his emotions, it would have been obvious that he'd enjoyed his work. My hand ran over him, and I almost came off the bed from the echo of that simple touch. Under that soft cotton he was hard as a rock. I would have thought I was incapable of feeling anything more, maybe for days, but I resonated with his need as if it were my own.

"You could use some attention."

"*Cela m'est égal,*" he murmured, removing my hand and placing a light kiss on it. I frowned. He didn't mind? Who did he think he was kidding? I wasn't accustomed to leaving partners unsatisfied, and at the moment I was feeling extremely generous.

I used my free hand to trace the lean line of a thigh muscle with a fingertip, stopping just short of the hem of the towel, and his whole body quivered in response. That was more like it. Louis-Cesare covered both my hands with his own, raising them back over my head as his lips met mine in a long, sweet kiss. "If you wish to please me," he murmured when we parted, his eyes amused for some reason, "obey me in this."

I was about to ask what he meant when I tried to move my hands. And found that I couldn't. "I will send for a healer," he said, getting up.

It took me a few seconds to process the fact that he had actually tied me to the bed. "These won't hold," I told him furiously, tugging on the sheets he'd used for rope. The high thread count didn't tear easily, though, and despite the fact that the headboard was already cracked, it didn't seem to be giving, either. I finally realized that Louis-Cesare had wrapped the sheets around the sturdier frame, and it was metal. "Son of a bitch! Let me go this instant—I mean it!"

"Do not thrash about, Dorina, you will only injure yourself further. I will release you when the doctor arrives."

I lay back, preparing to squelch the panic I should be

experiencing at being confined. It hadn't risen yet, but I had no doubts that it was only a matter of time. "There won't be anything of this bedroom left by the time she gets here!" I warned him.

"Under normal circumstances, perhaps not. But your strength is considerably under par at the moment."

"When I'm sane maybe," I said, wrenching on the sheets. All that did was to tighten them further. "But this is sure to bring on a fit. And you've seen how much fun those can be."

"Your control is not so poor, surely," he said with a frown. "Mircea did not mention—"

I glared up at him. "Claire has been missing for more than a month."

"What does that have to do—"

"She exerts a dampening effect on my fits. Without her, my control is slipping. Fast. Now let me up!"

He paused, but his eyes held what looked like genuine compassion, the earlier humor dissipating in the face of my distress. After a moment, he reached for the restraints. "I did not realize that the woman was so important—," he began; then both of us swiveled toward the door. I'd been so distracted that I hadn't heard it open, but the cooler wash of air from the hall had gotten my attention.

"I hate to interrupt," Radu said, "but I was wondering if either of you did anything to cause the wards to fail just now?"

Chapter Nineteen

"My lord . . . I can explain—," Louis-Cesare began, looking less than certain that he could do anything of the kind.

Radu held up a hand. "I am sure there is a perfectly good reason why my niece is naked and tied to her bed. I am also equally certain that I do not wish to hear it."

Louis-Cesare's hands fumbled a little, but they managed to get my wrists loose. I snatched up my jeans. "What's wrong with the wards?"

"They went down a few—" Radu stopped as the windows abruptly darkened, almost like night had decided on an encore. "Well, that's not right," he said crossly.

I got to the windows a half second before Louis-Cesare. The view wasn't encouraging. The sky boiled with greenish black clouds, laced through with silver streaks. The air pressure built in palpable waves, like a snake drawing its coils in closer and closer. A flash hit a decorative planting of three palms near the driveway, splitting one in half. The reverberation rocked the floor, sending vibrations up through my feet straight into my skull.

"This isn't the right time of year for storms," Radu was saying behind me. I didn't answer, being too busy watching shadows shift in the vineyards beyond the house. Dark shapes unfurled leathery wings like tattered cloth in a breeze. Cold little pinpricks started running up and down my spine.

" 'Du—when you say the wards fell, which ones exactly did you mean?" The shapes converged on the house, sweeping toward the window with the heavy wingbeat of large black birds. Below, I could hear something scrabbling with swordlike claws for purchase on the stucco.

"Why, all of them." He moved closer to see what had caught my attention. "They're on a common power source. I—"

A birdlike head on a serpentine neck smashed into the window, the glass distorting its face into a grinning rictus. Radu stumbled back with a small cry. The head disappeared and a talon-ended claw smashed through the window, reaching past me to grab at him. I beat at the thing with a bedside lamp, but it bounced off the leathery appendage without even leaving a dent, sending a throbbing pain up my arm to my shoulder.

Louis-Cesare grabbed the thing's leg and jerked it inward. Its wings stuck in the space between the window and the small cast-iron balcony beyond, keeping it from advancing. It also blocked its buddies from getting inside—at least for the moment. I got a good look into its greenish yellow eyes, but only animal intelligence looked back. I wondered where the smart one was.

Louis-Cesare had spun Radu out of reach. "You must raise the wards—quickly!"

"That will trap us in here with them!" The thing in the window began to scream and vibrate. A look out of the small side windows explained its problem—its buddies had started to rip into it with the viciousness of a pack of

wild dogs, rending the great wings as easily as black
cobwebs.

"Better that than allowing them to escape into the surrounding population! They are only dumb animals—we
will corral or destroy them."

Radu shook his head, and the flash of fear over his face
told me that I wasn't the only one to have noticed something odd about a few of those experiments. I found the
peasant tunic half-hidden under the bed and pulled it on.
"Is there something you want to tell us, 'Du?"

He swallowed. "I can't. The Senate—" The thing fell
out of the window, screaming, released by its buddies ripping off a wing. It was immediately replaced by several
others, their claws scrabbling for purchase on the delicate
balcony railing, their teeth snapping as their great wings
pummeled the air.

"The Senate isn't here!" I reminded him. "It's our
butts on the line! Come on, 'Du—give."

Louis-Cesare beat the things back with an armchair,
which he stuffed in the hole left by the shattered window.
I looked at it dubiously, doubting that wood and leather
would hold them for long. I'd barely had the thought
when the makeshift plug exploded through the room,
wedging in the open door to the hall, blocking our retreat.
One of the smaller creatures managed to scramble inside
the room, only to have Louis-Cesare grab it around the
throat and squeeze hard enough to cause its eyes to bulge.

"La salle de bains, vite!" He gestured at the bathroom
door, and I shoved Radu through with no ceremony.
There was a connecting door to the adjacent room, which
turned out to be Louis-Cesare's.

Unfortunately, a similar assault was taking place at his
window. A gust of rain-laden wind slapped me in the face

from the shattered panes as I pushed Radu toward the hall. I didn't make it. A long claw snaked in and plucked me off my feet.

I had a confused moment of disorientation as the bird creature launched itself off the balcony. Then one of my feet came into contact with the railing and I managed to get one hooked under an iron scroll. My leg was almost wrenched from its socket when the thing began trying to dislodge me, beating the air with its wings, throwing arcs of rain into my face, screeching in fury. Then its other claw struck me in the chest, hard enough to drive the air from my lungs and to fill my throat and sinuses with acid. Lightning crackled, the sky trembled and I couldn't breathe.

I let go, but before the creature could make any headway, someone jabbed a long shard of broken glass into the thin, leathery hide stretched over its rib cage. A long, red gash appeared on the black skin for an instant, before the drenching rain washed it clean. I had a moment to see Radu grasping for my hand; then the claw retracted and I was falling.

Halfway to the ground, I suddenly stopped. The pain of talons sinking into my calf let me know that I hadn't been miraculously saved. A bony claw held me suspended twelve feet over the ground, dangling helplessly. I had exactly a second to think about what I could do about it with no weapons when white-hot agony spiked down my back. Another set of claws had descended on my shoulders, talons sinking deep. I clenched my teeth on a scream as the two creatures began pulling in opposite directions. It didn't take a genius to figure out that much more of this would solve the argument by ripping me in two.

A long-handled knife came out of nowhere, severing the throat of the creature holding my calf. Unfortunately, it didn't retract its claw before plummeting to the ground, its weight taking me and the bigger creature along for the ride. We landed with a teeth-rattling crash, with me on top of the dying one. I ripped the knife out of the remains of its throat, but even though I had a weapon, it's hard to hit something you can't see. The talons sunk deep into the muscles of my shoulders ensured that I couldn't turn around to deal with my other attacker.

Luckily, one of the other creatures decided that the position also ensured that my attacker had limited movement, and tore into it. Its claws ripped out of me and I turned, sinking the knife deep between its ribs, angled upward. I felt the resistance as the knife cleaved the heart in two, heard the great muscle stagger and begin to fail; then the creature spasmed and fell, almost crushing me beneath it. I pulled out the knife and jumped back, just in time to meet my new attacker. How the hell many of these things were there?

This one was larger than the others, so big that its huge wings were useless appendages; it had had to wait for prey to fall to the ground. Prey like me. We slowly circled the huge rib cage of the dying creature, its torso heaving with shuddering breaths. The knife was so slick with blood and the now-pounding rain that it kept threatening to slip through my fingers. Even worse, this creature seemed smarter than the others. It didn't have the human eyes that had so disturbed me on the leader, but it watched me with calculation nonetheless, waiting for me to make a mistake. I had the feeling one would be all it took.

The electricity had come back on when the wards had failed, causing the landscape lighting to click on. The coziness of the golden light was in stark contrast with the angry silver streaking through the sky. It cast odd patterns

of brightness into the gloom, allowing me to see other assorted horrors slinking past, giving us a wide berth as
they moved toward the house. Louis-Cesare's face stared
down at me, a pale oval against the darkness, and called
out something. But his voice was swallowed by the
downpour, and I didn't have time to worry about it because the creature attacked.

It was like facing three opponents instead of one.
Leathery wings batted me in the face with the force of
solid punches, claws ripped at my skin, and that vicious
beak tore into the ground right beside me, carving a fur-
row in the earth where I'd been standing a half second before. I lashed out, but it moved with liquid speed, vampire
quick, and my knife only bit into a small section of wing.
It flexed its talons and its long, whipping tail, a piercing
scream of defiance issuing from its throat.

I quickly realized that it was faster than I was. It
seemed impossible—only master vampires could usually
make that claim—but there was no doubt about it. I got a
hand on it once, but the rain and the slick texture of its
flesh made it as slippery as oiled glass and I couldn't keep
hold. Within seconds, it became a moot point as I was
forced to give up all thoughts of attack. It took everything
I could do to avoid being shredded by those ferocious
claws or impaled by that razor-sharp beak.

My predicament wasn't helped by the fact that the
creature's clawed feet churned up the dirt of Radu's once-
manicured yard, mixing with the rain to create a slippery,
treacherous surface. Its greater weight gave it an advantage in keeping balance, one I didn't have, especially not
in bare feet. I swerved out of the way of a darting claw
and slid in the mud, ending up right beneath its under-

belly. Its tail snaked out, coils whipping around my neck, immovable as granite.

I took the only chance I had and slashed upward, hitting what felt like a bulging wineskin—a leathery exterior over a soft center. A flood of blood and ropy intestines drenched me in a sticky, sickening mass. I tried to fight my way free, but the creature wasn't dead yet, and it intended to take me with it—the coils of that deadly tail tightened until I couldn't breathe at all.

I slashed at it with the knife, finally managing to hack the tail in two and to draw a shaky breath when the coils slipped off. But although I was free, there was nowhere to go. The only way to avoid that deadly beak was to stay out of its way, and there was only one chance to do that.

The huge body had sagged over me. I widened the slit and crawled inside the split cavity, burrowing upward. I couldn't see, and trying to breathe was once more impossible. I fought blindly, the knife going ahead of me, ripping through everything in its path. I felt it in my arms when I hit bone, and pushed upward in a single heave. Ribs popped, flesh parted and the creature fell, its writhing jostling me this way and that, its screeches muffled by its own body.

Its movements finally slowed, but I had lost my grip on the knife in the upheaval. I began tearing at the tissue surrounding me with my hands. I was almost out of time—I had to breathe soon or suffocate—but I would likely be blind for a moment when I pulled out because of all the blood. I had to be sure the thing was in no shape for one final attack at that point, or I'd be as vulnerable as it was now.

I grabbed at anything, ripping and clawing, but my strength wasn't up to par and without the knife I couldn't do much damage. The body had stilled around me, and my lungs were burning in my chest, screaming at me to take the risk, to get out while I still had enough strength. I started moving backward, and then realized I had a new problem: the thing had collapsed onto its belly, closing the wound and cutting off the only exit I had. I pushed and fought from inside, but the leathery skin was impervious to all attempt to break through it. It stretched, but held, and my efforts were growing feeble as the burning in my chest spread weakness throughout my body.

One of my searching hands encountered something soft that had a familiar resiliency. Biting it open, I smashed my face against the cavity, and inhaled. I'd been right—the creature's lung had retained enough air for one breath, and despite being damp and fetid, it was sweet in my lungs.

It bought me some time, but not much, and my limbs still felt like they were moving through molasses. Then my hand closed around something long and sharp and hard, and I gripped it like the lifeline it was, even though the blade cut into my palm. I was trying to turn it, to get a cutting edge against that damnable hide, when a gaping hole was slashed in the darkness. A cascade of water droplets blew in on me, wetting my face, and I gasped in a great lungful of the cold, clean scent of rain.

"Dorina!" I was hauled from the bloody cavern, my body making a squelching sound as it tore free. "Dorina!" Blood was in my ears; I could barely hear, but the sound of Louis-Cesare's voice got through somehow. I pried open my eyes, blinking God knew what aside, and he caught me in a fierce embrace. His saber arm was crimsoned to the shoulder, and his other hand was gloved with gore. I'd never been so happy to see anyone.

"I'm okay," I croaked, wondering if it was true as the

world spun around me. I felt myself being lifted. One second we were by the carcass, the next beside the house. Louis-Cesare pressed me against the stucco, gripped my face in one large, muddy hand and kissed me. I fought free after a moment, gasping for air, trying to keep the heavy mass of hair dripping down his bare shoulders from suffocating me. "Not the time!" I choked.

"Est-ce que vous êtes folle?" His voice was harsh.

"No more so than you," I gasped, spitting out something squashy that I didn't look at too closely. "And considering everything, I really think you can use the familiar."

"I told you that I was coming—" For some reason, he was shaking.

I had a bad taste in my mouth. I spat and it was red, but I didn't think the blood was mine. "What? Did you think one little bird was going to do me in?" The liquid fatigue in my muscles forced me to lean against the house to keep from falling over. I took a deep, shuddering breath. "Hell, that was just a warm-up."

Louis-Cesare muttered something I didn't catch. Probably just as well. I ran a trembling hand over myself to check that all my parts were still there. I appeared to be okay, other than for assorted claw marks. The only ones that worried me were those on my abused shoulders. They were bad enough to limit my movement.

I tried to step out of the circle of Louis-Cesare's arms—we were under an overhang from the roof, and considering that I was soaked with bird goo, I preferred to stand in the rain. But he tightened his grip and glared at me. "You are not going anywhere!"

"Oh, okay. You're going to round up Radu's little horrors *and* guard him from whatever has already slunk into the house, *and* get the wards up all by yourself?" I gestured at the shadowy landscape, where all that exotic foliage was rustling menacingly. Some of that was due to the rain, but not all.

"I will do what I must." Despite his mud-splattered skin and the fact that the waterlogged towel was drooping dangerously, he managed to make it dignified.

I bit back a smile and a very inappropriate comment. "I can take care of myself."

His jaw clenched. "As you did a moment ago?"

I opened my hand and showed him the knife I still clutched. "Yeah."

Louis-Cesare stared at it for a long moment, expressionless. "You're hurt," he finally protested.

I brushed a piece of intestine off my shoulder. "It's hurt worse."

"You can assist Radu—"

"I know jack about wards," I said flatly. "I know a lot about killing things. You and 'Du get the wards up around the pen, and make sure they recognize me. I'll do the rest."

No answer, just the interlacing of warm, strong fingers with my own. The knife was tugged from my grip. I let it go—I needed something bigger anyway.

"Louis-Cesare . . ."

"No!"

"Louis-Cesare," I repeated quietly. "Look at me. I'm covered in blood and entrails. I just gutted a creature that would send most people into gibbering fits. And speaking of fits . . . well, let's not. The point is, I can take care of myself." I took a breath. "I'm not Christine."

I braced for anger about my prying. What I got instead was a look so far from anything I'd expected that it took a second for me to recognize it: the quiet, professional assessment of a colleague. "I will send you assistance," he finally said, "and once the perimeter wards are up, I will return to help you." A sword was pressed into my hand.

I nodded. "Deal." I glanced down and couldn't help but smile just a little. "And Louis-Cesare—get some pants on."

Geoffrey joined me a few moments later, as I was tying up something I'd fished out of the bushes. It was mostly tail and claws and a lot of bumpy protrusions. I'd eyed them with concern, but apparently they were just cosmetic, because nothing spurted or oozed out at me.

"We're going to need more rope," I told him, "a lot more. I found some in a gardener's shed, but there has to be a hundred of these things roaming around, and 'Du doesn't want us to kill any more than we have to."

"I will bear that in mind," he replied, and stabbed me.

I saw the blade coming. Unlike my own, deliberately dulled versions, he was using a nice, shiny one that gleamed like a beacon in the dim garden light. But I wasn't quite fast enough to completely avoid it. It bit into the fleshy part of my side instead of hitting my heart, not that that improved my mood any. "You're the traitor!" I said stupidly, stumbling backward.

"You should have died in San Francisco," he said furiously. I tripped over a garden hose and fell against a birdbath, while barely avoiding being skewered again. As it was, I lost the sword, which went flying out of my hand like a silver arrow. Either Geoffrey was faster than he had any right to be at his age, or I was slowing down. Either way, not good.

"Sorry to disappoint you," I told him, and threw a heavy earthenware pot, complete with hibiscus, at his head. He dodged and snarled. It looked really odd on that usually stoic face.

"Or at dinner—how did you know not to eat?" he demanded. He seemed highly incensed that I'd been so hard to kill.

"You poisoned Stinky!" Okay, now I was pissed. I drove the plinth from the stone birdbath into his gut, hard enough to make him fall to his knees retching. I looked around for the basin, which would hopefully be heavy enough to finish him, but in the few seconds it took me to locate it, Geoffrey was gone. His knee prints in the dirt were still there, rapidly filling with water, but there was no sign of the vamp himself.

"The freak ate from your plate—it was intended for you!" He fell on me out of the branches of a dripping bottlebrush tree, knife flailing, but I skipped back. One swipe of his weapon ripped a gash in the peasant top, but missed my skin. I had a second to be glad it was Radu's wardrobe being decimated this time, instead of mine, while Geoffrey went sprawling in the mud. Then he was up and coming at me again.

I brought up the basin like a shield, hearing the scrape of the knife on stone, then slammed it into his face and leapt back, skirting a trellis that ran along one side of the house. It created a small, very dark arbor, shadowed by grapevines as big around as my wrist. Something snatched at me from the foliage. I got a quick impression of a scaly body, a naked tail and a sharp snout with needle-thin canines. I retrieved my sword, which was still quivering from landing point first in the ground, and poked at it. It retreated, chittering in displeasure. Unfortunately, I didn't think Geoffrey would be so easy to

deter. After attacking me, he'd have to kill me, or Mircea
would rip him to pieces.

I scanned the garden, sword in hand, but didn't see
him. The inside of the arbor was like a dark wound beside
the brighter stucco—I couldn't see inside it, and the rain
and the ominous rustling of the vines meant that there
was little chance of hearing him. If he was even in there.

I glanced around, but there weren't many other hiding
places in the immediate vicinity. The palm trio was still
smoking, despite the downpour, and was no longer in a
position to hide much of anything. The graveled path to
the front was clear, and the nearest vineyard didn't start
for a couple dozen yards.

I saw something move among the vines, a black ripple
that darted between rows, silent and dangerous. Slipping
quietly on the wet earth, I moved out of the ring of lights
circling the house and into the darker reaches beyond. It
wasn't as dark as I would have liked—the lightning had
grown worse, flashing silver strobes across the landscape—
but it was better than remaining silhouetted against the
floodlit stucco, practically begging to be attacked.

The air quivered like something stretched beyond
bearable tension as I slowly crossed the yard, closing in
on whatever was hiding in the vines. These weren't
nearly as large as the venerable specimens in the arbor,
which looked like the conquistadores themselves might
have planted them. But they were mature enough to give
decent cover. It wasn't until I was almost on top of my
prey that I realized what it was.

A figure stepped out of the vines, wreathed in shadow,
its face only a pale smudge through sheets of rain. My
hair was plastered to my skin, my tunic heavy and waterlogged, but around the newcomer a bright pennant of hair

lifted on a gust of breeze. Eyes clear as water met mine.
I gripped my sword tighter and thought some very rude
things. Fey. Perfect, just perfect. Then the attack came,
blindingly fast and unbelievably strong, and I didn't have
time to think at all.

My sword was struck aside in the first rush, and went
spinning off across the vineyard. It had to have gone fifty
yards, and in the dark among the dense planting, I'd never
find it. Something slashed through my sleeve and I
jumped back, behind a vine that suddenly leapt off its row
to slither around my feet, dumping me in the mud. I
rolled aside and something silver flashed down, quick as
the lightning and just as deadly, missing me by maybe a
millimeter.

And then everything stopped. "Heidar!" The voice was
shrill. "What do you think you're doing? Stop it right
now!"

I sat up, and although mud and blood and a few bird
entrails that I must have missed fell into my eyes, I didn't
need sight to recognize that voice. "Claire!"

"Dory—where are you? Freaking rain! It's after nine
in the morning and I can't see shit."

I got to my feet and eyed the very abashed-looking Fey
in front of me. Lightning flashed, showing me blond hair
and pale blue eyes. Not the one I'd been dreading, then.
Claire burst through a gap in the vines and reinforced that
impression by smacking him on the shoulder. He had to
be six feet five and was surprisingly well muscled for a
Fey, but he cringed slightly.

"What did I tell you?" Claire was furious, and in char-
acteristic fashion, she decided to set him straight before
bothering with the pleasantries. I leaned back against a

fence post and waited it out. Luckily for Radu's future harvest, the vine kept its leaves to itself.

A few minutes later she wound down enough that I managed to insert a sentence into the tirade. "I've been looking for you," I offered mildly.

Claire's forehead unknotted slightly. "I knew you would. I was only gone a couple of days, but the damned Fey timeline isn't in sync with ours and . . . anyway, I hope you didn't worry."

I thought back over the last month, to the sleepless nights and the restless days, to the fights and the calls and the threats and the beatings, and I smiled. "A little."

"I'm really sorry, Dory, but you won't believe everything that's—" She caught me peering at her face and grabbed her nose, looking mortified. "Oh, God! Am I morphing? Tell me I'm not morphing!"

"Uh. No. Are you supposed to be?"

"Only in Faerie, so far." Claire looked relieved. "Don't stare at me like that! It freaks me out."

"Sorry. I just . . . aren't you supposed to have pointy ears or something?"

"Vulcans! Vulcans have pointy ears. Do I look like an alien to you?"

"No, but you never looked much like a Fey, either."

"I would like to apologize for my mistake, lady," Heidar said, jumping in during the nanosecond pause in the conversation. He'd obviously been around Claire for a while. "I was under the impression that you were a vampire."

"I get that a lot," I said kindly. "I'm Dory."

The Fey brightened. "Is this where I introduce myself?" he whispered in a loud aside to Claire, who looked horrified.

"Oh, God."

"I have been practicing," Heidar informed me proudly, then launched into a recital of what had to be fifty names, most with explanations.

"Never ask them their names," Claire advised as Heidar rattled on. "Just. Don't."

"Okay. It seems you've been busy." I poked her in the middle. "Anything in there I should know about?"

She blanched. It made her freckles stand out like spots on white paper. "How did you hear about that?"

"Are you kidding me? So far, I had that runt Kyle—"

"I hate him. I hate all vamps. That complete *toad*, Michael—"

"—tell me you were pregnant by a vamp—"

"—kidnapped me and—Kyle said *what*?"

"—and then a member of the Domi shows up and informs me—"

"The Domi sent someone *here*?"

"—that you're actually pregnant by the late king of the Fey."

"Late?!" Heidar squeaked.

I stopped and looked at him. His hair was miraculously still mostly dry, despite the downpour. Claire's, on the other hand, was as wet as mine, frizzing and straggling around her face like a dead animal pelt. It was hard to believe they were both half-Fey.

"Let me guess, you're Alarr?"

"It means Elven general," Heidar enlightened me automatically. "But, please, lady, I beg of you, tell us what you know of my father."

"I'm sorry, not a lot. Only that he's missing and presumed dead."

"That is impossible," Heidar said with conviction.

I didn't feel like arguing the point, especially when I suspected he might be right. "Okay." I looked at Claire sternly. "You want to tell me what's been going on?"

"It's a long story."

"Hit the highlights."

"Well, Heidar and I met at work—he'd come to bid on something—only my boss—you remember Matt, the gorilla in a suit?" I nodded. Her former boss at Gerald's did look frighteningly like a shaved ape. "He'd decided to sell me to Sebastian, who'd finally tracked me down, only it didn't work out quite like they'd planned. Heidar and I escaped into Faerie, but the damned Svarestri *attacked* us. We got away—you don't even *want* to know how— and made it back to New York, but when I stopped by the house, Michael grabbed me for the bounty—" She stopped suddenly, looking stricken.

"Which you failed to mention to me."

Claire rallied quickly. "I knew how you'd react, Dory! And you don't know what the family is like. They're . . . they can be very bad news."

"So can I."

"See!" Claire screeched. "See, I knew that's what you'd say! You'd have gone stomping off—"

"I don't stomp."

"—to see Sebastian, and my slimy excuse for a cousin would have had you killed! He was surrounded by bodyguards all the time, the little shit, and most of them were mages. With some of their spells, well, they can take down vamps, you know?"

"And we're talking about him in the past tense because?"

"Oh, Heidar killed him," she said, as an afterthought. I decided not to ask or we'd be here all night.

"So Michael kidnapped you and took you where?" I prompted.

"To Sebastian, for the bounty. Only of course Seb was dead and the family was busy fighting over the inheritance and couldn't be bothered. Michael was actually pissed at me, like I'd *asked* him to kidnap me or something. But I told him I was carrying a half-Fey child and that its father was the king, and he couldn't kill me then because the Fey would—"

"Separate his worthless head from his spineless body," Heidar managed to get in.

"So you *aren't* pregnant?" I asked for clarification.

"Um," Claire said. And stopped.

"Er," Heidar added, blushing.

I looked between the two of them. Obviously, Caedmon's story had been off by a generation. Then I recalled something. "A couple of *days*?!"

"Um, yes, well, it was more like a week, actually—"

I held up a hand. I was soaking and cold and my shoulders hurt. The details I could do without. "Just tell me how you got away from Michael. I know you were at the caves."

"That place," Claire said, wrinkling her nose in Virgo disgust for such disorder. "Michael decided to sell me to some dark mages he knew for a null bomb. He figured he could at least get something for his trouble that way, only the mages said they wouldn't touch me until they checked with the Fey. But Michael had been carting me around for over a day trying to get a paycheck and—"

"Where were you?" I asked Heidar.

He looked sheepish. "I opposed Claire's wish to return to your home. The Svarestri do not know the human world well, but they have occasionally ventured here. I considered the risk to be—"

"I was only going to leave a quick note," she said testily.

"So you ditched your only bodyguard with—let's see—the mages, the vamps and Fey after you?"

"There's no reason to take that tone, Dory. And anyway, this was *before* Michael. I didn't know the vamps were after me, too."

I let it drop. We were going to have a very long conversation at some point, but not now. "Okay. So you got away from Michael how?"

"I was trying to tell you." Claire glared me into submission. "*So* Michael got pissed at the mages, who wouldn't pay him until they were sure they'd actually be able to harvest me, and he trashed their place. You've never seen anything like it. Bodies everywhere, and so much blood and—you know how I feel about blood. I may have passed out."

I gave her a look. Claire gets nauseous from a paper cut. She sighed. "Okay, I did pass out. And when I woke up, I was being taken to the auction. Michael had found some guys who used to work for the mages who weren't the kind to ask questions—"

"And Drac found you there."

"Yes. He just took me; didn't pay or anything. Then we went to this total *rathole* of a motel—I mean that literally; it had rats. You could hear them in the walls—" I nodded. Drac must not have wanted to risk my leaking his Bellagio room number to the Senate and moved to the other extreme of the spectrum. "—and one of his men kept *eating* them, and I said I was going to be sick and went outside and they'd left the keys in the car—"

"They didn't have wards around the place?" As soon as I said it, I realized how stupid that was.

Claire raised an eyebrow, dislodging some water from her bangs, which ran into her eyes. "Damn contacts! That's the other reason I had to go home; I haven't been able to see anything for *days*. 'Extended wear,' my ass," she mumbled, fishing around in her purse for a pair of glasses.

"And you found me how?"

"I didn't. That's why I was so surprised to see you. Of course, I told Heidar all about you"—she thumped him again—"and said you might catch up with us sooner or later, but he never listens, and anyway, if you'd checked the answering machine, you'd have already known I was okay. I left—I don't know—like, ten messages, starting last night—"

"I've been kind of busy."

"And you never answer your cell phone."

"My cell had a little accident."

"Anyway, I found Heidar lurking around the motel— he'd found me but couldn't get through the wards—and we drove around until we saw this great hotel that does tours of the vineyards. Then I remembered when I was looking at that magazine article about the wine country, you said your uncle had a house around here, and I thought maybe he'd know where to find you. So we asked around and here we are."

I looked into her triumphant face and found myself utterly speechless. She'd been on a tour of the wine country. While half of Faerie chased her and I went slowly out of my mind, she'd been eating crackers and debating the merits of last season's merlot.

I finally managed to unclench my jaws enough for

speech. "Claire. This is very important. Did you accidentally take down the wards when you arrived?"

"What wards?"

"You might not have noticed, but Radu has a rather elaborate ward system."

Claire blinked at me. "Why would he need that kind of protection? I mean, he is a vampire, right?" She stopped abruptly and stared at me, a hand coming up to cover her mouth. "Oh, listen, Dory, when I said I hate all vamps, I didn't mean, you know, the *good* ones—"

"Svarestri," Heidar hissed, in a tone so unlike his previous cheerful ones that I looked around for a moment, expecting to see someone else. But I saw only dark leaves against a deep gray sky, and heard only sheeting rain.

Then, like the shadow of a shark just beneath the surface of the sea, fluid and dangerous, a shape appeared out of the vines. A gust of wind tangled my hair, carrying a scent like cold midnight that chilled me to the bone. A second shiver of darkness joined the first, then another, and then two more. It looked like we had company.

Chapter Twenty

Like a cold current in a warm sea, something parted the rain. I could sense everything going on around me with preternatural clarity: the scurrying of hoofed and clawed feet as Radu's terrors found something scarier than themselves; the rhythm of my own nervous breathing; the slight sucking sounds of light footsteps sneaking up behind me. I felt poised on the crest of a wave about to break.

"Get her out of here!" I told Heidar. "I'll slow them down."

"You'll do no such thing!" Claire was at her incandescent best. "I can help—"

I put a hand over her mouth and glared at Heidar. "Do you have a hearing problem?"

"You cannot win," he said hurriedly. "They—"

"Did I ask you that?" I grabbed him by the arm, hard enough to bruise. "If she dies, I'll rip your throat out."

He drew himself up, spine straight, and fixed me with a level gaze. "If she dies, I will already be dead defending her."

I nodded. "Good answer."

"Dory!" I'd passed Claire to Heidar, who was too busy

drawing a sword out of the sling across his back to muffle her. "You always do this! Other people have strength, too."

"Take her and go!" I snarled. Heidar silently passed me the sword, threw Claire over his shoulder and disappeared into the vines. I didn't see any of the dark shapes break off to follow them, which was both reassuring and a concern. Did they have others posted around the estate, to catch them unawares?

Then something dove at me out of the boiling sky. I lashed out at it instinctively, going on hearing rather than sight, and Geoffrey's head rolled to the ground at my feet. I nudged him with my foot, and anger raged in the still-living eyes. A master-level vamp could heal a wound like that, given half a century or so of excellent care. But Geoffrey wasn't a master, or at least, he sure didn't fight like one. A second later it didn't matter anyway. A booted foot slammed down on his skull, cracking it like a walnut and grinding it into the mud.

I jumped back, sword high. And looked up into pewter-colored eyes that shone with power like flickering starlight. Recognition was instantaneous, and I dove for him, but the sword literally jumped out of my hand and flew to him. I stumbled as a wall of cold slammed into me, so sudden and so chill that I had trouble breathing.

The Fey examined the weapon with a small smile. "The sword of kings, in the hands of a half-breed whore." The voice was low and musical, and strangely beautiful. "How . . . disturbing."

I managed to get to my feet, although the cold seared my skin like a branding iron. I glanced around, but there was no way out. In every direction, moonlight glimmered off pale faces.

"Do not be concerned." The Fey spoke to me, but his eyes were on the weapon. He tested it experimentally, gracefully slicing the rain. The clear surface glowed in the dim light, reflecting lightning along its razor edge like a warning. "Once, long ago, this blade took the head of a Svarestri king. I would not dishonor him by using it on you."

The burning chill was leaching my heat quickly. If I didn't do something soon, I'd freeze where I stood. But considering the odds against me, conversation seemed the best chance to give Claire time to get gone. "You should maybe use it on whoever set you on this wild-goose chase."

"What do you mean?" He was still more interested in his new toy than in me. I decided that was insulting.

"I mean, dumb ass, that I may be a half-breed, but I'm not a witch, I'm not a null and I am definitely not a six-foot redhead."

The Fey's head snapped up at that. "What?"

I bared fangs at him. "See these? Not standard-issue witch equipment. I'm a dhampir." I grinned. "You've been chasing the wrong girl, genius."

I guess he decided that the sword wasn't so holy, after all, because the next second, it was underneath my chin. "Where is she?"

"Why? You want to pay homage to your future king? 'Cause it's a little early."

"The half-breed son of that Blarestri buffoon can never rule, and neither can any child he sires on another mongrel." The sword point bit into the skin of my neck. "Give me what I need and you may live through the day. Otherwise . . ."

"I heard this speech once this week already. The other guy did it better."

"Have a care, dhampir." The Fey's voice was no longer musical. "You do not know with whom you are dealing."

Then again, conversation has never really been my forte. "Neither do you," I said, and lunged. I ducked under the sword of kings and went straight for the bastard's jugular. I threw everything I had into it, all my speed, and my fingers grasped the unexpectedly warm skin of his neck. But before my hand could close, something touched me, sliding down my spine like the blade of a cold iron knife. It took my speed, my strength, everything—as though all my senses had been cut off at once. I couldn't see, couldn't hear, couldn't feel. Everything was gone. Everything except icy nausea and bitter fear.

And then my senses returned, and it was worse. It was agony, like a thousand tiny shards of ice spearing me at once. My throat spasmed as his hand closed over it. He wasn't trying to strangle me—he wasn't even pressing hard enough to bruise—but it felt like I was suddenly choking on ice. My eyes told me there was nothing there, but my throat grew numb, and my gag reflex kicked in, closing the airway completely.

"You wish to test yourself against me?" The voice was flat and hard, like ice over cold, dark water. "Very well."

His hand came to rest on the front of my shirt, lightly, barely touching me, but it felt like he had spread his fingers and pushed them deep inside my flesh. Not tearing and ripping as an animal might, but in a slow creep like the onset of winter, stealing color and warmth and life. My lungs froze; I couldn't have taken a breath even if my air passage had been open. My blood slowed down to a sluggish icy soup. That phantom touch sank farther into my body, burning like dry ice, creeping into hidden recesses I hadn't even known existed until they cramped with it. Frost crept up my spine; ice encased my heart.

I fell, bones reverberating with a jarring shock when I hit the ground. It was no longer soggy, but hard as a rock with a thick layer of ice. The frozen mud glittered white and crystalline against my fingertips as my hand fell uselessly in front of my face. I was vaguely surprised that it didn't shatter into pieces on contact, like glass. I started to black out, from pain and lack of air.

"The Svarestri command the elements." The Fey kicked me onto my back with his foot, then crouched beside me. "Do you know the four elements, dhampir? Water, in one form, you are coming to know well, I think. Shall we try another?"

The pain changed from ice to flame in an instant. What had frozen before now boiled. I gasped as the constriction on my throat disappeared, and scalding air rushed into my lungs. A clinical pewter gaze watched as I arched in white-hot agony, my body bent like a bow as flames poured through me. Fire ate away at my nerve endings, but instead of deadening, the pain kept building, getting worse every second, until it felt like my bones would climb right out of my flesh.

The ice in front of my face melted and the puddle began to steam. It looked like the air itself had turned to fire, a boiling mass of knotted lightning. I was surprised that my skin wasn't doing the same; it felt like my blood was actually boiling in my veins. The Fey put his hand on me again, but where it had been ice before, now it was fire. My shirt began to scorch, as if the fabric had been left too long under an iron. I could feel my skin start to bubble beneath it.

Then, as suddenly as it had begun, it stopped. I collapsed to the ground, splashing in a puddle of water hot enough to burn. My flesh throbbed with every heartbeat; my breath hitched in my lungs as I tried to breathe. I choked on the acrid smell that rose from the burnt edges of my shirt, like the fumes of a candle that had just been extinguished. The Fey pulled his hand away and sat back on his heels. Part of my shirt had flaked away, exposing red, blistered skin that ran from my breastbone to below my belly button. It took me a second to realize why the shape of the injury was so familiar. The perfect imprint of a long-fingered hand had been burnt into me like a brand.

"If I wasn't protecting you, you would already be dead," I was told. "But we have two elements to go, do we not?" He wasn't touching me now, but a constriction was suddenly about my throat. My hands scrabbled at the burning sand beneath me, but I didn't have the strength to lift them to my neck—I couldn't even claw at the nonexistent cord. I bit the air, as if I could tear chunks out of it with my teeth, but nothing helped. Too many needs warred in my head—fight back, get air into my lungs, scream for mercy—

Almost as if he'd heard my last thought, the Fey leaned over to look in my eyes. "If you wish to save your life, tell me where the null is to be found." The constriction relaxed, and I could breathe, although my lungs almost felt like they'd forgotten how. He waited while I gasped and choked. "Nothing to say?" I stared up at him, too raw in every nerve even to glare. Helpless wheezing sighs accompanied my every breath, but I said nothing. I only wished I had enough water left in my parched mouth to spit.

Then I realized the fun wasn't over, as my lungs kept expanding even after filling to capacity. It felt like I had two balloons in my chest, balloons that were being stretched to their limit and beyond. They would soon burst; they couldn't possibly hold any more. My eyes blurred with pain and I couldn't stop a violent shudder. My vision began to fade. Something was screaming inside my head, a high, inhuman sound that had no beginning or end, a raw vibration of wet agony.

Just as I was sinking into blackness, the pressure stopped and I was allowed to exhale. I didn't cough this time. The air trickled out of me slowly, and I took a few weak, shallow breaths afterward, as if my lungs were afraid to try for more.

I'd hurt worse in the past, but this definitely made the top ten. I wasn't sure, but it might make the top three. The Fey regarded me thoughtfully, a finger tracing the burns on my chest delicately. "You surprise me. Most of your kind would have screamed themselves hoarse by now."

I wasn't about to give him the satisfaction of the truth, that my throat had locked up, that I'd been too choked on pain to scream. "You've never met one of my kind." It came out as a dry croak, but he seemed to understand.

"No." The storm-colored eyes narrowed. "I suppose I have not. Well, then." He stood up, and hauled me to my feet. I stumbled, but that iron grip wouldn't let me fall. After a moment, the dizziness passed and I found to my surprise that my legs would hold me. I was even more surprised that I hadn't dropped into a berserker rage. Pain of that magnitude had never failed to bring it on. I never had this much control, not unless . . .

Unless Claire was around.

I forced myself not to look. That triple-damned Heidar. I'd already promised to kill him, but for this I would kill him *slowly*.

"Since you act like a warrior, we will treat you as one,"

the Fey said. "I will give you the opportunity to die fighting." He draped an arm around my waist to keep me upright. The feel of it made the sweat on my body suddenly chill. "Do you see the house?"

Since it was lit up like a Christmas tree against the boiling darkness of the sky, it was a pretty stupid question. But then, the Fey didn't seem to have a lot of respect for human intelligence. I nodded. Anything was better than going on to element number four. I didn't know what form it might take, but somehow doubted I'd enjoy the lesson.

"If you reach the house, I will let you go."

"Reach the house?" My voice sounded thin and breathy, not at all like usual. But I was grateful for it. If my vocal cords still worked, I couldn't be as hurt as I felt. Right?

"My people will not try to stop you. But the fourth element will. Touch the house, any part of it, and we will leave you be. Fail—" He shrugged. "I will tell your people where to dig for you."

I assumed he meant that literally, since the only element left was earth. Goddamned Fey and their goddamned games. I'd heard the stories, but never thought much about them. I had certainly never thought I might die in one. Even worse, that I might die for nothing.

My eyes made a quick survey of the vineyard, but if Claire and Heidar were there, they were hiding well. But were they? The level of control I was somehow maintaining seemed to vote yes, but in that case, why were none of the Fey reacting? Heidar had known the Svarestri were here before I did; surely they would be able to detect him? And then the ground rose up on either side of me like black waves in the sea, and I ran.

I can outrun most things on earth, but not, I discovered,

earth itself. I made it to the edge of the rows of vines before a wall of dirt hit me like a club. I tried diving through it, but there didn't seem to be any end. Acres of soil crashed into me, over me, my overtaxed muscles screaming as I fought uselessly. I was drowning in fine particles that rose up choking thick around me. My abused lungs filled with dust, my eyes and ears clogged with dirt, and heavy clots rained down on top of me like blows from a hundred fists.

I struggled, clawing against the weight with everything I had, but I wasn't completely certain which way was up anymore. Was I digging toward air and life, or away from it? Was I helping to free myself, or digging my own grave? I couldn't tell.

Then something rough and hard twined around my ankle and tugged. The ground didn't want to release me, but the hard ropelike touch wouldn't be denied. It gave a massive heave, and I shot out of the mound of earth like a bullet from a gun.

There was too much dust in my eyes for me to see, but I felt it when I crashed into the vines like a trapeze artist falling into a safety net. They broke my fall, but not by much. What little air was in my lungs was forced out when I hit the ground, hard enough to rattle my bones. I just lay there for a moment, shocked and unmoving. Then I started to heave and cough up great streams of brown goop, in between trying to suck in whatever air I could.

I heard the sounds of battle going on around me, but it took several minutes for my brain to make any sense of it. Finally, I wiped my mouth on the back of my hand and fought my way free of the vines—including the one still securely wrapped around my foot—just in time to see Claire take on one of the Svarestri. I lurched to my feet, sure I'd be too late, certain she was dead. But instead, I saw the Fey stagger and fall to his knees, screaming. I couldn't figure out what Claire was doing to him—she wasn't even touching him—but he acted like he was being slowly tortured to death.

I staggered out of the vines, caked with dirt that kept falling into my eyes, and she saw me. She gave the Fey a vicious kick in the ribs and ran toward me, screaming something my dirt-clogged ears couldn't make out. Behind her, Heidar was battling two of the Fey, and looked like he was holding his own. What I couldn't figure out was who was dealing with the others—especially the leader. Then Claire crashed into me, sobbing and shaking. The impact was enough to loosen the land fall in my left ear, so that I would have been able to hear myself being royally told off if she had been at all coherent.

I looked around frantically for the leader, but didn't see him. What I did see was Caedmon, kneeling with his hands against the ground—no, in the ground. His fingers were buried deep in the wet, black dirt. Vines had wrapped themselves around his arms and across his back, flowing out like a living mantle behind him. He didn't see me—his features were twisted in an intense concentration that seemed to border on pain. Nearby, two Fey warriors lay unmoving, impaled on the infant grapevines that, even as I watched, grew up through their bodies to unfurl green, waving arms at the dark sky.

"—*ever* do that again, I'll kill you myself. My *God*, I thought you were *dead*—" Claire suddenly hugged me, tight enough to bruise my tender ribs. I grunted in pain and she let me go, looked at me for a second and burst into tears.

I spat more dirt and stared at her, not sure what to do.

I'd never seen Claire this upset; she was usually the calm one. I looked up in time to see Heidar behead one of his opponents before turning all his fury on the other. "Wh-where's the leader?" I managed to croak.

It seemed to be the right thing to stop Claire's tears. They turned at once to rage. "Æsubrand," she spat, her cheeks flushed and damp. "When I find the bloody evil cowardly bastard, I'm going to . . . going to . . . oh, God, I can't think of anything hideous enough right now, but it will be bad, really, really bad!"

Heidar had almost finished off his other opponent and I decided it was safe to collapse. So I did. And immediately regretted it when Claire burst into tears again and began shaking me. "I'm not dead," I told her as distinctly as possible with the inside of my throat coated in dirt.

"Water," she gasped. "You need water."

I needed a two-month vacation on a beach, but water would do. I nodded and she ran off in the direction of the house. I thought about what Louis-Cesare would say if he saw me now, after my declaration of competence, and decided to sit up. Caedmon had finished growing his crops—the two Fey were now vine-covered hillocks that had already started to form tiny green grapes. He collapsed beside me, looking smug for some reason.

"You're early," I croaked.

"It seems I was almost late," he replied, lifting my grimy, scratched and bloody hand. "My apologies." Then he drew me close and kissed me.

Power sang in the air. I felt it on my tongue, thick and syrupy and sweet, and then it flowed into me like a spring flood, and my body grasped it like a parched thing. Caedmon's hand smoothed down my side and my whole body tingled and came alive. I opened my eyes, but I couldn't see him. The creature holding me was a brilliant light in the darkness, bright as a sun, eternal as a mountain and utterly unmistakable for anything but what he was.

Gradually, the brightness faded and I came back to myself. My first thought was that Radu was going to need a new vineyard. The straight, symmetrical lines were no more. In their place was a riot of green—grapevines and small trees sprouted everywhere, and thin delicate garlands of bougainvillea and hibiscus draped over it all. Heavy with blossom, they swayed in the cool breeze, dropping an occasional orange or vividly pink petal onto the soft, grass-carpeted floor beneath us. The storm clouds had rolled back, and the sky was a pale, rain-washed blue.

"'Caedmon' means 'Great King' in Gaelic," I said, as a vine burst into flower over my head, like a living firework.

"Does it?" Caedmon looked mildly interested. Heidar gave a yell and chased a retreating Fey into the vines.

"And your loyal retainers would be where?"

The king shrugged. "Serving my interests in Faerie. That is why we were to meet tonight—I needed time to contact and assemble them. But when an informant told me the Svarestri had been seen in this area, I sent word to my people to join me here as soon as they might, and returned to be on hand in case anything went wrong in my absence."

We sat in silence for a moment while I picked red petals out of my hair. "Claire's uncle was part Fey," I finally said. "He couldn't have made all that wine, otherwise."

"Hmmm."

"And her father was Dark Fey. Making her just slightly over half-Fey." I shot Caedmon a dirty look. "You planned this."

His lips twisted wryly as he unwound an overly

affectionate vine that was trying to twine up his arm. "My dear Dory, I assure you, I did not plan for the deaths of two of my oldest retainers, nor for my own nephew to try to murder me."

"But you did plan for Heidar to end up with Claire. You sent him to that auction, didn't you?"

"What we parents must do to get our offspring happily settled."

"Why?" I asked in bewilderment. "Why not just introduce them?"

He shook his head, dislodging the flock of butterflies that had come to rest there. Some fluttered off, but one lit on his knee, fanning extravagant orange wings in voluptuous contentment. "Heidar is just over one hundred of your years old—a teenager, by our standards. And, like most young men of his age, the last thing he wants is to follow orders from his sire. Had I told him in advance that I meant her for him, he wouldn't have touched her—nor, in all likelihood, would she have had him." He smiled at me smugly. "As it was, their attraction had an irresistible forbidden quality to it."

"That resulted in an heir for you."

"Already?" Caedmon's smug grin widened. "That's my boy."

I refrained from slapping him. Just. "How is it that no one knew? I thought the Fey are obsessive about genealogy."

"Oh, yes, particularly among the noble houses."

"Then why did Æsubrand know nothing about Claire's uncle?"

"We are obsessive about *our* ancestry, Dory." When I still looked blank, he elaborated. "Light Fey ancestry."

It took me a moment to understand what he meant. "You're telling me Claire's uncle was Dark Fey?"

"I believe his great-great-great-grandmother was a quarter Brownie. It works out to a very small percentage for Claire, but enough to make any child born to her and my son more than fifty percent Fey. And therefore, by our laws, my legitimate heir. Assuming it is male, of course."

"And you think the Svarestri will accept a king who is part Dark?" I couldn't see someone like Æsubrand bowing to Olga or Stinky. Or anyone with similar blood.

"There is nothing in the old rules about what kind of Fey blood it must be," Caedmon assured me. "I suppose it was considered so obvious that it must be Light that it was never written down. As for the Svarestri, if I am right about their intentions, no Blarestri ruler will satisfy them for long."

"Which is why you've been skulking about, pretending to be dead?"

Caedmon grinned delightedly. "Skulking. Was I really? How . . . divine."

"Caedmon!"

He laughed. "Do you have any idea, Dorina, how long it has been since anyone has dared to address me so familiarly? Skulking." He laughed again.

Heidar came through the forest of vines, dragging an unconscious, or possibly dead, Fey behind him. He looked up and saw us, and a delighted smile broke over his features. It was so like his father's that it might have been a mirror image.

"That is why," Caedmon whispered as his son came closer. "If the Svarestri believed me dead, I thought there would be no reason for them to attack my son, who they knew could never rule. It would give me time to find him

and your friend while my retainers searched for Æsubrand. The only factor I did not anticipate was Claire pro-
claiming to all and sundry that she was carrying my
heir!"

"Which forced Æsubrand to go after her if he wanted
the throne."

Caedmon sighed. "My sister spoiled him; I always told
her it would end badly."

"But it hasn't ended. He's still on the loose, and now
he knows you're alive."

"There are always problems, Dory. That is why we live
for the few shining moments that make the rest worth-
while."

"Do you see, lady?" Heidar beamed at me, dropping
his trophy at his father's feet. "I told you he wasn't dead."
The Fey moaned, so I supposed he was still alive. "Where
is the Lady Claire?" He looked a little apprehensive.
"We . . . we have something to tell you, Father."

I looked around, frowning. "She went after water for
me." But that had been a while ago, hadn't it? I wasn't
sure. My time sense had taken a beating.

I looked toward the house, and it was eerily still. No
half-breeds, Fey or otherwise, roamed about outside, and
if anyone moved within, it wasn't obvious. Louis-Cesare,
I suddenly recalled, had said he would join me. And Radu
should have had the wards back up by now, only I hadn't
felt anything. I glanced at Caedmon. "I hope you enjoyed
the moment, because I think the problems are back."

Chapter Twenty-one

Oddly, the house looked more sinister in broad daylight than it had under an overcast sky. It also looked deserted. We paused in the little courtyard with the fountain, but the only discernible sound over the trickling water was the buzzing of a few insects hovering about the bougainvillea and my own breathing. It sounded loud and harsh in my ears. The Fey didn't seem to be breathing at all.

They had that in common with the corpse lying half in, half out of the shadowy hallway. The hair was black. I bent down and rolled the face toward me, but I didn't know him. Not one of Radu's humans, then.

I checked his shoulder and back, but there was no black circle tattooed anywhere I could see. Nor was there a silver. That didn't mean he wasn't a mage, of course. Just that he wasn't a very good one.

The cause of death was a heart attack brought on by the fact that someone had thrust a long, skinny blade through it. I looked up, and saw Caedmon noting it, too. Louis-Cesare may as well have signed his name to the body. Farther down the corridor, I saw a spill of gold against terra-cotta. Without being told, Caedmon started around the back and Heidar circled around toward the front entrance. I followed the trail of bodies into the house.

A blond and two brunets later, I was in the living room. The painting of Mehmed had swung out into the room, revealing an empty three-tiered shelf. Okay, so I knew where Radu had kept his power source, whatever it was. There were no bodies in the room, but a wash of blood-scented air slapped me in the face as soon as I entered. I didn't see any puddles, and it would take something that big to send off so much of an odor. But the door to the main entryway was open, and there was a cross-breeze.

I ripped the leg off a chair, getting a jagged but sharp edge, as I scented the air. The blood wasn't Claire's. That I would have recognized immediately. But it did seem familiar. I couldn't figure it out until I got close enough to see into the hallway.

"Do let him catch his breath, Jonathan."

"As you wish, my lord."

My eyes took in a succession of quick images: Radu being held off to the side by two vamps, the power signature around them unmistakably that of masters; no sign of Claire; a puddle of blood big enough to have drained a human in the center of the floor; and above it, hanging from the balcony railing, a nude, frighteningly pale body. I felt a chill so sudden and so cold that it rivaled anything the Fey had managed to summon. And I realized why the blood had smelled so familiar.

"The amount of blood he is losing will not do," Drac was saying. "We wouldn't want him to expire before our guests arrive."

"I wouldn't worry about that. I had him for almost a month once." The oily voice belonged to the blond-haired, gray-eyed human with a poker in his hand.

Jonathan. He stroked a hand down Louis-Cesare's bloody torso, and there was something sickeningly intimate about the gesture. "He'll survive—for a while."

I couldn't understand it—why was Louis-Cesare just hanging there? He had no weapon, but a master vamp *is* a weapon—a formidable one. And the restraints holding his arms to the balcony were merely rope—I could see where his weight had caused them to sink into the flesh of his arms. He'd been lashed to the ironwork balcony so that his body dangled downward, almost in a cruciform position, his toes not able to touch the floor tiles. He might not be able to get any leverage using his feet, but he could snap the ropes in an instant, as easily as a human might break a thread. So what was going on?

There were half a dozen mages standing around, several of whom I remembered from the Bellagio, and five vamps. But even outnumbered, Louis-Cesare should have been putting up some kind of resistance. I sure as hell would have been.

Jonathan was standing close enough that Louis-Cesare's unbound legs could have swung up, locked around his throat and snapped his neck, probably in the time it took to blink. Yet they didn't. Even when Jonathan worked the poker into Louis-Cesare's already mutilated chest, he did not so much as grunt.

My heart lurched sickeningly, caught between fear and outright panic. Was he already dead? Had one of the shafts sticking out of his chest pierced his heart? It was possible—he looked like some parody of Saint Sebastian, red wounds like gaping mouths over all that pale flesh. But no, he was still bleeding. I saw a light trickle seep out around the poker. And dead bodies don't bleed.

Jonathan traced the outline of the wounds he'd inflicted

on his captive's chest and belly, his touch an obscene mixture of delicacy and brutality. The new flow of blood seemed to dissipate into mist at his touch, a tiny wisp floating from Louis-Cesare's tortured form to wrap itself around the mage's hand. "Ah. It begins," he murmured, as my heart kicked hard against my chest, sick realization curling in my stomach. He was bleeding him of power, of life, little by little. Yet Louis-Cesare did nothing.

The only reason I could think of for the suicidal passivity was Radu's imprisonment. Maybe they had threatened him if Louis-Cesare fought back? It didn't make a lot of sense, as he knew perfectly well what Drac had planned for his brother, but it was the best theory I had. I grabbed the mage standing guard at the door, who had been too caught up in the little torture session to notice the wild-looking woman sneaking up on him. His neck snapped almost silently, any tiny sound covered by Jonathan's thick voice.

There was blood under the mage's fingernails as he caressed his prize, toying with the purple bruises and crusty blood around the older wounds. It slicked his hand and stuck his fingers together, thicker than honey as it dried. The urge to snap the thin man's neck made my fingers twitch sharply as he leaned in, staring at Louis-Cesare with a hungry look. "Do you remember how inventive I could be?"

I ignored the dull beat of anger throbbing behind my eyes and stowed the mage behind the sofa. I slipped into the entryway, careful to keep close to the wall. It was dark in the shadows, away from the chandelier's light, and my coating of black mud was good camouflage—for both sight and scent. Another mage was a few feet in front of me, watching the show.

In a sudden, savage motion, Jonathan pulled out the poker and was rewarded with a barely audible gasp, just a brief inhalation that was soft even to my ears. But the mage heard.

He smiled at Louis-Cesare tenderly, approvingly, his hands stroking down the long torso, smearing the spattered blood that stained his skin. "He died every day, and was reborn every night," he crooned, his voice a singsong, "like an ancient god, like Mithras himself." Without warning, he slid his finger into the gap left by the poker; I could see it moving under the flesh of Louis-Cesare's side. "I never killed him twice in the same way."

"You never killed him at all," Dracula said testily. Apparently I wasn't the only one to see the madness in those gray eyes.

Jonathan didn't seem to hear. "He died so beautifully, every time. Mostly in silence, but occasionally I would bring him to screams of agony, to passionate death throes." His free hand caressed Louis-Cesare's bare flank while his finger sank farther into its sheath of skin, to the base of his knuckles. "Will you scream for me one last time?"

Louis-Cesare shivered in revulsion, but he lifted his head to stare at him, haughty, defiant. I thought that's how the French aristocrats must have looked, going to the guillotine on the order of a middle-class bureaucrat, the blood of Charles Martel flowing in their veins. Then, over Jonathan's shoulder, he saw me.

He gave a sudden jerk and his eyes widened. The mage in front of me must have seen, because he stiffened and started to turn. I strangled him with his own scarf before he could sound an alarm. Only, if Louis-Cesare continued to look like that, no other warning would be needed.

Fortunately, Drac had never been known for patience.

He knocked Jonathan out of the way, grabbed a poker sticking out of Louis-Cesare's thigh and twisted it cruelly. "Enough of this! Tell me where Mircea is, or I will let this creature do his worst!"

Louis-Cesare said nothing, but he turned his face away from me as Radu's outraged tones echoed across the room. "I told you already—he isn't here! Let him go, Vlad. Your quarrel is with me!"

Vlad whipped his head around, almost as if he had forgotten Radu was there. But before he could answer, the front door opened, flooding sunlight over the bloody tiles. "Nonsense, Radu." At the rich, familiar tones, I stiffened. My head turned, very slowly. "As you know quite well, Vlad's quarrel has always been with me."

Mircea stood there, rapier in hand, smiling an antique smile. Like a glint of sunlight on an edge of broken glass, it was unmistakably a duelist's expression, with no hint of warmth. "Ahh." Vlad's hands dropped away from Louis-Cesare as if he had suddenly disappeared, which for him, I suppose, he had.

I had to give it to Caedmon—he was good. With all the blood and the carcasses of several of Radu's half-breeds scattered around, I couldn't tell if he'd gotten the scent right, but everything else was perfect. He might have fooled even me. My opinion of Fey glamourie shot up exponentially.

The vamp nearest me turned to say something to the now dead mage, and saw me. He wasn't a master, but the ragged-edged cry that tore from his throat before my makeshift stake cleaved his heart was enough to draw every eye in the place. Every one except Drac's. "Kill her," he ordered, his eyes never leaving Mircea.

I leapt for the chandelier to escape a barrage of spells and more mundane attacks. I wasn't sure I would make it.

Caedmon had undone the worst of the Fey's attack, but my strength was still at a low ebb and I ached everywhere. But crystals chimed under my hands as I grabbed hold, just as an explosion hit the wall where I'd been standing, blowing out a chunk of plaster and brick.

Caedmon darted out of the doorway toward me, but Drac intercepted him. They flowed into combat without a pause, evenly matched and darkly beautiful. There seemed little to choose from between them—Caedmon the more cunning, Drac the more savage. Then my attention was torn away by a spell hitting the chandelier, sending a whirlwind of tangled light dancing crazily around the room and causing the fixture's heavy ironwork to run like melting butter.

I dropped to the ground, leaping aside to avoid the slash from a vamp's knife. "Louis-Cesare!" I broke the arm of the vamp, but his weapon skittered across the floor, out of reach. "Some help here!" The chandelier fell, shattering in a thousand sparkling pieces that scattered like ice across the floor. Underneath it was the vamp who had attacked me, the molten metal of the fixture searing to his flesh as he lay screaming.

And still Louis-Cesare just hung there. Power was curling upward from every wound now; my skin prickled with it even halfway across the room. The mage seemed almost drunk on it, scooping up those coils of mist as fast as they flowed outward from his captive's body.

There were three mages and every vamp that wasn't busy holding down Radu converging on me. I was about to be toast if I didn't move, so I did—straight toward Louis-Cesare. I was hit halfway through my leap by something that felt like a club but, since I didn't see anything, was probably a spell. I smashed onto the tile, but somehow kept hold of my stake. Then two vamps were on me.

One was a master, but the other was not. The baby practically fell on the stake, puncturing his gut, by the smell. His shrieks added to those of the vamp still frying under the chandelier, and the clash of swords.

The baby vamp fell away, but the master had his head buried in my throat before I could move. I thrashed and struggled, but it was more the casing of dirt I still wore that kept his teeth out of my neck than anything I did. He bit down, but got only a mouth of dried mud for his trouble. And then he was sailing through the air, his head lolling at an unnatural angle. I looked up, ready to tell Louis-Cesare off royally, and met Radu's blazing eyes instead.

They turned amber, just like Mircea's when he was angry, I noticed. And at the moment, he was furious, with power sputtering around him like an electric field. Vlad might still think of Radu as his inept younger brother, but that was an image distorted by time. A second-level master could do a lot of damage, especially if the alternative was a sure death. I was glad to see 'Du finally putting some of those centuries of accumulated power to work, but what the hell was up with Louis-Cesare?

Radu helped me up, but tightened his grip on my arm when I started toward the balcony again. "I can feel the pulse deep within your body," Jonathan was saying, heedless of the carnage around him. His cheeks were flushed, and his eyes were fever bright. He had widened the wound in Louis-Cesare's side to a gaping hole. His hand disappeared in it up to the wrist. "That heart of yours, trembling against my fingertips. Beating, just for me."

The pain must have been excruciating. Louis-Cesare's

neck arched backward until it looked as though his spine would break. The glittering mist of power around him had grown, forming a thick shroud of pale silver light that threatened to hide him from view.

I fought against Radu's hold. "Are you crazy? Let me go!"

"It's a spell," he said quickly. "They're behind a ward. Break it and it will destroy Louis-Cesare!"

"He'll die anyway!" I'd met Jonathan's kind before. Radu released me and snatched up the sizzling vamp from the floor. He slung him, and the melted, smoking metal attached to him, at another, who had come at us so fast he was little more than a rush of air.

"Claire!" I realized that somewhere in all this was the one person who could bring down any ward, half the time without even realizing it. I grabbed Radu's arm. "Have you seen her?"

"Who?" He was watching Drac's troops, who were circling us warily. Their master had disappeared—I assumed from the ring of steel on steel coming from the dining room that he and Caedmon had taken their fight in there.

"A woman—tall, red hair, young—have you seen her?"

"No. But Chef was saying something about a girl invading his kitchen earlier—"

"Get to the kitchen. Find Claire and—"

Radu grabbed my stake and threw it at an advancing vamp. It hit the approximate center of his chest—not a heart blow—and although he skidded in the blood, he didn't fall. The second master, I assumed. Radu snatched the sword off the dead vamp and got it up in time to meet the one headed straight for him.

I crouched, stripping the vamp's body of a shorter weapon, but had to throw it at a trio of mages trying to get close enough to cast a net spell. Above my head, Radu's blade slid against the master's down to the hilt, twisting his wrist at an awkward angle. In the half second it took him to adjust, Radu pushed past his defensive plane and got inside his reach, driving an elbow against his throat. His sword work looked like it had improved through the years.

The vamp staggered and we were on him. Radu pulled the stake out of the middle of the vamp's chest and plunged it into his heart while I hacked at the neck. It wasn't a pretty job, but I got the head off.

It bought us a little time, as everyone paused, waiting for someone else to attack first. "*You* go to the kitchen!" Radu said, looking a bit crazed. "I'm needed here."

"I thought you said you weren't a fighter?"

"I've no desire to face my brother. Others I can manage. Now go, and tell Chef I said to let them loose. We could use a diversion."

"Let what loose?" I didn't get an answer because Radu was attacked by the two remaining mages with the magical net. If I'd had my backpack, I could have taken care of them in a second; without it, the best I could do was to avoid getting caught myself. Luckily, the mages seemed to view Radu as the bigger threat. I turned on my heel and ran.

The back of the house was an even bigger mess than the front. The hallway to the kitchen had been trashed, to the point that large pieces of it were missing. I leapt through a crack in the broken wall, thinking to save time by cutting through the pantry, since it was now open to the hall. But I had to immediately slow down. I already had several cuts in my bare feet courtesy of the chandelier, and the scene ahead of me seemed specially designed to add more. Broken bottles, smashed cans and crumbled shelving were everywhere. There was so much shattered glass littering the white tile floor that it looked like frost.

There were people, too. A lot of them had to be Drac's, because I didn't know them. But the handsome young human who had fed Louis-Cesare after we'd arrived was lying across the doorway to the kitchen. It looked like something had been feeding from him, because his rib cage was open and half his bones were licked clean.

I stepped over him and someone hit me in the head, hard. I grabbed the weapon and smashed the wielder against the wall, only to find myself face-to-face with an outraged human in chef whites, clutching a marble rolling pin. He did not seem to understand even after seeing me that I wasn't an enemy. I caught a glimpse of myself in the shiny stainless-steel fridge: mud-matted hair sticking up in all directions, wild eyes and a grimy body streaked with blood and sweat. Okay, maybe he had a point, but I didn't have time to explain.

"Where is she? Where's Claire?" He pointed the rolling pin at a steel-covered door across the room. "You put her in the meat locker?" I slammed him against the wall again. "Tell me she's alive!"

"Sh-she was when she went in. It was her idea," he babbled as I dragged him across the once pristine kitchen floor. It was now covered with dirty foot, paw and claw marks. Of course Radu's pets would find the kitchen. But they must have been there and gone, because none were in evidence.

I kept one hand on the chef, who was going to experience a world of hurt if he'd lied to me, and yanked at the door. The heavy seal parted only reluctantly, so I tugged harder and it flew open. Claire looked out at me through fogged-up glasses. She was sitting on the floor, surrounded by some of Radu's menagerie. I started forward with a shout, then stopped. Many of the half-breeds were dead, but one or two crawled through the wreckage of the locker, some missing limbs, others dragging blood behind them.

"Claire!"

She looked up, and her glasses slipped down her nose. Her eyes were huge, and she'd obviously been crying. "These poor things were just thrown in here together and when I got here, they were *eating* each oth—"

"Claire! Bring down all wards within this building! Do it now!"

"What?" She looked confused. "But the chef said the vampires were trying to rebuild—"

"All of them! Now! Claire, please—"

"But these things, Dory—they're all magic! I'm shielding as hard as I can and I'm still making them sick." She looked around miserably, tears trembling on her lashes. "I didn't know. I killed most of them when I—"

I caught my breath and screamed. "Claire!" I shook her by the shoulders. Jonathan or Louis-Cesare: one of them was going to die tonight. Louis-Cesare *couldn't* be that one. Because I hadn't liked Jonathan's "one last time" comment. I had a very bad feeling that, whatever he intended for Louis-Cesare, it wasn't something Louis-Cesare was going to walk away from. Not this time. "Listen to me! A person will die—very soon—if you don't bring down the wards. All of them. Now."

She looked lost, and more than a little shocked, but she nodded. Several of the creatures nearby tottered over and lay still. "Okay."

"Get on with it!"

She straightened her glasses. The creature closest to

her crumpled to the ground. It looked like the rat thing that had taken a swipe at me in the arbor. "I just did," she said sadly. "Dory, what *were* these—"

I didn't hear the rest—I was halfway back across the kitchen and flying for the entrance. I avoided the mine-field of a pantry and took the hall instead. It was longer, but would probably be faster. And it would have been except for the claw that snatched me off my feet and lifted me through a hole in the wall.

There was a brief moment of being airborne, giving me time enough to wish that I'd asked Claire to kill all the damn things, and then I was dropped onto the red-tiled roof. I hit with a thud, but didn't roll off despite a steep slant, which was good because a mage somewhere below began firing spells either at me or at Big Bird. I assumed it was me, since the creature was suddenly nowhere in sight. A spell burst against the window over the entranceway and sent a cascade of glass into whatever was happening there.

The tiles were still wet and slippery from the rain, but I managed to scramble for cover behind a chimney. I had to get into the entry. The ward the mage had put on Louis-Cesare was hopefully down, but I had no idea if that would be enough or not. He'd lost a lot of blood and God knew what had been done to him after I left. And Radu had too much to handle already to be much help.

The chimney looked like it connected to the living room fireplace, but there was no way I was doing a Santa impression. A cat couldn't have fit down there. I was eyeing the broken window above the entry, wondering if my posterior could squeeze through; then a beaky head peered over the peak of the roof. I stared at its chartreuse, oddly human eyes, and cursed myself for a moron. I should have remembered—in the fight at the pen, the leader had waited until the others exhausted themselves before it waded in. Like it had done now.

As soon as the one lidless eye on that side of its head got a good look at me, it let out an ear-piercing shriek and took off half the chimney with a swipe from its claw. I scrambled down the tiles backward, that wicked beak slashing down all around me, cracking any tiles it hit clean in two.

The creature's tail snapped and skidded across the tiles, sending a cascade sliding toward the roof edge with me along for the ride. Grabbing for something, anything, to break my fall, my hand encountered the rain gutter. Already overstrained from the flood, it ripped away from the roof, leaving me dangling over the courtyard right above the mage.

It was good to see that my luck was holding true.

A stream of dirty water flowed out of the pipe directly onto the mage, temporarily blinding him. I let go of the pipe and hit the ground, close enough to the man to get my arms around his waist. A dark shadow fell over the courtyard as the leader spread huge, leathery wings; then it was on top of us, its weight and momentum sending us crashing to the ground. I waited until I heard the mage's scream when the talons latched on to him, then scrambled out from underneath and bolted for the entryway.

Chapter Twenty-two

The heavy wooden front door was hanging off its hinges, letting in a flood of light, but there was no one to see. Bodies had fallen everywhere, but a quick survey told me that none were Louis-Cesare or Radu. The sounds of a sword fight echoed distantly.

My foot slipped in something, in someone, but I kept my balance and followed the sounds of metal on metal. The long, polished oak table in the dining room bore muddy boot prints, but it, too, was empty. Behind me, I heard the scuffle of claws on tile and glanced back in time to see the leader's head stick in through the door. I didn't think its body would make it through the narrow arch, but I didn't intend to wait around and find out.

Beyond the dining room lay a library, with tall windows on one wall and a floor-to-ceiling collection of books on the others. Weirdly, it looked almost untouched, the only damage a vase of flowers that had been knocked off a small table. I skirted the mess and went through to the next room, which I did recognize: the small antechamber leading down to the wine cellars.

Shit.

I peered down the stairwell. It gaped up at me like a maw. I really hate dark staircases, and this one had no light at all. I remembered that we'd dined by lantern light; maybe Radu had never had electricity run down there. Great, just freaking wonderful.

A crash behind me made me turn in time to see a huge, birdlike body topple over the library table and crush the fallen vase to splinters. Okay, there were things I hated more than the dark—like the things that prowl in it. I practically leapt down the stairs, slamming the door shut behind me.

The stone was cool beneath my bruised feet, and almost total darkness closed around me, sinking into my bones. I couldn't see anything while my eyes adjusted, but the stairs were evenly spaced and they went only one place—to the small wine-tasting room where we'd dined. Here, a few oil lamps burned, illuminating the room's only occupants: the hundreds of bottles that lay on their sides, many broken, leaking Radu's label all over the stones until I couldn't tell by sight what was wine and what was blood. I jumped up on the tabletop to get to the other side of the room without lacerating my feet. Behind me, the door at the top of the stairs burst open with the crack of splintering wood. I rapidly pushed on toward the sound of the fight, loud enough now that I knew I had to be close.

There was only one door in the room besides the one I'd just come through. I took it and found a stone corridor lined with barrels. It led, presumably, to the winery next door. The only light came from a far door at the end, which was standing wide open, and the faint glow behind me. Halfway down the rows, Caedmon, still wearing Mircea's face, battled Drac.

I started forward, so relieved I was almost sick, and fell over something. Or, more accurately, someone. Vivid turquoise eyes met mine, and I breathed in the faint scent of salt and ozone. "Radu."

"Dorina . . ."

A rustle of wings reminded me of what was behind me. I grabbed Radu and rolled to the side, putting a large barrel between us and the door. I was pretty sure the leader couldn't break through solid stone walls, but it might be able to squeeze through the opening.

"A weapon," I hissed, searching Radu's body. The only thing I encountered was blood, and the seeping warmth told me that at least some of it was his. "Don't you have anything?" I demanded, peering over the barrel. The half-breed appeared to be caught in the doorway, but I wasn't buying it. The one at the top of the stairs was no wider, and it had made it through that. And there had been more than enough intelligence in those yellow green eyes to think up a way to lure me out from behind the protection of the barrel.

A knife was slipped into my hand. It was a lot shorter than I would have liked, but better than nothing. "Stay here," I said. "I may be a few minutes."

The leader screeched as I reemerged, loud enough to reverberate off the stone in an eardrum-rupturing echo. I ignored the theatrics and darted out into the hall. It was clear; Drac and Caedmon must have taken the fight into the winery.

As soon as I was in the open, the creature tore loose from the door and came at me in a whirl of claws and wings. I felt a line of fire splash across my arm from that wicked beak; then the tail caught me in the gut and knocked me back against the stone wall, rattling every bone in my body. Before I could move, the creature was on me, a low, ugly sound of fierce delight echoing around us. I lashed out with the knife, almost blindly, and by sheer luck the blow connected. A dark rain splattered my face, blood-warm and slick as engine oil, and I twisted away.

As the impossibly graceful shape flowed upward to the ceiling, I realized that the damn Fey wine hadn't worn off completely. In a moment of sickening disorientation, I felt the touch of an alien hunger. I could hear it in my mind, half-human thoughts through a haze of fury. *Rend, pierce, kill. Hot blood spraying, teeth closing on something weak and soft . . . tearing the underbelly, where the slickest, thickest taste resides . . . violet looping entrails and wet sacks of meat, so sweet . . .*

I pushed the alien thoughts aside, panting, and realized I'd lost sight of the damn thing. Lightless black, the creature's color blended in well with the shadows, and the muffled sound of its claws on the stone ceiling seemed to echo from all directions at once. I couldn't see anything, but the hairs on the back of my neck started prickling. I learned a long time ago: never argue with instinct. I made a sudden leap behind a barrel at almost the same moment that the creature dropped out of the darkness. It crashed into the barrel but missed me. Burgundy flooded the floor, glimmering faintly in the poor light and sending the pungent odor of wine everywhere. For a second, the creature was caught, its beak buried deep in the wood, its great claws scrabbling for purchase. Then the barrel snapped in two and I vaulted behind the next one in line.

I kept my eyes on the creature until they watered, afraid to blink in case it moved. It sank to the floor, doubling over on itself with the bonelessness of a cat. It sidled a flowing step forward as I worked to get leverage under the massive barrel shielding me. The huge dark outline came closer, blocking out what light there was. I knew I'd only get one chance at this—it was too smart to fall for it twice—so I took my time. I braced my back against the wall and put my feet on the barrel, ignoring the way the muscles in my thighs protested the deep crouch. When I could no longer see anything but blackness in front of me, I pushed with everything I had.

The barrel flew off its holder, crashed into the creature and forced it into the unyielding stone wall opposite. I heard the crunch of bone, then silence, but didn't trust it. Circling carefully, I reentered the tasting room and grabbed the biggest of the lamps. Taking it back with me, I set it on the top of the barrel, trying to see the thing's head. I intended to put the knife through at least one of those disturbing eyes.

Then time seemed to stand still as I caught a glimpse of the bloody blade, shining bright with reflected lamplight. It was the knife from my dream, with the family crest half-obscured by blood. Fitting, I thought, my head spinning. But before I could reason it out, Radu screamed my name. I scrambled back to where he lay in the middle of a puddle of his best stock. I felt a grip, hard as steel, on my wrist. "Jonathan has him," he gasped. His voice sounded funny. "The damn mage hit me with something. . . . I think he believes me dead."

"It looks like he's half-right." I realized why his voice was strange—Radu's chest was all but gone, the red-streaked white tissue of his lungs clearly visible through his shattered ribs. There was no place for sound to resonate.

He grinned up at me weakly. "Don't believe it. I'm hard to kill."

"Radu . . ."

He gripped my hand, hard. "I never had any honor, Dory. I've been sneaky and underhanded and downright dishonorable my whole life. Just like Father." A quiver of mad laughter bubbled up from his throat, along with a lot of blood. "I only ever . . . I did one thing right. One thing . . . don't let that bastard take him away."

Before I could answer, the air shivered and broke apart, shattered by a soundless scream. Somewhere nearby, power had been unleashed—a lot of it. Louis-Cesare, I thought, and forgot everything else. I ran.

The winery was equipped with bare-bulb lighting overhead, but it was currently out of commission. A few lanterns burned here and there instead, seeming almost unnaturally bright as I exploded out of the dim corridor. The place was larger than I'd expected, on two levels, with the lower housing the stainless-steel vats used for fermentation. They lined the walls like chubby sentinels, their shiny surfaces reflecting my own face back at me multiple times. Up a set of wooden stairs was a catwalk leading to the rest of the building. At the moment it was ringed by faces—Caedmon, Drac and Olga were looking down, not at me, but at the crumpled body in the center of the floor. A mage lay in a twisted pile, like a doll thrown down by a two-year-old. I didn't need to check to know that he was dead. Unfortunately, he wasn't Jonathan.

Drac recovered first and lunged at Caedmon, who sidestepped the blow, his sword back up in the space of time between thoughts. Even in the narrow confines of the catwalk his fighting form was perfect, a smooth flow of muscle and sinew, every motion exquisite. Drac's style wasn't nearly as pretty, but it seemed effective. Caedmon was bleeding in several places, while Drac was bloody only on one arm. Too bad it wasn't his sword arm.

My brain was so focused on what was happening ahead that I didn't notice the faint rustle of wings behind me until the room was suddenly filled with the tuneless howl and fury of the leader. It came at me out of the dark, trailing one wing uselessly, but it didn't need it in the confined space. I leapt backward, away from those slashing claws, and then I saw them, Louis-Cesare, Jonathan and some flunky on the floor near one of the huge vats.

At almost the same moment, Jonathan glanced up, probably at the sound of the leader slamming into the vat beside me, and our eyes locked. He huddled over the vampire's unmoving body protectively, like a predator over his latest kill. Before I could move, he drew a knife from his boot and cut a deep gash across Louis-Cesare's throat.

A white hiss of panic crowded rational thought from my head for a stunned moment, as blood flooded down the pale torso and across my vision. But one thought got through clearly enough: challenge had been made. I couldn't see if Louis-Cesare still lived; all I knew was that he wasn't moving, and it was more than enough. Challenge was accepted.

As I started forward, Jonathan threw a hand out, shedding a trail of fox fire in its wake, and something exploded around me in a wave of red sound. Power rolled over me, knocking me to my knees, turning the room hot and vivid and scarlet, until I was drowning in the blood-ripe taste of it. I tried to reinforce my shields, but I couldn't sense them, couldn't sense anything but the crash of those waves across my body. Somehow, I'd ended up on my back. I watched Jonathan start to drag Louis-Cesare toward the wooden staircase leading to the upper areas of the winery while my pulse throbbed in my ears and I struggled to breathe.

"Dorina! Behind you!" The shout came from the fight above—Mircea's voice. I was still so disoriented that it took a moment to realize what he was talking about. The creature had righted itself from its wild ride into the vat and begun to stalk me with quiet, deadly intent. I could see it getting larger, a black hulk reflected in the nearest vat, lurching at me across the floor. But there wasn't a damn thing I could do about it.

Jonathan had hit me with a souped-up disorienting sphere. I'd seen them before, but never been able to afford one. Apparently, the mage had a bigger bank account. I could throw off the usual kind in a matter of minutes, but this version was a wartime weapon used to take out whole groups of mages at once. I had no idea how long the effect would last, and it didn't look like I'd live long enough to find out.

Above me, blades clashed hard enough to strike sparks, and Caedmon gave way first. Drac pushed him back using sheer force, striking with hammer blows that Caedmon met but didn't have the strength to return. So much for the Fey's boast about his dueling ability. I struggled to move, but couldn't even manage to sit up. I felt a presence behind me, and braced for the attack.

It never came. Olga tossed something over the balcony, and a gray blur hit the floor with a graceful roll. Before I could identify it, the tiny whirlwind was streaking across the floor at me, snarling and snapping useless fangs and launched itself right over my body. It took forever to figure out which way to turn my head to see what was going on. When I did, I was treated to what even a baby Fey can do when it's really and truly pissed.

Stinky's long, twiglike fingers had found purchase on the leader's neck. His tiny body was saved from that vicious beak by the simple method of hiding behind the creature's own head. Stinky was little more than a fuzzy bump on the vast expanse of leather-like back, safe from beak and claws as he slowly choked the creature to death. It was a great plan, except that the leader realized that the game was up and decided to try to take me with him. Instead of moving forward, in a vain attempt to cross the last few yards to me, it suddenly sprang backward, directly into a huge holding vat. It had dented the thing earlier; now the force of its final assault punctured the steel, letting loose a river of wine that spilled outward in a crimson flood, threatening to drown me.

Finally, the madness I'd been expecting, but which Claire's presence had prevented, washed over me. Only this time, it didn't pull me under, didn't make me black out. I'd never in five hundred years had a chance to find out what happened during one of my fits, other than to examine the carnage afterward. I found out now.

The disorientation didn't go away, but the animal that lives in my veins was far less affected by it. I didn't manage to stand, but I didn't need to stand. Hands and knees got my head above the wine, and propelled me in a drunken crawl toward the staircase. I caught a glimpse in another vat of a crazed-looking creature with matted hair, gleaming fangs and mad, amber eyes staring out of a black-streaked face. I hoped it was me, because I really didn't want to fight it if not.

Movement made the disorientation worse, as my

confused inner ears tried to keep track of new sensory input when they hadn't yet sorted out the old. Colors, shapes and sounds all ran together around me. I ignored them and stayed focused on Jonathan, who had almost reached the top of the stairs with his prize.

I knew I'd reached the bottom step when I felt old wood under my hands. I dragged myself onto it by feel alone. Jonathan was trying to heave Louis-Cesare's dead-weight the last few feet while fighting off an attack by Olga, who had positioned herself in front of the door leading out. He didn't see me, but the mage helping him did and panicked. Instead of throwing a spell, which might have worked, he grabbed the nearest lantern. The oil lamp arced through the air, straight at my wine-soaked clothes. I caught it in the air and whipped it right back.

It hit the mage, but glanced off his chest to shatter on the hard wooden slats of the catwalk. The oil spread rapidly over the wine-spattered floor, fire caught and within seconds the circle of boards was a ring out of hell. The mage backpedaled, batting at the tongues of flame that had landed on his shirt and trousers, the soles of his boots aflame and starting to singe. He bumped into Olga, who tipped him over the balcony with a casual motion of one huge hand. There was a sudden whoosh, and the wine-soaked floor exploded in flame.

I caught sight of Stinky, scaling the side of the vat like a little monkey, well ahead of the flames. He leapt from the top of the vat to the catwalk, and turned to stare at me, as if to say, what's taking you so long? My legs were like rubber, but I made headway using my arms, scraping my palms as I dragged myself slowly upward.

Caedmon had been driven back almost to Olga's position, and his perfect form was starting to falter. His eyes kept straying to the burning catwalk, and the fire that was quickly spreading their way. Drac, on the other hand, was shining with power. His sword strokes were easy, and he ignored the smoking hot floor beneath his feet as if the threat didn't exist.

The two of them reached Olga at the same time that I topped the stairs. Caedmon made a misstep and dropped to one knee, Drac surged forward for the kill and Olga's hand shot out, palm forward, as if she thought she could merely push him back. Drac looked at her, his flat expression saying as clear as words that he was considering how best to snap her neck. I would have screamed if I'd had the voice—no matter how strong she was accustomed to feeling, there was no doubt Drac was stronger. But then I saw that there was something in Olga's hand.

It flared to life the instant it touched Drac, and within seconds was so bright I could see it through the flesh of her hand, like sunlight through butterfly wings. Drac dropped his sword and stood staring down at his chest. He looked up at Mircea, and there was something in his eyes for a second, something that looked almost like triumph. A shudder started at his head and ran to his feet, gathering force like a fist about to land. And then he exploded from the inside, raining blood and bits of flesh over everything.

Something fell to the catwalk and rolled off, bouncing down the stairs, boring and dull once again. It hit my foot before disappearing into the flames below—just a tiny piece of stone, gray and unprepossessing. I looked up at Olga, stunned and impressed as hell. I should have remembered: she'd been married to one of the big names in the illegal-weapons trade. Of course she'd have brought a few nasty surprises.

"You outbid me." It looked like Mrs. Manoli and her cursed gravestone had claimed one last victim. Considering the number of women Drac had murdered in his time, I thought she would have approved. Olga merely shrugged. "Did you see Jonathan?"

"No." She glanced over the railing, unconcerned. "He not leave. Maybe fall off."

I didn't think so. With a final heave, I dragged myself onto the landing. The boards were uncomfortably warm under my hands as I stayed on hands and knees for a moment, panting harshly. Stinky ran down the smoking railing, his long toes clutching the wood as surely as hands, until he reached me. He hopped off, chattering about something in an unknown language, or maybe it was the Fey equivalent of baby talk. He grabbed my hand and started tugging me toward the door and I got the idea, but my head was swimming and I still didn't trust my legs.

I held up a shaking hand. "Give me a minute."

Olga grabbed Stinky by the scruff of the neck, and scooped up Caedmon, who was leaning in utter exhaustion against the wall, surrounded by a ring of burning boards. He wasn't in any real danger that I could see, but for some reason he was staring at the fire with as much terror as a vamp. She tucked him under one sturdy arm and carried him and Stinky into the light-filled outer portion of the winery.

I sat on the smoking catwalk and waited. Olga had been between the mage and the door; no way had he gotten past her unnoticed, especially with Louis-Cesare in tow. Which meant they were still here.

My eyes scanned the circle of wood, but saw nothing. That wasn't too surprising—cloaking spells are fairly standard—but they hold up only as long as you don't move. Unless he planned on suicide, Jonathan had to move and move soon, before the merrily burning catwalk collapsed completely. And when he did, he was dead.

I'd no sooner had the thought when fog billowed up in front of my nose, thick as cotton, leaving me facing a featureless sea of gray. I could hear chanting nearby, echoing weirdly off the walls, but couldn't pinpoint it. Power pulsed through the air with dangerous strength, pounded at my temples like a headache, made my ears ring. Crazy Jonathan might be, but there was no doubt that he was strong.

But there was still only one way out, and I was sitting right in front of it.

Chapter Twenty-three

"Louis-Cesare!" I yelled as loudly as I could, but the billowing wall of white threw it back in my face.

If he heard, there was no sign. But someone else did. Like a bad microphone, tinny and too loud, Jonathan's voice was suddenly everywhere. "Your Fey friends are outside, dhampir. No, no, can't go that way." He giggled, as if being stuck in a building burning down around his ears was funny.

Fear replaced the fury behind my ribs. I could talk my way out of most things, but no one could reason with a madman. Especially a high madman. But I didn't have a lot of other options. "Jonathan! Give the vampire to me and we can talk."

More high-pitched giggles echoed everywhere, as if the walls were laughing. Jonathan was on a power high, and likely to do anything. I had to get to him before he decided he could fly, or something equally crazy, and got Louis-Cesare roasted in the process. I flexed my muscles, feeling tiny pinpricks of pain in my legs as sensation returned. Little burn marks, mostly from floating ash, peppered my jeans, but there was no real damage. As long as I didn't run into any more spells, I ought to be okay. How Louis-Cesare was holding up was another question. If he was unconscious, he couldn't even bat away flying particles. A single cinder, if it caught, might be enough to finish him.

I couldn't wait Jonathan out. Olga appeared in the doorway, looking at me quizzically. Probably wondering if I had a death wish, to be sitting in the middle of an inferno. "Jonathan's here," I told her. "He has Louis-Cesare. If he comes this way—"

"I kill him."

I nodded. Jonathan might still have some tricks up his sleeve, but then, so might Olga. And his magic would be a lot less effective on a Fey than on someone from our world.

I dragged myself to my feet using the wall for support. I swayed like a tree in a hurricane, but my legs held. I stared into the fog resentfully. The only real advantages I have, other than faster-than-human healing, are enhanced senses. That's all; that's it. I've heard of others of my kind that developed additional abilities with age, but I wasn't among them. It's the main reason I hate the dark—or anything else that deprives me of even one sense. It takes away one of the few weapons in my limited arsenal.

What the hell. There's always a last time for everything. I took a deep breath and moved cautiously forward.

The unnatural gray blanket almost immediately cut off sound and light as if a door had been dropped shut behind me. Weird flickers of flame from below occasionally broke through the fog, like hell's version of the northern lights, but were not bright enough to see by. My eyes were useless, so I closed them. I concentrated on feel, moving away from the current of slightly cooler air drifting in from outside.

Smoke mixed with the fog, acrid and sharp, making it

hard to breathe. I counted steps, trying to ignore the brittle feel of the boards beneath my feet. I passed what I guessed was a quarter of the distance, a third. . . . I hadn't made it quite to the halfway point when something moved across the current of air I was using as a guideline, disrupting it. I lashed out with the knife, but encountered nothing but air. Then a billow of fire erupted behind me, turning the boards I'd just crossed into charred, papery things that collapsed in a cascade of particles.

Backing away from the dangerous edge, I tripped over something on the floor. I looked down to see the outline of a man, surrounded by faint flickers of what looked like electricity. It cast an ethereal light against his face where indigo eyes, fierce as the wildest storm, met mine. Louis-Cesare.

The room swayed. The sudden pounding of my heart was making me dizzy. I dropped to my knees, and reached out to cup one bloodstained hand around his cheek before drawing it down, curving around the skin of his throat, whole and smooth and warm. I didn't understand it, but I was not about to question fate. "I thought I told you to get some pants on," I said, my throat threatening to close on the words.

Pain showed all over his face and in the lines of his body, but a weak smile lifted the ends of Louis-Cesare's mouth. I could detect the small movement because another billow of flame had erupted on the other side of us. I could see Jonathan silhouetted against it for a moment, safe on the somewhat sturdy side, until the boards he'd just set ablaze collapsed into dark dust. The piece of catwalk remaining to us groaned and started pulling away from the wall, the heavy screws that helped to hold it in place overtaxed without the support of the beams on either side.

"Jonathan doesn't lose gracefully," Louis-Cesare said.

I watched the shadow of a man dart along the far wall, the flames from below catching and magnifying him to giant size. "Neither do I."

I pulled Radu's knife out of my boot and weighed it in my hand. It wasn't my preferred size for throwing, but it was heavy and solid. More so than my arm, which felt alarmingly like jelly. But at this range, I could hardly miss. I tracked Jonathan until he paused at the sight of Olga in the doorway. With her weight to consider, she was staying well clear of the weakened causeway, preferring to balance on the stone threshold. But her bulk almost completely filled the opening, barring his retreat. I took my chance and threw.

A shudder went through the wood below us as it slipped another inch or so. It wasn't much of a movement, and I should have been expecting it. But my whole attention had been on the mage. It shook my arm at exactly the wrong moment. Jonathan hadn't seen me move, but the vibrating knife sticking out of the wood only an inch or so in front of his nose caught his attention. He and I both stared in disbelief at it, quivering in the side of a support beam. I couldn't remember the last time I'd blown a throw that easy.

Jonathan recovered first, and laughed, wrenching the knife out of the wood. And I realized that I'd essentially tossed away our only weapon. Louis-Cesare had struggled to his knees, his head dropped forward, panting harshly. I grabbed his shoulders and pushed him flat again. "Stay down!" I hissed as the mage's arm went back. I could only hope his aim was as bad as mine.

I never found out. The boards under his feet suddenly crumbled. He grabbed desperately for the railing, which

miraculously was still in place due to the more solid
boards on either side. But the charred wood splintered
under his weight, sending him reeling over the edge. It
happened so fast, I never even heard him scream.

A second later, the room tore apart. The mage had
made no sound, but a shredding howl of torment spiraled
up from below as if formed from wind and fire alone. The
power he'd stolen boiled up like a cauldron bubbling
over, spilling out, filling the room with a cold silver glow
that cut through the fog and smoke like a searchlight,
putting the light of the fire to shame. It took a few seconds for my eyes to adjust, and when they did, I saw a
snake of pure energy, hovering like a vast and brilliant
cobra, ready to strike.

I stared at it, mesmerized by more power than I'd ever
seen manifested at one time. I had a chance to think, *So
that's what's inside a master vampire,* before a shattering
hammer of light crashed down. It sank into my bones and
blood in an ice-hot blast: Louis-Cesare's stolen power, all
coming back home to roost. And it didn't wait for me to
get out of the way first.

I found out real fast why it was possible to get addicted
to power. A hot silvery rain poured around me, into me,
energizing my tired body with a rush. Suddenly, I could
feel everything, all my senses hyperfocused, hyperaware.
The brush of a piece of ash against my arm felt like a
slap, the heated air rushing into my lungs was fire, and all
around me, ripples of blue-white energy arched over my
body.

I fell to my knees, trying to ride out the sensations,
bracing myself against the rough wood of the floor. It was
not a good move. Under my hands, the old boards came
alive. It felt like I was sinking into them, able to sense for

a moment what it was like to *be* a tree. Only, with my usual luck, I was lying on a section that had been struck by a bolt of lightning before being cut. And I *felt* it, knew the way it had spread like liquid fire through the tree, searing living tissue into dying, charred cinders. . . .

Louis-Cesare pulled my shaking body against his chest: one arm around my waist, the other in my hair, tucking my head protectively under his chin. It didn't help. Along with the writhing, boiling mist of power came memories. I couldn't even start to comprehend all the images that rushed into my mind. Unlike the tree's one searing impression, this was centuries of love and hate, triumph and loss, dreams attained and hopes dashed and, beyond everything else, the feeling of being bereft, abandoned, lonely. Or maybe those were just the memories that made the most sense to me, that my mind could most easily process. The energy storm raged around us, but I could barely see it anymore. Vivid pictures slid across my vision, scenes captured once by another pair of eyes; then the world streamed away into brightness.

A little child with golden curls tottered on unsteady legs toward a richly dressed woman in embroidered satin. She picked him up with a delighted laugh. "My little Caesar. Someday, you will outdo your namesake!" Other images in the fast-moving stream showed the boy listening, day after day, for the sound of horses' hooves on a dirt path that would announce her return visit. A visit that never happened from a mother who had prudently forgotten he ever existed. Because he hadn't fulfilled the prophecy—he hadn't ruled, imprisoned instead by a brother he had never met.

A new scene, a pair of turquoise eyes in the darkness, a gasping breath that forced air into lungs that had lain unused for days. An elegant, pale hand on his brow, feeling hot next to his chill, smoothing tumbled auburn curls out of his eyes. A slow understanding dawning of his new state, disbelief giving way to hope of belonging, of acceptance, of finding in death what had eluded him in life. Only to discover that this new father wanted him no more than the old. Memories of tracking him across the continent, of finding him repeatedly, only to see him turn away again and again.

I jerked away from Louis-Cesare, hoping the loss of contact would also stop the flood of memory. But it didn't seem to help. The pale body was still limned in fire, but the power was fading fast, withdrawing back into him, becoming part of him again. Yet the memories didn't go with it. They soaked into my skin, saturated my mind, bearing down on me with the weight of centuries.

The wood shuddered beneath us, the power that had spilled into me also shaking the overburdened catwalk. I had a moment's lurch of dizzying vertigo as we slid sideways, toward the hellish pit the winery had become. But I couldn't seem to move, could barely breathe, as Louis-Cesare's memories melded with my own.

Another century, a pair of flashing hazel eyes, a brief, heady affair, only to have her taken from us. Tracking her through the streets of Paris, to an old door, pulpy with rot, that hid far worse decay inside. Finding Jonathan, a mage who hid centuries of cunning behind a boyish face. He'd prolonged his life by seeking out the unprotected, by stealing the power that flowed through their veins. Christine should have been protected from such as him, by the one who said he loved her, yet had allowed this to happen.

We made the bargain, agreed to return, to become a victim once more for her sake. We took her to safety, only to learn that the doctor's couldn't save her, that we had arrived too late and failed once again. Making the decision to change her to save her, only to see the horror when she awoke and realized what she was. What we were. Monster, she called us, and damned and wicked, before fleeing into the night, leaving us behind.

Louis-Cesare caught me as I started to tumble over the edge. He had a one-armed grip on the last support beam still clinging to the wall and the other hand grabbed my wrist. But the strain on his face was evident; he'd lost too much blood to hold for long. I tried to climb up his body to get a hand on the beam myself, but another wave of memory crashed into me.

Going back to Jonathan almost felt right. Perhaps the jailers had spoken truth when they whispered in our ear— it was all we were good for. We'd believed it, even when the blistering agony of a blade thrust through our back stuttered up our spine. We'd looked down to see a blood-slick blade sliding back inside our chest as a hand shoved between our shoulder blades, drawing it back out. We watched the pulsing arc shimmering in midair, like a spill of rubies, until the mage sang to it and it dissolved like smoke. We'd believed, because night after night, the torture continued. And night after night, no one came.

Until a voice out of the darkness, shrill with fear. Until a lone figure stood over us like a wolf protecting its young, snarling with a rage and possessiveness that was close to demonic, until the mages ran. Until Radu took us away, hid us while we recovered—and then left us once again.

"Dorina!" Louis-Cesare's voice cut through the fog, and I gulped in a deep breath of hot air. I met eyes full of pain, but not enough. Not nearly enough. I stared at him, dumbfounded. The wine had worn off; he didn't know what I'd seen. "I can't hold you!"

I nodded, head swimming, trying to work against the effects of the disorientation sphere and the distraction of the memories. My brain kept giving orders, but my limbs were slow to carry them out, and my eyes didn't seem to want to focus. And then it didn't matter. With a crack like a gunshot, the beam tore away from the wall and we tumbled into the flames below.

We hit the bottom with a jarring shudder and a splash. The small section of the catwalk somehow held together, but didn't serve as much protection. It caught fire immediately, turning into a jagged square of flame as wine gushed over the dried boards. I stared around frantically, looking for a spot anywhere that wasn't already burning. I didn't see one. Then Louis-Cesare grabbed me around the waist and jumped, straight into the middle of shin-deep burning liquid.

"Are you crazy?!" He ignored me, spinning us toward the tunnel through knee-deep flames. They licked at my legs, hot and bright and hungry, but for some reason, I didn't feel the burn. Shock, I thought distantly as Louis-Cesare made a final jump that landed us both in the dark, barrel-lined hallway leading to Radu's cellar.

He sat me down, leaning heavily against the wall for support, his disordered mane obscuring his face. I grabbed him, my hands batting at flames that I only slowly realized didn't exist. He looked like ten kinds of death, but for some reason, he wasn't burning. "What did you do?" I demanded, willing my knees not to collapse.

"I used a huge amount of power to shield us for a few seconds," Louis-Cesare said shakily. "I trust we won't need it again. It has left me . . . somewhat weak."

"But alive." I still couldn't believe it.

Louis-Cesare slowly pulled himself into a half-standing position against the side of the winery. "What? Did you think one little mage was going to do me in?" He swallowed hard. "Hell, that was just a warm-up."

I stared at him. A joke. Louis-Cesare had made a joke. The very thought left me dizzy.

And then the barrels started to explode. The ones closest to the inferno of the winery tore apart with the sound of a dozen cannons going off, raining wine and sharp bits of wood all around us. Louis-Cesare pushed me into the wall, shielding me with his body until I kneed him in the groin. "Wood!" I screamed into his outraged face, yanking out a sliver that had embedded itself in his shoulder, and waving it under his nose. Every time one of those barrels went off, it threw out the equivalent of a hundred or so flying stakes.

The cellar was suddenly a vamp's worst nightmare, and I didn't like it much better. If we didn't get out soon, we were toast. Louis-Cesare must have figured it the same way, because he wrenched the top off the nearest barrel, picked me up around the waist and ran.

Hammer blows sounded against the makeshift shield as another row exploded behind us, the flames from one set of barrels igniting the next in line. Weird red shadows, like leaping fingers, grabbed for our heels as we all but flew toward the cellar door. I scanned the floor for Radu, but didn't see him; it looked as if he really was hard to kill. Like the rest of the family, I thought as Louis-Cesare slammed the heavy oak door shut behind us, just as a volley of explosions rocked it from the other side.

We stood, panting and half-fainting against the scarred wood, knowing we should get farther from danger but too exhausted to move. Dizziness pushed through my body as I stared dully around, looking for the next challenge, the next threat. All I saw were two outraged turquoise eyes staring at me from the darkened stairs. "Dorina! What did you do to my wine?"

An odd rumbling started from my right. My head whipped around and I stopped, staring. The strangest event of a very strange day met my eyes. The last thing I saw before I keeled over was Louis-Cesare. He was leaning against the door, naked and bloody. And he was laughing.

Chapter Twenty-four

We were still arguing about wine two days later. Radu and I were on our way to Benny's wake, held in his cramped office despite the crowd because the warehouse was still sporting several large holes. The remainder of Benny's Occultus charms had been sacrificed to keep the large number of usual visitors arriving at the small store-front from raising too many eyebrows.

I watched a mail truck trundle down the street, looking fairly innocuous until it suddenly took a left turn and squeezed itself through the front entrance. I wondered idly what was big enough to need to use a truck as camouflage. It was better than listening to Radu whine about having to buy wine, "and an inferior vintage at that," because his stores were sitting on zero.

Then I saw a familiar, arrogant stride coming down the street, cape swirling around booted feet. A few last rays of natural light were still peeking over the edge of Vegas' neon horizon, so the hood was up, but it didn't matter. I knew Mircea's walk as well as my own. I had a swift, ir-rational flash of gut-wrenching panic.

"Don't even think about it." I didn't realize I'd turned away until I felt Radu's grip on my shoulder.

"I guess saving a man's life isn't the debt canceler it used to be."

"Not when you also blow up his cellar and destroy his house."

"I had some help with the house."

Radu gave a snort and steered me into the office. There was a giant squashed in a corner, a long beard like smoke down his chest, who I assumed had been the truck. A couple dozen trolls, a few humans who were definitely shape-shifters, judging by the buzz they gave off, and a few lesser demons made up the mourners who had assembled so far. I mumbled a swift condolence to Olga, who was looking regal in black satin and a veil, and headed for the relative safety of the tiny kitchenette.

It was crowded with offerings of food that I didn't examine too closely and barrels of beer stacked to the ceiling. Radu's bottle looked insignificant by comparison, like something a troll might drink for a chaser. I was nonetheless searching for an opener when the bottle was taken smoothly out of my hands.

"You are going to miss the eulogy." The smoky voice was rich with fondness. It was almost certainly fake, but it still tugged at my heart. Damn it. I silently passed him a glass.

The eulogy ended up being a series of stories, each more outrageous than the last, that followed one another in quick succession. They and the beer lasted well into the night, as we were joined by an endless stream of visitors. Children came with their parents, fell asleep on fathers' shoulders, listened entranced with their heads in mothers' laps. Benny was remembered, drunk to, admired. Every crafty deal was praised, every shady transaction celebrated with toast after toast. Tears glistened on cheeks even as people roared with laughter. I didn't know if this was normal for Faerie, or if, being so far from home, people naturally drew together. Either way, Benny received quite a send-off.

Mircea had found us a perch in the middle of a family of trolls, and ended up holding a small child on his lap. He looked totally at home, as if he babysat trolls every day. The long, slim hands soothed the restless child with ease, until she fell asleep with her head on his shoulder. I glared down into my empty glass and got up to refill it.

"I guess we won't be doing one of these for Drac," I said a few minutes later, draining my third mug of beer. Radu's wine was long gone and the Fey beer was the only alcoholic beverage around in unlimited quantities. It had a kick like bootleg moonshine, but despite my very serious wish to get drunk, it wasn't obliging.

"This is for family," Mircea chided.

"Drac was your brother," I pointed out tersely.

Mircea handed the sleeping child to her mother, who simpered at him past a luxurious brown beard. He took my hand and pulled me outside, into the garden Olga cultivated in the tiny space between buildings. It had a porch swing in a corner, facing a slate patio with a few tubs of greenery. Enough light seeped through the slats in the office blinds to stripe the patio in orange and umber, while the full moon on the pavement turned everything else silver.

"He wasn't a brother," Mircea said. "He was a disease, from which the family suffered for centuries."

"So that's why you killed him?"

Mircea watched me, eyes liquid black in the dark. "I thought your Fey friend did that."

I gave a laugh so hard it hurt my throat. "Don't try it.

Drac grew up fighting you; there's no way he could have mistaken Caedmon's style for yours."

I should have read the signs sooner: Drac accepting Mircea without question, Mircea calling him "Vlad" when Caedmon had never heard that name, the fear of fire no Fey would have had. But it hadn't been until I'd spoken to Caedmon that I figured it out. Æsubrand had jumped him halfway around the house, trying to finish what he'd started and remove his main obstacle to the throne. Caedmon joined the party only after the excitement was over, once he and Heidar had beaten the bastard into submission.

"Louis-Cesare asked me to take a look at your mysterious Fey," Mircea said, not attempting to deny it. "He thought Caedmon might really be Æsubrand or Alarr, bringing their war into our world. And because of the work I do for the Senate, I have met both of them."

"That's not what I asked."

"I did not kill Vlad, Dorina. The lovely Olga did that."

"After you maneuvered him into position." He raised a brow and I scowled. I wasn't in the mood for games tonight. "I've never seen you fight that poorly," I said flatly. "You wanted him to die, but you didn't want to do it yourself. Why?"

"Because it was what he wanted."

"I don't understand."

"He wanted to die by my hand. Wanted to force me to do what I blamed him for, and fracture the family yet again. I denied him that."

"What family?" I asked, my voice bitter.

"We *were* a family, Dorina, however dysfunctional. We watched each other's backs; we killed for each other; we saved each other's lives again and again. And, yes, sometimes we hated each other. But we did *not* betray each other. We did not prey on each other. Only Vlad did that."

"Radu attacked him first."

"No." The air between us suddenly felt tangible. "The family was broken long before that."

I swallowed, the fear in my throat thick enough to taste. I'd asked to meet him—demanded it, really—but now I wasn't certain it had been such a good idea. Maybe if I just let it go, refused to acknowledge those stupid dreams as anything important, I could ignore it all a while longer.

Cool fingers closed on my wrist. The odd lighting cast strange shadows on Mircea's face, leaving him lean and elegant, but also austere and forbidding. I decided I wanted another drink. "Dorina . . . be very sure."

"It's my right to know," I said automatically. Taking the opposite side from Mircea was so ingrained that it was out before I'd really decided anything. And then it was too late.

"I left her," he began simply, without preamble. "I saw to it that she was financially secure, but I left. I couldn't begin to comprehend what had happened to me; how could I ask her to do so? I didn't want to see her turn away when she realized . . . what I had become."

I didn't even try to pretend that I wasn't following him. "And when you came back?"

Lounging in the swing, Mircea looked completely at peace, though there was a tension to his body that spoke of leashed energy, as if staying so perfectly still was a matter of conscious will. "When I came back, I found her village burnt to the ground and its people dead, of 'plague' or so I was told. It was not implausible, such things had happened before. And yet . . ."

"You didn't believe it." Mircea lied. It was what he did, what he'd always done, one of his essential tactics for survival. And when unavoidable circumstance forced him to tell the truth, he told as little of it as possible. If anyone could spot a lie in another, it was him.

"No, I didn't believe it."

Suddenly, I couldn't take it anymore. The pressure welled up in my throat until I thought I would choke on it. Whatever it was, I wanted it over—I wanted to *know*. "Just tell me!"

"After I left, your mother realized she was with child. She intended to keep you, but once your . . . condition . . . became known, she was subject to a great deal of pressure by superstitious villagers to give you away. It was an act she almost immediately regretted. But you weren't in a fixed location, at a home where you could easily be retrieved. The Gypsies wandered where they would, often even across borders into other lands. She looked for you for years, spending most of the money I had left her in the search, but to no avail. Finally, in desperation, she went to Tirgoviste."

"Why?" No Gypsies in their right minds ever went there. Drac had viewed them as leeches on the landscape.

"To beg Vlad to help her." Mircea's voice was raw.

I stared at him, not sure I'd heard correctly. "She went to Drac? For *help*?"

"I was his brother; you were his niece," Mircea said quietly, his eyes bleak. "She had reason to think he would be receptive."

I shook my head in shocked disbelief. She must have either known nothing about the man or been criminally naive to think she could show up with a story about his undead brother and a half-vampire bastard and expect anything except . . . my blood ran cold. "What happened?" I whispered, knowing what the answer had to be.

"He ordered her executed for telling slanderous lies." Mircea's voice was winter, but what I saw in his eyes was a hate so pure it burned. "He left her writhing on a stake for days. They said she died still calling out my name. But I wasn't there. I didn't come." The hand that rested so casually on his knee clenched into a fist. I stared at it, air suddenly in short supply. "Dying was a laughably inadequate punishment for his sins."

I closed my eyes, seeing that frozen corpse again, the stiffened limbs tossed about by the freezing wind, the glazed, staring eyes. Starbursts of bloody violet flared behind my eyelids. I half rose from the chair, to do what, I don't know. She was dead; the monster who killed her was dead. There was nothing left to do, not even a grave to visit. Nothing. I felt a hand on my arm, pulling me back down, and I followed its direction blindly.

After a long moment, Mircea continued, voice as calm as if that moment of uncontrolled anger had never happened. "When I returned, Vlad realized that she had told the truth, after all, and that he had murdered my mistress. He was . . . concerned . . . that I would find out. In an attempt to keep his secret, he tracked down everyone who had known her, and put them to death."

Painful clarity dug sharp fingers into my mind. "Everyone?"

"He hired some men to find the Gypsies who had adopted you and kill them after drugging their wine," Mircea confirmed. "They were supposed to kill you, as well, but were too superstitious to touch a dhampir, even though you were as unconscious as everyone else. They

left you where you lay, assuming you would die of expo-
sure or starvation, with no one to care for you."

"And you know this how?"

"Because you told me. Enough, at least, for me to discern the rest."

"I don't recall that conversation."

Mircea ignored the implied question, and I was still in
too much shock to call him on it. "Once your adopted
family was dead, you determined to track down your real
one. You arrived in time to pick through the burnt-out ref-
use of your mother's village."

"He killed her entire village on the chance she might
have mentioned him to someone?"

"He knew what would happen if I found out the truth.
He circulated a rumor that they had died of plague, and
that he'd burnt the village as a precaution against it
spreading. As I said, I did not believe him. Despite being
a pathological liar, Vlad was remarkably poor at it."

"Everyone else believed him."

"Everyone else found it prudent not to question his
word," Mircea corrected. "But I began to investigate, and
discovered there had been a child. But years had passed
by then, and Vlad had killed most of the people who
might have been able to tell me any details. I was left with
the dilemma that had faced your mother. I had no idea
where to look for you."

"I'm surprised you bothered." He must have known
what I was. Must have realized that even if I wasn't a raving lunatic consumed with bloodlust, I wouldn't be happy
to see him.

"Comoara mea—"

"Don't call me that!" It was a growl, half-choked, but
at least my eyes were dry.

Mircea drew me close. The warm leather of his blazer was buttery smooth against my face, and the thumb that stroked my cheekbone was gentle. "And why not? You are my greatest treasure, Dorina." There was honey and gold in the soft tenor, and sincerity so real I half believed it. "You always were."

Mircea could talk the sun out of rising, but he wasn't going to distract me. "How did you find me?"

"I didn't. Before I could begin my search, you found me."

"Poenari." The dream had been true, then.

"Yes. You somehow infiltrated a castle universally considered impregnable, intent on killing the man you believed was responsible for Elena's death."

Something stirred, like an itch on the skin of my memory. "Elena."

"For Helen. Her family named her after Helen of Troy."

"I don't remember her." Not an expression, not a tone of voice. Nothing. My recall was usually razor sharp, but not about this. Fractured pieces were the best I could manage, and that hadn't happened without help. "Did you take that memory, too?"

"Dorina—"

"Don't lie to me! Not about this. You altered my memory." It was the only answer that made sense.

"Because I didn't want to lose both of you. You were determined to kill the murderer of your mother. You had found a knife with the family crest near the remains of her home. Vlad told me later that he must have dropped it when a desperate villager attacked him. He hadn't noticed at the time, but it was enough."

Poking at the half-glimpsed images was like raking cold fingers through my brain, but I pushed it. I didn't want to be told; I wanted to *remember*. "I didn't get all the facts straight. . . . Everyone just said it belonged to the *voivode*." It was a title, that of the local strongman, not a name. I had assumed Drac was my sire—I'd learned from the Gypsies that my father was a son of the old *voivode*—and gone looking for some revenge. But I found Mircea instead.

"You were almost dead already. Why?"

"Vlad knew his story had not convinced me, knew that I was searching for the truth, and he was afraid he had missed something. He decided to strike at me before I could do the same to him. Only he didn't dare attack me directly, in case he failed. He used assassins, and they found me somewhat more . . . resilient . . . than they'd expected."

"Why not kill him?" I demanded. "Once you'd gotten enough from me to figure it all out, once you *knew*, why protect him?"

A tender hand brushed my hair. The caress was as light as a kiss of wind, soft and infinitely comforting, but it was the soothing peace that followed it that I fought with all my might, determined not to lose myself. "I told you, Dorina. Death would have been ridiculously inadequate recompense for his crimes. Thousands had died, murdered so that he might gain or retain power. It was a bloody time, and some of those he killed undoubtedly deserved their fate—but not all. Not most. Not her."

"So you locked him up? If death wasn't bad enough for him, why was imprisonment?"

"It wasn't only about finding something 'bad enough.' Justice said that he should die once for each of his victims, but how do you kill someone more than once?"

I thought about Jonathan and Louis-Cesare, but said

nothing. "I do not see how any imprisonment could be worse than death."

"You forget, Vlad spent most of his childhood locked away—he hated confinement more than anything. For him, there was no greater punishment."

"But Drac wasn't a vampire then. You couldn't trap him without having him age and die on you. And you were only a newborn yourself, and not strong enough to change him—"

"I took you and fled, before Vlad could decide to kill us both. We went into hiding, and I . . . adjusted . . . your memories. I was afraid that if I did not, you would return to make another attempt on his life and be killed yourself."

I listened to the faint sounds of traffic, and fought against the bone-deep sense of well-being and rightness that Mircea's presence evoked. He was spending a lot of energy to soothe my volatile emotions, to make this talk possible without my descent into comfortable, familiar madness. But it had the side effect of also making his answers sound oh-so-reasonable. Of blunting the truth with his usual ease. That wasn't going to work. Not tonight.

"Or perhaps you were afraid I'd mess up your plans and give him an early death."

"Perhaps." Mircea's voice was light, giving nothing away. "In any event, I waited several decades, until my power had grown, and returned to pluck him off a battlefield, before the Turks could behead him or the nobles assassinate him."

"So why kill him now, after so long? Why give him what he wanted?"

"Every time he escaped, Vlad tried to hurt me by attacking those I loved. I finally had to ask myself how much I was willing to risk for his continued pain." I numbly watched Radu through a crack in the office blinds. The wake had reached the maudlin stage, and he was being crushed against the huge bosom of a sobbing troll woman who made Olga look petite. He took out a handkerchief and gently dried her eyes, as Mircea's voice caressed my painfully tattered nerves. "I realized . . . some things are worth more than revenge."

I abruptly stood up. I was so angry I could barely see straight. "Well, I'm thrilled you had that epiphany!"

"Dorina—"

"How many people died for your revenge? How many suffered? You could have ended this centuries ago, spared us all, but no. The great Mircea is always right!" I raged at him, finally giving voice to everything I'd known for years and that he had stubbornly refused to see. I'd waited for this moment, dreamed of it, and now that it was here . . . it rang strangely hollow.

I could still see Louis-Cesare's mutilated body, with Jonathan tenderly stroking the multiple wounds he'd inflicted. I understood what Mircea meant; one death was far, far too good for him. I'd have loved to give him one for each and every scar, but wasn't sure I'd given him even one. He'd fooled me with the illusion that Louis-Cesare was dead. No vamp healed an almost decapitation in a couple of minutes, not even a master. Especially not a master so drained of power he couldn't even stand up. What I'd taken for a challenge had been Jonathan's attempt to convince me not to risk my neck trying to save a corpse. Too bad for him that I don't reason well in the midst of a killing rage.

Now I was faced, just like last time, with cleaning up the mess Mircea's revenge had left behind. Was Jonathan really dead? Or had it been another illusion? We'd found several charred bodies that might have been his, but could just as easily have belonged to one of his little helpers. No one seemed to know exactly how many mages he'd brought along, how many bodies we should expect to find. I had no choice but to play it safe and assume that I now had a revenge-crazed dark mage after me, along with who knew how many other people. All because Mircea had to do it his way.

He started to get up, a hand outstretched toward me. "Don't," I warned him. "Just. Don't." The hand fell to his side.

It was too much, after centuries of ignorance, to have this all dumped on me now. Along with Louis-Cesare's memories, I probably had nightmare material for at least the next millennium. Even worse, there wasn't a damn thing I could do about any of it. It was over, except for the mopping up. And suddenly I was so very tired.

We stared at each other for a heartbeat. Despite the gloom, I could see the faint lines of exhaustion etched onto that ageless face. Mircea looked as tired as I felt, and the sad, almost defeated look in his eyes was one I'd never seen. My hands clenched, and it was with a kind of horror that I saw one fist come up, the knuckles brushing lightly across the smooth line of his cheek. Then I whirled on my heel and started for the door, desperate to get away before I showed a weakness I'd regret.

"Dorina. Where are you going?" The voice was soft, careful.

"Back to New York. Back to my life." I paused, my hand on the aluminum facing of the door. "And Mircea—the next time you need a favor . . . *don't* call me."

Postscript

He didn't call. He wrote instead. Although I almost didn't get the letter.

Ever since an unfortunate incident involving a lack of morning coffee and the postal uniform's uncanny resemblance to Byrthinian demon battle dress, my mail is thrown in the general direction of the house while the carrier books it down the street. This morning, I fished one piece out of a hydrangea bush and another off the porch roof. Then I prized Mrs. Luca's poodle away from Stinky and took him back inside.

I added the letters to the ones I'd collected that morning from the basement. Claire was in Faerie for the moment, but she still sent regular notes through the portal, which her uncle had used as a conduit for bringing in bootleg supplies. Because of the timeline difference, I'd found three letters that morning, each dated several weeks apart. They all said the same thing: she was fine; Heidar was fine; Caedmon was impossible—apparently, no one fusses over an expectant mother like the Fey, especially when the mother in question is carrying the heir to the throne.

As Claire said, she was still pretty freaked-out, both about the pregnancy and, even more, about all the creatures she had killed at Radu's. A strict vegetarian, she was having a hard time accepting that she had drained most of the experiments dry of magic, and thereby of life, without even realizing it. The only ones who had survived were those, like Stinky, who were at least part Fey. Her gift seemed to have less of an effect on them. I supposed that was just as well—a part-human null was going to have enough trouble being accepted at court without draining the nobility dry.

She also wrote that she's looking into possible Fey cures for my fits. A word was all it took for Caedmon to have a lab set up where she could explore the new flora to her heart's content. Pretty soon, she's going to have him as whipped as Heidar.

Of the other letters, the first was from Mircea. Purely a business proposition, he said, with no family strings attached. I raised a brow at that, but read on. Claire's disappearance meant the bills were now all coming in my name.

Mircea wanted to know if I would be willing to work with the task force the Senate was forming to deal with problems caused by the war. Specifically, I would help to hunt down more of the dark's special experiments and see that they were taken to Radu for examination. I might also assist in rounding up illegal immigrants from Faerie before they started snacking on humans. And, of course, ensure that the import of Fey wine was strictly prohibited.

I poured a tiny amount of the contraband stuff into my coffee mug. Luckily, I had about a five-year supply in the basement, courtesy of Claire's uncle—God bless him. I drank a salute to Pip and resumed reading.

The Senate had been convinced to employ such a

disreputable type as myself because of two recommendations. Mircea had somehow persuaded them that our recent adventures, and the fact that I am currently babysitting a Duergar, qualify me as a Dark Fey expert. The second came from Caedmon, although perhaps *recommendation* isn't quite the right word. It seems that he'd flatly refused to deal with anyone else. That had me narrowing my eyes and wondering what the crafty old bastard was up to. I had a feeling I was going to find out.

The other piece of mail was a brown-paper-wrapped package sealed with the family crest—in bloodred wax, of course. I smiled as I slit it open, and smiled more when I saw the contents. Radu had thoughtfully sent me a little gift along with his letter, which consisted of two paragraphs explaining about the task force, and eight more bitching about the facilities/people/pressure with which he was forced to work. He was back at MAGIC while his place was undergoing massive renovations. I winced at the thought of what he'd build on what was now virtually a blank slate. It boggled the mind. I couldn't wait to see it.

He also wrote that Mircea was twisting arms trying to get Louis-Cesare back, at least for the duration of the war. He'd gone off chasing some rumor about Christine, much to Mircea's annoyance. He wants him for the task force, which, as it was his idea, Mircea is expected to staff. He told Radu that it's been tough going—most people don't want to deal with the Fey. The Senate was desperate enough to employ a dhampir; what was next, trolls? I grinned and made a mental note to introduce him to my new secretary as soon as possible.

No explanation was given for the enclosed item, but then, I didn't really need one. Radu had sent me a box of butterscotch candy. My favorite flavor. I stood there for a moment, thinking of schemes and plans, oaths and family. But mostly about a pair of blue, blue eyes.

I hadn't been surprised to find out when I woke up at Radu's that Louis-Cesare had done a disappearing act. I might have been hurt, if I hadn't had his memories. If I hadn't known to expect it. Somewhere along the line, he got tired of people lying to him, betraying him and leaving him. So he pulled the classic response. He became the one who left.

I should have been furious that someone who could be accepted chose not to be, that he shied away from the closeness I was denied merely to avoid the possibility of hurt. But I had those damn memories, and they weren't fading with time. If anything, they seemed to be settling in for good, revealing stray glimpses into another life, another world, when I least expected it. And understanding another person, I was discovering, makes judging him a lot harder to do.

I finished my wine-laced coffee, then put through a call to Daddy. The vamp answering the magical mirror hissed at me, showing a lot more fang than he probably would have if I'd been there in person. I smiled back, which made him twitch. Finally, I got my request across and Mircea came into view. I told him that, with certain guarantees, I really thought I could make the time.

KAREN CHANCE

TOUCH THE DARK

The first novel in the Cassandra Palmer series

Cassandra Palmer can see the future and communicate with spirits – talents that make her attractive to the dead and the undead. The ghosts of the dead aren't usually dangerous; they just like to talk . . . a lot.

The undead are another matter.

Like any sensible girl, Cassie tries to avoid vampires. But when the bloodsucking Mafioso she escaped three years ago finds Cassie again with vengeance on his mind, she's forced to turn to the vampire Senate for protection.

The undead senators won't help her for nothing, and Cassie finds herself working with one of their most powerful members, a dangerously seductive master vampire – and the price he demands may be more than Cassie is willing to pay . . .

KAREN CHANCE

CLAIMED BY SHADOW

The second thrilling novel in the Cassandra Palmer series

A recent legacy made Cassandra Palmer heir to the title of Pythia, the world's chief clairvoyant. It's a position that usually comes with years of training, but Cassie's circumstances are a little . . . unusual. And now she's stuck with a whopping amount of power that every vampire in town wants to either monopolize or eradicate – and that she doesn't dare use.

What's more, she's just discovered that a certain arrogant master vampire has put a *geis* on her – a magical claim that warns off any would-be suitors, and might explain the rather . . . *intense* attraction between them. But Cassie's had it with being messed around and anyone who tries it from now on is going to find out that she makes a very bad enemy . . .

Karen Chance

EMBRACE THE NIGHT

The third novel in the Cassandra Palmer series

Recently named the world's chief clairvoyant, Cassandra Palmer still has a thorn in her side. As long as Cassie and a certain master vampire – the dangerously sexy Mircea – are magically bound to each other, her life will never be her own . . .

The spell that binds them can only be broken with an incantation found in an ancient text, the Codex Merlini. The Codex's location has been lost in the present day, so Cassie will have to seek it out in the only place it can still be found – the past.

But Cassie soon realizes the Codex has been lost for a reason. The book is rumoured to contain dangerous spells, and retrieving it may help Cassie to deal with Mircea, but it could also endanger the world . . .

He just wanted a decent book to read …

Not too much to ask, is it? It was in 1935 when Allen Lane, Managing Director of Bodley Head Publishers, stood on a platform at Exeter railway station looking for something good to read on his journey back to London. His choice was limited to popular magazines and poor-quality paperbacks – the same choice faced every day by the vast majority of readers, few of whom could afford hardbacks. Lane's disappointment and subsequent anger at the range of books generally available led him to found a company – and change the world.

'We believed in the existence in this country of a vast reading public for intelligent books at a low price, and staked everything on it'
Sir Allen Lane, 1902–1970, founder of Penguin Books

The quality paperback had arrived – and not just in bookshops. Lane was adamant that his Penguins should appear in chain stores and tobacconists, and should cost no more than a packet of cigarettes.

Reading habits (and cigarette prices) have changed since 1935, but Penguin still believes in publishing the best books for everybody to enjoy. We still believe that good design costs no more than bad design, and we still believe that quality books published passionately and responsibly make the world a better place.

So wherever you see the little bird – whether it's on a piece of prize-winning literary fiction or a celebrity autobiography, political tour de force or historical masterpiece, a serial-killer thriller, reference book, world classic or a piece of pure escapism – you can bet that it represents the very best that the genre has to offer.

Whatever you like to read – trust Penguin.